A Dream Come to Life

"Oh!" A man's voice rasped beneath her.

The hard thud of her landing jarred Magda's senses back to her. She was kneeling astride a man in bed. His chest was warm beneath her flattened palms. A light dusting of hair bristled softly through the thin flannel of his nightshirt. Shadows flickered in the dim candlelight, exaggerating the intensity of his black-eyed gaze.

"You?" Shock choked her voice into a squeak.

"Aye." His voice was groggy with sleep, but the rest of his body seemed to be rousing to wakefulness beneath the covers. "Me indeed."

James shook the bed-mussed hair out of his face and broke into a devilish smile as his eyes devoured the length of her. "But do tell, love, who are *you*?"

His hands glided up Magda's legs, disappearing easily under the folds of her dress, thumbs roving to stroke the insides of her thighs.

She studied his face. *Just like the portrait.* It had obsessed her, hadn't it? No wonder her unconscious mind would summon a vision of this very man.

"Still here, love?" James prompted, giving her thighs a quick squeeze.

Jerking her h̶̶̶̶̶̶̶̶̶̶̶̶̶̶̶̶̶̶̶̶̶̶̶̶̶̶̶ right and stared down at ̶̶̶̶̶̶̶̶̶̶̶̶̶̶̶̶̶̶̶̶̶̶̶̶̶̶̶ the darkness. The slight̶̶̶̶̶̶̶̶̶̶̶̶̶̶̶̶̶̶̶̶̶̶̶̶̶̶̶ d amusement. Despite ̶̶̶̶̶̶̶̶̶̶̶̶̶̶̶̶̶̶̶̶̶̶̶̶̶̶̶ umbs, he seemed to be v̶̶̶̶̶̶̶̶̶̶̶̶̶̶̶̶̶̶̶̶̶̶̶̶̶̶̶ ve.

"I know who you are̶̶̶̶̶̶̶̶̶̶̶̶̶̶̶̶̶̶̶̶̶̶̶̶̶̶̶

His smile flared to life. "But of course, love." He winked. "All the lasses do, don't they?"

Berkley Sensation Books by Veronica Wolff

MASTER OF THE HIGHLANDS
SWORD OF THE HIGHLANDS

Sword
of the
highlands

Veronica Wolff

BERKLEY SENSATION, NEW YORK

THE BERKLEY PUBLISHING GROUP
Published by the Penguin Group
Penguin Group (USA) Inc.
375 Hudson Street, New York, New York 10014, USA
Penguin Group (Canada), 90 Eglinton Avenue East, Suite 700, Toronto, Ontario M4P 2Y3, Canada
(a division of Pearson Penguin Canada Inc.)
Penguin Books Ltd., 80 Strand, London WC2R 0RL, England
Penguin Group Ireland, 25 St. Stephen's Green, Dublin 2, Ireland (a division of Penguin Books Ltd.)
Penguin Group (Australia), 250 Camberwell Road, Camberwell, Victoria 3124, Australia
(a division of Pearson Australia Group Pty. Ltd.)
Penguin Books India Pvt. Ltd., 11 Community Centre, Panchsheel Park, New Delhi—110 017, India
Penguin Group (NZ), 67 Apollo Drive, Rosedale, North Shore 0632, New Zealand
(a division of Pearson New Zealand Ltd.)
Penguin Books (South Africa) (Pty.) Ltd., 24 Sturdee Avenue, Rosebank, Johannesburg 2196, South Africa

Penguin Books Ltd., Registered Offices: 80 Strand, London WC2R 0RL, England

SWORD OF THE HIGHLANDS

A Berkley Sensation Book / published by arrangement with the author

PRINTING HISTORY
Berkley Sensation mass-market edition / June 2008

Copyright © 2008 by Veronica Wolff.
Excerpt from *Warrior of the Highlands* copyright © 2008 by Veronica Wolff.
Cover art by Aleta Rafton.
Cover design by George Long.
Hand lettering by Ron Zinn.
Interior text design by Laura K. Corless.
Text composition by ReadSmart® from Language Technologies, Inc.

ISBN: 978-0-425-22248-5

BERKLEY® SENSATION
Berkley Sensation Books are published by The Berkley Publishing Group,
a division of Penguin Group (USA) Inc.,
375 Hudson Street, New York, New York 10014.
BERKLEY SENSATION and the "B" design are trademarks of Penguin Group (USA) Inc.

PRINTED IN THE UNITED STATES OF AMERICA

10 9 8 7 6 5 4 3 2 1

For my mother,
who tends skinned knees and catches dropped plot points
with equal aplomb.

In loving memory of my dear friend
Anna Livia Brawn.

Acknowledgments

This book would not be what it is without a lot of help from the wonderful team at Berkley. My heartfelt gratitude goes out to Cindy Hwang for giving me my shot; she's a passionate reader and an exceptional editor, and I am beyond lucky to have her in my corner. Special thanks to Leis Pederson, whose quick and kind responses to the random questions of a beginner never made me feel foolish for asking.

My sincere thanks to my agent, Stephanie Kip Rostan, for helping nurture my career with such enthusiasm and for reminding me that I'm writing fiction and, at the end of the day, I can just make stuff up.

A tremendous thank-you to the extraordinary Kate Perry, who became my critique partner and friend when I found myself sorely in need of both.

And also to Monica McCarty, for her generous support, and always making sure I know who's who and what's what.

A shout-out to Kim Green, for eleventh-hour feedback, despite her own babies and deadlines. One to Kalen Hughes, for so happily fielding the most obscure of historical questions. Also to Bella Andre, for such joyful encouragement. And to Rudy Reyes, for everything.

I am also grateful for the advice, camaraderie, and brainstorming powers of the following women: Jami Alden, Barbara Freethy, Carol Culver, Tracy Grant, Candice Hern, Anne Mallory, and Penelope Williamson.

At times I've needed to reach out, and I've been touched and overwhelmed to find such generosity out there. I owe my thanks especially to Tom Cameron, Rebecca Cusworth, Brody Lee, and Áine Minogue.

I'm blessed with the greatest family ever, especially my mother, who doubles as a gifted plotter, and my father, whose support is unflagging. My thanks also to my in-law cheering sections, particularly Ivan Wolff and Joey Wolff.

And finally, my thanks to Adam, always Adam. Honestly, without him, I don't think this book would be in your hands.

He either fears his fate too much,
Or his deserts are small,
That dares not put it to the touch,
To gain or lose it all.

—JAMES GRAHAM,
FIFTH EARL AND FIRST MARQUIS OF MONTROSE

Chapter 1

The image of Magda's brother stared back at her from the bathroom mirror. Gripping the counter, she leaned in closer. Though it had been only one year since his death, she had a hard time picturing his face in her mind. But, staring at her reflection, she could summon Peter to memory, layering features one by one into focus. They'd always been a pair, with the same broad forehead and full mouth. She could just picture his hair, red, but many shades lighter than her own, and smooth like dark copper.

Magda pushed away from the sink and stood straight. That was also like Pete, an erect posture to match the patrician nose.

The ringing phone startled her back into the present. Moments like this, feeling the grief claim her suddenly, came less frequently now, and so when they did she always let herself experience the full force of her pain. Bring it out, study it fresh, see how it might have changed.

"Hey, Magda," Walter's tinny voice warbled on her ancient answering machine. "Ya there? I know you're there."

The disembodied voice paused and Magda heard herself murmur testily, "Coming," even though there was no way her boss could hear. Having lived alone for so long, she increasingly caught herself mumbling around the apartment. She supposed it was how people ended up with cats.

"Hi, Walter." Phone tucked at her shoulder, she reached back into the bathroom for her hairbrush, the powder blue phone cord strained tight. "I'm here."

The old-fashioned telephone never posed much of a problem in her Manhattan studio, because she was able to reach three of the four walls while tethered to its base in the kitchenette. That

Magda lived in such a tiny apartment aggravated her parents to no end. She told herself it was because she liked to live humbly, but somewhere in the back of her mind Magda also knew she stayed in the place to goad them.

"I need you in here." Walter was typically curt, his thick Long Island accent, ragged from decades of cigarettes, at odds with his lofty position as one of the principal curators at the Metropolitan Museum of Art.

"That's what you always say, Walter. Please. It's Saturday." She tugged the brush through the length of her hair. "I pulled a twelve-hour day yesterday, in case you don't remember. Contrary to popular opinion, I do have a life, you know." Her eyes roved the room, scanning the morning's paper, the tepid remains of a cup of coffee, the stack of overdue library books, and a pile of dry cleaning. She winced. "Kind of."

"Yeah, so you insist on telling me. Now, we got an anonymous bequest, and it's got a couple of plums that'll be perfect for the new pastoral exhibit. I just need you to come in and clean these bad boys up for me, so be a honey, okay, and get your butt in here."

"But Walter . . ." Magda protested weakly. She looked around the apartment again. Peter was suddenly everywhere. Tossing the brush aside, she plopped on the loveseat and nestled down, trying to push her brother from her mind. But she could just picture him, flopping back on that very sofa, making one of his cracks about its hideous pink and green flowers. She would've swatted his red Converse high-tops off the upholstery.

She hugged a silk throw pillow close to her chest. "Walter, the pastoral exhibit is ready to go. There's not an inch more space. Besides, it takes weeks to properly restore a painting, I mean, I assume you're talking about oils, right?"

"Don't sweat it. They're all oils, recently restored too. It won't be much work at all."

She almost caved, but then thought how she was always the last one out at night. The only one in on the weekends. Since Peter's death, she'd immersed herself in work. It was why Walter called on her alone for just this sort of emergency. Because Magda alone responded.

But the stabbing grief and disbelief that paralyzed her after the accident had begun to dull. It was as if some crucial part of her had grown numb, like a deadened limb she knew was a part of her yet was unable to rouse. She'd begun to question what all that work meant. Why she should even bother. "No way, Walter." Magda surprised herself with the vehement reply.

"Aw, come on, kiddo," he persisted. "They're in bang-up shape already. Just get your tools, and I'll meet you here."

She looked around again. She'd learned how to tuck away her brother's memory, but it had surged to the surface that morning with raw force. There he was again: She could almost see him rummaging through her freezer. Or making his too-strong coffee and leaving the grounds scattered on the counter for her to clean up. His freckled face would've broken into an apologetic grin.

The prospect of another weekend alone yawned long and grim before her. Another weekend where Magda would tick away the minutes until Monday when she could dive back into her job.

"Fine." She didn't even try to conceal the defeat in her voice. "I'll do it."

"There's a honey!" Walter's patronizing be-a-doll this and you're-a-peach that would feel more condescending if he hadn't been so sensitive just after Peter's death. He'd treated Magda like the kindly uncle she'd never had. It was a fine line, though, between pleasantly familiar and flat-out presumptuous.

He added, "I'll see you in . . . how's thirty minutes?"

"Thirty?!" Magda aggressively plumped the pillow in her lap.

Her boss let the silence hang.

"Okay, Walter." She silently cursed him. It wasn't the first time he'd used dead air to get her to do something she didn't want to. "See you in thirty."

Grumbling to herself, Magda shuffled to the kitchenette. "We finalized that exhibit weeks ago. What does he expect? I mean, he can't just give me forty-eight hours to make something museum-ready."

She stood and stewed for a moment, then banged the phone into its cradle. Anger seeped into her voice as she continued, "Is there mold, discoloration, varnish, dirt, peeling? Are the paintings on canvas or board? And he'd better just need them cleaned, not restored." Her eyes widened at that prospect. Even the slightest bit of inpainting could take days.

It used to be that she worked hard because of her ambition. She'd once been hungry to claim a life as grand as her parents'. But she had vowed that her glory would be gained from hard work alone. Not because of her last name, or her trust fund.

If only she'd gone with Peter the weekend he died. Maybe she could've prevented the accident, saved him somehow. But she'd worked instead, and it was her work she clung to now, to stave off the despair. Filling her days with rote activity was the one thing that managed to push her brother back into the recesses of her mind.

Taking a few breaths to gather herself, Magda stood straight, flipped her long red hair over her shoulders, and smoothed her hands along her simple cotton dress. She crammed all that hurt back down deep, and applied her work-self as she would the shellac on one of her paintings.

She slipped on some sandals and was halfway out the door when the ghost of a smile touched her face. She strode back into the kitchen and then was on her way out again, a loaf of bread tucked firmly at her elbow.

❀

The immense sign mocked her. Even though Magda's taxi was still a couple of blocks from the Met, she could see the advertisement fluttering high above the museum's entrance. *Finding Arcadia: Pastoral Paintings of the Seventeenth Century.*

"You can stop here." She grabbed a crumpled ten out of her purse and thrust it at the cabbie. "I'll walk the rest."

Clutching her toolbox and the now mashed bread, she marched down Fifth Avenue, her irritation with Walter dissolving as she began to anticipate what treasures might be waiting at the museum to suck her in for the weekend.

Her wealthy childhood had afforded her the luxury of studying fine art, but she'd bristled at the cliché. Magda had resolved to be more than the little rich girl who knew her way around pricey antiques, and made sure she gave no one the excuse to think her anything less than a rigorous academic.

When she was first hired as assistant curator of European Art, a few of her coworkers had looked down their noses at the girl who'd been chosen for her last name. What museum in their right mind would turn down a member of one of Manhattan's more philanthropic society families? And so Magdalen Deacon had made it her mission to be the best of the best when it came to identifying, cleaning, and restoring old paintings.

She entered a side door to avoid the typical throng of Saturday morning tourists. The heat of the Manhattan summer was claustrophobic enough; given a choice, Magda would avoid a crowded, enclosed space every time. Savoring the sweet blast of air-conditioning, she flicked on a single light switch and walked down a flight of stairs to an antiseptic hallway. Door after door of restoration offices lined a hall that, during the week, had the feel of a busy hive, its workers buzzing around independently and with intense focus. Empty, though, it was like a tunnel; the tiles that glared white during work hours now shimmered gray under the single row of buzzing fluorescent tubes.

She'd been amazed the first time she visited the employees-only area. Dozens of rooms lined the bowels of the museum. A number of them housed mismatched sculptures like a millionaire's garage sale, while others felt like bank vaults, with temperature-controlled facilities housing drawer after drawer of prints and drawings. Her favorite, though, was the painting storage, where hundreds of priceless works hung on panels that she could flip through, much like browsing posters in the museum shop.

"Thanks, kid."

Walter's voice startled Magda and she smiled at herself. She always had a tendency to get a bit fanciful whenever she was among so much art. The empty rooms and dim lights only intensified it.

"No problem," she said, realizing that it was true. Now that she was there, it really wasn't a problem. Magda was actually quite curious about the paintings that would drive Walter to call her for such a fast and loose cleanup job for a ready-to-go exhibit.

"They're in here." He rattled through the dozens of keys hanging from his belt. It was yet another surprise for a curator. Generally a tweedy set, they weren't inclined to janitorial-grade key chains. "They arrived by courier late last night, anonymous bequeathal. All Scottish pieces, which is unusual."

Walter fumbled along the wall for the light, continuing, "Frankly, my dear, I don't give a damn what their provenance is; they're a perfect fit for the exhibit. We've got Flemish paintings coming out of our ears, but we're short on Britain. I even see some Scottish Highlands here, which is unheard of for this time period."

The lights flickered on and Magda drew in her breath. The table was cluttered with dozens of miniature landscapes, each bearing some romantic vista on a small scale: seascapes under bright blue-saturated skies, idyllic farmlands dotted with sheep, storm-clouded castles, purple heather-tangled moors, and emerald green rain-drenched glens.

"Don't have a cardiac, kid. I don't want you to clean the lot of them. There are just two that I have to have. The rest is gravy.

"Besides," he added, picking up one of the small paintings, "they look like they were restored not too long ago." He held the piece horizontally up to his eyes, shifting it under the light, scanning the surface for imperfections. "You should get these under the UV, see what's what. Otherwise, they should tidy right up with a superficial cleaning."

But Magda wasn't listening. Nor had it been the number of paintings that had made her gasp. It was the portrait that held her attention, looming so incongruously alive among the pool of formal landscapes. Leaning askew against the rear wall was a life-sized painting of a man, pictured from the waist up, against a background of dense, impermeable black. Only the man's face was illuminated with color, and his features seemed to emerge from the darkness. White paint slashed dramatically across his left breast, as if he'd been lit from below, a candle's flicker cutting through the shadows, turning his suit of armor into a dull gray.

He was handsome, but not too perfect. His features were fine, except for his nose, which was just a fraction too large and gave his face a strong, masculine appearance. Brown hair hung in loose waves to his shoulders, making him appear somewhat more disheveled than these sorts of portraits usually depicted, as if the painter had just caught his subject in mid action. His black eyes stared, and they were painted with such vitality the man seemed about to break into a wicked grin, charisma pinning him to the surface of the canvas like a magnet.

"You hungry or something?"

Magda jumped and looked at Walter as if seeing him for the first time. "Huh?"

"You really are an absentminded professor, kid." He nodded toward the loaf of bread crushed under her arm. "You on an all-carb kick or something?"

"This?" Magda looked down and seemed to come back to earth. "Oh, yeah, we're so short on time, I thought I'd bring out one of my favorite cheats."

"You're on a diet?"

"What? No, of course not. It's a trick I use, for the painting. Dough can clean better than any solvent. You just wad it up, and—"

"Okay, whatever, I get the picture. Now just get to work. And get your eyes off Mister Universe over there. You're only interested in these two." Walter pointed to a small matched pair of landscapes depicting the same Highland glen at different times of day. "You don't see that kind of thing a lot, at least not before the Impressionists came along."

"Walter, wait." Magda stopped her boss just as he was walking out the door. "Who is that guy anyway?" she asked, staring again at the portrait.

He huffed an exasperated sigh. "I take it you're not going to concentrate until you know, huh?"

"Hm?" She looked at him distractedly. "What was that?"

"Mag," he grumbled, shaking his head. "The things I do for you." Putting his briefcase down, Walter shuffled through a stack of papers. "Aha. That is . . ." He took out a small, yellowed note card and read, "James Graham, first Marquis of Montrose."

"They had marquis in Scotland?"

"Yeah, I guess so." He saw from her expression that she wasn't going to let him go without more information so, scanning the paper, Walter enumerated the pertinent facts to Magda. "Let's see . . . seventeenth-century nobleman . . . Scottish . . . started some group called the Covenanters . . . something about the king and religion . . . ah . . ." Walter was silent for a moment.

"What?" she asked impatiently. "*Ah* what, Walter?"

"Looks like the guy switched sides . . . led a bunch of High-landers to battle . . . That must've been a sight, huh?"

Magda glared.

"Okay, let's see . . . ech." He finished quickly, "Captured, imprisoned, and hanged in Edinburgh."

"That's hideous!" Magda exclaimed.

Walter looked up at her. "Yeah, I'd say. So much for your Mister Universe. Glad you don't live in seventeenth-century Scotland, huh?" Closing his briefcase, Walter demanded, "Now, take your Wonder Bread, or whatever that is, and clean my paintings."

The door whispered shut behind him.

Chapter 2

"But what of Yvette?" Tom tugged at his coat, clinging tight from perspiration, and shuffled quickly to keep up with his companion's long strides. "She was a lovely, porcelain-complected lass."

"Aye," James agreed merrily. He eyed his friend's state and slowed down. "A lovely lass indeed, were I in want of a wife."

"And ze French accent, James, ooh la la!" Tom patted at his flushed cheeks with a handkerchief. "Would that I had family eager to find me a titled young maiden. Och, man," he added, "slow . . . down."

James Graham came to an abrupt halt along the edge of Parliament Square. In a habitual gesture, he flipped the hem of his overcoat to reveal fully the basket hilt of the broadsword at his side. He stood taller than most, and the morning sun cast sharp shadows on his face as his eyes roved over the mob that was rapidly forming.

"And with that French coat on your back"—Tom, chest heaving, caught up to James's side—"how could you not want a bonny French bride?"

"If you're so enamored, you should wed her yourself." A mischievous light danced in James's eyes as he focused on his friend. "Yvette is a blooming flower, but I'm not yet done smelling the roses, aye?"

"James!" he howled. "You scoundrel!"

"You find me indelicate?" James beamed, and the force of his presence crackled through his open, handsome features. "Just wait until you hear what I've to say to the king's man."

He abruptly pushed into the growing mob, now chanting and shrieking its fury. It had become a single shuddering organism, crushing in on the center of the square, drowning the blare of royal trumpets that began to trill over the din.

Tom's hand caught at his friend's sleeve. "Mind your words, James," he warned. "This isn't your parlor and these are not your friends. Speak the wrong words to unsympathetic ears and you seal your fate."

"I'm but a Scotsman." James was suddenly serious, his intensity like a flash fire. "And my Scottish king has fashioned himself England's king. So tell me, Tom"—his blithe expression hardened to match the vehemence of his words—"to whom do I give my loyalty when my ruler sits on a fat London throne and changes the religion of Scotland?"

"Oyez, oyez," the town crier shouted, ringing his bell from a platform atop the Mercat Cross. Clapping his hand onto his feathered tricorn hat, the man leaned over the elaborate stone parapet, visibly relieved to be so high above the throngs pressing in around its stepped base.

The Mercat Cross was a hub of merchant activity halfway down the Royal Mile from Edinburgh Castle, and was named for the pillared cross jutting high above the structure. The main attraction was its scalloped balcony resting atop a stout, two-story octagonal tower, from which royal proclamations were made and royal enemies executed.

The crier leaned back and, with one last clang of his brass bell, intoned in a mannered and resonant voice, "Charles, by the grace of God, King of England, Scotland, France, and Ireland, defender of the faith . . ."

The crowd's anger kindled anew, and over outraged shouts, he persisted, "Hereby proclaims supreme the new Book of Common Prayer. His Majesty decrees the Church of Scotland will minister from this book alone, to the exclusion of all others. Henceforth, no prayer shall be said without royal sanction."

With a final peal of his bell, he announced, "Clergy found in defiance will be punished for high treason. As decreed by His Majesty King Charles the First, on this day, February twentieth, in the year of our Lord, sixteen hundred and thirty-eight."

The crowd raged, pelting the crier with rotten vegetables and shouting, "Popery!"

James kicked over a nearby barrel. The velvet of his brandy-colored overcoat couldn't conceal the flex of his lean muscles, and the fabric pulled tight at his biceps and shoulders as he leapt nimbly atop it. He unsheathed his sword and rapped the base of the Mercat Cross.

The hiss of whispered voices swept like a wave over the crowd, and their cries dulled to a low hum.

"Good sir!" Feigning confusion, James shouted louder, "I beg your pardon? Yes, down here, my good fellow."

He flashed the frightened crier a dazzling smile. Despite the strong carry of his voice, James's tone was equable as he continued, "So, to clarify, my good servant of His Majesty, is it that Charles, by the grace of God, King of England, Scotland, France, etcetera, would have ministers read to their flocks from behind pistols cocked upon red velvet pillows?"

The crowd, which had for a moment been mesmerized by the cavalier Scots nobleman, surged into renewed outrage.

Shouts of "Popery!" and "A papist plot!" resounded through the square.

A drunken voice cried, "Keep your bloody English . . . popish . . . mass service book away from the Scots Kirk!"

"Aye," another slurred, "dinna fash the Scots Church!"

Laughing, James resheathed his sword. "There's the spirit, lads!"

"James!" Tom scolded, grinning despite his shaking head and furrowed brow. He jabbed an elbow in his friend's calves and pleaded, "James, get down from there. I swear, you'll not be at rest till you yourself be lifted above us in three fathom of rope."

"Why, Tom!" He hopped down from his perch. "Dear man, you flatter me! But you are the thespian, not I. Do you think it possible that I could play the hero in the court's next spectacle of public humiliation and shame?" His friend grimaced, but James only laughed.

"Come now, Tom." He clapped his friend on the shoulder. "Fear not. You're of brisker stuff than that, I know." Tom was sweating mightily in the press of people, and a stripe of perspiration ran down his back, darkening the fabric between the shoulders of his tightly buttoned coat.

Market sounds gradually replaced the hum of the crowd as the mob began to thin and merchants resumed their daily business. "It looks like you could use some refreshment, my good man. I'd spot you a pint. Or," James added, "think you that the king has outlawed ale in Scotland as well?"

"*Wheesht.*" Tom silenced him, looking around nervously. "You'll be the death of me, James Graham. If you manage to keep your own self alive so long."

"Nerves, man," James exclaimed. "I'm a Scotsman in the middle of Edinburgh. My king cannot hear me when he's nowhere to be found."

"Hush, I say. The king's men are everywhere, and I'll not join you on the gallows." Fleshy cheeks blotching crimson, Tom pursed his lips in thought, his normally jovial demeanor turned solemn.

James barked a quick laugh. "But I've upset you!" He hugged his friend to his side. "Let's see to that pint, aye? I'd have a spot of refreshment before we go."

"And pray, where are we going?" Tom asked with exaggerated dread.

"Back to my home in Montrose." James walked them briskly to a public house on the edge of High Street. "I need some time by the sea before we fight."

"Alright, James." Tom stopped in his tracks, and the apprehension in his voice belied the lightness of his words. "You have my attention. Before we fight whom?"

"And who else?" James cocked a single brow as a rakish smile split his face. "Before we fight our king, of course."

Chapter 3

It was a pleasant walk from the Fifty-eighth Street library to the Met, surrounded by the whir of traffic on one side and the happy squeals of kids and distant thumps of boom boxes emanating from Central Park on the other. The early morning brought a light breeze, and Magda was reminded how much she loved New York City. Long walks buffeted by the sounds of the city always blunted the sting of loneliness she'd felt since her brother Peter died.

The rare ringing of her cell phone shattered her serenity. Spying the number on the caller ID, she girded herself to answer. "Hi, Dad."

"Magdalen, dearest! How's my little butternut?"

"Oh, I'm alright," she sighed. "I—"

"Your mother is very upset with you, you know."

And just like that, her father executed his greatest signature move, the sudden flip from Daddy-boisterous to Daddy-business. It was a skill she could just picture him using in the boardroom. Skip Deacon lets them in with his chumminess, gets their defenses down, then goes in for the kill. And damned if she didn't get sucked in every time.

"We had a lovely time at last night's Founder's Gala," he added, "though your presence was sorely missed."

"Uhhh . . . oops." Magda had forgotten her mother's latest benefit. The usual parentally induced headache seized the top of her skull. Rubbing between her brows, she couldn't stop herself from asking, "Remind me, what'd mom found this time?"

"Magda, you know how much your mother does for the community."

"Sorry," she said. And she did know, having witnessed her mother's glory from the sidelines as she was raised by a series of well-meaning, albeit thickly accented, nannies. "I got pulled into a project at work and couldn't get away."

"Your mother and I do not understand why you keep that job. If you're so set on a museum, join your mother on the board. You'll never—"

"I know, I know," she interrupted. "I'll never meet a nice man cooped up in the basement at the Met. I said I was sorry I missed it." She'd dated her share of well-to-do boys in school, and then moved on to rising young businessmen after college. None of them ever quite took, though, and now her folks no longer even bothered to be subtle about their matchmaking.

"She'll be happy to hear it. Call and tell her yourself."

"You mean actually speak to her?" Magda's attempt at humor fell flat, and she added, "How about I just send some flowers instead?"

"Call her, Magdalen," he scolded. "Though flowers would be lovely too. And please?"

"Yes?" she asked, the trepidation clear in her voice.

"Don't forget, it's off to Saratoga come June!" And there he was, Daddy-boisterous peeking his head up again. "I don't expect you to make it for the Tipton auction, but I'll see your shining face in our box for opening day."

"You guys don't even own a racehorse." She massaged her temples, squeezing her eyes shut tight. "Your fascination with the track is beyond me."

"Don't be difficult, butternut. You know your mother likes to summer on the lake, and many of her friends have their own boxes."

"I'll go to the races." She stopped walking. Hand still on her forehead, her vacant gaze landed on a street vendor selling Indian-print skirts and scarves. "I'll even wear one of those ridiculous hats, but I refuse to join you at your lake house."

"*Our* lake house," he chided. "Try as you might, you will not forget you are a member of this family. Saratoga opens at month's end, and we expect you in attendance there and at the lake after-ward. And this time you will dress in a manner appropriate to a young Deacon daughter." And there it was, the full shift. Daddy-business was back, and he stuck his landing.

After a moment of tense silence, Magda pleaded, "Please don't make me go to the lake. You know I hate it there."

"Well, we all need to move on. Your mother and I are in terrible pain every day, but it's what Petey would have wanted."

"Move on?" she blurted. "I can barely make it through the summer and you suggest I *move on*?" Magda knew that even though they mourned differently than she did—in fact, did most things differently than she—her parents had been heartbroken at Peter's death. And yet she heard herself say, "Meanwhile, you and your pals toodle around all season in your boats—"

"That's quite enough," he snapped. "Just . . . just . . ." Flustered, he fumbled for words, then finished, "Just promise you'll make it to opening day. Now go send your mother some flowers. She's on a peony kick."

"Sure. Bye, Dad." Magda flipped the phone shut before he could say any more.

Growing up, she'd idolized her father. He'd appear in their Upper East Side apartment every night, just about the time she was about to slip into bed, and scoop her onto his lap for a goodnight hug and kiss. She had visceral memories of these moments: tracing her small fingers along the top edges of his crisp shirt collars, hugging her nose into the powdery dry-cleaning smell of his suit jackets, rubbing her cheek along the cool silk of his ties.

Magda walked on, pushing away the memories. In some abstract way she loved her parents, and in their way they loved her, but that only meant they knew the most effective ways to hurt each other. Mostly they were just strangers.

She silently thanked Walter for giving her work to do that weekend. Her routine reassured her—padding around the workshop barefoot and silent with just a cup of tea and her tools for company—and slipping into it was like shrugging on an old cardigan.

Missing last night's fund-raiser was a gaffe, but her mother spearheaded so many organizations and boards and benefits, they were impossible to keep straight. Magda had always had her brother for reality checks after those sorts of missteps with her parents. The two of them had gone away to boarding school for their high school years, and it'd been best for everyone. Their mother could tend to her busy social calendar without the complications of messy childhood faces and feelings, and Magda and Pete had forged their own, however unconventional, mini nuclear family.

But now that he was gone, the only thing that managed to bring her back to the realm of the ordinary was, ironically, her very unordinary work. She'd felt aimless since Peter's death, as if some inner light that once filled and guided her had been snuffed out. Tunneled in her workroom and immersed in a single painting, though, she'd wonder at all the emotions the artist had poured into the work and feel her old vitality return, imagining the energy that had been directed toward the subject, musing whether the artist had been happy, or aloof, or moved, marveling that each brush-stroke was a purposeful gesture made by that person so long ago. She could almost sense how it might be to tap into such a consuming passion, remembering for a moment what it had been like to feel joyful, expansive.

The landscapes had taken her all of Saturday and into the night, but, in all, the job had been surprisingly easy. A bit of melted beeswax took care of a small area of flaking along the edge of one of the paintings, and she was able to bypass solvent completely when cleaning the other. Walter had been right: The pieces had been in almost mint condition already. Somebody had restored them not too long ago, and done a decent job besides. The only flaw she found was some repair putty, visible only under the UV light.

Some brushes and her wonderfully unorthodox bread took care of the light cosmetic cleaning. Wadded-up bits of dough pressed methodically along the surface pulled the soil right off. It was her favorite trick, and she'd learned it not in graduate school, but from the Deacon family housekeeper. Followed with a dusting from a clean, soft paintbrush, the paintings were exhibit-ready.

She'd thought to spend Sunday catching up on rest and errands, but dreams of the mysterious man in the portrait had haunted her sleep. That roguish face, captured on canvas, came alive in a dream to break into a mischievous smile. In another, the silk of his shining brown hair was wavy and soft under her fingertips.

And what had startled her awake over and over through the night: witnessing the flint in his eyes dampen to a flat black stare, as he stood to face his fate on the gallows.

She'd woken that morning compelled to return to the museum. She needed just one more look at that curious portrait before Walter took it and stowed it away. And so she was off to her basement workroom, by way of the library for a book on Scottish history, to pay a visit to the brown-haired Mister Universe.

She flipped through the pages as she walked and was surprised to find that James Graham was actually a famous figure. He had been a man of wealth and status when he sacrificed everything to fight for Scotland. He'd fancied himself a poet, and Magda pored over lines he'd written that now felt tragically prescient.

> But how to conquer an eternal name:
> So, great attempts, heroic ventures shall
> Advance my fortune or renown my fall.

She whipped her head up at the careening trombone blare of a car horn, just as she felt the collar of her sundress tug tight against her throat.

"What the hell, lady?" The man took his hand off the back of her dress and stepped back as if Magda were infectious. He had pulled her back from stepping blindly into the crosswalk, right in front of a speeding cab.

"I . . . I . . ."

"Yeah, well, I'd come back to earth if I was you. This is New York, not some walk in the country, so watch it."

"Yes, I . . ." Magda's heart was pounding from the near miss. Cheeks flushing red, she mumbled a quick thanks and darted across the street as the light turned green.

❁

The unnerving intimacy tightened her chest, constricting her breath. Magda had brought the portrait into the windowless workroom where she examined everything under ultraviolet light. She didn't know why a painting of a man long dead would be different from any other work of art, but her hand trembled over the remaining light switch. She felt vulnerable, like some preyed-upon animal, sharing such a small, dark space with his unblinking gaze.

Magda shook her head, flicking the light off and the UV wand on. The painting buzzed to life in an eerie, Technicolor glow. Immediately engrossed, Magda slipped off her sandals and, squinting her eyes, leaned in to study the bright hum of light wavering across the painting's surface.

She scanned for signs of tears, punctures, or even old repairs, but remarkably, there were no telltale dark purple blotches under the ultraviolet light. What she did see were centuries of grime and soot that had discolored the varnish and now glowed in a pale greenish yellow UV haze. Dust, visible as small bullets of electric blue, jangled across the surface.

"Where have you been? All these years"—switching the UV wand off and the lights back on, her eyes roved the surface of the portrait—"and not a single bit of harm done to you."

Magda studied his face, and her cheeks flushed at the strange feeling that those black, almond-shaped eyes stared back. Though his brown hair waved to his shoulders, it wasn't styled in a way she imagined court fashions required, falling loosely around his face and tousled over his brow. Magda studied his mouth intently and fought the sensation that, if she stared hard enough, his lips would curve into a slow smile.

Without thinking, she broke a cardinal rule of museum work and extended her ungloved hand, touching the utter blackness of the portrait's background. Gasping, Magda pulled back as if stung.

The painting was cold.

Maybe she was just chilled, she thought, as she chafed her hands together. Although cool to the touch, paintings definitely did not generate their own temperatures.

Magda slowly lowered her palms to the portrait, one on either side of the man's face, and she drew in a breath with the shock of it.

The portrait's black background wasn't just chilled—it was a raw, dead sort of cold. An ache crept up Magda's forearms as she tried to puzzle out the growing impression of damp paint under her fingertips. She eased her hands along the surface. The typical hard peaks and valleys of any oil painting were absent. Instead, Magda had the sensation that her hands would sink into the paint if she let them, like penetrating the surface of an inky black pool.

The fluorescent tube overhead began to flicker, echoing the dull hum that had begun in the back of her head.

Once again she pulled her hands back, but slowly this time, and her eyes met those of the man in the portrait. The urge to touch him overwhelmed her; she had to feel the smoothness of his cheek, trace the light arc of his eyebrow beneath the muss of hair that rested on his brow. Magda flexed her hands and, mesmerized, reached out, hovering just over the painting's surface.

The drone in her head became a loud buzzing as she stretched a single fingertip out to brush his face. A breathy sigh escaped her. Magda had known, somehow, that it would be warm. That *he* would be warm.

Dizziness nagged the edges of her consciousness. Magda fought to focus on the painting, her compulsion driving her. She gently cupped the side of his face with her palm, and again, it wasn't like touching dried paint on canvas. Unlike the cold black of the background, his face felt as if it had been heated by that candle's glow, warm and soft like velvet under her palm.

The dizziness burst through her, consuming her, and Magda flung both hands out to steady herself on the painting.

Vertigo whirred in her skull like a fan's blade as she fell through the cold blackness.

Chapter 4

"Oh!" A man's voice rasped beneath her.

The hard thud of her landing jarred Magda's senses back to her. She was kneeling astride a man in bed. His chest was warm beneath her flattened palms, his breathing deep and even, in the languorous rhythm of sleep. A light dusting of hair bristled softly through the thin flannel of his nightshirt.

"A good evening to you . . ." His voice was a slow, rolling Scots burr. Shadows flickered in the dim candlelight, exaggerating the intensity of his black-eyed gaze. She felt the heat of his hands through her thin dress, as they came to rest lightly on her thighs. "You wee jade."

It was the man from the painting. She was dreaming of James Graham.

"You?" Shock choked her voice into a squeak. Jerking her hands to her chest, Magda stilled, even as her heart exploded into high gear. *A nightmare.*

"Aye." His voice was groggy with sleep, but the rest of his body seemed to be rousing to wakefulness beneath the covers. "Me indeed."

She tried to master the pounding at her sternum, assuring her body it was just a dream and dreams always pass. She forced air in, driving the reluctant rise and fall of her rib cage. She'd had nightmares before. Had them often, in fact, since her brother's death. Her conscious mind knew the drill: Convince the body to get ahold of itself while she watched and weathered the nightmare through, riding it like rapids that would sweep her along till its course had run.

Her eyes darted around the large square bedroom. It was unnervingly realistic for a dream. The furnishings were simple but lush. A maroon and gold duvet was draped over the mattress. A gold-tasseled tablecloth and ceramic pitcher topped a wooden nightstand. A desk and darkly upholstered chair sat in the corner. Heavy draperies embroidered with a fleur-de-lis pattern hung on the far wall, and by the sound of distant waves, Magda imagined that, if her dreaming mind could will the cutains open, they'd reveal a generous view of the sea.

She didn't remember going to sleep. *Where was I? The museum. At work. What happened?*

James shook the bed-mussed hair out of his face and broke into a devilish smile as his eyes devoured the length of her. "But do tell, love. Who are *you*?" His hands glided up Magda's legs, disappearing easily under the folds of her dress, thumbs roving out to stroke the insides of her thighs.

Her muscles tightened. His thick duvet gave with the pressure, and Magda could feel the solid warmth of his torso gripped between her legs. *An erotic dream?* Could she relax into it, let it pass . . . maybe even enjoy it? She tried to give her conscious mind sway, let it take over, steer the dream either to action or to an ending.

She studied his face. That same loosely tousled hair. Black eyes that caught and held hers. The mouth, slightly full, fighting not to curve into a smile. *Just like the portrait.* It had obsessed her, hadn't it? No wonder her unconscious mind would summon a vision of this very man.

She'd been dizzy, violently so, like there was a chain saw buzzing through her brain. Some people had bad visual side effects from working with ultraviolet light. Photic seizures were not unheard of. *A seizure, then. From the UV light.*

"Still here, love?" James prompted, giving her thighs a quick squeeze. He studied her, his eyes bright in the darkness. The slight tremble of his lips betrayed his puzzled amusement. The look in those eyes alone identified him, unmistakably, as the man from the portrait. Magda fought the urge to smooth the rest of his hair from his face.

Though it made sense that she'd dream of this man, Magda couldn't recall ever having had such a vivid one. *Postconvulsive hallucination.* She felt herself relax a little. *Wake up now.*

He cocked his brow as if to ask a question then appeared to think better of it. Despite continuing to stroke her legs with his thumbs, he seemed to be waiting for Magda to make the next move.

Wake up.

She couldn't bear the silence. "I know who you are," she blurted out.

His smile flared to life like a newly lit candle in the darkness. "But of course, love." He winked. "All the lasses do, don't they?"

"You're James Graham. This is a dream."

"Well,"—he caressed her thighs in renewed earnest—"I'm glad you find it so agreeable."

"No, I mean . . ." She shook her head. *Time to wake up now.*

The room was dark, but so detailed in the shadows. She was in too deep. *Wake up.* She shook her head again, vigorously this time.

"Where am I?" Panic intensified her voice, and she hopped off the bed in a daze. "Why can't I wake up?" It all felt too real to be a dream. Needles prickled the soles of her feet and up the backs of her legs. She slapped at her thighs, waited a moment, then pinched her arm hard.

Magda turned to him. "Wake me up," she demanded. "I don't belong here. Why can't I wake up?" She stomped her feet then paced a quick circle around the room. She froze.

"This!" She ran to a painting hanging over his fireplace. It was the portrait. *Her* portrait, from the Met. And the man sitting on the bed behind her was clearly the subject, with the same dark eyes and the nose and the mussed brown hair. The blood leached from her hands and the crown of her head, leaving her fingertips like ice. Frantic, she reached up, slapping her hands over and over along the surface. But the canvas lacked the energy she'd sensed at the museum. It was room temperature now, simply a painting hanging on a wall.

Had she been kidnapped? Did someone break in to the museum, steal the painting, and take her? Except Walter said that the man in the painting died in . . . What was it? Sometime in the seventeenth century?

"Wait." She stepped backward. "What's your name? Who are you?"

"Back to this, then?" He moved toward her, and she flinched. He looked around the room as if he could find some answer there, then focused back on her. "James, love," he said slowly. "Still James."

"James Graham?"

"Aye." He canted his head, a funny smile lighting his face.

"The marquis?"

"The very one."

She tentatively leaned closer, craning her head to analyze him more closely in the candlelight. Could he be a descendant? A look-alike distant relative? "So, like a great-great-grandson of the real James Graham?"

"No." Patience and confusion elongated the word from his mouth. "Simply James Graham. The very first and only Marquis of Montrose, at your disposal." He gave her a lighthearted bow. "Look here, love," James soothed, "it appears you like to stroll about in your sleep, so"—he put his arm around her shoulder and began to steer her to his door—"why not sleepwalk back to your room and there'll be none the wiser."

"I have no room." The pounding of her heart weakened, growing as shallow as her panting breath, until it skittered into the light tap-tapping of a sharp steel nail in her chest.

"No?" James retrieved a fresh taper, and the virgin wick crackled brightly and briefly as he touched it to his bedside candle. He looked her over. "You're truly frightened, aren't you?"

Magda clutched at the skirt of her sundress, nodding frantically. "I'm having a nightmare."

"Be calm, hen. No harm will come to you." He reached his hand out as if to touch her, then, hesitating, brought it back to his side. "What's your name?"

"Magdalen . . . Magda." She hesitated, seeing his blank look.

James tilted his head and gave a quick smile at the unusual name. "Well, Magda, I think it best that you rest here, and we'll sort you out with the dawn."

"But . . . but I am asleep already, aren't I?" Magda was trembling now, her limbs cold and bloodless.

"Aye, so you shall be." He steered her gently toward his bed.

She flinched away from him, her panic giving one last desperate flare. Anxiety was smothering her, pressing down on her chest. "I . . . I . . ."

"You . . . you"—he smiled—"need to rest your head a wee."

James wrapped his arm firmly about her waist and eased her down to sit at the edge.

"Come now, hen." There was something about his masculine voice, murmuring so gently in the dark; Magda felt herself unspooling, ready to lean in to him. Adrenalin had barreled through her, leaving her exhausted, unsteady. *This is how the nightmare ends*, she thought with relief. This strange man had been on her mind before she collapsed, and now he'd come to her dream, calming the chattering of her thoughts, easing her back into a mindless sleep.

She felt the bed's warmth at her seat, luring her, and she turned, crawling like a willing child under the covers. They still held his heat, and her body gave a single violent shiver as she nuzzled down low. Only then did she realize how chilled she was, how the utter cold at her feet had turned into a bone-deep ache. *Sleep.* She'd wake from this. But first, *sleep.*

❀

He stared at the pale foot peeking out from underneath the blanket and imagined what it would be like to slide up that long, smooth leg.

James gave a quick shake of his head. The lass had been truly frightened. Now was not the time to let his mind wander. And yet the feel of those creamy thighs under his thumbs kept coming to him, bringing fantasies of slipping his hands farther up, under the bodice of that dress, so thin, and hanging loose enough at the neck for tantalizing glimpses of flawless ivory décolletage.

Unsettled, James shifted in his seat. He didn't recognize her. With that strange accent, she wouldn't be a part of his staff. And what of the revealing shift she wore? The fabric was fine, a rich blue like the color of lapis, and surely hard to come by.

A friend of his sister's perhaps? But she'd seemed terrified, and quite plainly out of her element. He'd felt her panic in her rigid legs, saw it in her eyes, flitting around the room as if she were a trapped animal.

Perhaps she was sick. That was the likeliest explanation, in fact. A blow to the head could cause such disorientation.

But there was the matter of her personal effects. Tucking the covers around her, he'd felt a hard object in her pocket. Baffled, he sat there now, turning it over in his hand. It was hard as a rock and shone a uniform red, but wasn't crafted from any stone he'd ever seen. A silver band with a small pewter wheel capped one end of the device. The wheel sent sparks like flint, and James couldn't imagine what its use could be.

It was her peculiar bracelet, though, that had most troubled him. Ugly and black, it seemed some sort of magical contrivance, bearing dark numerals that flashed menacingly on a gray face.

James leaned in, staring at the woman on the bed as if that would give some clue as to her identity. Though leaner than his tastes ran, she was a beauty, with long hair the color of leaves in fall. When her broad, smooth brow had furrowed in fear, James thought his heart might break for the poor creature.

He was intrigued. His unflappable nature was a source of personal pride, but this Magdalen flustered him, and James found he savored the novel sensation.

Perhaps it was growing up so close with his sister, or maybe his many dalliances through the years but, until that moment, James had found few of the female sex who'd held much mystery.

Crossing his feet on the edge of the bed, he smiled. Any woman who could unsettle James Graham was one to keep close indeed.

Chapter 5

Magda rolled onto her side. With her eyes still shut, she gathered one of the bed's many pillows between her legs and burrowed more deeply under the covers. A faint musk lingered there. She pulled the sheets higher over her shoulders and neck, tucking a cool patch close to her breast, and savored the scent of woods and dark spices.

A man's scent.

With a sharp intake of breath, her eyes shot open.

"Ah, she arises."

Magda bolted up onto her elbow, the icy gust of reality blasting away sleep's warm fog. *Him. Still him.* With that shoulder-length brown hair tousled from sleep, and a blue and green tartan wrapped haphazardly underneath his nightshirt.

Last night's panic had driven a deep rut; her body remembered it, instantly flooding once again with adrenalin enough to tremble her hands and warp her vision. She felt the chill returning, her face blanching and fingertips prickling into numbness, as if her body were being drained of blood.

Her eyes darted around the room. The same room from her dream. He'd drawn back the thick draperies, revealing a bay of three rounded windows. Though narrow, they stood taller than a man, and the morning sun shimmered over the glass with a blinding white haze that obscured the view to the outside world. The seaside sounds she'd heard the night before were even louder now, made richer by the heavy brackish scent that hung, not unpleasantly, in the room.

"You?" she managed. The man from the portrait did not suffer in the light of day. The body that had been hidden in shadow was impossible to ignore now, with long, lean muscles and the bearing of an appraising panther. "But you . . ."

James regarded her with eyes more wide set and somehow even blacker than they'd been painted, and Magda thought distantly that the portrait hadn't done them justice.

"Aye, lass"—he chuckled—"'tis still I, though I do recall we've already conferred at length on that topic, or were you well and truly sleepwalking?"

Pinning her with a disarmingly unreadable gaze, he added in a soft voice, "I knew the dress would match the eyes."

"D-dress?"

"Indeed," James said, shifting back to his cavalier tone. "I've procured some more . . . *suitable* . . . clothing, aye? You cannot very well troop about in your current state." He nodded toward a lump of predominantly green fabric heaped atop his desk in the corner. "Now, speaking of emeralds, hen, from what stone on earth has this little treasure been conceived?"

Magda couldn't tear her own gaze from James. His scrutiny over, he was biting absentmindedly on his lower lip, which, she only now noticed, was slightly fuller than the other.

"Magdalen?"

"Huh?" She looked down at her red lighter, weaving smoothly in and out of his nimble fingers.

"Oh, my lighter. I was using it to melt wax when I . . ." Magda took her head in her hands. Something about the man from the portrait tugged at her, and that nagging sense of familiarity had momentarily put her too much at ease.

"But . . ." Magda looked up, forcing her eyes to sharpen and meet his gaze. "I'm still dreaming."

James considered her, and their eyes met and held for a moment. Morning sunlight cut in at an angle, catching his profile, igniting the stubble along the edge of his strong jaw into flecks of gold and amber. Inexplicably, a brilliant smile dawned on his face. "No dream, I'm afraid." He hopped to his feet.

"You need some food in your belly," he stated authoritatively. "I'll have something brought in shortly to break your fast. I've set Cook to preparing something more savory than the godforsaken bannocks she insists on serving each morning. You'd think we were on campaign." He pointed at her and added, "Kippers, black pudding, and a buttery. That's what a man needs."

He walked slowly to the door. "A lighter, you say? You'll not mind if I keep it in my possession a wee spell longer?" Considering the object closely, he added, "I'd have you demonstrate its uses."

"Oh," Magda replied, disoriented. "Of course." She smiled weakly, shaking her head at the absurdity, and thought wouldn't her parents be proud of the good breeding that maintained polite civility even in nightmares.

Thinking her smile for him, James rekindled one of his own, the corners of his eyes wrinkling with the pleasure of it. Her breath momentarily faltered, very nearly knocked down by the force of his charisma. Heart thumping to life, Magda instinctively pulled the duvet tight to her breast.

"In the meantime"—his eyes ran over the covers concealing her body—"as pleasant a sight as you make in my bed, we'll need to sort you out. I've, shall we say, a date with my king and I'm away within the fortnight."

He added quickly, "If I cannot jar loose your memories, then I'll do you the courtesy of leaving you with someone who can."

"But . . ." She swallowed. Her mouth was sour with fear, burning like bile in the back of her throat. She hadn't lost her memory. She just couldn't make sense of it. Couldn't make sense of the fact that she'd somehow been transported from Manhattan to—what did Walter say?—seventeenth-century Scotland. She'd dreamt of this long-dead man, and now she'd literally fallen into his lap and into a dream from which she couldn't wake.

He turned for the door.

"Wait. What do I do?"

"Don't fret." James laughed. "I'll send a maid in to help you ready yourself."

She looked at the formidable mass of green plaid and white lace that he'd left for her. "But whose is that?" she asked, feeling the hazy tide of this nightmare pulling her in.

Peeking his head through the closing door, James said with a wink, "I've some ladies in my acquaintance who are always happy to oblige."

❀

She let her body sway with the maid's relentless tugging and pulling. Magda looked down the length of the absurd green dress to her slippered feet. *Barefoot.* She'd been barefoot. In her workroom. *The UV light.* Fragmented images came in a rush, and standing there, being dressed by some stranger, Magda had plenty of time to sort them through. She'd had some sort of episode from the UV light, but couldn't seem to surface from this peculiar dream.

There was barely a pause between the brisk knock and the door swinging open. "Ladies!" James announced, surveying the room. He'd dressed for the day, and somehow the sight of his clothes startled Magda even more than donning her own period dress had.

His britches were tight, made of a crimson and butter yellow plaid that was a perfect match to the hose hugging his calves. A high-necked yellow vest concealed most of his torso, its double row of buttons snug along his belly and chest. His jacket was crimson, with large metal buttons, and he wore a cravat tied jauntily at his neck.

Seeing James again was a shock, yet oddly reassuring too. Each time Magda saw him, he became more real in her mind. She decided to let herself flow with it. If she was going to be stuck in this imagined seventeenth-century world, she might as well be open to the experience until its conclusion. It didn't seem to be a nightmare, and she couldn't help but hope the dream would finally take an erotic turn.

Magda traced her eyes over all those buttons and the plaid. Rather than make James seem foppish, the extravagant clothing only made him appear all the more imposing. The fabric hugged his body, highlighting the tautness of his stomach, the lithe muscles of his arms and shoulders, and the hard silhouette of muscle so clearly visible along his calf and thigh. Fighting to avoid resting her eyes on the tasseled sporran hanging prominently and somewhat suggestively from his waist, Magda heard herself ask, "Yes?"

"Do forgive the interruption," he said with an easy smile, "but you'll need to stop your preening sometime this afternoon or we'll never make it to my physician."

He strode across the room with a proprietary air that was all too familiar to Magda, and she wondered if the real James Graham would've been that way, or if her dreaming mind had plucked the attitude from somewhere deep in her subconscious. He comported himself with the same confidence she'd seen in countless of her parents' wealthy friends, whether skimming through a champagne brunch or commanding their staff. James walked around like he owned the place. Because he did.

He raked his eyes over Magda in admiration. After hours of tightening, cinching, smoothing, and more buttoning than Magda thought possible, she had to admit she looked quite pretty in the forest green plaid he'd procured for her.

An off-white shift kept the wool from feeling itchy. The maid had stared overlong at Magda's bra and, embarrassed, Magda had allowed herself to be crammed into a corset with a readiness that she now regretted. The top of the dress was snug, and between the deeply rounded neckline and the stays holding her into place, her curves appeared healthier than they ever had. Despite the stiff bodice and the elaborate prep time, she was surprised to realize how comfortable it was, and how well suited for staving off the definite chill in the room.

In fact, the most trying part of the outfit had been her hair, which the maid had parted tightly down the middle and somehow gathered and looped into curls despite the fact that Magda's locks had never seen a wavy day in their life. And she'd endured it all as if she were plodding through a murky dream, waiting to wake up, or for her circumstances to magically change.

"Una, dear heart," James said, addressing the maid who now studied the ground, blushing furiously, "you are capable of wonders!"

Magda stared openly, spying the surreptitious pat he gave the young woman's bottom.

James's laugh was slow and deep in his throat. "Shame on me." He leaned close to Magda's exposed neck and shoulders, and catching her eyes in the mirror's reflection, trapped her gaze to his. His black eyes smoldered, the look on his face grave with intent. "We cannot overlook the real wonder in the room."

She felt the brush of his hair soft on her neck. With James so close, the musk that had hung on his sheets lingered now on the edge of her senses, and Magda felt the blood rush to her head, the faint dusting of freckles along her nose and on the apples of her cheeks flaming dark russet.

"Just look at you, *mon peu de mystère*, with a blush like a ripe plum." He inhaled deeply and added in a husky voice, "I'll wager you're as juicy as you look."

The feel of his hand stroking along her lower back brought Magda back to herself. Breaking their gaze, she hopped away from him with a startled gasp.

James's laughter erupted through the room. Magda looked to Una for support, but the maid who'd earlier been so sweet-tempered with her assistance now glared at Magda as if considering the many ways she could murder her.

"Come, hen," he announced merrily, donning a pair of broadly cuffed black gloves. "You're off to the doctor."

❊

James filled the carriage's silence with details about the town of Montrose. It lay on a spit of land surrounded by water on three sides: the North Sea, the River Esk, and the large tidal basin which Magda stared at now, glimmering steel gray and stretching into the distance, its glassy surface interrupted only by clumps of coarse bracken and the occasional hump of marshland peeking out from the water to announce low tide.

The brackish scent she'd detected in James's room was particularly heady now. Fresh bursts of the brisk sea breeze whirled into the carriage's open window, carrying that salty smell, rich and thick with life. Birds cawed overhead, and Magda watched as they lazily swooped and dove over the enormous tidal basin.

"You like it."

"Hm?" Magda realized she'd been staring quietly, mesmerized by the desolate view of the marshland reaching out toward the sea in the far distance. The landscape soothed her. The absence of civilization made it seem possible that she was looking at any seascape, anywhere in the world. The sense of familiarity was an assurance that she would soon wake to find her world the same as when she left it. Her body was no longer capable of sustaining such heightened panic, and her senses had dulled into a blunt concern that would keep vigil until this dream passed.

"The salt marsh." James's eyes were kind as they studied her. "Your cheeks bear the kiss of the sea." He touched his fingers to her chilled face. "Her breath is brisk, and it's rare the lass who appreciates it."

His attentions unsettled her. He was so . . . *vivid*. His actions so specific, so focused on her. Looking away quickly, Magda replied, "I . . . yes, it's lovely."

She felt his smile at her back, but doggedly stared out the window rather than once again face that frank gaze.

"You don't seem to recognize where we are," he said solemnly. "Is it that you're newly arrived to Montrose town?"

She huddled closer to the window, pretending his question didn't exist, willing the chill wind to stop the tears that threatened to fall.

"You can place your trust in me, hen." Magda felt his hand warm on her wind-whipped shoulder. "You truly don't know this place? Don't know where you are?"

Magda merely sat in silence, willing her situation back to normal. *It's time. Wake up.*

Speaking over the rattle and creak of the carriage, James graciously changed the subject, pointing out the town of Montrose growing visible in the far distance.

"Well, then, I shall tell you of it. You have before you my favorite burgh in all Scotland. And a fortuitous thing too." James edged close to the window and scanned the horizon. A thick cloud of geese swept across the sky, while a lone carrion crow hopped and jerked its head, pecking for mussels hidden in the rocks along the shore. "For I am its marquis."

Magda squinted beyond the stark panorama of brown and gray and into the distance. As the vista gradually resolved more clearly into Montrose town, her nerves nagged at her with greater intensity. *I couldn't really have gone back in time, could I?* Panic barreled back to the surface, blotting out the tired desolation that had suffused her just a moment ago.

Of course not. Wake up now.

She could just make out the rangy line of mismatched buildings that sprang up between the bleak marsh on one side and the frigid water of the North Sea on the other. A seascape was in the realm of the familiar, but these scant buildings were not.

The past? Alarm hummed along her body like a plucked violin string, dizzying her.

She heard James continue, unaware of her swelling hysteria, "Montrose offers an abundance of gentlemen's pursuits. Golf, fishing . . ." He looked at Magda and tucked an errant strand of hair behind her ear, his touch jarring her already piqued senses. "Aye, gentlemen's pursuits abound," he sighed, "yet mostly what I do is return the Lowland cattle our mischievous Highlanders insist on reiving."

He mistook the bewilderment in her eyes for a question, and added, "You see, Graham family lands form a bit of a wedge between the Highlands and the Low. Highlanders yearn to put themselves in harm's way, and when skirmishes are scarce, such thieving in the night is a bit of a sport for them. And can be a rite of passage, for the younger lads. Though I'd wager they prefer claymores to cattle, generally speaking."

Dozens of cottages slowly came into view, low-slung and hugging the shore as if bracing against the wind off the sea. The number and variety of boats bobbing idly near the gray stone pier proclaimed Montrose a vibrant fishing community. Several roads spoked out from the harbor and connected further up in a winding, haphazard maze.

Just a very old town.

Two- and three-story buildings huddled over thoroughfares so thin they seemed perpetually cast in shadow, and yet Montrose didn't appear forbidding. Rather, the preponderance of red-tiled roofs and buildings painted the color of yellowed linen made for a cheery backdrop, despite the close quarters.

Not the past. Just a dream. A vivid dream.

James had said his physician was off of High Street. As they traveled there, ambling down a path that grew more claustrophobic with every turn, Magda fought the sensation that, like Alice, she'd fallen down her own rabbit hole.

"Pray, what is this material?" James asked, leaning toward her intently. The warmth of his leg along hers jolted her attention to him like an electric shock.

When she'd been alone in his room, Magda had been able to deny what was happening to her. The simple luxuries of his home were recognizable enough, and what had transpired was so surreal, it had been easiest to let the experience happen to her, to watch from outside herself, all the while waiting patiently to awaken from her dream.

But now that they'd left his home's luxurious confines and traveled beyond the serene landscape, nuances plucked from a history book overwhelmed her. Horse-drawn carts clattering along side streets; the thick brogue chants of fishwives hawking their glassy-eyed wares from mucky street corners; and the occasional person leaning out a window for a shout and a quick smile, showcasing vaguely soiled clothing and a number of brown jagged teeth.

Like a seventeenth-century town.

She craned her neck out the window, ignoring the frank stares she'd provoked. *No cars. No cell phones. Not even a damned bicycle.* Instead, Magda was assailed by foreign images, sounds, and such a stink. The astringent reek of old fish mingled with the sweet smell of refuse, turning her stomach.

"This red material, hen?" James prompted her, gently drawing her back in. He held the lighter in his palm.

"What?" She took it from him. Her growing panic made Magda impatient, and without thinking, she flicked the wheel. "Plastic," she told him testily.

How could he not know that? If I dreamt him up, wouldn't he somehow know that?

James gasped at the tiny blue and yellow flame. "What magic is this?" he whispered.

He wouldn't know that if he were from the past, a small voice nagged.

"And this item," he asked quietly, pulling back the cuff of his glove to reveal her digital watch, "from your wrist?"

"My watch," she replied, more haltingly now, taken aback by his reaction, and growing more distraught by the minute.

He stared blankly. In lieu of an explanation, Magda took his arm and tried to reset the buttons, but the watch merely continued to blink 12:00. "The time, it tells the time," she added, her voice growing manic.

"A miniature clock, is it?"

She nodded frantically, and his normally cavalier manner suddenly stilled. "Where is it you're from?" he asked. "Who are you to have such precious objects?"

Suddenly it became very important to Magda that she be able to set the time. She was done with this . . . this experience. She needed to be home, needed everything back to normal, needed to be away from this unsettling man who was the focal point. If she could just get this one thing to work normally, she thought, then everything else might jar back into place.

Frantic now, Magda dug her nails over and over into the watch's tiny black buttons. "I . . . I can't seem to reset it."

A relentless beeping shocked the carriage, its modern screech shrill in contrast. The numbers still flashed midnight. Magda's throat ached with the unshed tears she realized she'd been convulsively choking back.

"I don't know what happened. I was cleaning a portrait, your portrait, and suddenly I'm . . ." A sob escaped her, and with a deep shuddering breath, Magda's tears finally came in a rush. Hysterical now, she rapidly glanced from James to the carriage interior and back again, as if there might be some way to wrap her head around the situation if only she'd find it. "I dreamt myself back in time, but I can't seem to wake up."

"In time?" James grasped her hand hard, quieting her fingers that still fumbled wildly with the watch. "When is it you think you're from?" His voice was tender, and the cavalier good humor that ever animated his features flickered out, replaced by genuine concern.

Magda looked at James as if finally focusing on him. She said in a quiet but steady voice, "I live in New York City. In twenty-first-century America."

The carriage came to an abrupt stop, and James caught her easily before she knocked her head against the wall of the coach.

The need to flee consumed her. Rational thought was pushed out of her mind, and all Magda could think was that she needed to run, to escape once and for all from this nightmare.

Before the footman could open the door, Magda dove at the latch and tumbled out. Cool mud gave beneath her feet and oozed into the fabric of her shoes, and she stood for a moment, dumbfounded by the oddly recognizable sensation.

Chaos whirled around her in a cacophony of foreign sounds and movement. The inside of the carriage had been insulated from the clamor of the town, and Magda stumbled forward as her brain attempted to connect the two.

A strong arm seized her from behind. James had her tightly about the waist and tugged her to him just as a horse trampled by, its rider cursing unintelligibly, close enough to fill her nostrils with the earthy smell of horse and to feel the whoosh of its jangling harness in her hair.

Almost run over, again. Her eyes darted up and down the street. *But no taxicab in sight here.*

James breathed heavily, his cheek warm against her chilled skin. She crumpled against his strong chest. *No modern buildings. So many horses . . .*

His thumb stroked absent circles on her upper arm. She perceived the very real pounding of his heart through her wool dress. *Not a dream.*

Not New York. Just carriages and horses and period clothing as far as the eye could see.

The past.

James held her firm as she fainted in his arms.

Chapter 6

"She needs a doctor, James!"

Magda had half heard the woman, clearly agitated, carrying on for some time in a hollow drone, as if speaking from the end of a very long tunnel. Her voice, surprisingly deep for a female, slowly resolved into intelligible words that pierced Magda's consciousness.

"You have a care," she shouted, "who you bring under your roof, young man!"

"I'm no longer a young man, Margaret," James replied wearily, "and you're not our mother to speak to me so."

"*You have a care*," she enunciated, heart set on continuing her train of thought, "who you bring under your roof! You are not the only one bearing the name of Graham of Montrose."

"Last I checked, dearest sister, your name is now Napier."

"You understand my meaning!" Magda heard a swat, sounding much like a glove hitting a man's head. "And you are lucky I called today, or you might have made an ill-informed decision. Now you will get that maid in here and send for a physician at once!"

"No doctor." Magda's eyes fluttered open, and once again her first sight was James, sitting at her side, a cool cloth pressed to her wrist, concern etched in the corners of his eyes. He gave her a quiet smile that shut out the incessant nattering in the background.

"I find you once again in my bed, hen." His voice was gentle as he began to lightly stroke the damp cloth along the sensitive skin of her inner wrist and palm.

"Not in front of me, you scamp," the woman reprimanded, wagging a beige glove at James. "I'll not have you endeavor your latest conquest in my sight!"

Magda turned and had to smile at the person attached to the scalding voice. Hovering on the other side of the bed was a woman with an uncanny resemblance to James, bearing his black eyes and longish nose on plump cheeks that wore an easy smile despite her constant admonishments. The woman leaned across the bed and playfully whacked James on the back of the head for good measure.

"Magda, may I present my sister Margaret?" James nodded hesitantly toward the women, trepidation clear on his face. "Margaret, meet Magdalen." Magda gave her a warm smile. She recognized a big sister when she saw one.

Then her smile faltered, the light in her eyes going instantly cold at the memory of her own little brother, and the constant bickering that had belied her fierce love for him. She never knew when Peter's loss would surge to the forefront; it was always the more brutal when so unexpected.

"James!" Margaret shrieked. "The poor creature withers in front of us even now, and you!" She pointed a thick finger at her brother. "You'll get your physician now, James, or I swear I'll—"

"No, really," Magda interrupted, "I'm fine." Her eyes met James's, and she added softly, "Really, I am."

Tossing the cloth aside, he gripped her hand in his. "Leave us, Margaret," he said, eyes not leaving Magda's face.

"Well!" she announced with mock anger. "I'll be right outside this door if this beast offends you in any manner."

A weak but encouraging nod from Magda sent Margaret out of the room in a rustle of skirts and dramatically beleaguered sighs.

"What *about* your doctor?" she asked immediately. For some reason, she'd implicitly trusted James and dismissed Margaret's urging for a physician. "Weren't we . . . What happened?"

"You fainted dead away. And," he added gravely, "from what you showed me, I fear you need more than merely a practitioner of the healing arts. Though," he added with a shake of his head, "I don't know the path whose destination does not feature your bonny self tied at the stake for witchcraft."

"Witchcraft!" She pulled her hand from his.

"Hush." James stood to secure the door. "Aye, hen, witchcraft indeed. And you'll mind your voice if you don't want to bring un-wanted attention to yourself. I've more than a few Lowlanders in my employ, and they're particularly skittish when it comes to talk of scrying the future, or any other sort of witchery."

"I'm"—she lowered her tone—"I'm not a . . . a witch." Magda flopped her head back hard on the pillow. She felt trapped. Relentless panic had ravaged her, leaving her desolate, sapped, her body out of adrenalin. "I told you, I'm not from here."

"And that is why you thought you were dreaming?"

She merely nodded.

"That would explain your fear. Your confusion." He stared out the window for a moment, lost in thought. "Aye, to be trapped in a nightmare . . ." he finally said. "A chilling thing indeed."

She nodded more vehemently.

"But perhaps you've merely suffered an injury?"

Tears spilled down her cheeks. He didn't believe her. If she couldn't convince him, he could put her out, and she had no idea how she'd survive.

"Your family might be looking for you even now."

"My family's not even born yet." She sniffled and wiped her face with the back of her hand. She was beginning to feel like she'd gone insane. She tried to pull it together. James was her one connection to this world. He had to believe her. She *needed* him to believe her.

"If I'm not from the future, how do you explain my lighter?"

He sat silently, appraising her. James took the lighter from his pocket and idly flicked it lit over and over. "I thought the world—*my* world—had such marvelous inventions. Clocks and spectacles, the printing press, the telescope." He tucked away her lighter and retrieved her digital watch. Shaking his head, he pressed the button lighting its face. "But none such as this."

"You're right." Magda sat up suddenly, nodding. "It's all new. That's all modern-day technology. Things like digital watches and lighters weren't invented until the twentieth century."

He studied her. "Tell me, Magdalen, how is it you find yourself here? You mentioned something of painting when you claim your world fell away?"

"Yes." The formal sound of her full name on his lips drew her eyes to him. She saw the trust on his face, knew then that he wasn't merely placating her anymore. And if he believed her, he could help her. She felt her shoulders loosen at the thought.

"Well, no, I wasn't painting anything. I work in a museum. I was cleaning your portrait. That portrait," she said, pointing above the fireplace. Magda craned her head toward the hearth, and the portrait hanging above it. James in armor, with lace at the collar, his hair worn loose, and black eyes pinning her where she lay. "It was right in front of me, and then . . . then *you* were there instead."

"How is it you encountered a portrait of me almost four hundred years hence?" Bewilderment and something looking like fear played on his face.

"Four hundred . . . What year is it exactly?"

"It is 1638, hen, with spring on the horizon."

"More like three hundred seventy years then," she stated, expressionless. "The painting. It felt . . . special. I couldn't keep my eyes from it."

She blushed fiercely at his self-satisfied nod.

"Aye, the artist did a fine job."

"Not like that," she added quickly. "It was powerful somehow. You seemed . . . alive." Her gaze roved from him to the portrait and back again. Her eyes pored over his features then over the fine brushwork that depicted the intensity of his gaze, yet still captured his easy informality. Feeling something tighten in her belly, she stumbled on quickly. "But it's different now. It's just a painting again."

He bit at his lip, and Magda found herself abruptly looking away to concentrate on some vague point on the far wall.

"'Twas one of the Black Friars who painted it," he said somberly.

She looked at him quizzically.

"Named so for their black robes, aye?" He explained, "They've a monastery in Montrose, and earn a modest income teaching, but mainly they're scholars of a sort, and a rare sight outside monastery walls."

Seeing Magda's interest, James bent a leg to sit more fully on the bed and, leaning in, continued, "They've a wee plot for tilling but, on occasion, circumstances require the men to beg in order to supplement their coffers. Though not a papist myself," he interjected quickly, "I'm drawn to men of letters and had the occasion to meet one of these friars, a fellow named Brother Lonan."

A wistful smile softened James's features as he continued, "He'd given me a livelier debate than I'd had in ages, at least without the benefit of ale to hand, and I saw fit to make a goodwill gesture, with some coins from my purse and a promise of goods from my cellar. 'Twas a small thing for me," he assured her, "and soon forgotten, but not so Brother Lonan.

"The man came round one evening—nearly frightened the staff to death"—James laughed, his handsome face breaking into an easy smile—"appearing in the dark as he did, like some tormented spirit in a black robe and bearing a tattered valise reeking of paints and oils.

"He insisted on repaying my kindness by painting my portrait, of all things. Claimed he was short on subjects yet long on time and would I do him the honor. Well, seeing fit to prolong our discussion, I agreed, and an invigorating debate it was."

Visibly moved, James was lost for a moment in thought. Abruptly, he asked, "But what has this to do with anything? The man seemed a canny artist, if a trifle dark." He grinned. "But certainly not capable of transporting lovely young lasses back in time to my very own bed. Had I known the means by which Black Friars express gratitude, I'd have tithed to the monastery years ago."

"Please be serious," she pleaded, her voice flat.

"Oh, but I am always serious, hen," he said with mock gravity. Cheerfully disregarding the daggers in her eyes, he asked, "You were telling me what role this strapping portrait played in your arrival?"

"Yes, well, I was cleaning it, and"—she hesitated—"well, I felt the need to touch it."

"To *touch* it?"

"Yes."

"I see," he said, rubbing his chin thoughtfully. "You needed to touch the painting."

"Yes."

"Of me."

"Yes," she faltered.

He pressed, "What did you touch?"

"I told you," she said. "I just touched it."

"But *what*," James asked, leaning in close, "did you touch?"

"I . . ." She stumbled, feeling the blood creep into her cheeks. "I felt compelled to . . ."

"To?"

"To touch your face. Your face," she added quickly, "in the painting. And when I did, something happened. It was like I fell through it and," she finished quickly, "there you were, and well, here I am."

"Here you are indeed," he said, his voice low, eyes glittering as he studied her face. "I take it that is why you attempted to slap my portrait senseless upon your arrival?"

She nodded, willing the tears that blurred her vision not to fall.

James lifted his arm, hand poised over her cheek as if to cup it. Slowly tracing his finger along her jaw, he asked, his voice a husky whisper, "And what would you say if I told you I felt the need to touch your face now?"

"I-I," she stuttered, feeling the heat from his palm like a caress. Lips parted, the rise and fall of her chest became an effort as she felt her breath mingle with the heat of James's thumb, threatening to graze along her lower lip.

Staring at her mouth, his own lips moved ever so slightly, as if pondering a thought that hovered there. Magda's gut felt suddenly hollow, as some long-neglected need fluttered to life in her core, tightening her breasts, speeding the pounding of her heart. "I-I'd say no."

James's laugh was a low and sultry rumble. "You, hen, are a delight indeed." Clapping his hands to his thighs, he pulled back from Magda, seeming not to notice the embarrassment and fury waging battle on her face.

"I'll send word for Lonan," he said. "I'm still unable to fathom what's transpired here, but a lengthy chat with the good Brother is in order." He added sternly, "I'd know what dark arts he's about, and why he's chosen to play at them under my roof."

He rose to leave. Still reeling from their exchange, Magda

stopped him. "James," she said through clenched teeth.

"Aye?"

"Will you please no longer refer to me as a barnyard animal? I have a name, and it's Magda. Or Magdalen, if you prefer," she heard herself amend, cursing her habit of resorting to politeness in even the most extreme of circumstances.

He flashed her a rakish grin and countered, "I'll consider myself advised, hen."

❁

"I tell you, good man, this is different." There was a muffled sound of dulled steel as James pulled his sword from its scabbard. "I am completely and utterly charmed." Elbows at his waist, James held his practice sword poised in an easy stance, bobbing lightly on the balls of his feet.

"Aye," Tom teased, "I've heard similar words fall from that mouth of yours before." Taking his time to fit each finger into an elaborate pair of leather gauntlets, he warned, "You'll have scandal at your door if you install a mystery lass in your bed."

"She's not in my bed," James said dismissively. "Now, place that sword in your hand. You've delayed this moment long enough."

"You know I prefer my pistol to all other weapons."

"Aye, and your enemy prefers you out of gunpowder, standing dumbly with an unseasoned blade in hand. Now," James commanded, "spar."

Tom swept his blunted practice sword out, striking a tentative blow. Flicking his blade to the side, James easily deflected the other man's strike.

"You must tell me who she is if I'm to leave you be. You've found an exotic princess from a foreign shore, perhaps?"

"No princesses, sorry to disappoint." James swung his broadsword around slowly, giving his friend the chance for an easy block. "That's the way," he encouraged.

"Tom," he added in a grave whisper, "she claims to be from the future."

"Oh, James!" Tom shouted, seized by laughter. The point of his blade dropped to the dirt. "That's rich!"

A light film of sweat already coated Tom's brow. He tugged

at his collar to help catch his breath. "I think, my friend, you've been ensorcelled by a bonny lass with an eye to becoming a marquise."

"This is no jest," James said flatly. "I saw . . . the wonders she has . . ."

He was cut short by another sudden hoot of Tom's laughter. "She's flashed her *wonders* already? I told you, a clever marquis hunter—"

"Hold your tongue," James snapped. "And raise that blade to me or I vow I'll end this lesson and give you some true sparring. Now listen, man." They slowly circled each other, heavy broadswords held in both hands, their blades touching lightly. "She had on her person objects that defy reason."

James twirled his blade overhead and slashed downward, forcing Tom to raise his sword high in a block above his head.

"She wore a miniature clock on her wrist, lit from within yet not hot to the touch, capable of making a sound fit to puncture your ears."

Tom's face was a fixed, blank mask as he parried James's increasingly aggressive volley of sword thrusts.

"And a fire that she kept in her pocket. Aye, man," he asserted in answer to the skeptical look that Tom managed over his blade. "A small bonny thing, like a jewel, cool in the fingers, that builds a flame with the turning of a wheel.

"Keep your guard up!" James shouted abruptly. "That's it, thrust, thrust!"

Short of breath, Tom sputtered, "Is this a scheme to back out of your quarrel with the king?"

"You'll not jest so." James drove at his friend from the side, bringing his sword down with a crash onto Tom's quivering blade just at eye level. "Ever."

"Careful, James," he yelped. "Mind the face!"

"I'd no sooner misjudge my blade's mark than unintentionally cut mine own hand off." James's sword dipped up and down in an effortless feint. "My feelings are unchanged, Tom. My intentions regarding our king remain deadly serious. I'd sooner not battle Charles, but if he'll not abide the sensible thoughts of sensible men, I see no other choice."

James punctuated his last thought with a strong thrust of his sword, and Tom skittered backward.

"I'm a thespian, not a soldier," Tom panted, holding his blade in a defensive posture. "So please just have a care."

"I thought you were a philosopher," James quipped.

"Ah, that was last year."

"Not so much hopping, Thomas. You'll tire. Your advantage is size."

"That's not what I'm told." Brows furrowed with exertion, Tom swung his blade around, and James easily ducked back to avoid it.

"Come, man, thrust! Throw your weight into it." Taking his heavy sword into one hand, James canted his body to the side and propelled himself forward, the long, lean muscles of his legs stretching into a wide V. "Attend the left side!" he shouted, and back utterly straight, breath coming as easily as if he'd just risen from bed, James slapped his sword lightly onto his friend's side.

"Och, man, I've just killed you." James stuck his blade into the ground and leaned into the hilt. "When I take my weapon by a single hand, what is it I've lost?"

"Not the battle, surely," Tom huffed, gratefully resheathing the blade at his hip.

Ignoring his jibe, James explained, "Placing my sword in a single hand, I have the advantage of reaching you from a great distance. But, in so doing, I lose strength and speed. Yours was an opportunity lost."

"Aye, James, once again you've bested me. I hope you're well pleased."

"What would please me is if you'd put your back into it. I'll not be able to mind you on the battlefield."

"And you'll thankfully not have the need to," Tom replied quickly. "I'm eager to be a font of wise counsel, but when it comes to the fighting, I prefer taking refuge in the outer ranks." Pausing, he retrieved a small square of linen from his pocket with which to wipe his eyes. "So you sincerely intend on going to battle over this?"

"We've signatures plenty on the Covenant, and the University at Aberdeen will surely provide us with even more," James said, referring to the manifesto they'd drawn up with a group of like-minded men. With it, they hoped to rally support—and signatures—throughout Scotland in an effort to protect their country's religious freedoms. "King Charles cannot, *will* not, ignore the reason of so many of his countrymen."

The king had married a Catholic, and Scotsmen viewed his new prayer book as but the first of many offenses. As crosses and chalices of gold began to adorn more altars, many feared the integrity of their own kirks were in danger.

"What if you find Aberdeen lacking in sensible men? And," Tom asked, his voice treacherously low, "what if you find that your Scottish king now listens only to his *English* countrymen?"

"Aye," James responded gravely, "that is when you and I will talk of battles."

❁

He knew he'd puzzled his friend with his talk of Magda, but James couldn't spare it a second thought. Tom, rightly, had steered them back to discussion of the king and their Covenant. Tom had not believed him and his story of Magda, likely never would believe him. And that was oddly acceptable to James.

He swirled his port, the liquid shimmering off the faceted crystal of his glass like a dark purple jewel. His hair was still damp from bathwater as scalding as he could bear. Stretching his legs out from the folds of his thick robe, he savored the languid feel of worked muscles beneath hot skin.

He knew the lass was special. Had known it the moment he'd seen her, leggy and spooked like some gorgeous chestnut filly. Her explanations defied reason, but so too did her strange and wonderful treasures. She claimed to be from the future, and he found he believed her. Enough, at least, to have had that devilish portrait stored away for everyone's protection, despite the fact that her repeated touching of the thing had been futile.

The situation was a test for any true romantic, and James was nothing if not that. Poetic words and deeds inspired him, drove him, and James challenged himself as to why her extraordinary tale should not be so.

Besides, she was different from anyone he'd ever known. Other people rarely caught James off his guard; for another person to astonish him so was a rare joy. Indeed, with her charmingly tentative poise, she was a refreshing contrast to the usual society women. Rather than fill the air with empty chatter, Magda gave word to economically chosen remarks through lips full and swollen as if just kissed, and James found he'd likely believe her if she claimed to be Mary Queen of Scots returned from beyond to seek her vengeance.

He saw clear the tempest that lay dormant in her eyes, shimmering like lightning on the horizon, giving lie to her studied outward calm. James was sorely tempted to be the man who'd set spark to flint, releasing Magda from her precise and tightly coiled exterior.

Contrary to Tom's cautioning against ambitious lasses in search of titled husbands, Magda seemed unimpressed by the luxury of her surroundings. Most other unmarried women of his acquaintance ingratiated themselves to James, cooing over his clothes, estate, furnishings—even his bloody horse wasn't above notice. Although not a vain man, James couldn't help but be aware that his affable nature and pleasant looks had opened many a door—not to mention a few petticoats—for him. But the things that elicited fawning titters from her female peers instead set Magda's eyes to a slow burn: a playful pat on the rump, a flirtatious word, or a prolonged glance drew that pretty jaw of hers into an ill-tempered pique that drove James to distraction.

And what was he to do with her? He'd sent for Brother Lonan, knowing his duty was to help her find her way home, yet he found he did not enjoy entertaining that thought.

But James and his men had penned the National Covenant merely weeks ago, and it was an issue he felt with the utmost urgency. The king had to be stopped immediately from making an ill-informed decision that would impact every kirk in Scotland. Indeed, he seemed set to sabotage the very notion of religious freedom.

To stop the Covenanter momentum now would be like an incomplete thrust of the sword. There was no time to spare: James had a dispute to kindle with Charles, and that meant he'd a woman with whom he needed to dispense.

He gave his port one last swirl and tossed it back.

Political concerns could wait till the morrow.

He had some hours left to him yet, in which to contemplate the set of that pretty jaw.

Chapter 7

"Come in," Magda said from her seat in the window. James had set her up for the time being in a small but sweetly cozy room of her own. Remaining in his room had clearly not been an option, even though he did make more than a few jokes at the prospect.

Restless and unable to sleep, she'd risen with the dawn and passed much of the morning perched on the cascade of small downy pillows that were piled in the window seat. The sun glimmered over the sea on the horizon, and Magda was comforted by the familiar pulse of the tides in the distance.

The sound of the seashore was such a simple thing, and yet she clung to it now. Its constancy reassured her, grounded her, gave her hope that she was still sane.

"You wee mouse, I thought I'd find you here!" Margaret swept into the room, and Magda thought how grateful she was that James had procured dresses for her in comfortable but lovely tartan wool patterns, rather than the more fashionable satin that his sister preferred, the constant rustling and crinkling of which only added to the impression that Margaret was formidable in both personality and size.

"Och," Margaret grumbled, "my brother is far too lax for my tastes, particularly when it comes to the bonnier maids in his employ." She bustled over to the bed and began tugging sheets and thumping pillows. "I come to call on you for a spot of midmorning tea and I find you sitting here like some sort of bereft hound." She added accusingly, "And I'll wager you've not yet eaten."

Magda shook her head, and not feeling particularly bereft or houndlike, she began to see why James was quick to bristle at his sister's badgering.

"You poor lass! Without food," Margaret gasped, as if missing breakfast was the greatest of deprivations. "My word."

"I've been fine, really." Magda straightened in her seat. "I haven't been hungry at all." She attempted to smile and failed, and not because of her hunger. Rather, Margaret's entrance was a concrete reminder of Magda's surreal and decidedly unsettling circumstances.

"And sitting here all by your lonesome," she continued, mistaking the reasons for Magda's dispirited mood. "Well, lass, you need to make your demands known."

Peeking her head out the door, Margaret hollered, "You there! Yes. Hurry it up, girl." She paused for a moment as, Magda was certain, some maid presumably scampered to attention as James's sister demanded, "There's a poor lass in here who's not yet been fed. Where's my brother? Who's in charge here?" She rattled on without taking a breath, "No matter, no matter. Bring up a tray." Magda heard timid murmuring outside the door, then, "Yes, please. And fetch some of that lemon curd as well."

Turning to Magda, she asked, "Do you fancy some quince jam?"

"I-I've never had it."

"You've not had quince?" Margaret looked at her in exaggerated puzzlement, then quickly ducked her head back out the door to shout, "And some of your quince jam. Oh, and I'd like bread enough to go round this time!"

She added in a mutter, "The way Cook metes out food. I say," Margaret turned to her, voice imperious, addressing Magda as if she actually had a say in the matter, "you've to demand exactly what you want! Men know nothing of running a proper household. You don't see cooks skimping on breads and jams when a woman's about.

"Now!" With an elaborate swoosh of her shiny rose-colored skirts, Margaret settled herself on a small upholstered chair across from the window seat. She arranged the table between them in anticipation of the tea and, facing Magda with a broad smile, announced, "It seems we've to get ourselves acquainted!"

A queasy feeling bloomed like a rancid flower in the pit of Magda's belly. "Has James not told you anything?" she asked, dread and uncertainty making her light-headed.

"No, lass, but what better way to get to know you than over a nice cup of tea, I say. And, oh dear"—she leaned in close, shading her eyes from the sunlight shining through the window—"you seem quite pale. The tea will be here not a moment too soon."

Magda couldn't decide if Margaret's concern was annoying or endearing.

"And what a rare sight you are. For all his comings and goings and female"—Margaret cleared her throat—"*acquaintances*, I've never seen my brother so thoroughly install a young woman under his roof. Now, tell! Tell! What of you, dear? How is it you've so captivated the elusive Marquis of Montrose? I'd hear it from you," she added conspiratorially, "as men leave out all the interesting details, don't you agree?"

"Yes, I—"

A knock at the door saved her, announcing the startlingly fast arrival of the tray. The food was whisked in by a wiry older woman who greeted Margaret with an ingratiating enthusiasm that clearly pleased her.

"Ah, mum! What a pleasure it is to have you here, and what a sight you are," she gushed, shaking her head as if in disbelief over the glory of James's sister. "And doesn't that dress just bring out the roses in your cheeks. I'd swear you were the younger of the Graham siblings."

"Oho," Margaret tittered. "Rona, you do flatter! Now, you must tell me all the scuttlebutt of the day."

Magda watched in fascination as the maid deftly set about serving the tea, doling out biscuits and jam, chattering good-natured gossip, all the while maintaining the veneer of mistress and servant.

"Tut-tut," Margaret responded to one bit of salacious news involving Una, whose name Magda recognized as that of the woman who had helped her dress the other morning. "I say," she went on, "my brother needs to keep a firmer hand on the goings-on under his roof. And just where is the layabout this morning? I sincerely hope he's not still abed."

"Och, no, mum," the woman explained, "he went off to the links with the dawn."

"Golf, again!" Margaret exclaimed. "It's a wonder he gets anything accomplished, he's so smitten with that forsaken game. I imagine he went with that, that *thespian*," she spat. "That Tom Sydserf, he and his exploits, I cannot keep up." She turned to Magda. "He says he's a Renaissance man, but I say he's an idler. First he's for journalism, then poetry, now theater. It's shameful."

"Well, mum," Rona interjected, "he's applied himself well and good to your James's Covenant."

"Aye, there's that," Margaret agreed. "My brother enlisted his help with this Covenant manifesto they've devised. Dangerous work, I say," she warned. "It's meant to capture the king's attention." Noting Magda's puzzled look, she asked, "You've not heard of it?"

Magda shook her head, and Margaret elaborated, "Charles has decreed that every church in Scotland forsake their teachings in favor of services with a more, shall we say, Catholic flavor. His wife the queen is a papist, you know. My James has it in his head that, if he gets the support of enough men, the king will suddenly have a change of heart." She squinted at Magda. "You've truly not heard tell of this?"

"Well, mum," the maid interjected in a conspiratorial whisper, "Master James sent for Tom late last night, said he needed a word, and quite upset he was too. A messenger arrived well past supper, most peculiar it was. Come from the Black Friars with tidings that didn't sit well with the master."

"From the monastery?" she asked, incredulous. "What sort of tidings would they have for my brother?"

"I don't ken, mum," she added quickly. Magda gathered that spreading rumors about one's employer to the employer's sister was a potentially risky enterprise. "'Twasn't my business."

Margaret glared pointedly at the woman, inspiring her to remember the rest of the tale.

"Och, mum," the maid suddenly recalled, "I did gather that it was something about a Brother." Apparently keeping household gossip *from* the master's sister was an even more treacherous path. "Seems the marquis had sent for one of the friars, but the man's disappeared. Taken off for Aberdeen they say."

There was a crash as a small blue-patterned teacup slipped

from Magda's fingers onto the silver tray. The maid stared aghast at the cup's broken handle, sitting in a puddle of brown tea that was beginning to dribble onto the floor.

Magda had only been half listening to the story, her mind otherwise occupied with strategizing a means home, and fighting the growing despair that nagged at her. But the maid's last bit of news had startled her right back into the conversation, bringing with it a wave of disbelief. This couldn't be happening. Had she and James discovered the portrait's author, only to find out he'd disappeared?

"Do you know this Brother?" Margaret asked kindly. She mused, "Perhaps herein lies some clue as to your mysterious origins, aye?" She shot a sly look at the maid, then continued, "For whatever reason, my brother hasn't revealed the nature of your home or family, and"—she examined Magda, her eyebrow cocked—"you seem to be as tight-lipped as a willful child facing a dram of medicine.

"Och," she sighed, "up with you. Rona"—she waved a hand at the older woman—"clean this mess up. I've had enough of my brother's intrigues. We're off to find James."

❁

The morning had dawned unusually clear, with a gentle breeze off the sea pushing thick white fluffs of cloud across a turquoise sky. James inhaled the brisk mingling of brine and grasses. He'd received bad tidings last night—Brother Lonan had apparently up and disappeared—but rare was the news that could bring him down when he'd a few holes of golf to look forward to on a fine day.

And nothing was more efficient at pushing all thoughts from a man's head than the links at Montrose. Cradled in the bosom of the North Sea, the course was bolstered by a wall of sand dunes along one side and peppered with hazards like sand, gorse, and long, impenetrable tufts of wispy dune grass that devoured golf balls like an insatiable demon. And the turf, so green as to provoke an Irishman's envy, was rippled by shallow hills like a sheet billowing gently to the ground. Wind could assail an unsuspecting golfer from all sides and gave the course its teeth, demanding complete vigilance of even the most talented players. It was an unusually large course, and James marked a banner day as one in which he had the opportunity to play every one of its twenty-five holes.

"How's your traveler from the stars this morning?" Tom asked, with laughter in his voice.

"You'll not fash me on such a bonny morning," James replied easily, a smile on his face as he scanned the horizon, distractedly tapping the shaft of the wooden club in his hand.

"I'll not fash you, unless your new lassie has replaced thoughts of Aberdeen." Tom adjusted his hands along the suede grip of his club as he took a few tentative practice swings. "You said we'd be leaving within the fortnight, and that was nigh a fortnight ago."

"Aye, and so we are off, and soon. I've not forgotten." James took his swing and was away down the green to the next hole when he turned and blithely added, "I fear we must bring the lass, though." He paused for a second, then said nonchalantly, "The wind is showing us mercy today, aye?"

"You'll not change topics on me, James Graham," Tom scolded, huffing down the hill after his friend. "What say you, bring the lass? To Aberdeen? Are you mad? You're off to wage war on the"—his voice shifted into a panicked whisper—"on the king! And then there's the Campbell to treat with."

"Now you're the one fashed, dear Tom." James squatted, studying the curve of the ground. "I'll not be waging a war, exactly. We're just off to . . . capture the king's attention." He stood and deliberately drew his club back to swing. "Inspire him to a bit of sense, aye? If he's a wise man, he'll listen. Ha!" he shouted, finishing his stroke. "A braw shot!"

Not waiting for his companion, James was off again across the fairway.

"But . . . och! Confounded game!" Tom cursed, fumbling his shot in his haste. "I'll ask you again, man," he pressed. "What do you plan if the men of Aberdeen have no mind for protesting their king?"

"Then, Tom," he declared, stopping short to address his friend, "that is when you and I shall talk of war.

"As for Archibald Campbell," James added, turning to amble leisurely toward his ball, "he'll stand with us. The Campbell has

vexed me in the past, and his days of mischief making are surely
far from over. But mark me, he will place his name on our Covenant." He sneered. "That lout won't miss an opportunity to wave
his pistol about in a skirmish, anyone's skirmish."

"What of the lass, James? The only gentlewoman on the road
with a troop of men! Is her presence truly necessary?"

"Aye," James replied, "if I'm to get her back home, the secret
lies with an errant friar who, I'm told, is to be found at the abbey
in Aberdeen."

Tom's brow furrowed. "So you persist in this fantasy that she's
a traveler from another time?"

"Observe her for yourself, my good man." James beamed. "For
here comes my bonny riddle now."

Magda was briskly making her way toward them across the
green, with James's sister Margaret trotting a few paces behind,
her red face contorted with effort.

James's blithe humor faded and sharpened into something more
intent, his eyes narrowing in rapt attention to take in the sight of
the approaching woman.

And a sight she was. Light glinted off Magda's hair, flowing
loose and smooth behind her like molten metal, the sun igniting
the dark russet into bright sparks of copper and burnt orange.

An unexpected hunger drove to his core, and James wondered
what it would be like to tangle his fingers in that red hair and bring
her mouth to his. Would she maintain that veneer of propriety and
stiffen in his arms? Or would she meld to him with a fire to match
the challenge that burned bright in her green eyes?

She had hiked the hem of her tartan dress up to accommodate
her long-legged stride, and her single-minded advance only exaggerated the lithely rigid line of her posture.

James wondered at what marvels Magda kept at bay. Certainly,
he mused, the more unyielding the façade, the greater the passions
it hid.

He exhaled sharply. They were soon leaving for Aberdeen, and
he would keep these unbidden desires in check. He'd always been
able to moderate the needs of the flesh, and now was not the time
to find himself fixated on a woman.

Placing a smile on his face, he donned his own façade. The

devil may care, James assured himself, but he would not.

"'Winsome she was, as is a jolly colt,'" he recited, a sexy tease in his voice. "'Long as a mast, and upright as a bolt.'"

"Excuse me?" Magda asked impatiently.

"'Her mouth was as sweet as honeyed drinks,'" he added seductively, eyes lingering over Magda's lips. "'Or—'"

"James!" Margaret reached the party in time to be scandalized by her younger brother's impropriety. "You'll not speak thusly!"

"What, dear sister, not a fan of Chaucer?" He winked rakishly at Magda.

Margaret merely stood there, jaw flapping wordlessly like a fish out of water.

"I've not had the pleasure," Tom interjected, deflating the tension. Reaching his hand out to her, he said, "I am Thomas Sydserf, and you are clearly the lovely Magda."

Looking a bit thrown off, she took his plump, damp hand and nodded.

"Though James has been remiss and neglected to inform me of *your* surname."

"I've been trying to extract her origins for the better part of an hour," Margaret interrupted in a chiding voice.

"Oh. Yes, of course, I'm sorry." She gave a small bob of her head to James's sister. "It's Deacon. Magdalen Deacon."

Margaret stared, puzzled. "Is that an Irish name?"

"Her father was a man of the cloth. Some sort of missionary," James said quickly. "Now, dear sister, we'll have plenty of time for your tittle-tattle, but the sun waits for no man and it's currently hastening its way across the sky, taking my game with it. So," he announced, wiping a chunk of turf from the head of his club, "if you've some business with me, you'll need to take it up as I play. I *will* get in a good game before we leave for Aberdeen."

"Wait," Magda exclaimed, startling everybody. "Isn't that where that friar went? And . . . you're going?" she asked, forcing calm into her tone.

"You can smooth the worry from that pretty brow." James looked at her with a glimmer of amusement in his eyes. "You're coming with us."

His sister yelped in disbelief.

"Aye, we'll discuss the details as we play."

"Pardon me?" Two bright spots of color flamed Margaret's cheeks. "Our Magda most certainly cannot play your wretched game."

"I, well," Magda interrupted hesitantly, "actually I *can* play."

Feeling an inexplicable mixture of pleasure and pride, James seized her with a look, thinking that somehow he'd expected that very response.

"Come, Margaret, we will be a foursome," he announced merrily.

"I think not," his sister replied, aghast at the thought. "Women do not play golf."

"Not true, not true." Tom tapped his fingers to his lips thoughtfully. "Mary Queen of Scots, in fact, played a fine game."

"We'll play a match of foursomes so you'll not have to take a shot each go," James said, trying to convince his sister. "You can forfeit any of your turns to your partner, Tom, here. But . . ." He gave a dramatically gusty sigh. "I suppose if you're not up to it, it's good-bye for now. I'll try to grab a moment before I leave Montrose to—"

"All right," Margaret announced, exasperated. "I'll walk with you, but I'll not touch that filthy ball, nor will I muck about in the wet sand."

"Fine, fine!" James grinned.

Magda shot a solid game straightaway, and James watched in frank admiration as she strode confidently across the fairway. She seemed to find comfort in their brisk walking. It was obvious that she knew her way around a course, and James surmised that something so mundane and familiar as a game of golf could be just the thing to loosen her up.

"It's a birdie," she announced, as her ball sank into the hole after a slow and uncertain roll in its final inches.

"I beg your pardon, hen?" James squinted, looking up in the sky.

Magda looked confused for a moment. "No, not a bird. I birdied."

His face was open but puzzled. There were few people more conversant than he on the topic of golf, and yet he found he wasn't surprised that this elegant, auburn-haired mystery was able to confound him on that very thing.

"You don't call it that yet?" she asked.

"I suppose not." Squatting, he shaded his hand over his eyes to study the slope of the ground. "Though it was a superb shot."

By the sixth hole, Magda and James had an easy camaraderie, fueled by what was becoming a thorough trouncing of the other pair. Magda, though quiet, seemed to be enjoying the fresh air, and more than once James had spied her with her eyes shut and face turned toward the sun. Another oddity, he thought. Most women shrank from sunshine, and it was refreshing to see one savoring its warmth on her face.

James watched as Magda swung her club back and forth over the ball in extended deliberation, and he finally yielded to temptation, sneaking up behind her to cover her eyes with his hands. He'd taken her by surprise and, guard down, Magda unthinkingly bumped him away playfully with her hip.

"Well," he laughed, taken aback himself, "if you're going to waggle so over that ball, I'll not be able to help myself."

They strolled across the fairway in amicable silence, enjoying the sun on their backs and the pounding of the sea in the distance.

James sunk a particularly difficult pitch shot, and Magda startled them both by yelling, "Nice putt!"

Mouth cocked in a half smile, he looked at her, his face unreadable.

She paused, uncertain, and asked, "That is a word you've heard of, right?"

"Please, hen." He grinned. "The Scots taught the world to putt, aye? 'Tis a Scottish word forbye."

Tom approached, his mood uncharacteristically somber. "I lost the bloody ball in the rough." By the end of the front nine, he'd taken over Margaret's half of the game, yet still was well over par.

James's sister had given up feigning interest in the game, and struggled toward them, navigating her way through the bank of gorse that had swallowed Tom's ball.

"Tom"—James pinned his friend with a serious look that said he'd brook no disagreements—"you and Margaret find that ball of yours. Magdalen and I will move on." He found he wanted to spend a bit of time with her not under his sister's disapproving eye.

They crested the rise, and James bent to stick his tee in the grass. "Now, hen, if you'd be so kind as to take this shot for me . . ." He held his breath for a moment, then, throwing caution to the wind, shot her an exaggeratedly sultry gaze. "I'd see how smooth your stroke is."

Magda's cheeks flamed. "My stroke is just fine, thank you," she managed.

"Oh, but I'd be happy to coach you." He stood behind her, slowly drawing his fingers down her arms to take her hands firmly in his. What had begun for him as a playful challenge intensified, and he was struck with the shock of it. His voice was low in her ear when he added, "But I'll first work on your grip."

"There's really no need." Her knuckles were white beneath the light touch of his hands. "My . . . my grip is fine."

Magda held her ground, and yet James heard just the slightest waver in her voice. Something vulnerable. A need there, belying the self-proclaimed strength and independence of another era. He was fluent in the language of seduction, knew how to beguile a woman and what it was to feel temptation in return. But suddenly, surprisingly, this was about more than just a game.

He wanted Magda. Wanted her soft and open beneath him. Wanted to see an invitation in her eyes, and an easy smile on her face. And he'd not be satisfied until he knew what it was that had made her so severe, had hardened her so.

James knew his breath was hot in her ear. It took everything for him not to nibble that delicate skin, not to trace kisses down her neck, nor draw his tongue along that creamy slope of collarbone. Not to feel her smooth flesh give between his teeth.

He was losing control. His want for her was maddening, pushing all thoughts from his mind. He found his hand smoothing the seat of her dress, cupping her in his palm. Felt himself slowly turn her in his arms.

"But . . ." she murmured weakly. Magda made a small noise in her throat, and it nearly unmanned him. He pulled her more tightly to him, felt the hard ridge of his cock push angrily along her hip.

He wanted to stop, knew he should stop. Yet he heard his voice, husky with desire, whisper, "Don't fret, hen. I thought we might work on your stance."

He vowed to stop at any moment, yet found that he kneaded her gently, her derrière rounded but firm in his palm, and was easing his hand slowly down between her legs. He sensed her respond to him, felt her breath, quick and shallow, on his cheek. And he found his mouth at her ear, saying, "I fear we must spread these splendid legs of yours apart if you're to—"

"I . . ." She stumbled out of his embrace. "You shouldn't . . ."

James stared at her intently, as he came back into himself.

"I just came to find out about . . . about that monk."

"Aye," he cleared his throat. "Yes, of course." He shut his eyes tight a moment, then swept her a deep bow. "You have my sincerest apologies. That was quite boorish of me. I . . ." His voice was remote. "I've no idea what possessed me to such coarse behavior." And truly dumfounded he was that a wave of such unbidden lust could overcome him, making him lose his senses in such a way.

"Do you accept?"

"What?" she responded, still reeling from his touch.

"My apology, do you accept it? It is sincere and I hope it finds your pardon." A gentle curve touched James's lips, as he willed himself back in control. He vowed to acquit himself in a manner more seemly for the Marquis of Montrose. "I do still hope to finish the game. Our Tom thinks himself a better player than he is. I'll wager this routing will take him down a peg."

Magda considered him. "You're maddening."

Taken aback, James let out a laugh, genuinely amused by her response. He'd expected her to slap him, or kiss him, but not this. Not this inscrutable dare in her voice.

"Aye, I am that."

"And you won't touch me like that again?"

"You've my word."

"And you promise to find this friar of yours who can maybe get me home?"

"Posthaste."

"All right then," she smiled weakly. "Play on."

❖

James tossed onto his side. It was rare for sleep to elude him so. A brandy by the fire, and he was always out by the time his head hit the pillows.

But tonight was different. Tonight brought with it Magda, appearing over and over in his mind's eye. He'd watched her from behind as they golfed, and fragmented images spilled into his thoughts now. How she'd knit her brow in concentration, unconsciously flicking her tongue along the corner of her mouth as she contemplated the course. How the tight bodice of her dress had highlighted the gentle curve of her waist and the long ivory line of her neck as it rose elegantly from the neckline.

Her power and poise had awed him as he'd watched her swing her arms down, pivoting her body to connect with the ball. And more than once, James had to force himself to look away from the forward jut of her pelvis as she followed through.

He'd let himself go too far with her. James had known many a woman, and never had he lost control in such a way. The urge to touch Magda just a moment longer, to slide his hand a trace deeper in her skirts, to grip her to him that much harder, had seized him like a madness.

He had to harness his desires. Magda had a home, and he needed to return her to it. She was too much of a distraction. He had responsibilities. His obligation to his country far outweighed anything—or anyone—else.

The thought brought with it an unexpected stab of melancholy. No woman had ever surprised him; none had ever caught him unawares with merely a word or a look. Were it another time, he'd perhaps keep her close, unravel the mystery of why a single lass could humor him so.

He worried for a moment whether taking her to Aberdeen might not be the wisest course. He'd a duty to his country, though, and sometimes speed outweighed sense.

Surely they would find Brother Lonan in Aberdeen, and James would deposit Magda with him.

With his regrets.

Chapter 8

"I beg your pardon?" The distant lapping of the waves on the shore had mesmerized Napier, still fogged and trying to chase the remaining tendrils of last night's sleep from his brain with a cup of tea. The air was particularly brackish that morning, as if the receded tide was a blanket pulled back to release the strong scent of seaweed and shells that lay beneath, littering the stark stretch of wet brown sand. He'd just taken another sip when he thought his wife had begun to broach the topic of golf, of all things. "It sounded as if you said—"

"I did indeed," Margaret interrupted. "Which you would know already were you abed at a reasonable hour last night, instead of partaking in more of these tiresome political ruminations you seem to be obsessed with of late." She paused to pick up the teapot and, with great deliberation, warmed their cups. Margaret and her husband would soon go down, as always, to join the rest of the household in breaking their fast, but to sit each morning on their balcony, overlooking the seashore and greeting the sun with a spot of tea, had become their treasured routine. Dawn had well and fully broken, and a rod of white sunlight glared along the wet sand. "I did indeed say golf." She blew on her tea and sipped it gingerly.

Napier hid a smile. He could always tell when his wife had some juicy bit of news. He knew she enjoyed the telling of it, and he'd let her prolong her pleasure. She'd been a beauty in her youth, and he had been shocked when she'd chosen his quiet reserve over one of the many men more outgoing in their charms who'd courted her. Napier vowed he'd never give her cause to her regret her decision. They'd never been blessed with a child, and though Margaret didn't hesitate to make her opinions known, she'd not once complained of her lot. So, if his wife wanted to delight in telling him her gossip, he'd delight in the hearing of it.

"But I thought nothing vexed you so much as to hear about your brother's golf games," he said.

"Oh, you've the truth there," she replied tartly. "But I'd endeavor to play at swords and longbows if I thought I'd gain some insight into my brother's heart. We've tried for years to find him a suitable match, and he shows up one morning with some accented beauty."

"A beauty, eh?" Napier raised his brows with affected gusto.

"Archibald!" Margaret swatted her husband with her napkin and, not missing a beat, continued, "I tell you, this Magda is a peculiar one. But I dare say, I quite took a fancy to her. Do you know she plays golf as well as a man?"

"Not so." He'd been feigning his interest somewhat, but now Napier leaned in, truly intrigued.

"So indeed! She played golf with the men." Margaret put down her teacup to free her hands for broader gesturing. "As did I."

Napier's usually stoic demeanor shattered as he let go a brief and explosive laugh.

"I most certainly did," Margaret huffed. "That Sydserf and I were a duo. I made quite a pretty shot on, what do you call it, the fairway."

"Dear heart, women don't—"

"Women most certainly do. Why, Mary Queen of Scots herself was quite the golfer."

"Oh really?" He chuckled. "My Margaret playing golf." Napier shook his head. He looked at his wife, ever amazed that he'd been so blessed with a woman who never ceased to surprise him. He wasn't a naturally joyful man, but his wife made him more of one each day. Napier's mind turned to coarser things, and he mused he'd risk much to catch sight of that plush rump of hers bending over a tee. "Well, that would be quite a sight."

Margaret flushed. They'd been together nearly twenty years now, and he knew she recognized the look in his eyes.

After savoring her discomfort for a moment, Napier asked, "But who is this lass then?" He'd finished with his tea, and set to smoothing the corners of his moustache up and the length of his goatee down. He knew that such vanities only emphasized his thin, elongated features, but he knew too that his Margaret's preference was a well-tended and fashionable man. "Who—and where—is her family?"

"She claims the surname Deacon. I think it's Irish."

"And are we to welcome this rudderless lass into our home?"

"Well," Margaret exclaimed, "we shall of course be gracious as always."

Napier recognized that even Margaret herself hadn't known until that moment where she would stand regarding the strange and wayward woman.

"But of course we'll do whatever you say, my beauty." He smiled warmly, a rarity generally seen only by his wife. Beautiful she was too, he thought. Her glossy brown hair was not yet grayed, and she bore the Graham family regal height and carriage. She'd grown in girth since their youth, but he loved her all the more for it. Margaret was lush refuge for his tired bones, though he'd never dare breathe as much to her, knowing how prickly she'd grown about her weight. "You are my one and only mistress, and you know I live only to please you."

"Good." Margaret's eyes sharpened. "Then you will refrain from this Aberdeen madness."

"Ah." Napier girded himself. He'd known she wouldn't be happy about his departure, and had been fearing this exchange. "Go I must, dear heart. To protect your brother, at the least."

"My brother," she grumbled. "And what of your very own wife? You don't even agree with all this Covenanting nonsense."

"No, I do not. It's true."

"And yet you go all the same? When I've explicitly asked you not to?"

"Your brother needs me, Margaret. Even in his youth, he was a lad of principle. But a man can be blinded by his good intentions. James doesn't suspect the knife at his back, wouldn't think to. And yet I fear that with his Covenant, these Lowland noblemen see their opportunity. His virtuous movement has become an adder's nest of callous and opportunistic ambition."

"Will there be a fight?"

"I hope not." Napier's usually unreadable face creased with concern. He hated to see his wife worry so. "Fret not, Margaret." He took her hand. "I travel not as a soldier, but as a guardian. If this Magda is to travel with us, we'll need to install her well outside Aberdeenshire limits."

"Well, do care for yourself, Archie." Margaret sniffled.

"Of course, pet."

"I'd die without you."

"And I you."

"And you'd best vow to bring my scamp of a brother back to me alive."

He laughed and took her hand to his lips for a kiss.

"Perhaps I am wrong. Perhaps James has the right of it. I hope so for his sake. Regardless, I will be an ally at his back."

"To watch for that knife?"

"Yes, dear heart." Napier placed her hand back in her lap with a gentle squeeze. "To mind that knife."

❋

"Lowland nobles gather even now, and the weight of our war purse grows heavy." Archibald Campbell rattled a small leather purse, disdain beading his small, close-set eyes and quivering his thin, bloodless lips. "The gold your little German princeling paid you was surely no more yellow than ours."

Campbell grew vexed. He'd summoned this general-for-hire all the way from the warring on the Continent, thinking that Alexander Leslie's Scottish heritage might inflame him to the cause, but Leslie only played as shy as a maiden at her first dance.

"Aye, gold is good, but I care no more for this prayer book than I did for Gustavus," Leslie replied, referring to the Swedish king and would-be German princeling who'd last bought his military services. "Should King Charles march on your Covenanters, he might well have more men at his back than I ever faced in Germany."

"The religion of your country is under siege." Campbell pulled his face into a mocking pout, exaggerating the sag of his thin skin and his droopy, overlong nose, making his face seem a thing carved from wax left too long in the sun. "Are you to tell me that

Alexander Leslie, celebrated sword-for-hire, cares solely for his own hide?"

"And who else's?" Leslie replied matter-of-factly. "Campbell, I've no care for your cause. Spare me talk of king and kirk. I fight for the highest bidder, so save your sanctimonious breath for those precious noblemen of yours. I don't see many of *them* raising broadswords for this Covenant." He kicked a stool close to sit across from Campbell at his ornate desk. "But double your payment in gold, and you've my sword and my word." He carefully twisted the ends of his long moustache, letting the statement hang in the air.

"You crooked little man," Campbell muttered, reaching in a drawer for additional purses. "But"—he snatched the money back before Leslie could grab it—"I'd have your word that my coin also buys me the services of some seasoned men. If Aberdeen refuses to sign the Covenant and sides against us, I'd not belabor this. I shall need you to fight them. With hired men at your back, the townsfolk should scatter like leaves in the wind."

"I'll thank you not to call my ability into question. I can gut the Aberdeen townsfolk, if you will it. My father was a captain, as was his father before him."

"Yes, but your mother was a wench."

"Och." Leslie snatched the pouches from Campbell's hand. "You'll have your men," he spat. "And pleased they'll be for a day's work in their native land for a change. But what of you, Campbell?" he sneered. "Whose back will you be guarding the day we take Aberdeen? As I understand it, you favor the taste of blood."

Campbell's face soured, and he stared blankly at the mercenary seated in front of him. "I'll have my own . . . *concerns* . . . that day."

He shuffled through papers on his desk as if already dismissing the soldier. "But you do remind me," he added offhandedly, "there's a small matter of sharing your command. There will, in fact, be some of your *detested* nobles fighting that day, and they'll not follow a mere sword-for-hire." He eyed Leslie derisively.

"Aye, I feared as much, though it might cost you more coin." Leslie strode to the door, his presence more commanding than his small, wiry frame might suggest. "Especially if I'm expected to keep your noblemen alive. I'm a soldier, not a caretaker."

"Despite your contempt, they're men of reason and class, who will want to follow one of their own. James Graham will march with you. The Marquis of Montrose. I suppose he's a skilled enough fellow," Campbell added. "He's learned in the arts of war, with the teachings of battle in his head, if not the taste of it in his mouth. You'll stand with him, Leslie."

"You send me to battle with a man who knows no more of war than what he was spoon-fed by his betters?"

"Ho!" Campbell silenced the general's protestations with a raised hand. "Protocol demands you've a nobleman as second in command. And I tell you, the Graham will suffice."

"I see." Leslie's face was dark. "Is that all, Campbell?"

"One last thing. Pray, remind me, what was that word you learned on your continental campaign?"

"Aye," Leslie smiled broadly, "'tis a German word I've come to hold in high regard.

"*Plunder.*"

Chapter 9

She was tired, her face was cold and stiff from squinting, her hands covered in an oily grime of horse and dirt, and she hadn't been that saddlesore since she'd taken her first long trail ride at the age of nine. And it was only the end of their first day.

Magda hunched low in her tent and wrenched herself into a cross-legged position. She felt the slick of sweat under her arms and scowled as a fresh cloud of her own body odor filled the enclosed space.

"A problem, hen?" James scratched on the flap of canvas that gave her some semblance of privacy. "You're muttering like an old woman in there."

"I am not muttering."

"So say you."

She heard his chuckle and angrily pulled the flap aside. "I smell."

He inhaled deeply. "Like a rose on the vine, you are." James laughed then, and Magda swatted at him with the scarf of plaid wool she'd worn knotted tight at her chin all day.

"Come."

"You've got another thing coming if you think I'll follow you again. I've followed you enough for one day."

"Come, come." He reached his hand into the tent. "I'll not bite." He waggled his hand for her to take it. "No need to be churlish. I've prepared your bath, m'lady."

"A bath?" Magda ignored his outstretched hand and crawled from the tent.

"Aye, there's a wee burn not half a league hence."

"A burn?" She halted. "That's like a stream, right?" She

began to edge back under cover. "I don't do burns. And a league sounds really far at the moment, so don't worry about me. I'll be fine."

"What, a braw lass like you, worried by some wee burn?"

"But I think it's getting too late in the day . . ."

"Och, it's never too late. Come, my fair lady, perform your ablutions in nature's temple. You'll find a quick wash with naught but the sky overhead good for the soul." He took her hand from the dirt and gave a gentle tug. She didn't budge.

"I'm not great when it comes to water and the great outdoors."

James considered Magda for a moment, peering at her in the shadows of her tent. He gave a slight nod. "Then I promise to stay by your side. Come." The playfulness was gone from his tone, his voice kind as he guided her back out. "You'll feel the better for it. Truly. Less than half a league and you can lean on me as we go."

"But . . . won't the men look?"

"They dare not." He took her arm, and Magda let him lead her, walking in silence across a broad glen. It was lush and green and, at that moment, it felt very wide-open. She imagined the men's gazes at her back, no less keen for the distance they were putting between them.

"The men will be able to see," she muttered finally, deeply concerned over how exactly she was supposed to manage in some surely frigid burn, and looking for any excuse to back out.

James barked out a loud laugh and, catching her hand in his, tugged her into a run. She gave a startled shriek, then raced to keep up with him.

"If you'll not believe me, see for your own self." They jogged up a low sloping hill and Magda had to pump her arms to make it to the top. By the time they crested, she was winded, and laughing despite herself.

"You see?" A stream wound its way around the other side of the hill. Though small, she wouldn't have called it a burn. It rushed along quickly and, even though a cluster of gray rocks choked one section into a narrow channel, the water didn't look very shallow. James pointed to a small copse of trees on the nearest bank. "Your bath, fair lass."

The walk downhill was more precarious, and she tentatively picked her way down, as much to avoid slipping as to come to terms with what lay ahead.

"I'll not disturb you." They reached the trees, and James began to back away.

"No!" Magda put her hand to her mouth, self-conscious at the shout that had escaped her. "I mean, no. I . . . um . . . I don't have any soap."

"What is it?"

"You don't have soap in the seventeenth century?"

"Och, lass, of course we have soap." He stepped closer to her, taking her chin between his thumb and finger. "I meant, what is troubling you? I can see that the matter is not merely that you want for soap."

"Well . . . I'll need it to wash."

"Soap is not what's fashing you at present, hen, and we both know it." He playfully tilted her head from side to side. "No, I see some other worry robbing the peace from your bonny face."

"I . . ." She turned her face from him. "I guess I'm a little afraid of water."

"Afraid of a wee burn such as this?" He began to make light of it, then cut short. Magda was wringing her hands in front of her, looking back up the hill as if fantasizing about her escape. "You *are* frightened," he said with astonishment. "Whyever for?"

"I'd rather not go into it."

James didn't pause a beat before giving one quick nod of assent, and she was grateful. He simply took her hand and began to lead her toward the trees clustered along the water's edge.

"But what are you doing?" Anxiety hitched her voice again.

"Fret not. You shall have your bath." He removed his coat and used it to sweep the damp, leafy debris from one of the larger rocks, then sat her down atop it. "And your soap too."

Her fingers curled around the edge of the rock, cold and sharp beneath her, and she shot him a wary look.

"Trust me." He disappeared farther into the trees. "I'll be but a moment," she heard him shout from a distance.

Magda sat on the rock, trying not to panic at the sound of burbling water. She felt cursed that such a tranquil thing could be such a source of angst. That she couldn't do something so simple as bathe outside without having a panic attack.

"Oh!" she cried. James had returned, startling her with a light touch to her shoulder.

"Easy, hen." Cradling her elbows, he stood her up and led her a few paces downstream to the other side of the rocks. The water sounded even louder there, dashing against the large gray stones, whirling into eddies on the other side. She stiffened in his arms.

"I swear to you, this is the shallowest part. I'll be right here with you." He nodded to the rock she'd just left. "You have but to call if you need me. And, on my honor, my back shall remain ever turned." He winked at her, crossing his heart in earnest. She eased a bit, and even managed a crooked half smile.

"Remove what you will. No men will see you here. Or just knot your skirts if you prefer. You'll see—you'll be as fresh as a flower. Ah," he added, patting his coat pocket. "I'd almost forgot. You understand I've no soap to hand . . . We discussed that at length already, aye?" He gave her a wicked grin. "But I did gather these for you." White petals appeared in his palm with a flourish, bringing a burst of rich, sweet perfume. "Scotch rose for a Scottish bath."

She hesitated, confused. "What do I do with them?"

"Oh, I don't know the ways of lasses, hen. I thought you could rub them on yourself perhaps? Use them as you will. Or not, if you don't wish it. Whatever gives you pleasure." He placed the soft white petals in her hand and, with an elaborate bow, turned to sit on the rock, his back set firmly to her.

Magda stood paralyzed at the water's edge. She studied the soft petals in her hand and laid them in a careful pile on the ground. She looked at James then, studying his back, trying to imagine the expression on his face. He would be gracious, patient, sitting there for as long as she'd need him. She glanced at the stream, and then down at her feet. She really did need to wash. If she remained standing, she'd be okay. The water was moving quite slowly, especially on the other side of the rocks. She could pretend it was just a large bathtub. A large, cold, and relatively dirty bathtub.

Magda slid one leather slipper off, followed by a low woolen stocking. Cool mud crept between her toes, sending a shiver of pleasure up her body. She was so sore, and so dirty her skin itched with it. She could just dunk her feet in, at the very least. The cold might even soothe the aching in her legs.

She squirmed quickly out of her other shoe and stocking, had her skirts in a knot, and was in the knee-high water before she could give herself a chance to rethink it.

She looked at James again. His feet were kicked out on the rock in front of him. Late-afternoon sunlight shone weakly through the trees, dappling the buff color of his britches in shades of yellow and gray. He leaned back on his hands, his shirt pulled tight at his shoulders and over his outstretched arms. He'd hear her splashing. She imagined he'd smile at the sound of it.

James was right there. No harm would come to her. The other men were far away, and she trusted he'd have their hides if they tried to sneak so much as a peek. Magda trotted back out of the water and, before she could change her mind, tugged the laces of her bodice free and slipped her dress over her head.

"Done already?"

"Don't turn around!"

He chuckled quietly, a husky, masculine sound almost out of earshot. "I'd not think of it, hen."

She splashed back in, feeling suddenly exposed despite the shift that was as long and as thick as any dress she'd have worn in her own time.

Magda leaned over and cupped her hand in the water. She stood there, watching the crystal clear stream flow over her palm, the image of her hand fracturing and wavering under the swirling water. It was brisk, but it felt so good, invigorating her after such an arduous ride. She splashed up, rubbing under her arms and chafing along her calves. She soon adjusted to the temperature and was lost for a while in the sheer pleasure of cool water sloughing dirt and sweat and horse from her body.

"You'd have more luxurious accommodations than this, then."

She froze at the sound of his voice and peered at him. He'd eased back farther, leaning on his elbows.

"Where you're from," he added in an easy voice. "You would've washed in much grander baths, I'm certain."

She relaxed a little. He clearly had no intention of stealing so much as a glimpse of her. "How can you tell?"

"How could I not?" James laughed. "Considering the fear you bring to such a wee trickle as this, it's not difficult to imagine you don't often find yourself bathing en plein air."

"No." She examined the dirt packed hard at her fingertips. "Not exactly." She plucked a yellow leaf from atop a nearby rock and used the stem to scrape her nails clean. "Though I guess this isn't so bad."

"Not so bad? You're a funny one, hen. Just give a look around. Not so bad indeed."

Magda stood straight. Her feet and calves were numb to the cold now, but she found she liked the sensation, and burrowed her feet more deeply into the powdery silt of the streambed. Alder trees reached high all around, their rounded leaves fluttering in the breeze. She focused her senses outward, attuned to the occasional plop of their tiny cones dropping from branches high above. She breathed in, and crisp air filled her lungs, rejuvenating her. When was the last time she'd stood among the trees like this? Seen trees in someplace other than Central Park? Surely not since her brother's death.

Peter. What would he make of all this? Would she be nearly so calm about this whole situation if Pete were alive, at home waiting for her? No, she'd be hysterical. Stomping, raging, freaking out. Not bathing in an idyllic babbling brook with some famous hero of old.

She stared at James. The strong triangle of his back. He inhaled deeply just then. She could see the rise and fall of his rib cage. He tilted his face up to the sun. Just then she wished she really could see the look on his face. His eyes would be closed. She imagined she'd see his pleasure written in the subtle change in his features. In the smoothness of his brow, the slight curve to his lips.

She rubbed her wet hands briskly over her face. No, the degree of panic she felt definitely did not match what her current predicament called for.

"Magdalen?"

She cleared her throat. "Yes?"

"Merely ensuring you've not turned into some gorgeous red-feathered creature and flown away."

"No," she said tentatively. His attentions made her self-conscious, and she bent again to the water, rushing to finish. "I'm still here."

❁

It was supposed to be just a quick peek. James had promised he wouldn't look, but after her prolonged silence and much internal debate, in the end, his concern for Magda had won out. He'd wanted to ensure she was still there, sound and upright.

And was she. He'd intended a brief glimpse, and instead she'd taken his breath away.

She'd knotted her petticoat to just above her knees, and though the water concealed most of her legs, the simple white gown clung to her, revealing modest curves at her hips and breasts. He watched, mesmerized, as her delicate hands reached to cup handfuls of water, stroked up along elegant stretches of pale arms, down her long throat, and back again, a smooth curtain of auburn hair hanging down all the while, threatening to graze the surface of the water.

He wanted to look away, but kept telling himself just one moment more. She'd spotted the tumble of rose petals at the water's edge. He smiled as he watched her give a shrug, then bend to scoop a handful. The wild roses were much smaller than their formal counterparts, but he knew the petals were no less soft. He watched her crush them, bring them to her nose, shutting her eyes to breath in their perfume. They would be like suede in her fingertips. The scent lush, and likely familiar.

He turned away quickly then. She'd begun to rub the petals over her arms and chest when James remembered himself.

It was clear the lass was terrified of water. And worse, her fear seemed tied to some greater issue close to her heart. She'd not told him what the matter was, and he hadn't pressed, but he'd thought to be on the alert for whatever might come to pass during what should've been a quick dunk and splash in a stream. But instead he found himself adjusting his position on the rock, uncomfortably aroused by the unexpected and intimate glimpse.

He felt her grow still at his back. Would she be looking at him? he wondered. She was likely just examining her dress, or perhaps adjusting a stocking. But, turning his face to the sun, James fantasized that she watched him from behind instead.

Eyes shut, he listened intently to the rustle of clothes as she began to dress. He breathed in deep, imagining he could smell the roses on her skin from far away. There was the rasp of cord against fabric. She'd be lacing her bodice then. How would it be to untie those laces, set free that bosom into the cool air, see Magda clothed just in sky and the shadows from the trees above?

He felt the cool spill of shadow over his legs and opened his eyes. Magda stood before him, clean and dressed, and he couldn't stop his gaze from raking up the length of her. Nervously pleating and smoothing a swath of her skirts, she seemed almost embarrassed to stand before him. He found her self-consciousness endearing, took it as a sign that perhaps she too had perceived the intimacy of his close proximity.

"Better now?" He hopped to standing and in a flash was inches from her. He sensed the chill of her skin against his warmth, noticed the slight shiver that trembled up her torso. He chafed her arms softly, to lend her heat. The barest scent of roses teased him, and he paused.

He couldn't help himself. Leaning down, he tucked his nose close at her neck and breathed deep. "I see you found some use for those petals, hen."

"I . . ." She felt the cool pull of air along her skin as he breathed in. All rational thought emptied from her mind and Magda shivered. "I . . ."

"But here, you're chilled." He swung his coat over her shoulders and pulled her unnecessarily tight to his side. "We shouldn't tarry now. The sun sets early this time in the season."

The coat around her shoulders was warm. She pulled it tight around her, and the smell of him lingered in her senses. "I can walk," she managed.

Though he nodded, James didn't loosen his grip. As they emerged from the trees, Magda gasped, halting them where they stood. She felt him instinctively put his hand to his empty scabbard, sensed him scanning the land before them. But she couldn't spare him a glance. She could only stare up at the sky, awestruck.

The evening was only beginning to purple into dusk, yet already she could make out millions of stars surfacing into clarity like spirits materializing from the twilight. And bisecting it all was a spectacular flume of starlight, a dense, swirling cloud cutting across the sky.

James gave a throaty chuckle at her side. "Not generally let out after dark, hen? Or is it that there are no stars in your time?"

"No . . ." she murmured. She began to walk forward slowly, not taking her eyes from the sky overhead. "I mean, yes. There are stars. But not like this."

"Well then, we shall bide a wee." He ushered her to the base of the hill, sitting them both down. "You must tell me how it is the stars can have changed over time."

"It's not that they've changed. Stars are stars." Magda slowly leaned back to lie against the sloping hillside. "It's the sky that's changed. Because of electric lights, the nights are no longer as dark as they once were."

He lay back, waiting silently beside her, and she finally pulled her eyes from the sky to look at him. "Oh. Electricity." She sighed. "In the future, we have electricity. Like . . ." She looked back up, scanning the sky. "Like the power of lightning harnessed at your fingertips. Because of it, our homes have lights that burn brighter than any candle. All you need to do is walk into a room, flick a switch, and it's bright as day."

"Doesn't that get . . . hot?"

"No!" A startled belly laugh escaped her and she turned to him. He'd edged closer and was looking intently at her, his expression open, eager to share in her mirth. Their eyes met, and she grew still. "Oh . . ." She glanced away quickly. "Um, no, not hot. Just . . . bright."

"Ah."

She could feel that he hadn't moved, that he still faced her. She could hear his breath, felt it tickle her cheek. Her stomach gave a flutter. She sensed his eyes on her, wondered what would happen if she'd but turn her head the slightest bit. But she kept her gaze locked on the sky above.

The light dimmed quickly now, the sun winking below the horizon, and Magda felt tiny beneath the darkening sky. After all she'd been through, seeing such a magnificent explosion of stars above, it was impossible not to think about the more distant past, all those who'd come before, seen this same vast bowl overhead.

"I see why they named it the Milky Way." She realized she'd been fidgeting and forced her hands to still. "It is like a big swirly cloud of . . . well, of milk."

"Aye." James shifted, and though she sensed his gaze turn from her back to the sky above, she felt the warmth of his arm near her side. "Greek legend has it that it *is* a river of milk." He pointed his finger and traced the thick line streaking across the night sky. "They say it appeared while the goddess Hera held her infant son Hercules to her breast. While the baby suckled, Hera discovered he was Zeus's bastard from another woman. She pushed the baby away, and her milk spilled in a great stream, forever marking the heavens above."

"Oh." Her voice was quiet. He had enthralled her, his voice masculine, but gently thoughtful, transporting her to another time.

"So there aren't many stars in your time?" His question brought her back to the moment.

"Well, I suppose there are. We just can't see them as much. Unless you go far into the country, and even then, it's nothing like this."

"So you're not from the countryside?"

"Oh no." She sighed, thinking of Manhattan. "I'm from one of the biggest cities in the world."

"And that's where your museum is?"

"Yes. There are a lot of museums where I live. And stores and bagels and buses and hot dogs . . ." Her voice trailed off.

"Dogs?"

"No," she chuckled. "Hot dogs. A kind of food. People sell them from carts. On street corners. They're like . . . like tubes of meat. Delicious tubes of meat."

"Ah, like a blood sausage."

"Oh yuck!" She laughed. "Nothing like blood sausage."

"So you don't see many stars whilst eating these . . . hot dogs?"

"No. You can't really see the stars in New York City."

James was silent for a time, then said, "I'm not surprised."

"That we can't see the stars?"

"No, hen, that you come from a city. You seem . . . not readily impressed, aye?"

She did turn to him then, without thinking, and smiled.

"Well this . . . these stars impress me." *You impress me.* She gazed back at the sky and thought how grateful she was not to have missed this. *Not to have missed you.* Regardless of what she'd been through, in some small measure, this had made it all worthwhile.

"Thank you."

"Whatever for, hen?"

"For this."

Chapter 10

"Does your friend Tom know?" Magda hammered her heel into the solid barrel of her horse's belly to catch up. It had taken the full two-day ride to Aberdeen for her to realize that the trick to the lazy, gray mare was forceful persistence.

She and James had set out that morning for King's College on the outskirts of the city, and though it was early yet, the old horse was already asserting her stubborn streak.

"Where you come from? Aye, he knows. And," James added with a smile, "if he didn't believe it before, watching you golf brought the truth to your words. I've not seen him beaten so handily in quite some time." He ran his eyes up and down Magda sitting erect in the saddle. "And wouldn't the jackals of society chatter to see such a fine stroke from a lass? One look at you, and golf would become the latest infatuation of every woman at court."

She found herself smiling at his compliment. Between the lethargic horse and her awkward saddle, Magda had lagged behind the men on the road to Aberdeen. James had circled back to check on her frequently, and his tireless attentions were chipping away at Magda's reserves. She was finding it difficult to maintain formality around his amiable chatter, and the two of them slipped once again into easy conversation.

"Of course I can play," she replied dismissively. "A talent for worthless pursuits was the currency in a family like mine. Golf, horses, skeet—you name it, we prized it."

Though, hearing herself say it, Magda realized how different the situation would be in the seventeenth century, where an ability with horses and guns would've been a matter of life or death.

"Horses!" he exclaimed. "So you say, hen, but I've yet to see your skill as an equestrienne. Though"—James pulled his reins, swinging his mount toward Magda to more fully examine her— "you do sit a horse quite prettily."

"You try riding this silly thing." Magda scowled. Despite her protests, everyone had insisted she ride a ladies' sidesaddle. Though beautiful, she considered it to be an entirely preposterous contraption, featuring an uncomfortable hook from which to dangle her leg, elaborate baroque stitching, and to top it off, a small, red-leather-lined pocket she was informed could be used to store a handkerchief.

James nodded, gesturing his hand to her, palm up, as if to say she'd won on that point.

Magda gave him a warm look in return. She didn't know what dark magic it was that had brought her to this man's side. Or, she mused, what brand of sorcery was casting a spell on her now, because home sure was a blurry memory at the moment. She supposed she loved her parents, and was fond of her job. She certainly knew she missed hot showers—yesterday's dunk in a frigid stream hadn't even begun to touch the soil that clung to her skin like an extra layer.

Magda reminded herself that life for seventeenth-century women wasn't all tea biscuits and silk duvets, and that it was James's wealth and status that cast her new surroundings in an unrealistic light.

She knew she wanted to return to her world in Manhattan, *had* to return, but the urgency she'd initially felt paled when compared to the fantasy she was fulfilling. The art historian in her was thrilled to be getting such a detailed, real-life glimpse back in time. History was alive around her, with a cast of characters and costumes like something from a movie set, and with a previously unimagined depth that no painting she'd ever seen could bring to life.

Magda had landed in a world where the pace was slow, and yet the stakes were dramatically heightened. Minor injuries could be fatal, a simple change in weather could pose an inordinate obstacle, and people regularly staked their lives for the things they believed in.

And James Graham was about to do just that. She knew in

her head that he was just a man, but she marveled at the invisible thread that had pulled her through time to him. A bond that she could just almost feel tied snug around her heart, continuing to draw her close to his side.

Something had happened between them yesterday. First while she studied that broad back during her bath, then later, under the stars. She'd felt the heat of his body radiate to hers and sensed his face turned to her, so close. She shivered, remembering the feel of his breath on her cheek. She'd been so afraid to look back at him, to meet his gaze and the intensity she knew she'd find there.

What would it have been like if she'd turned to him? To be held in his strong arms, feeling that breath mingle with her own, leaning her body into his, hearing his passionate whispers for her alone?

Like a dramatic punctuation to her thoughts, the clock tower of King's College Chapel peeked through the trees in the distance, and the sight took Magda's breath away.

"Magnificent, aye?" James pulled his horse to a halt. He seemed pleased by her awe.

Unlike the predominantly granite buildings that made Aberdeen city proper feel so stolid and uniformly gray, the chapel was constructed of sandstone, and from a distance appeared a warm, mottled yellow and brown. Inexplicably delicate prongs and ornate embellishments topped a gigantic stone crown at the top of the tower.

"How did they do that?" she gasped.

"With great precision, I imagine. It's said there's a sundial up there somewhere, though you'll not be able to see it from the chapel itself."

"And you think Brother Lonan is there?"

His voice was suddenly subdued. "I'm told he's somewhere about, aye."

Something in her heart clenched at the realization that this was almost good-bye. Magda looked down, studiously examining the reins in her hands. Anything to avoid catching James's eye.

"So, hen, shall we?" He kicked his horse to a slow trot. "Let's be off with you then."

Off with her?

The tenderness that had claimed Magda just a moment ago was doused by the cold truth. James was all handsome ease, his blithe flirtations without thought. She recognized his type. James was nothing more than a rich playboy. One who just happened to make her blush every time he directed his attentions her way. The episode on the golf course, with those experienced hands of his doing what they did. Then she'd thought they'd shared a moment gazing at the stars. Of course her feelings had gotten muddled.

The remorse she'd felt at leaving crystallized into anger. What could she have been thinking?

Magda did not relish strife, and before meeting this man, she'd led a peaceful life. After her brother died, she'd put away once and for all the last of those crude and messy bits of herself—her passions, her desires, anything that required her to relinquish her practiced armor and bare the vulnerability beneath.

It had been the reason she'd fashioned herself into something more like a courteous associate of her parents rather than a loving daughter. The reason the most exhilarating moments of her life took place alone in a darkened room with nothing but her tools at her side.

There had been times, perhaps, when she'd not stood up for herself enough, but all in all, Magda's little world had been calm and conflict free. How could she have let that world recede so far into the corners of her mind?

She'd reclaim it. It was back to reality now. They'd find this Brother Lonan and solve the mystery of what brought her here and how. He'd paint a picture of her, or do whatever it was he needed to do to get her home. He had to.

She realized there was a part of her that hadn't fully accepted the reality of her situation. It was that part she clung to now, refusing to entertain any doubts that this Lonan could—*would*—help her find her way home.

That would be Magda's single focus from now on. Not James, not his politics, and definitely not his easy chatter.

Off with her indeed.

Chapter 11

"Notebooks?" Magda exclaimed. "That's all he left behind? Page after page of doodles and ramblings?"

Hurt sharpened her voice. She was impatient and just wanted to get home, and now this. The monk had disappeared again, and all that was left of him were some small bound notebooks, a sheaf of yellowed vellum, and innumerable bits of scattered sketches and papers.

It seemed the men of King's College had more than heard of Brother Lonan; they'd housed him for a number of weeks prior, as they did many of the scholars who came for study, drawn by the silence of the vast library collections, or the academic camaraderie of noisy philosophical arguments over meals. Lonan had favored the former, sticking primarily to the library and to the dimly lit cell that was his temporary bedroom.

"Now, hen, don't lose heart. There may be some clue, aye?"

He sat next to her, Lonan's thin woven cot creaking under the added weight. The room was a cramped rectangular space with walls of damp stone, lit by a single small slit open to the outside. The only furniture besides the cot was a rough-hewn oak desk.

Lonan's fellows had been baffled by the man's sudden disappearance, and more so by the fact that he'd left behind his prized journals. Magda pored through them, both baffled and increasingly enthralled by what amounted to hundreds of pages of cramped writing. Despite the thick blots of black ink that stained most every page, his notes were remarkably legible, if not utterly coherent tracts on everything from Greek musical scales to cycles of the Viking calendar.

But it was Lonan's sketches that transfixed her. She recognized a number of patterns plucked straight from ancient art history. Chevrons rimmed many of the pages, the tightly drawn arrows stacked atop each other, hemming in his notes with their mad repetition. Many sheets bore what Magda knew were meanders, interlocking lines and boxes looking like miniature mazes that intertwined and repeated with seeming infinity. There were other maze shapes as well. Sanskritic swastikas—like those the Nazis had subverted—marched across the pages. Lines branched out from many of the swastika shapes, forking off at right angles to create elaborate labyrinths.

And over and over the same image appeared amongst the patterns. That of a snake eating its tail.

"He's mad." James's harsh whisper echoed off the dank cell walls.

"Or brilliant. Look." Excitement twinged Magda's voice. "Maybe it's just because I'm looking for it, but"—she riffled through the pages with increasing speed—"all these symbols represent time. Like the swastika here: For many ancient peoples this was a sacred symbol of the equinoxes, or a representation of the sun, moon, and stars, or the passing of the seasons.

"Or these Egyptian symbols: The obelisk, this crescent moon, all represent the passing of time."

"What of this? It's common for the old Scots." James pointed to an elaborate interweaving of vines and dragons. "I've seen its like on the old stone crosses."

As she flipped farther along in the notebook, the Celtic designs that James had noted began to lose their detail. Drawn in an increasingly primitive manner, they eventually morphed in the final pages into the single image of a serpent swallowing its tail.

"Or this." Magda ran her finger over the circle made by the snake's body.

"Aye, he seems to favor that one."

The drawings became even more rudimentary until, on the last page, all that remained was a circle, with a crudely rendered female figure at its center.

Greek symbols dotted the shape, and underneath Brother Lonan had written a single phrase.

"*As many points on a single wheel, Time abides.*"

❈

James silently damned Lonan. He needed to help Magda back to her own time, and the brother alone held the key. Though his notebooks had been intriguing, they were useless without their author.

His country was on the brink of war. It was a dangerous place for any woman, not to mention a foreign lass with no notion of how to survive. Magda had no friends, no family. Nobody but him to rely on, and he was off to a battle from which he might not return.

He'd been letting himself get too comfortable with her, increasingly finding himself looking forward to talking to her, and to the challenge of goading a smile onto that bonny face of hers. Now he feared he was getting too close, and felt the need to send her back to her own time with sudden urgency. When he was by her side, the sensation of some epic change glimmered vague on the edges of his mind, some unrealized potential that was just within his grasp. And the feeling scared him.

He would not cast Magda out to face the Fates alone. No, he would keep her close until he could see her ushered home to safety. And not just for her own protection, but for his own good as well.

He could not forget his duty to his country. He had pressing responsibilities, his own world and his own time, going to hell on the throne of Charles. He needed to focus on Aberdeen. Then afterward he'd return to his home by the sea, and his golf and books and other pursuits. He might even finally let his family find him a decent match among the fine flowers of Montrose.

James would remember what he was about. And that was not a wayward lass from a distant land.

❈

"These . . . what do they call themselves now?"

"I know not, Your Highness." The painter stepped back to admire his work. Never had he met a person so besotted with his image as this king of England. In fact, the whole of the English court kept him busy with their commissions, and he'd not enjoyed an idle day since his arrival from Antwerp.

"Flemish you may be," King Charles scolded, "but you are in my court now, and best you begin following the goings-on. I talk of the Covenanters, man. I call them spoiled whelps in the midst of a tantrum." The king waved his hand impatiently. "Parliament chafes under my reign; these Lowland nobles buzz about like flies. They are all children, the lot of them."

Charles once again fluffed the lace at his collar. "Tell me, Anthony, what does a good father do when a child has a tantrum?"

The court painter Van Dyck remained silent, merely continuing to look from subject to canvas and back again. He was used to the king's outbursts, and knew his questions were merely rhetorical. The man seemed to use the time he sat for his portrait as an opportunity to think aloud, working through the growing conflicts: with the Church, with Scotland, with Parliament. Charles seemed to be having a run of missteps that was slowly tripping up the whole of his kingdom.

"A good father ignores the tantrum, Anthony. But when pressed"—Charles shifted out of his pose to face the painter directly—"when pressed, the father has no choice but to discipline the child."

He shifted back into his pose, chest puffed and back arched to elongate his short stature as much as possible.

"Aberdeen shall be my test. My children fight all around me, but I shall be the good father and step back. To see what happens in Aberdeen will tell us which way the wind blows."

Chapter 12

"You cannot be serious, lad." Napier slammed his cup down on the crude wooden table before him.

"Ah! If you could but stand up to my dear sister in this way—"

"You'll not be impudent with me, James. A mere in-law I may be, but I am still a man of knowledge and reason."

James tried—and failed—to suppress a smile as he studied his brother-in-law. The first Lord Napier was lean where Margaret was plump, somber and stoic to her animated sentimentality. Not a hair was out of place on his thinning pate. The man was precise comportment in contrast to his wife's bluster, and the poor sot loved Margaret more than life itself.

"I'll not know why you insist on your present course of action," Napier continued. "The town officers have denied you support, so now you're after Aberdeen like a pup worrying a rag. Don't you see?" He lowered his voice. He'd installed himself in a crofter's cottage not far outside Aberdeen, and it would do no good for the wrong ears to overhear. "The townspeople are merely the pot our king has placed over the fire so that he might better test the heat without risk to his own flesh."

"You've changed topic, dearest brother-in-law."

"Och, James, the topic? My topic is your folly. Your lass needs to return to Montrose. I could ferry her back tomorrow, safe into Margaret's care."

"You'll not fight with us?" James cocked his brows encouragingly, but his brother-in-law remained as stolid as ever.

"You know I'll not, James."

Napier let the statement hang before continuing, "I love you as my own blood, but I must speak with candor. I've been following the news from Edinburgh. As the days pass, it seems your Covenanters are becoming more like a gang of selfish and despotic nobles who've spied their chance to seize power."

"How could that be when they've asked that I lead? You ken me well, Napier." Opening his arms, James raised his brows in mock innocence. "Am I so tyrannical?

"Truly, brother," James continued in graver tones, "the king threatens to dictate the Church of Scotland. I'll not sit idly by."

Napier thoughtfully stroked the thin flesh of his cheeks. "You claim Charles has overstepped where the Kirk is concerned, but you need to see with your eyes, James, beyond the appearance of a thing, to its true nature."

"My elder you may be," James snapped, "but you'll not patronize me. I indeed see the truth of what I fight for. I'm driven to battle for a principle, honor-bound to ensure Scotland's religious freedoms are protected. It is that honor that will find us victorious."

"Then at least let me take Magdalen. I fear she's a distraction, and distractions kill, lad."

"I said no, Napier. Believe me. I would that she were home—away to her *own* home." He stood abruptly, curling his hands into fists then dropping them loose to his sides. "But until that time, I'll not cast her to the winds. These are dangerous times. She was sent to me and shall remain under my care."

"Sent by whom? Och," Napier grumbled when met with James's silence, "I wish you weren't so mysterious about this whole business."

"You must trust me on this. The lass has none but me to turn to. I'll not send her off until I have more of an . . . understanding of her situation. She can bide with you well outside Aberdeen while I fight."

"She can bide with me in Montrose."

"I'd keep her close to me." James slammed his open palms onto the table in front of him, leaning close to his brother-in-law. "And that is the end of the matter."

Napier stood to face him. "Who knows how many troops Charles might be marching toward us even now?" He pleaded, "You've no reckoning of the fight that could lay ahead."

"Magda stays," James said with finality. "Whatever my thoughts on the lass, I'll not leave her."

❧

"We march on the morrow," James announced, settling himself next to Magda on the grassy riverbank. "Our troops are rallied well beyond the Brig o' Dee under a General Leslie." He nodded toward the bridge in the distance, whose low, stout arches spanned the River Dee.

"We have some men of high birth, and a goodly number of swords-for-hire, but I doubt we'll need to resort to such gross tactics."

"You act like you're excited about this," Magda grumbled. She didn't relish watching him march into the sunset, nor did she want to be shuttled back to Montrose either. Fate had sent her to James, and somehow she'd come to trust him. Despite the close proximity of battle, she'd stay with him as he'd asked. At least until they could find Lonan, and a way back to her own world.

"A chance to trade doublet for armor? Aye, I am excited. But," he said, swooping up onto his knees, "I'd take a charm for the fight."

Magda gasped at his suddenly unsheathed broadsword.

"Goodness, that's some weapon."

"Aye, indeed it is." His wicked wink brought an indignant blush to her cheeks.

Balancing it on his forearm, James held the sword aloft. Sunlight glinted sharply off the blade, a couple inches wide at the base and tapered to a deadly sharp point.

"'Twas a gift from my father. He'd wanted to gild the basket," he said, referring to the thick filigree work that protected the hilt and ultimately would guard the swordsman's hand, "but I prefer the look of raw steel."

James moved so quickly, she didn't have time to protest. One swift flick of his sword, and a small strip of Magda's hem fluttered between his fingers.

"For luck, aye?" James deftly tied the light blue strip of silk into a knot and pinned it to his bonnet. "You'd not deny the warrior a wee talisman, would you?"

He smiled and reached out to gently pinch her chin. "Don't look so dire, hen. You'll keep safe with Margaret's husband while I fight."

"So that's it then?"

If only she'd listened to Walter more. Magda remembered that day at the museum when he'd told her of the horrible fate that James Graham had met.

Would meet.

Was this that moment? Would this next fight bring his death?

She stared sullenly at the river, concentrating on its noisy rush, willing the pounding of water over rock to deafen her to the thoughts in her head.

Tears stung her eyes as renegade memories crept in to stab her unexpectedly, and Magda wondered if she'd ever be able to look at the water the same way. Or if Peter's death had ruined her forever.

And now James was off, more reckless than her brother ever had been. Magda didn't think she could bear to watch yet another man cut away from her. She couldn't withstand more grief.

"To what horrible place have I lost you?" The gentle tone of James's voice brought out a husky Scots burr. He sat, setting his bonnet on the grass by his side, and the soft brown waves of his hair tousled loose in the wind. "You seem as if you're the one who's off to battle. Tell me your mind, hen."

She tried to inhale deeply, her breath coming in shudders as she fought back the tears. "It's my brother."

"You've a brother then? I thought you said—"

"Had a brother. He drowned." She took the ragged hem of her dress and twisted it between her fingers.

"Ah." His face went still. "That's it then. The reason you were so stricken at the stream."

"Yeah, I don't think I'll ever again be able to be near the water without thinking of him." She spat out a mirthless laugh. "Sucks for me, huh? Seeing as the world is made of water."

Ignoring her dismissive laugh, James caught her eyes with his and held Magda with his solemn gaze. "How did it happen?"

"He was visiting my folks. He'd just gotten back from South America. Ever the adventurer, my brother." Magda gazed blankly at the rushing water. "He helped build some school." She shook her head. "Adventurous and charitable."

Dropping the hem from her fingers, Magda switched her focus to stare intently at her hands as they brushed along the top of the grass. "Not me, though. I had to work. Or . . . well, I chose to work that weekend. Work, work, work," she added in a fake bright tone.

"He went to visit my parents, and I didn't." She shrugged. "They had . . . they have . . ." She fumbled for a moment, suddenly intent on finding the proper tense. "They've got a retreat on Lake George. Peter—my brother—was camping with some kids. Just a bunch of stupid rich kids. They'd set up on a small private island on what we called The Narrows. They'd been drinking, of course. Probably something stupid like cheap light beer. It made them feel superior to think they were slumming it."

Realizing she'd been rambling about what were likely some pretty foreign concepts, Magda paused for a moment to see if James was registering her story. Somehow she wasn't surprised to find his eyes holding hers steady, her pain mirrored in his drawn brow.

"Anyway, a couple of them went for a midnight swim, and Peter heard one of the girls get into trouble. He went out to help. Neither of them came back."

She paused for a moment and froze, willing away the ache that inevitably clutched at her throat at the thought of her brother. James slowly placed his palm flat on the grass, just a blade away from touching.

She stared at his hand so near to hers. "I can't figure it out," Magda finally continued. "The others said they heard her screaming, flailing. She must have pulled him under. That's really the only explanation. He was a strong swimmer. We both were."

"Were?"

"Yeah, well, I sort of lost the taste for swimming after that."

"Aye."

Magda was grateful for his firm nod, as if there could be no other response.

"The thing is," she said, desperation in her voice, "I can't get over that I wasn't there. I don't even remember why I thought it was so important I go to the museum that weekend. And if I'd been with Peter instead, maybe I could've saved him."

"No, you couldn't have," James replied firmly. "There's none stronger than a panicked swimmer. If you'd gone in after your brother, it would have been the both of you pulled under."

"Well, that's not what my parents said."

"Och, your bloody parents were wrong!"

A shocked laugh burst from Magda. She'd beaten herself up over Peter's death for a year now, holding herself secretly accountable, and here was this man she hardly knew, saying just the right thing to momentarily blunt the pain.

"Thanks," she said. "*My bloody parents.*" She smiled at James through her tears. "What's the other thing you say? Like, they bother me . . . ?"

"Aye," he laughed, then said in an exaggerated Scottish brogue, "they *fash* ye!"

"Aye," she replied with a twinkle in her eye. "They do at that. Or," she added quietly, "they *did . . .*"

Chapter 13

He woke at sun's first light, with the strains of the regimental piper keening in the distance, and inhaled the crisp dawn air that smelled of the brilliant blue sky to come.

James knew battle tactics well, and was an expert swordsman and champion archer. Today he'd don his armored breastplate, trading bonnet for a helmet of steel. Today was the day he would lead an army in defense of church and country, and he thought his chest would burst from the joy of it.

He and General Leslie broke their fast with oatcakes and cold rashers. They'd not risk smoke from a fire that morning, even though the townsfolk would have to be hidden under some pretty large rocks not to know what was about to hit Aberdeen.

"The Brig o' Dee guards the main approach, aye?" General Leslie nodded to the bridge in question, then paused to clear his throat, thick from the early hour and hoarse in the way of a man who lived hard.

He spat, then continued, "They've dug in around the city, but 'tis a blind man who wouldn't see our approach. You can be sure they'll marshal forces at the mouth of the bridge, and that's where we'll dance."

James had harbored hopes that the townsfolk would see reason and, greeting the Covenanting troops as protectors, sign their fealty to the cause. But scouts had brought news that the men of Aberdeen had raised a militia, now entrenched in various key points on the outskirts of the town.

The dry food stuck in his throat, and James washed it down with a swig of icy water from the Dee. He was sorely wanting a cup of tea, and he believed it would be one of the first things on his mind at the battle's conclusion.

Nodding at the general's words, James looked around at the men in their charge. A few noblemen had come to stand at their side, in their armored kit, second sons the lot of them, he'd wager.

The rest of the men were in various states of traditional clothing. Hardened by their years fighting in Germany, Leslie's hired mercenaries had forsaken heavy armor, instead donning additional weaponry and clothing that allowed for agility and speed. Most wore close-fitting trews and a leather vest, with a musket on the shoulder and sword at the hip.

A small band of Highlanders had gathered for the cause as well, and James had to smile at the audacious lot of them. He hadn't seen the men set camp—they'd merely disappeared the night before, reappearing like mist with the dawn. They dressed like true Scotsmen in belted plaids; some bore only tall hooked pikes, others carried dirks and scarred shields, and a few wore claymores strapped at their backs.

"I hope I'm not interrupting your repast, gentlemen."

James and Leslie looked up at the source of the sarcasm to find Campbell standing over them. A long royal blue waistcoat, knee breeches, and hose announced that he would not be seeing battle that day.

"I see I've dressed for our side this morning," he added snidely. Inspired by the blue talisman James had pinned to his bonnet, dozens of blue ribbons had sprung up in just as many shades, knotted from bonnets, or worn as sashes across chests.

"Aye," James replied smoothly, "the men are calling it the Covenanting blue."

Campbell looked in the distance, disdain souring his features. "I see not everybody has been informed of your winsome badge."

A group of Irish, many no more than boys, had gathered not far from them. James had been surprised to find that Irishmen had come to bear arms with them, and was told merely that they'd come to repay a debt. They had stood out at once from the crowd, having all, inexplicably, donned long yellow shirts for battle.

"Aye," Leslie answered slowly, picking the oats from his teeth. He studied Campbell's coat. "We need all the swords we can get today, seeing as not all stand at the ready."

Ignoring the jibe, Campbell said, "Ah, you remind me." Pursing his thin lips, he shrieked out a whistle and a young boy appeared with a dog at the end of a cloth leash.

Campbell thrust his hand toward the boy, making him balk. "Come, lad," he scolded. "I've not all day."

Face crumpled in a mixture of terror and anger, the young boy reluctantly handed the whimpering dog to Campbell.

"I find it auspicious to greet a day of battle having fleshed my maiden sword."

His blade, a showy broadsword with gilded basket and filigreed base, swept down, catching the mutt at the shoulder, clumsily cleaving his head from his body.

The young boy let out an anguished cry, and James jumped to his feet, hand poised on the sword at his side in outrage and horror. "What are you about, man?"

"Don't just gape like an idiot, lad," Campbell chided the young boy. He nudged the limp body with the flat of his blade. "Take this thing away."

General Leslie merely looked away, bored distaste playing across his features, as he continued to pick at his teeth.

"So guileless, James?" Campbell laughed. "Do you think that title of yours was a reward for noble goodwill? No, Marquis, your wealth was bought with the blood of those who came before you. You're off to battle today. Now act it."

James remained standing, jaw set and steel in his eyes.

"Now, Leslie," Campbell continued as if James were no longer there, "how do you plan to manage today's affair?"

"We march on the bridge," the smaller man replied, spitting some bit of food from his mouth. "We use musket fire first. What doesn't scare off the townsfolk will thin them. We hold fast in the center. Once it gives, we charge in and finish it."

"The townsfolk shall be offered clemency," James interjected. "My desire is for order and civility above all. Provisions shall be replaced, and none will suffer needlessly. Once Aberdeen fully understands the king's folly, I am certain they will accede."

"Is that how it will be?" Campbell asked, his tone inscrutable.

"Aye," James replied. "And how else?"

❦

The sound of so many marching feet echoed loudly off the stone bridge, strafing the gently rushing river below. The Dee was in flood, and Leslie had decreed they'd charge on the bridge, forgoing any supplemental attacks from the right or left flanks.

It was a brutal firefight lasting hours, the muskets of the Aberdeen militia having proved unsettlingly tenacious, biting leisurely into the ranks of the Covenant soldiers whenever they attempted an advance.

By day's end, the town's spirits ran high. The accidental realization that their militia could hold their defenses intact against a well-funded attack bolstered them with newfound confidence.

James, however, felt as gutted as his ranks. Many men had fallen. Walking through the camp at day's end found the injured tending themselves in grim silence, binding—and in the worst cases cauterizing—their wounds.

Those who'd survived the day despaired of the fight. The Highlanders, armed mostly with hand-to-hand weaponry instead of guns, were disheartened that Leslie hadn't let them see much of the fighting at all.

The Irishmen, defying all reason as well as a dozen briskly shouted orders to fall back, had charged the bridge on foot and had been first to fall in the line of fire.

James scrubbed his face and hands in the frigid river water and returned to his tent to find Magda there waiting for him. A sense of relief hummed through him at the sight of her, and rather than send her away, he thought to allow himself the pleasure of the distraction.

"Good evening, hen." His voice rasped from a day of shouting over the din of battle. "I thought I'd left you in Napier's care. You should be in a croft far from here, if I'm not mistaken."

"I . . . I had to see if you were alright. Don't blame Napier," she added quickly. "I've promised I'd let him return me after I saw with my own eyes that you were alright."

"I'm glad of it." He stared at her for a moment. He'd thought to muster a smile he didn't feel, and instead let the concern writ on her face be a balm to his soul. Abruptly, he looked down and began to disarm.

"For something that preserves me, och"—James fumbled with the leather straps connecting the breast- and backplates of his armored vest—"this fool contrivance will surely be my death."

Magda instinctively reached to help him shoulder out of his gear.

"Ah, I am most indebted, kind mistress."

Pulling the front flap of his tent aside, he tossed his armor in with a loud clatter, then turned back to find Magda staring at him, frozen. Glancing down, James saw that the torso of his quilted coat retained its pristine buff color, a jarring contrast to the gore spattered across its sleeves and collar.

She clutched her arms to her chest as if suddenly chilled, roving her eyes along his body to ensure he was intact.

Moved by the look of worry pinching her broad brow, James said in a deep Scottish burr, "Och, you'll not fash yourself, lassie." He smiled. "It worked, aye? I got your bonny mouth to twitch up at the edges a bit. Now let's see a light in those green eyes."

James paused for a moment, his own despair rising once again to the surface. "I *need* to see your smile, hen."

"How was it?" she asked, still visibly taken aback by the reality of battle.

"Bide with me." Crumpling his coat into a ball, he threw it into a far corner of the tent and eased himself down just inside. With a heavy sigh, he stretched his powerful legs through the opening. He'd worn close-fitting trews that day. The brass buttons that had studded along his outer leg were now missing, and Magda quickly glanced away from the hard, sinewy patch of thigh revealed through the tear.

"'Twas a bit of a disaster, aye? But, truly lass, first I'd hear of you. I see you survived my brother-in-law."

"Of course I survived." The hint of a smile played on her face. "But he is a serious type, isn't he?"

James had to chuckle at such a kindly understatement of the uptight Lord Napier. Magda seemed encouraged and, sitting down, embellished, "The man must have worn out the soles of his shoes with all the pacing he did. And packing that small bag of his, and unpacking, and packing again, whenever he got new word about what was happening on the bridge."

James stilled for a moment as the dreadful thought dawned on him that he had put Magda in harm's way after all. He hadn't even conceived that they could lose the battle. The horror of what could have befallen her had the townspeople gotten the upper hand chilled him. Napier's restlessness hadn't been high-strung at all. It had been wise.

Pushing that thought aside, James forced ease into his voice. "Aye, that is a peculiar wee valise he has. Margaret would have bought it for him."

"And you can imagine how he approaches packing the thing. The word *tidy* doesn't begin to cover it—" Magda stopped.

James had been trying his best to be amiable, hoping to push the pain of battle to the back of his mind, but images of the day's senseless killing kept rising to the surface.

"Can you tell me what happened today?" she asked quietly.

"Magdalen," he began, moderating his breathing as moments from the day came to him in a rush. "I spent a lifetime in hell this day. I spent years studying, training, preparing for a day such as this. To lead soldiers into battle, protecting the rights of my country, its people."

He caught her eyes and held them. "But the horrors I saw, lass. These men . . . many of them boys yet. They'd pledged their life's blood for my battle, *my* dream. And yet, at day's end, there were only but a few familiar faces among the fallen. These men died under me, and I didn't even know them."

She was quiet for some time, then finally ventured, "You could get to know them. Should get to know them. It would make you a better leader."

"Aye, you speak true. I thought to follow the general. But a man—a true man—stands alongside, not behind. I ken he's a seasoned soldier, Leslie is, but he doesn't know most of the men he fights with. I'll not accept that a general can have success on the field if he's no true knowledge of the weapons in his arsenal."

He touched his hand to hers, squeezing it briefly, then pulled back. "So many men, and bedlam all about. The Irish boys took off like a flock of loosed pigeons. The hired men fired muskets and hoped for a fair spot of luck. And the Highlanders. Och, the most blooded of all of us. With nary a musket among them, they were forced to spend the day seated upon their hands as Leslie demanded that the brunt of the attack come but from the center, while we were choked on that bridge like a cork in a bottle."

Magda hesitated, "Do you have to fight on the bridge? Can't you fight somewhere else instead?"

"What?" James looked at her flatly.

"Just, I don't know," she stammered, looking nervous to say the wrong thing. "Move the battle or something. You know, just come at them from a different place, maybe?"

"It's impossible." He shook his head. "The plans have been drawn. The Dee is in flood. Our strength is firepower; we'd never get the men and their weapons across a swollen river."

"Well, you don't have to use just the guns, right? I mean, people cross rivers all the time. And most of your men have swords anyway. You just said the Highlanders don't even have muskets."

James started to dismiss her once again, then began to think. "I suppose it could work," he said after a time. "So simple, aye?" He nodded now, considering. "With the Dee in flood, they'd never expect us from the right flank." He began to think out loud, passion renewing his voice. "We scout downriver a bit. Surely we'll find some place to ford across. The ponies could manage it. And I know just the lot of men for the job. So simple. It's brilliant, lass."

He enthusiastically cupped his hands on Magda's cheeks and planted an offhanded kiss on her mouth.

He pulled away quickly, and they both froze. James memorized her face, so close to his, and her eyes, glittering green like a cat's in the evening twilight. He marveled at their vibrancy, alight like some rare gem. He looked into those eyes for just a heartbeat too long and felt panic skitter through him. He sensed himself in a very different kind of danger, even as her gaze pierced him through and warmed him to the soul. And it was in that instant James realized he was capable of loving, truly loving, a woman.

Something flickered on the fringes of his mind, urging him to flee, to avoid at all costs this vulnerability. To be rid of this sudden feeling of want that he hadn't known possible.

Instead, unwilling to help himself, he reached out to her. Tangling his fingers through the fine auburn silk of her hair, he cradled her head and brought his mouth roughly to hers.

She was so soft in his arms. Her full lips opened to him with an eagerness that nearly undid him. He inhaled deeply, hungering for as much of her as he could take, wanting to consume her, to feel Magda's tongue in his mouth and her breath in his lungs.

She wrapped her arms about his neck and pressed herself against him, her breasts firm against his chest. His hand trembled as he drew it carefully from her hair, grazing down her cheek and jaw, her skin as soft as those rose petals beneath his fingers.

Magda stretched higher, pulling closer, rubbing against him, and more than anything he wanted to bring his hand down and tear the dress from her, taking those breasts in his hands, his mouth.

"Och." With a groan he pulled himself from her. "Good Christ, lass, but I want you so." He brought his forehead to hers and tried to calm his thundering heartbeat. He breathed slowly, deliberately. "I'm a ruined man, Magda. Like an angel you are, sent to me from some place beyond my ken, and you've doomed me to forever crave your touch."

"James." She whispered his name, and tracing her tongue along his lip, she beckoned him back.

"Magda," he murmured. "Lovely Magda." He brought his mouth to hers gently then, and the taste of her moan in his mouth broke him.

He couldn't do this. She didn't belong there, in such a brutal, uncertain time. He'd not ravage her in some tent on the eve of battle. He might be a man forever destroyed by her touch, but he'd not bring her down too.

"I must go." His voice was a hoarse whisper. James rose from her, had to turn his back to avoid seeing what was the most powerful temptation of his life. He knew if he were to look once more at her, see the invitation he knew he'd find in her eyes, there would be no going back. He'd not be able to stop himself again.

With a muttered oath, he wandered blindly away, to lose himself in the gray smoke of the soldiers' camp.

Chapter 14

Even in her confusion, Magda's face flushed as she thought of James, of last night. His kiss had crashed over her, consumed her, his mouth urgent to taste every part of her.

And she'd felt the same hunger. Magda had wanted to take him to her, to touch and taste away all the rest, to forget the world of the future, and the pall of death that hung like a physical thing over their present. His fingers had traced with unexpected gentleness along the curve of her cheek, down the slope of her neck. She'd longed for them to ease lower, sliding down the front of her dress, fantasized how it would feel for his roughened palm to chafe her breast and take her in hand.

They'd pulled apart reluctantly. James had rested his forehead on hers, murmuring words of adoration that, though entirely new to her, had felt familiar and right.

But then he'd left so abruptly, and she'd returned to the smells and din of the crofter's cottage, where she stayed with a few of the cooks and grooms not far from the soldiers. The bizarre transition from something so intimate to a situation so foreign left Magda feeling unreal. James had insisted on her privacy, and the embarrassment she felt at having an entire room to herself while the others made do on the floor in front of the hearth was only more isolating.

Adjusting her plaid shawl one last time, Magda stepped into the clearing before she lost her nerve. She'd left her room before dawn, knowing that if Napier saw her, he'd never allow her to venture to the soldiers' camp. But she had slept fitfully the night before and wanted, needed, to see James before he was off. She had to find out what the kiss had meant to him. What she meant to him. Even if she discovered what they'd shared had been nothing more than a flare of lust, the knowledge of where she stood would be something solid to hold on to.

She heard James before she saw him. A broad laugh rising above the voices of others. He had clearly heard something that delighted him, and she had to smile at the sound of it. His easy pleasure was a constant surprise, reassuring, and welcome like a chance break in the clouds in an overcast sky.

"The sun, she rises." James snuck up behind her, his breath hot on her neck in the chill morning air, and traced his fingers lightly up and down her spine. Her body shivered, nipples pulling taut against the rough fabric of her dress.

She turned to look at him. Dawn was beginning to filter through the trees, and the shapes of things slowly appeared out of the fading dark. The early morning mist shrouded the camp in an unearthly haze, James a gray silhouette standing close by her side. A shiver crawled through her, terror of the coming battle like a spear in her belly, even as the sight of James—long and handsome, donning armored breastplate like some magnificent hero of old—made her feel like a woman undone.

"To what do we owe this honor?" His voice was suddenly formal. Then she spotted a stoic group of men who'd appeared and were heading toward them.

"I wanted to wish you good luck," she said, cursing the anxiety that seeped through in her voice.

"I cannot imagine a greater boon than your bonny self, hen. Though," he added with a laugh, "Napier will surely burst a vein to find you gone from your room."

"Come, I'd have you meet some of the newest men in my acquaintance." Winking, he added, "A learned sage once instructed, 'a stranger does not a good leader make.'"

Magda noticed at once that these men were dressed differently from the rest, in muted tartans, a few wearing low boots or leather shoes and hose, though most were barefoot. About a dozen of them carried dirks and small rounded shields, but there were also a few with hooked pikes, as well as two archers in the group.

"Have you ever met a true Highlander, lass?"

"I . . . I can't say that I have," she said nervously, instinctively tucking herself closer to James's side.

One man stepped to the front, locking his eyes with James so sternly that Magda might have laughed had he not looked so dangerous. He stood solidly, with feet apart and hands at his waist, an enormous claymore strapped to his back. Magda estimated he was still a teenager, despite his already great height and the deference the other soldiers seemed to pay him.

"This would be Ewen Cameron, chief . . . rather, soon-to-be chief of his clan." The men exchanged nods.

"You Lowlanders tarry, even as the sun breaks the sky," the young warrior growled in a deep and thickly accented burr. "I'd be off while Aberdeenshire is still abed. Uncle"—Ewen nodded at an older, much grizzled man in his party—"did you scout the right flank?"

"Aye, lad, there are wee shallows a ways downriver fit to cross."

"You can take the ponies," James suggested.

Ewen's uncle merely glowered, incredulous. "We're not traveling to England, lad. God gave Highlanders two feet, and we ken how to use them."

"Fine." James nodded. "They'll be paying mind only to the front line."

"Aye. My thought as well," Ewen said. "While you busy them with musket fire, we'll split them in two at their flank, and the battle is done, quick as you please."

"Do it," James ordered. "Leslie's hired men are eager to repay yesterday's humiliation. Let them. What they don't know of you Highlanders won't hurt them."

The Highlanders all nodded solemnly. "'Tis the greatest courage of all, sending men into battle," Ewen said, the gravity of his hushed words a contrast to his young age. "But you'd not kill a trout with a cannon, aye? The town's defenses demand stealth, and my Cameron men are unrivalled overland."

"What a pretty wee meeting." General Leslie appeared, approaching leisurely, wiping his teeth with a rag. "Is the lassie leading the charge now," he asked, his eyes, overfamiliar, roving down Magda's body, "or has she appeared just to muddle the men's minds?"

"Have a care," James growled slowly.

"The men are in formation and ready to march," Leslie said, disregarding the last remark. "You've not lost your stomach after yesterday, have you? I'd as soon test Aberdeenshire hospitality and bide my day with a warm lass on a soft bed, but it's your nobles who've called for the attack."

Ewen regarded the general, and his granite-still features narrowed to a scowl. "*Tapadh leibh*, Marquis," the Cameron said, turning slowly to face James. "We'll not let you down."

"It seems you've been busy, lad," Leslie snarled after the Camerons disappeared into the trees. "What scheme have you set our enterprising Highlanders to?"

"I'm sending a small outfit downriver."

"Are you indeed?"

"Aye, Aberdeen will not expect a charge from her side. We'll hold the bridge, and the Camerons will deliver a surprise attack, effectively splitting their defenses."

Blood leached from Leslie's face, his lips pursed white with outrage. "What makes you think you've the authority to order my soldiers about?"

"Those Highlanders are Scotland's men, not yours," James warned, steel in his voice. "You are merely an opportunistic musket-for-hire with *my* coin in your purse. *That* is the source of my authority. You will just have to bear up, aye, General?"

❀

"You will sup by my side tonight, I'll wager." They stood not far from a cluster of readying soldiers, and James cast his voice for her ears alone.

Magda's mind raced. James was off for another day of battle, and she was unable to staunch the cascade of morbid scenarios that filled her head. Her brother had always been off trying to save the world, and here Magda was again, about to say good-bye to another who would live, and quite possibly die, doing the same.

She tried instead to commit the moment to memory. The mossy smell of the earth beneath the trees, birdsong growing louder with the dawn, the creak of the leather straps on James's armored breastplate. His near-black eyes and the steadying force of his presence. And the light dusting of stubble, bleached yellow from the sun, along his mouth and jaw.

"Something of interest, hen?"

"Excuse me?" She was startled back into the moment.

"You were staring at my mouth."

"Oh." Magda looked away, tears stinging her eyes.

James glanced around quickly, then, grabbing her arm, whisked her just within cover of the trees.

Hands on Magda's waist, he pushed her back up against a tree, his touch gentle as he slowly rubbed his hands up her side, thumbs grazing along the sides of her breasts, then stroking up her arms until he held her hands overhead. Pine filled the air, a green, astringent scent that cut like memories of another time. The tree was an ancient, magnificent thing, and Magda felt her hair catch in the deep furrows of its bark, thick and silvery brown in the morning light.

James eased close, then dipped his head to take a sudden kiss that stole Magda's breath, his mouth on hers snuffing all else out, filling her senses with the taste and smell of him. The freshness of woods on skin, a faint tang of sweat, and an amber, musky scent that clung lightly to him like a whisper of sex in the dark.

The sound of men calling his name echoed through the trees, and James pulled away reluctantly.

"Dawn has come and gone," he murmured, voice ragged. "It will happen fast now." James brought his hands down to cup her face and kissed Magda tenderly on each corner of her mouth, then lay one, chaste and lingering, full on her lips.

"You'll not fear for me. I will return to you unharmed, this very night. I swear it. How could I quit such a precious gift bestowed by the Fates?" A smile lit his features for just a moment, then he was once again somber.

James tugged a strip of blue silk from beneath his chest armor, the bit of hem he'd snatched from her dress just two days prior. He took the talisman and held it to his lips, eyes not wavering from hers.

"I will come back to you," he whispered, and disappeared through the trees.

Chapter 15

"Tom, my good man!" James boomed, his arms outstretched. "Come, come! I've set aside a dram of the good brandy."

Hopping up from his seat by a small bonfire, James ducked into his tent for his flask.

"A moment, James . . ." Tom hesitated.

Peeking back through the canvas flaps, James feigned astonishment. "Such dire spirits! Don't you know we've won the battle? I understand you fancy yourself more spy than soldier, but even you can't have missed that we've more men left standing than our opponent has, aye?" He laughed heartily, then added, "As my emissary, perhaps you'd be so kind as to root out a fine set of clubs. I'd give the links at the Royal Aberdeen a try before returning to Montrose."

"James," Tom said again, with more surety. "We'll not be playing any golf."

"What madness is this?" James asked broadly.

The grin on his face slowly dissolved into bewilderment then concern. "What is it, man? Has something happened to Magda?"

"No, no, it's naught to do with the lass. As far as I know, she remains under Napier's watchful eye." Tom scrubbed a hand over his forehead. "It's Aberdeen, James. They've razed it."

James stared blankly, so Tom continued. "After the bridge fell, Leslie and his men disappeared. You'd gone off to salute the Camerons; soldiers were going every which way. It was mayhem all about, James." Tom pitched his voice as if to offer consolation, earnestly trying to convince his friend of something. "You can't have accounted for every man."

"Just tell it," James said through clenched teeth. "What is it you're telling me?"

"The general and Campbell, and some of their men . . . They've laid waste to Aberdeen, James. Thievery, mostly. But there was some, well . . . Leslie's men are savages, many of them."

"Och, hell." James dropped to the ground, legs crossed, cradling his head in his hands. "The accursed Campbell. Napier warned me, aye? Warned of men drunk on newfound power." He ran his hands over his face and through his hair. "I need to make it right. I'll not abide barbarism. Releasing a pack of wolves on my own country was never my intention."

He rose solidly to his feet. "I must go, have an audience with the king himself, make him listen to reason. The fall of his supporters in Aberdeen should have captured Charles's attention." James paced a few steps, and then turned to face his friend. "I started this madness, Tom, and now I will finish it."

"But there's more," Tom said quietly. "The king and his Catholic wife have divided more than just Scotland. Parliament has risen against him. Charles has fled London and set up a military court in Oxford."

James was silent for a moment, then said, his voice steady, "Then it's to Oxford we go. Now."

"You're mad."

"I've been told as much."

"I cannot come with you this time, James."

Silence hung between the two men. Just the slow popping of the dwindling fire filled the late-afternoon air.

"Aye, I've anticipated this day."

"What of the lass?"

"I'll keep her by me, of course."

"You cannot."

"And why not?" His friend had situated himself by the fire, and James stepped closer to stand towering over him. "The lass has a sound seat on a horse. She'll make the journey just fine."

"Aye, the lass has a pretty seat indeed," he said, and James's glare was deadly in return. "Listen to reason, man." Tom rose to face him. "It's been pure good fortune that nothing has befallen her thus far. Think you, what would've happened had today's battle gone the other way? Who would've protected her?"

Tom let the thought hang heavy in the air before continuing, "The battle in Aberdeen has opened a Pandora's box. Traveling as a stranger, and on the road to England? Men will be on the look-out, and with hatred in their eyes, for any sign of a Covenanter. Others will want vengeance against any Royalist they can find. And then there are those who'll merely be suspicious of everyone." He met his friend's eye with uncharacteristic challenge. "And what of you now, James? What of your Covenant now? How would you choose, if you were forced to pick a side?"

He placed his hand on James's shoulder. "I know you'll want the lass by your side," he added quietly. "But for her safety, you must part."

"Aye," James said finally, his voice ragged. He flinched his shoulder from beneath Tom's hand. "I'll return to Montrose and gather Will Rollo. I'll need another man at my side." Turning his back, he spoke, staring into the fire. "I must leave at once. If I ride through the night, I can be there by dawn. I'll gather some provisions and head to the land of our king."

❦

"She's not here, lad," Napier said, perplexed. James had finally found his brother-in-law in the crofter's cabin, all its other inhabitants gone to the soldiers' camp to celebrate the Covenanters' victory. "We thought surely you'd be raising a toast to your great triumph by now. She went off and about with the cook. Magda has no shortage of questions for her. I don't know what manner of missionaries her parents were, but it seems your lass wouldn't know the difference between sustenance and certain death when it comes to living off the land."

James only nodded absently, so Napier elaborated, amused by his own story, "Cook only just stopped her from poisoning us all with a basket full of spindle berries. She finally decided simply to take Magda on one of her foraging walks. I've not done wrong to let her alone?" he asked, sudden panic seizing his voice.

"No, no," James replied, his tone distant. His eyes scanned the room once more, as if Magda might somehow magically appear. The single cookpot. A lone cot. Grit and dirt on the cold stone floor. She didn't belong there, in such an untamed land. How would she survive it? She'd want her museums and grand baths, not spindle berries. She'd want to return to her home.

"You did well." James's voice was rough. He raked a hand through his hair and began again. "These past days. You did well, tended Magda well. You've my thanks. It's been a great relief to me. But . . ." He clasped his hand to Napier's shoulder. "I've one more favor to ask of you."

"You know you have only to ask."

"I need to be off. And soon."

"Can you not wait for Magda's return? It can't be more than a matter of hours."

"I have no choice." James paused, blinking his eyes shut tight. When he opened them, his gaze was sharp on his brother-in-law. "I need to leave for Montrose at once. You were right about the Covenanters. It appears we've created a many-headed beast. Even now, Campbell razes the town, and the king has lost London to Parliament."

"Civil war?" Napier asked incredulously.

"That is the question, aye? I'm off to Oxford to treat with Charles. Gather what I might about the situation. But Magda . . ."

Napier nodded, knowing.

"I'd wanted to see her once more . . ." His voice trailed off, remembering the vivid green of Magda's eyes. In them he'd seen the promise of something greater than just a man and a woman lying tangled together. But whatever potential he might feel with this strange, wayward woman, he knew she had to return home. That England was on the brink of civil war only confirmed it. To keep her in his world would only put her life in jeopardy.

James inhaled deeply, gathering himself, then focused once more. "The lass needs help. Return her to Montrose for me, offer her my every hospitality." He added somberly, "Help her find the way home."

"Anything, James, of course."

"Ask her story. And Napier?"

"Yes, lad?"

"I would that you believed her."

Ignoring the other man's confusion, James continued, "Take her to the monastery. My hope is the Black Friars might lend assistance."

"Where exactly is the lass from?" Napier asked uneasily.

"In good time, man, in good time . . . Ah, one last thing." James reached down, and extracting a small knife from the cuff of his boot, he sliced a navy and gold enameled button from his coat. "Give her this from me," he said, pressing the button into Napier's hand.

"A trifle to remember me. When she finds herself home, I'll be long dead."

Chapter 16

James smiled for the first time since Aberdeen. It felt so good to be by Rollo's side once more. They'd grown up together, and he'd missed the man who'd become like a brother to him.

"Have you need of assistance?" he asked, seeing Rollo struggle with his saddle. Though a riding accident as a child had damaged his friend's back and left his legs without much feeling, the near-constant spasms had rendered them unusually strong. Sheer determination and grit drove him and, once seated, he was one of the greatest horsemen James knew.

"I'm lame, James," he bit out, "not a half-wit." Rollo pulled himself into place and, bending to adjust the thick straps, grumbled, "I think I am capable of buckling my own leathers."

He sat up, nodding grimly at James. Will Rollo cut a regal figure, sitting tall on his gray-speckled stallion, an unusual, and pricey, mount for a Scotsman. If it weren't for so many straps and the extra-high pommel and cantle of his custom saddle, one would never guess the pain and stiffness he suffered.

"I find you cheerful as ever, my dear friend." He erupted in laughter, which Rollo answered with a begrudging smile.

James inhaled, savoring once again the tang of sea in his throat. Though the coast was at his back, he could feel its distant pulse like the snore of a slumbering monster, and it was something that never ceased to bolster him.

Abandoning Magda to Napier's care had been a blow, but he'd seen no other choice. Though he hoped he'd ensured her safety by leaving her, it did nothing to ease the torture of separation. Traitorous thoughts had flickered, taunting him. *Perhaps Napier won't find Lonan. Perhaps she'll choose to stay. Perhaps, when this madness is through, she'll be in Montrose. Waiting.*

He pushed such notions from his mind. They were too painful. He needed to focus on the task at hand. If James couldn't have Magda in his life, he'd sacrifice his life to his cause.

Seeing Will Rollo again had done much to take the edge off his melancholy, but it was something about the rhythm of the tides that reminded him of his true calling. That pounding of wave on rock was as much a part of him as it was a part of Scotland. And it was for Scotland that he rode now, to pursue what was best for his beloved country.

"I will hear news of Montrose," James said, nudging his horse into a brisk walk. "I find I've yearned for the sea."

Rollo appeared beside him, staring sternly at the road ahead. "As Margaret tells it, you've been yearning for something considerably more feminine these past days."

Astonished, James swung his head to look at his friend, whose mouth was still set in a grim line. "You devil!" Standing in his stirrups, he leaned back to clap Rollo's horse hard on the rump.

And even Rollo spared a laugh when both horses broke into a gallop, as the two friends rode south to parley with the king.

❀

"The spires of Oxford!" James shouted, pointing across a tangled field to distant towers that rose to elegant points on the horizon.

"It's been a fortnight of hard riding," Rollo said dourly, leaning to massage his legs. "I was beginning to doubt their existence."

"Such a lack of faith." James *tsked*, pulling his mount up to ride shoulder to shoulder. "A fortnight is superb time for such a distance."

"Now we just need to cross these mucky fields," Rollo grumbled. "Another fine pasture of sheep dung. I weary of the sheep dung, James."

"Don't sound so fashed. I promise to find us a good pub upon our arrival."

"Well at least, miraculously, there's no rain to greet us. Merely gray spires in a gray sky."

"There's the spirit," James said sarcastically.

Wary of the uneven meadow, they kept their mounts to a tentative trot. The meadow was rutted and muddy from winter's melted snows, and it would do no good to lame a horse so close to their journey's end.

A short ride brought them to Oxford proper, and the men looked around in disbelief as they walked their horses slowly down Broad Street. Gone from Oxford was any sense of scholarly atmosphere, nor was there much indication that it had ever functioned as a university at all. Soldiers roamed the streets as far as the eye could see, and the town seemed to James a tinderbox of bored men anxious for battle.

"We'll find ourselves a pay house and settle in."

"Aye," Rollo replied, "if the town is taking civilians." He looked around warily. "King's men as far as the eye can see. If I hadn't called myself a Royalist before, I shall now."

❁

"These infernal Puritans. So hostile!" The king distractedly held a small gilded looking glass above his head to study the fall of his hair atop his broad lace collar. "I have enough to concern me here in England without Scottish noblemen stirring the pot."

"Your Majesty?" The painter gestured, gently reminding him to return to his former pose.

"Yes, yes." Charles nodded impatiently. Settling back into position, the king canted his head slightly to keep one eye on the man pacing the room. Colonel Sibbald was an old soldier, and just the sort he'd need to subdue the Covenanters. The king had thought the militia in Aberdeen could put a neat stop to Campbell and Graham, and had been surprised when the city fell. The Covenanters had relied on more than might that day; Graham led them, and exercised military tactics more refined than Charles had expected.

But word had it there was now dissention between him and the Campbell. If Charles could convince Graham to leave the Covenanters and join his Royalists, it might give him hope of quelling this uprising once and for all.

"So this Graham comes for an audience?"

"If it pleases Your Majesty," the colonel replied, surreptitiously pouring his third glass of brandy.

"I'm told he's a confident sort." Charles scowled. "Perhaps a bit overconfident, I say."

Sibbald shrugged. "Might I remind Your Majesty that you snubbed him at your first and only meeting? I recommend a more politic reception this time round." He tossed back his drink and placed the empty snifter on a tray. "The Marquis of Montrose could be a real asset to your cause."

"Perhaps I should side with the Campbell instead." The king glared a moment at the colonel, who stood almost a foot taller than the diminutive monarch.

"Have a care, Your Majesty." The colonel adjusted his waistcoat, clearly uncomfortable in the formal dress appropriate for a royal audience. "Rumor is, his men have taken to calling him *King Campbell*."

Charles huffed, and turned to take out his aggravation on his court painter. "You." He stabbed his finger toward the man. "I desire a mythological theme, something grand, and I'd not be distracted this time by sylphs and those chubby-cheeked babes you so favor."

"But of course, Your Majesty," Van Dyck deferred, "you will be as Apollo himself, virile, and fresh from the hunt."

"Your Majesty," the colonel interrupted, ignoring the insolent stare from the court painter. "If you can make peace with Graham and somehow convince him to fight for you, he will need men to lead. I fear the English are not much in the mood for war."

"Well, Sibbald, we'll just commission them."

"The gentry haven't been commissioned into service in decades. With respect, sir, I fear that could be a treacherous course of action. Many Englishmen already agitate against you."

Charles waved his hand testily. "I've made arrangements." He rose from his carved mahogany seat. "A thousand head of Irishmen are come to assist me."

"It will be seen as a Catholic conspiracy." Astonishment tinged Sibbald's voice. Returning to the tray, the old colonel tried to exact a final drop from his empty glass.

"What would you have me do otherwise?" Charles asked. "The Kirk and nobles rebel, and the only men at my back are professional soldiers like you, a handful of Irish, and whatever help my dearest queen might procure from abroad."

He caught Van Dyck's stare, as the painter waited expectantly for the king to reassume his position. Charles's cheeks blotched red with impatience. "I'm done for now." He shooed the painter away angrily. "Leave us."

The artist bowed silently, and hastily gathered his paints into a box, leaving his easel where it stood in the king's private chamber.

"Once again, I encourage you to listen to the Marquis of Montrose," the colonel said. "He will, of course, expect you to make concessions on your religious mandates, but with Parliament splintering the south and the Covenanters raging in the north, the question of religious freedoms seems to be the least of your concerns at the moment."

Sibbald wandered to the abandoned easel and examined the half-painted portrait of the king, seated atop a great white stallion, his stubby legs elongated under a gleaming sheath of imaginary armor, tiny frame now towering over all he surveyed. Concealing a smirk, the colonel quickly added, "I knew James at the military college at Angers. I have every confidence in him. The marquis was a gentleman, and seemed a bright enough sort."

"Bright enough to beat his peers at their own game?"

"Aye, Your Majesty, we can hope."

❁

A night in Oxford hadn't done much to compose James and Rollo. They'd discovered pub curfews were now nine o'clock, liquor sales being directly related to late-night brawling within the ranks. They had found a small rooming house near New College, which, they'd been told, now functioned as the king's main magazine, housing all military provisions and artillery.

"Good Lord," James exclaimed, retrieving a small handkerchief from his pocket. "Do I smell cattle?"

They had entered the main gates of Christ Church. Though he had a cane crafted specifically for him, Rollo's progress was slow, and James strolled leisurely at his side.

Distant lowing echoed off the staid stone buildings that enclosed the courtyard in a vast square. "I hear them as well," Rollo said.

"Good sir," James called, flagging down a young soldier. "If you would please be so kind as to enlighten us, pray tell, what are livestock doing in Christ Church?"

Though tall, the soldier was a rangy lad, and James guessed he'd not yet even reached his full height. "We've need of something to eat, aye?" the boy said.

"Yes"—James concealed a smile—"but of course you do."

"They've filled the church with cows," Rollo marveled under his breath.

"Royalist cows, surely." James smirked, bemused by Oxford's bizarre transformation. "Let's find Charles. Perhaps he's tending turnips in the cloisters. They'll have want of a royal side dish."

"Caution." Rollo laughed softly, looking around quickly to ensure nobody had overheard. "Or it'll be your head on a platter for dessert."

There wasn't a cow to be heard or smelled in Charles's temporary court, though, which they eventually found installed, with royal extravagance, in St. Frideswide's Priory.

"You may enter," a footman said, soon after James and Rollo's arrival had been announced.

"So quickly?" Rollo asked under his breath, brows raised.

"Perhaps he will look me in the eye this time."

"Why, James Graham," Charles said as they entered the library, which had been fashioned into an impromptu royal sitting room. He reached his hand out, offering his ring for a kiss. "To what do I owe this surprising honor? Last I knew, you were routing my people in Aberdeen, under the banner of your Covenant."

"Campbell worries good Scotsmen in his teeth like a dog, and I can no longer stand with him," James replied, ignoring the king's sarcasm. "What I began as a noble venture has become a crass purloining of as much of my beloved homeland as he and his greedy lords can devour."

"Oh, my." Charles laughed. "Such righteousness!" He looked to his footman, gesturing that chairs be brought to his side.

"Sit, sit." The king studied Rollo as he struggled into the chair, legs unbending. "What of you?" Charles asked him, skeptical distaste pursing his mouth. "I'm told your name is William Rollo."

Rollo gave a curt and wordless nod.

Charles turned to James and asked, "You bring me a cripple?"

"And none other." James clapped his friend on the shoulder, his easy smile a challenge to the king's doubt. "Rollo is an unrivalled horseman and the finest soldier I've known."

"It is my understanding that Aberdeen was your first rout." An oily smile split Charles's lips. "How many soldiers can you have known, James? No matter, no matter." The king's hand fluttered, shutting down James's response.

"Music!" he shouted to nobody in particular. "Bring Nicholas," he said to the first of many scattering attendants who caught his eye. "I'd have music."

Turning to James, he said, "We shall rival Parliament in more than our wisdom. We are men of taste!"

Charles carefully preened his moustache and goatee away from his lips. "I would have you raise Scotland for me."

"And," James replied without missing a beat, "*I* would have your assurance that Scotland will retain the sanctity of her Kirk. Just as the clergy should concern themselves solely with matters of the spirit, the monarch should rule over matters of the state, and the state alone."

"Touché, young man." The king steepled his fingers at his chin, a calculating look wrinkling his brow. "I care not for bishops either, James. I shall grant your Scotsmen their ecclesiastical freedoms. You just subdue these rebel nobles and restore order to Scotland."

Charles appeared distracted, watching his court musicians set up to play. "And now I've word of a Parliament-backed army to contend with."

James began to speak, and Charles stopped him with a raised hand. "Parliament has raised what they're calling the New Model Army. And, James, here's the whimsical bit. They've donned matching coats of red. *Twenty thousand* matching coats of red, to be precise." The king's patronizing smile didn't reach his eyes.

"You see, Marquis, you'd be wise not to be so dismissive. These red-coated soldiers are the jackals who will feast on the carcass your Campbell leaves behind."

Charles rose and looked down at them imperiously, his short

stature barely clearing the heads of the seated Scotsmen. "A Campbell who, I might add, appears to have Scotland's nobles tumbling over each other to swear him fealty. Your Covenanters," he said, pointing at James, "now hold significant cities in the Lowlands."

"Held by the Covenanters?" James asked, voice like steel. "Or is it that the Lowlands simply lie in wait for a true leader?" He let the near-treasonous statement hang. "I'll raise your standard," James continued, "by the same principles of liberty and self-determination that committed me to the Covenant. Just as you had no right to play politics with the religion of Scotland, Scotland has no right to depose her king. I'll rout the vermin who would destroy my country." James stood, towering a foot over the monarch. "The Highlands will stand with me."

"Give us men and horses enough to cut through to the north," Rollo said, his voice gritty. "We hold our line there."

"I'm afraid you'll have but the mounts you rode in on." Charles wandered away from the men toward his court musicians, playing quietly in the corner. "I will spare you my Colonel Sibbald, an old military man who will prove helpful on the campaign. James, you shall be named my viceroy and captain-general—"

"No," James interrupted.

The king spun, his face blackened into a cold stare.

"Respectfully, Your Majesty," James amended, "I decline your offer. I shall indeed raise Scotland for you. But I find I've become a man skeptical of empty titles."

James walked toward Charles and bowed with a flourish. Raising his chin, he looked his king hard in the eye and said, "I need naught but my own name to fight for my country."

❁

In his half doze, he shifted yet again, having a remarkably difficult time getting comfortable for a man who'd spent the past two weeks sleeping on the ground. A tense day followed by a sickeningly lavish meal with the king had left James exhausted, and yet Magda's face kept rousing him, appearing in his mind, denying him a deep sleep.

Back in Aberdeen, James had felt privy to a prized secret. Only he had held Magda close enough to discern the yellow flecks that brightened the emerald green of her eyes. And surely only he had noticed how the sun had pricked light brown freckles across the bridge of her nose, a faint dusting of color to soften the sharp lines of her features.

He pushed away the memory of that soft, broad mouth crushed beneath his, and rolled onto his belly, pressing himself into the bed, seeking relief from the hardness that seized him.

With her, he'd had the sensation of being on the brink of some great unknown. It wasn't in his nature to turn from such tremendous possibility. Walking away from her had been like abandoning another life, relinquishing it to a sort of eternal stasis, forever unlived. James felt Magda's loss keenly, their parting no less tragic for its necessity.

Mercifully, the mad pulse at his groin dulled to a distant ache, and James fell, finally, into a fitful sleep.

They began as flashes in the gray half-light of dreams, fragmented images, and his subconscious snatched hungrily at them. His body began to hum, as his fantasies slowly bloomed with color, and texture, and taste.

Magda walking toward him, inexplicably illuminated under a black sky. Her sheer shift rippled close against her breasts as she walked, nipples tight in the night breeze, and her arms opened to him, face open and serene.

Then Magda was in his arms, facing away from him, cradling his hands at her belly. There was a bright sun overhead, warming his shoulders and infusing him with a sense of equanimity, pleasant and right. The smell of her rose to him, a rich musk, and he became a hard ridge at her back. A knowing laugh was quiet and low in her throat as Magda turned to face him.

James stood, now in Montrose, looking out the windows of his room, watching the sun glint off the sea. He felt the distant rumble of the surf on sand reverberate through the core of him, and was content. He knew Magda lay on his bed at his back, heard her naked skin slip against the sheets. He turned to face her, a presence lingering bright just out of his line of vision.

Now she straddled James, finally naked above him, grass rustling at his sides, tickling the backs of his knees, the fresh smell of it filling his senses. Magda laughed, musical and joyous, and he reached up to cup her breasts. Her body was out of focus, but the feel of her was soft and full in his rough, callused hands.

It was dark now, and her image was robbed from him. But his other senses were amplified, and the sounds of their breath, heavy and close, filled his head. The scent of their mingled bodies and the velvety expanses of thigh and stomach sliding under him raised him to a fever pitch. Her wetness enveloped him, and it was like succumbing to some primal force, hot and magnificent, drawing him in to drown. James pinned her hands beneath his and leaned forward to taste her, and the remembrance of her was a visceral thing, her breath in his lungs, the rough and smooth of her tongue. A hard bolt of desire impaled him as he drove into her, ravenous and fierce with want.

And James was freed, finally, with glorious release.

He slept hard until dawn, when he was taken again by restlessness, images of Magda once again colorless fragments haunting his sleep. She had disappeared from him, and James was riding hard to find her. The Scottish Highlands stretched cold and desolate along the horizon as the crest of every hill, and the sunlight at the end of each stand of trees, brought glimpses of yet more emptiness.

And James rode on, hard, until he bolted upright from his nightmare. Awake, confused, body drenched and heart pounding, he asked, "What have I done?" as the emptiness echoed in his soul.

Chapter 17

Magda fingered the button, hard and cold in her palm. Curves of navy blue enamel formed a simple decorative pattern, thick and smooth atop the gold background.

"I don't understand." For the first time in her life, she'd been captivated by a man. Magda had found someone she admired, who was also capable of sending delicious shivers through her body. She felt connected to James. She'd found an easy intimacy with him that led her to believe that she could, for once, shed her armor to let a little life in. And he'd gone away, leaving her a button. What was she supposed to do with that? He was off, his death likely on the horizon, leaving her to navigate the seventeenth century with a button?

"Nor do I, lass," Napier conceded. "Though I was fairly hoping you might be able to enlighten me."

He took the button from her hand and held it to the window, and the late-afternoon sunlight shimmered along its surface.

"Our James, when he gets an idea in his head . . ." Napier shrugged. "We shall return to Montrose forthwith."

She studied James's brother-in-law. How his tight, upturned moustache exaggerated the sharpness of his features. His eyes, measured and earnest. It was a face that, she'd noticed, softened only at the mention of his wife.

"You're anxious to get back to Margaret, aren't you?"

"Aye," Napier admitted. "I am that."

"That's nice." She choked up, and turned as if to stare out the window. Magda had thought she had found someone too, but she had apparently been fooling herself. Maybe she'd imagined their shared connection. James had gone off, endangering himself once again for his cause. If he didn't face his death on this foray, it was sure to come eventually. The thought made her tears spill hot on her cheeks.

Napier rushed to her side, and placing his arm gently at her back, he steered her to a chair by the fire. "Poor girl. I'm told you have a story for me. I'd hear it as we return to Montrose. I vow you'll have my every effort to return you home, safely and soundly."

"But." Her voice wavered, uncertain. "I'm no longer sure I can go home," she said, thinking how they'd been unable to track down Brother Lonan. Then she realized, even more so, she couldn't go home because she had to know what would become of James. It had been slowly dawning on her that she needed to witness his fate for herself.

"Well . . ." Napier was flummoxed, and his generally impeccably genteel demeanor was no longer doing much to mask it. "We'll get you back to my Margaret," he announced, suddenly sure. "She will help us sort this to rights."

Magda merely stared at her hands clenched in her lap.

"You'll not fret, dear girl." Napier spoke softly and surely. "James shall return to you, a king's army at his back."

❀

She stood, chafing her arms by the hearth, greedy for the last of the fire's dying heat. Magda knew she should rest—they were to leave for Montrose at dawn—but she wasn't ready to lie down for the night.

James had said she should go home, but she knew now that she couldn't leave him. He thought she was the one in danger, but Magda knew it was he who faced the greatest risk. She'd fooled herself, thinking it was merely the historian in her who needed to see it through, who needed to witness history happen in real time. But now Magda knew the need ran even deeper. She had to stay for herself. And for James.

She had considered what it would be to turn from his fate. She could simply go home, choosing to read his end in the pages of history.

The thought sat like ice in her belly.

She imagined it, how she'd return to her time only to search hungrily for any painting, or book, or artifact that would tell his story, delivering him to her side. But reading history wouldn't truly bring James back. The answers she'd find would leave her hollow, the pages at her fingertips, her might-have-been.

Or, courageous, she could seize her own fate.

James wanted Magda to find her way home, but he thought he had a battle to fight, triumphant. He'd have her out of harm's way. Little did he realize that he was the one who was truly in danger.

She stoked the fire one last time, suddenly warmed through. For the first time in her life she'd stand her ground. She thought of Peter, and how she hadn't been able to save him. Considered her parents, and how they'd tried to have a say in every aspect of her life, from dictating which schools she'd attend to steering the right men her way. But now was her time to take an active part in the living of her life. She wouldn't just study history; she would be a part of it.

Magda laughed quietly to herself, and turned to scamper into bed for the night.

Where a strange man sat, staring at her, lips curled into a feral half smile.

"What the—" Magda instinctively clasped her arms to her chest, concealing herself under her thin nightgown.

"I see your swain has abandoned you. Pity," the man said, running his eyes hungrily up and down her body, lit from behind by the fire's soft glow. "We find ourselves in rough countryside, the sort where a woman has want of a man, and yet it seems yours is no longer in need of you."

"Excuse me!" she said, finding her voice. "Please leave this room now."

"And so, as I was saying," he patronized, "I've decided to take your care upon myself." His lips, thin and shining as if just licked, peeled apart to reveal the tip of his tongue clamped between small teeth.

"You see, I too am abandoned," he continued in mock despair. "Your paramour has taken us all unawares and is reportedly off to meet the king. No man turns his back on me," he growled. "Who knew the Marquis of Montrose had such pluck?"

"James is not my paramour, and I have no need for a caretaker, so if you'd please just—"

He barked out a laugh. "*James*, is it? So"—he assessed her thoughtfully—"you are indeed *intime* with our marquis. An interesting development."

Ignoring her outraged gasp, he oozed, "Oh, but where are my manners? I must introduce myself. I am Archibald Campbell, Marquis of Argyll, at your command."

Magda stared at the jowly letch in front of her, speechless. This wasn't supposed to be happening. The kindly Napier was going to come for her tomorrow morning. She would wait for James, or she would return home. She wasn't supposed to be caught helpless in a real seventeenth-century nightmare.

"Help!" she shrieked, bolting for the door. "Somebody, help!"

Campbell was on her in an instant, his chubby hands gripping her upper arms like two vises.

"Tut-tut." He shook his head, his tone one of exaggerated dismay. "Poor duck. Your companions have all gone to Aberdeen. To celebrate *my* victory. And you here, alone. Oh," Campbell added brightly, "not completely alone. Just you and that old sot Napier, who seems to find himself knocked insensate at the moment."

Panicked, her eyes flicked around the room, looking everywhere but at his face. Was there something she could use as a weapon? Some tool by the fireplace?

Campbell gave her a strong shake, pulling her close. "What is it?" he asked playfully. He'd pulled her face near to his crimson velvet coat. "Ah, have you eyes for this trinket?" He let go one arm and fingered a long, straight pin stuck garishly at his breast. A reddish brown stone at its tip shone dully in the firelight. "It was a . . . gift"—he chuckled salaciously—"from a fine Aberdeenshire lady. If James can have his blue rag, I thought it best to have my own emblem." He stroked her cheek with his knuckles. "If you show me your every kindness, perhaps I will make you a gift of it."

"The only thing I require of you is your exit," Magda snarled. Her escalating fear spiked her confidence, and she spit at him and clawed for his face. He grabbed her wrist and jerked it down to her side. She struggled frantically, kicking at his calves with her painfully bare feet, trying to knee him and shake her body free from his grip. "Get out!"

"I think not, dear." Campbell pushed her backward. "But fear not. Your fate is in your marquis's hands. I'll not sully myself with you. Yet." He wrenched both her hands up, pinning them against the wall with his forearm over their heads. He took a swath of her hair, wrapped it once around his fist, and slowly pulled it through his hand. "I find I've a taste for battle, not for used whores with hair the color of rust."

He leaned his face close to hers, and the sour stink of his breath turned her stomach. Campbell ducked to take her earlobe between his teeth and bit down hard, silencing her shriek with a damp palm pushed hard to her mouth. "We'll make our way back to my lands in Argyll." She felt spittle on her cheeks as he whispered in her ear, "Clans along the way shall kneel, or enrich my coffers."

❀

"But he's a Campbell!" Tom shouted, frantic. "How could you let a Campbell take our Magda?"

"I—" Napier was stricken. Rubbing the lump on the back of his head, he deflated, sitting on Magda's bed to reread Campbell's note yet one more time. "He claims the lass as his own. Says James has discarded her, and he is the storm that sweeps the chaff from the field."

"The bastard dares be poetic."

Tom sat by Napier's side. "'Twas not your fault, I know. He caught you unawares. The Campbell is capable of great treachery. Now up with you," he added, mustering an optimistic tone. "We must get word to James."

"Don't you see?" Napier asked, subdued. "James will be gone from Montrose by now."

The other man began to speak. "Aye," Napier interrupted him, anticipating Tom's next thought. "We can—and we will—send word to Oxford. But open your eyes, Tom. That girl is as a cloud of smoke on the wind."

Chapter 18

"Eat." Campbell nudged the tin platter toward her with his foot.

Magda contemplated the hard bread and white cheese on the ground before her. Two days had passed since being captured by the Campbell clan, and she hadn't consumed much more than water.

Even when Campbell had hustled her roughly onto his horse and off to his distant camp, she'd been in a fog of disbelief. It had quickly shattered, though, on her first night. She'd heard a struggle and, straining her eyes into the darkness, had spied a girl no older than twenty rushing from Campbell's tent, torn dress clutched to her chest. The sound of the girl's sobs, convulsive and reedy, had pierced the night, robbing Magda of her appetite, even as she'd felt a remote kernel of resolve crystallize deep inside.

At first, she'd hoped for rescue, fantasizing that every hillock or copse of trees along the road concealed James, who would surely burst out at any moment to save her.

He was out there, somewhere. Did he think of her, she wondered, or was Magda just a brief chapter, now concluded, in his greater adventure? Would he rescue her, if he knew? Or perhaps he already did know of her capture and chose instead to continue on his current course. Her throat closed at the thought, and she blinked rapidly. She'd rather die than let Campbell see her tears.

Campbell squinted at her. His thin, perpetually moist lips peeled from his teeth. "Too good for my food, is it?" He tapped the plate once more with his foot. "I can see to it that you're offered none, if that's your preference."

Knowing she needed to preserve her strength, Magda lifted the cheese to her mouth and gnawed off a bit from the corner. Tart with age, it flaked onto her tongue, its sourness turning her stomach. She made herself dissolve the dry lump in her mouth, and swallow.

"That's it," he said, sneering. "Need to keep your strength up. I've plans for you, lass. Big plans."

She eyed him wordlessly, willing him to disappear, not bothering to mask her contempt. Campbell laughed, amused by her impotent outrage. "Eat fast, woman. We've a hard day of riding ahead."

Later, when Magda spotted the girl from the tent—her young eyes empty despite the bright face she tried to don for her equally young husband—the glimmer of resolve she'd felt exploded into a determined rage.

Magda was all alone now, and the one person who'd risk helping her was as good as a world away. It would be up to her to save herself. She'd spent her days plotting, but could come up with only one simple strategy: run.

❈

Another day passed, and Magda's opportunity never presented itself. They stopped to camp for the night and her dignity demanded she force herself not to limp, pushing the stiff ache in her legs to the back of her mind and rallying muscles that felt wrung out from a day coiled in anticipation.

They'd traveled south along the coast, and it had been hard riding, rocky and treacherous, and spectacularly terrifying with the sea pounding relentlessly, always somewhere to their left.

There would've been no way for her to outride the Campbells on such terrain, even if she had been left alone once all day. Even relieving herself had been humiliating, as anonymous clansmen pretended not to watch avidly her quick squats behind those rare tangles of coastal brush that'd been thick enough to conceal her. She swore that, by day's end, Campbell was choosing such desolate areas for their breaks on purpose.

Her resolve was beginning to blur into something more like despair and she knew she had to escape, immediately. Though Campbell was the only man who had a tent, Magda had considered herself lucky to have been given a swath of broadcloth she could use to protect herself from the elements. She'd been shocked that Campbell had allowed her that concession, and she suspected it was a gesture to his clansmen that she was off-limits. He'd said he had big plans for her, and Magda shivered to think how this temporary protection was related to Campbell's grand scheme. She had a hunch he was saving her for himself.

She relied on that stretch of broadcloth now, using the semiprivacy to disguise a meager lump of branches and brush as herself, fast asleep under the covers.

Though frightened to leave in the night, she was more terrified of the fate she imagined at the hands of these men. It seemed she waited an eternity for the sun to set, looking out from her scrubby nest, the cold earth intensifying the feverish ache of her muscles. As the granite-colored sky deepened into an indigo bowl overhead, she thought of that night with James under the stars and was comforted to imagine him settling down for the evening underneath the same sky.

A band of light the color of eggplant lit the horizon. It appeared so slowly, Magda wondered if it hadn't been there all along. But then there was a flicker, like the curtain of the night sky parting, and green lights shimmered overhead. The purple halo cupping the horizon intensified and seemed to shoot up from the earth even as the green swirled overhead like vapor in a witch's crystal ball. Magda felt humbled by this unexpected gift: her first sight of the Northern Lights. And it emboldened her, its grandeur somehow a reminder of how minuscule humanity was in the scope of things. Campbell and his men seemed suddenly absurd, simply men, fallible, who'd been long dead by the time she'd been born.

Magda sprang from her refuge, feeling gloriously like a wild animal, and ignoring the slap of branches at her cheeks and the bite of rocks at her feet, she ran hard into the night.

❀

"Whatever could you be thinking? That's good beer, you daftie." Sibbald whacked James with his riding crop.

"You'll not strike me, old man," he said, turning his back to the colonel. James stepped closer to his horse, as the beast continued to lap enthusiastically at the bucket of ale.

"Aye, there's no stopping him," Rollo said. "What began as the whimsy of a bored rich boy has become a habit surrounded by no less superstition than an adder spied on an old woman's doorstep."

"You call me an old woman?" James kicked the bucket to the corner of the impromptu stall, and slapped his horse on the neck affectionately.

"Aye, I am that." Rollo shooed away a stableboy who'd come to help him onto his saddle. He clambered onto the mounting block just outside the door to what was once a Christ Church dining hall, now a royal stable. He stopped struggling once he got his belly to his mount, as Rollo used his extraordinary upper-body strength to seat his uncooperative legs in the saddle. "And you move as slow as an old woman on Sunday too."

"You'll cease your complaints, Will. At least you're not the one disguised as a groom." James nodded to his costume. While Rollo and Sibbald were outfitted like noblemen, James wore threadbare, colorless clothing appropriate for a stableman.

"I've always wanted to give you orders." Rollo's face cracked into a rare smile. "Now can we move from this place?"

"What?" James asked. He inhaled deeply. "Has Oxford's rich bouquet become too unbearable for your delicate sensibilities?"

"I beg you to reconsider your obsession with Perthshire," Rollo said, ignoring his friend's joke. "Can we not strike at Campbell from someplace closer to Oxford?"

"Perth is a hub of money and politics," James said, the smile gone from his face. "To triumph over the Covenanters there would be to command victory.

"What's more, we need to fight a battle of our own choosing. We've no artillery, and no cavalry but our own piteous mounts, and that will be our advantage. Our want of metal and mount shall find us fleet of foot. The Highlands will be our weapon, her people our blade." James smiled. "Why battle in the south, my friend, when we can lead Campbell on a merry ride through the Highlands?"

"A bloody ride, more like," Sibbald said, thoughtfully stroking the balding crown of his head.

"Aye," James said, "bloody indeed."

And he sent up a silent word of thanks that Magda was somewhere safe from harm.

Chapter 19

Magda had been running for what felt like hours when she heard the muffled sounds.

The momentary bravado she'd felt had quickly turned back into terror as her side cramped from running, and she realized she had no way of knowing where she was headed. She'd fallen more times than she could remember, scrambling down hills of scree then through glens damp with night's moisture. Her palms and feet throbbed with scrapes and embedded gravel.

She tuned her ear to the night, and attributed the sounds to a trick of her fatigue; fright and exhaustion morphed the noise of her huffing chest and the snapping of brush underfoot into something more sinister.

And then Magda heard it again, more clearly now, a sound like laughter. She froze, her heart pounding. The countryside was finally clothed in darkness, and her eyes strained to make out human shapes among the muted grays and blacks around her. Adrenalin poured into her, dizzying her with the horror that she was no more able to defend herself than a frightened deer.

And again the laughter, coming from all around now, the sound surrounding her as it shattered the night's silence.

"Can I help you find somethin'?" a tentative voice shouted, and was met by titters that echoed around her.

A hand swiped at her arm, and the sensation of movement so close spurred her into action, as the hysteria of the initial adrenalin spike honed into instinctive flight.

Magda fled once again through the darkness, thighs straining as she slid down a hill, then feet slapping against the dewy grass yawning before her. Again she felt a slight stirring of air at her back as someone swung for her. Thrown off balance, she tripped and was momentarily airborne, then thudded hard to the ground.

Someone kicked at her shoulder. "Rise and shine, lassie." She struggled to pull breath into her lungs, paralyzed from the impact of her dead weight falling to the unforgiving glen.

Two sets of hands grabbed her roughly under the arms and pulled her to standing. She saw them in the moonlight. Not much more than boys, they laughed nervously, stealing feels of her breasts and legs and sides.

"Campbell says we're not to touch you overmuch." She felt a hand grope hard between her legs.

"I reckon he wants the first taste for himself." The stench of foul breath surrounded her as one of the boys opened his mouth wide and licked her neck with the flat of his tongue.

She shuddered.

"You like it!" He cackled and reached over to punch his friend's shoulder. "She likes it, aye?"

Magda merely stood still, erect like a statue. She knew that fear could kill her, and she racked her brain for some plan.

"Lads." The word was a threat cutting through the night, stern and deadly. The clutching hands at her arms loosened, but she still wasn't free.

A horse chuffed in the darkness, and Magda heard someone approaching. Her heart leapt to think help had arrived, that James somehow, inexplicably, knew she was in danger. That he had come back for her.

Instead, the shadowy figure that emerged was shorter, stouter. He warned again, "In time, lads. In time." Campbell's features slowly materialized, and he brought his face close to hers, gray and spectral in the darkness.

"You pulled me from my bed, woman."

Magda began to turn her face from him and he grabbed her, pinching her chin hard between strong fingers.

"I've no patience for insolent females." He gave a quick shake to her chin. "I intend tomorrow to be a day of magnificent triumph for Clan Campbell. I already have big plans for you, but if your escapade tonight diminishes me or my men in any way, you'll pay."

He released her chin and stroked slowly down to her throat. Campbell's hand twitched, gripping her in a sudden choke hold, and he leaned in to kiss her with exaggerated tenderness on each cheek. "And I will exact payment in ways you could never have imagined."

❉

They cut inland the next day, and the rocky coast gave way to yellow green glens and rolling hills. It had been impossible for Magda not to notice the massive forces gathering under Campbell. His ranks had swelled in their trek down the coast, and she now estimated they numbered in the hundreds. Some rode Highland ponies, stout, blunt-nosed creatures that looked absurdly diminutive beneath the lot of scowling, surly men. Most, however, were on foot, and the pace had slowed considerably. Campbell had let Magda continue to ride her own mount, and watching the ponies, she was grateful of the creaky old nag's long gait. Though, why he'd chosen to grant her such a luxurious allowance as a horse baffled her. A now-familiar wave of revulsion curled through her, as she imagined what fate Campbell was preserving her for.

She could feel the battle hunger of all those men pressing at her back like a physical thing, and it made her jittery. She tried to distract herself with fantasies of what seemed to be increasingly improbable escape attempts.

The mood had shifted dramatically among the clansmen, and they no longer pretended to hide their lascivious glances. Someone mentioned they weren't far from Montrose, and memories of James's gracious home gutted her, her belly heavy with mourning, for the life she had in New York and even for a life in Scotland that could have been.

"Let's pay a visit to the Ogilvys, shall we?" Campbell shouted to the masses as he reined in. "I hear our good earl has taken a little trip out of country. Seems he wants naught to do with the Covenant."

"Aye, aye," he said to the grumbling crowd, "Ogilvy thinks his best strategy is to ignore us. Let's see if we can convince his sons otherwise."

The men erupted into deafening cheers.

Campbell turned to her and said, "Lady Ogilvy must be sorely wanting for company, wouldn't you say, Magdalen?"

She looked to the valley below. A manor house sat idyllic in a tree-edged glen, surrounded by modest cottages, a barn, and those other buildings necessary for running an estate. Her breath came shallow as she realized what she was about to be witness to.

"Gather some torches, gentlemen. Today we lunch at the bonny House of Airlie, and I'd have a nice fire to take the chill from my bones."

There was a brief commotion followed by distant screams as wave upon wave of Covenanters spilled down the hill toward Ogilvy lands, leaping and hollering their bloodlust. Torches appeared all around as if from nowhere, and already Magda saw tentative flames biting at thatched roofs.

A few dozen men had the main house surrounded, struggling with fire too stubborn to ignite such a large building. She heard a window smash, and a burst of flame belched from one of the first-story windows as someone thought to set their torch to the draperies. The sound of shattering glass echoed through the valley, as more men tossed in their torches, hopping in and out of the burning house with deranged glee. The smashed windows released the sounds of the screaming women within, and Magda slid from her horse, legs crumpling beneath her in her horror.

❀

The Ogilvy estate took hours to burn. Serving women climbed from high windows. Those who landed safely only suffered a worse fate at the hands of the men who snatched and dragged them into the trees.

Unable to fathom such butchery, Magda turned and stumbled from the scene, a knot of clansmen ever at her back, grumbling now to be missing the festivities.

Her hearing dimmed, and Magda instinctively cupped her ears. Her hands felt clammy and numb, as if she were being touched by someone else's chilled, damp fingers instead of her own. Remote thoughts quivered in the back of her mind, that she must be going into shock, that she'd soon pass out. And yet she couldn't muster concern for herself. Her heart fluttered a frantic beat, and she felt weak, insubstantial, that if she'd just let go, she could disperse, vaporous, into the air.

She found she'd slumped to the ground at the foot of a tree. Magda curled onto her side and shut her eyes, not quite caring if she lived or died.

❀

Her body felt languorous, and warmth pulsed through her as a slow throb began between her legs. She longed to kiss James, to taste him, but she had to be satisfied with the feel of his hands, massaging her breasts, pinching gently at her nipples. Magda arched slightly, leaning into him. He pulled down the neck of her dress and cool air touched her skin, tightening her, beading her into rigid points. His fingernail flicked the tip of her exposed breast, and Magda slowly began to emerge from her sleep, aching for more.

The fingers pinched her with sudden roughness, and her eyes flew open, at once wide-awake, the sight of Campbell's looming face dousing the warmth that had filled her in sleep with cold shame and anger and fear.

His thin hair was pulled into a tight knot, exaggerating his broad forehead and the thick jowls at his chin. Magda began to shriek, and was silenced by Campbell's mouth, gnashing at her in a violent kiss. His lips were so thin she felt nothing but the stubble above his mouth and his teeth grinding into hers. He pushed her away.

"As lovely a sight as you are, I'd have you washed. You smell foul, woman."

Terror hammered her heart thin and fast in her chest. Magda quickly tugged her dress back up over her exposed breast.

"Yes," Campbell sneered. "Do cover yourself. We can't have any men eyeing your wares. You're *my* whore now."

Despair unfurled in her, smothering even her fear, leaving her gasping to pull air into her lungs. Magda thought now that she would risk anything to escape this man. Any other fate was preferable to remaining his captive. She'd get away from Campbell, or she would die.

"Up." He slapped Magda on the side of her hip. "We're a day's ride from Gloom, my base in the Lowlands." He stood and turned to mount his horse, held in stoic silence by a young, filthy-looking boy.

"Tonight you sleep in *my* castle. A proper wench in my very own bed." He laughed, trotting off.

❀

She'd ridden the day in numb silence, unable to wrap her mind around all that had befallen her in the past weeks. Born to wealth in Manhattan, could she really be destined to die as the property of a cruel seventeenth-century clan chief?

Campbell's castle loomed high on a hill in the distance, and the sight of it brought fresh terror pounding through her veins. She refused to believe this. Refused to accept that she'd been sent back in time to *this*.

The castle wasn't a pretty one. It emerged, solid and sharp edged, high above a craggy, tree-tangled valley in the Ochil Hills. Unlike the romantic whimsy of other European castles she'd seen, this one seemed almost to portend a dreadful fate. Like something out of a fairy-tale nightmare, it featured a large, rectangular tower rising into the gray sky, its stone face and scant windows declaring the impossibility of escape.

Her horse skittered, and a burst of panic brought her back into the moment, her heart thumping to realize how close she'd come to the edge of a gorge yawning below her. The ravine was steep, and covered by a thick web of moss, leaves, and a few tenacious saplings fighting to take root. A thin stream of water burbled obliviously at the bottom.

"The Burn of Sorrow, aye?"

"What?" Magda asked, startled.

"That there's called the Burn of Sorrow." The anonymous clansman winked at her, as if merrily sharing an insider's knowledge of her future in Campbell's care.

"Is that a joke?" Magda tried to sound outraged, and she cursed the weak, warbling voice that escaped her.

"No, lass." He adopted an informative tone that annoyed her, and she felt a flicker of gratitude at feeling something other than the dread that was permanently lodged like a stone in her gut.

"The Marquis of Argyll, he's a powerful big man in Scotland, and he's keen to chill the bones of any who'd think to attack his lands. He's holdings aplenty in Scotland, aye? Inveraray Castle is his main seat, but we're off to his Castle Gloom now, of course. Oh aye," he said, seeing her look of astonishment at the name. "Long ago they'd renamed it Campbell Castle, but our marquis prefers the sound of the old name. The Campbells have a flair of mystery about them, aye? We've the Burn of Sorrow, Castle Gloom . . .

"Don't be fashed," he giggled, "there's always the Burn o' Care on the castle's far side." Chortling, he kicked his pony and jarred into a trot away from Magda and toward the front of the line.

The castle was as squat and stolid as it had appeared from afar. A stone wall surrounded the structure, enclosing a large courtyard, what looked like gardens, and a few buildings. All aspects of it were connected to, and dwarfed by, the enormous stone tower rising high above the rest like a medieval prison.

Once she got within the castle confines, that would be it for her. She knew it without a doubt.

Hearing something, she turned to see a man, about her age, smiling at her, his hand outstretched.

"What?"

"To the stables?" He nodded toward her horse, his shaggy pink-blond eyebrows raised in question. "Shall I take her to the stables?"

She sized him up. He was short, but he had a wiry look to him, all tendons and thin ropes of muscle from a life spent training horses and hauling hay.

Magda looked around at the mobs of people milling about, some taking their own mounts to the stables, others handing theirs off to disappear into the shadows of the castle. The men who had been posted as her guard that day were busily tending to their own horses, seeming confident that she'd never leave these gates again.

Her mind worked frantically, scrambling for some final escape plan. But in her desperation, all she seemed to come up with was the hollow echo of defeat. "Um, do you mind . . ." she began, hoping for any excuse to postpone the inevitable.

She dismounted as gracefully as possible given the long day's ride, and mustered a sweet smile. "May I please take little . . . little Silver myself?" She patted her horse's neck, hoping an impromptu pet name might make her request more convincing. She thought it critical she be allowed to tend to her own horse. Buy herself just a few more minutes before disappearing into the castle's black depths.

"I've become so attached to her. I'd love to wipe her down myself. Maybe even steal a bit of oats." She shrugged her shoulders and grinned, praying it looked more coquettish than the grimace she feared she was producing.

Disarmed, and probably more than a little puzzled by her strange accent, the groomsman flashed her a ragged smile and, nodding frantically, gestured broadly to the stables.

She forced her shaking legs one in front of the other, keeping her clenched smile frozen on her face. She shot a sideways glance at the stableman. He wasn't leaving her side. "Alright then," she mumbled, thinking that would've been way too easy.

It was much quieter inside. Unbidden memories of her parents burst to the front of her mind, bringing tears to her eyes. They'd loved horses, loved visiting the stables at the track.

Stop it. She didn't have time to get sentimental now. She had to find a way out before they locked her inside Campbell's preposterously named Castle Gloom. While she still had a chance.

Her body moved mindlessly as she slipped the saddle from her horse, replaced the bridle with a rope halter, and tied her off once again, all the while eyeing the far end of the stable where a slash of sunlight cut through the dimness. *An exit?* Motes of hay floated in the air like sparks, beckoning her as if promising the last warmth of freedom. Clouds of dust puffed from the animal as Magda flicked a stiff brush along neck and belly. There had to be a way to get over there without detection.

She felt the heat of a body close in behind her and her mind slammed back into the present. She was Campbell's prize, and she was crazy to think she wouldn't become fair game for the rest of the men of the keep. She needed to escape. Now—or not at all.

The groomsman pressed his groin in at her back as he reached over her shoulder, making like he needed to instruct her on some element of grooming. She heard the rasp of his breathing.

Her eyes scanned around her, alighting on brushes, a bucket of water, stretches of rope and leather. She'd led her life with such formality, had worked to cast herself with such reserve. But reserve wouldn't save her now.

She choked out a coy giggle, bumping gently back into him. He was hard already, his stubby cock stiff at her rump. She caught his eye and forced a pouting smile. "Now, now."

She ducked under the horse's neck, popping back up to gaze at the groomsman from the other side. Magda tried to hold his eyes so she could scramble for anything usable as a weapon, her hands just out of sight. She felt ridiculous summoning all manner of pouts and winks and simpers, but her efforts seemed to have shocked him into rapt attention. She sensed the bench behind her and spun to grab a brush and a length of harness from it. The man moved to walk around to her, and Magda stopped him, redoubling her efforts, teasing his fingers with little touches as she smoothed the brush down the horse's back in as seductive a manner as she could muster.

She had a lead line in her other hand. Carefully, she let it slide down the length of her palm until she felt the cold steel hook at her fingers. Magda gave him a brilliant smile then, even flicking a bit of tongue at the corner of her mouth. Circling her wrist, she wound the length of rope around her hand, securing the hard metal clip at the end in her grip. She stepped back then, sliding her hand slowly from the horse's back, raising her brows in her best come-hither look.

The groomsman licked his lips and bobbed quickly under the animal's neck to join her. As he stood, Magda slammed the blunt end of the hook into his temple, left hand at her right wrist to bolster her strength, and he fell at once.

The horse reared, spooked, and she quickly patted her, settling her back down. Magda looked back to that ray of light cutting into the far end of the barn. Turning, she walked slowly down the corridor, horses in stalls on either side chuffing and whinnying quiet greetings. She came to the source of the light. Magda realized that what had looked from a distance like the far wall was actually a half door. Though the bottom was clicked shut, the top half was cracked ajar and the source of her sunbeam. Pulling the latch, she stepped through to an outdoor paddock, its resident horse grazing intently on a well-manicured lawn.

He heard her approach and glanced up, chewing and blinking at her lazily. He was a magnificent animal, tall—at least seventeen hands high, she thought distantly—and his chestnut coat gleamed, the late-afternoon sunlight picking out shades of red and yellow silk.

She walked to him, and he stood alert, not afraid, but simply focused on her presence. Magda couldn't help but reach her hands up to tangle her fingers in his deep orange mane, and she leaned her weight onto him, his solidness reassuring her.

The horse whickered quietly, nudging her with his powerful head, and Magda felt her breathing deepen and her pulse slow for the first time in days.

Magda knew horses—any number of expensive mounts had been at her disposal as a young Deacon family heir—and this was a fine stallion. He was surely a rare animal by Scottish standards if all those Highland ponies were any indication.

She turned, knowing already what she would find. A leather bridle, just cleaned, hanging from a hook to the side of the door. No saddle was in sight, but an old woolen blanket was folded neatly beneath. Excitement pricked at the back of her mind. She looked around quickly. The half door had drifted shut behind her. The paddock was at the far end of the stable, and enclosed by a low wooden fence. She'd jumped higher in her time, and would bet this horse had too.

Magda cursed herself—she'd been in a daze when they'd arrived—and she hoped now that she remembered correctly, that the stables stood along the edge of the castle compound and that the only other gate she'd need to jump would be the stone wall surrounding the compound. Though she recalled seeing portions that were low enough to clear, she hoped they weren't too wide. Magda had been quite the equestrienne in her time, but jumping bareback was a killer, and her leg muscles were already thrashed.

It took a moment to slip the bridle over the horse's head. Magda imagined that he knew what was coming; she sensed his anticipation as he readily took the bit into his mouth and stood still while she settled the dusty blanket in place of a saddle.

With a grudging thank-you to her horse-loving parents, Magda hauled herself onto his back. She might kill herself trying this, she thought, but it beat anything that Campbell had in store for her.

The horse pranced, his muscles coiled, tense with ready energy. "Oh, yeah," Magda purred, remembering what it was like to ride a horse of this caliber.

She wove the reins lightly around her fingers, and he responded with a nervous side step, his mouth sensitive to her every move. A slight tensing of her thighs and he was off like a shot. Magda had to swallow her cry of joy, feeling this animal beneath her, imagining her freedom just over the fence.

She kicked him into a gallop, and he began to hesitate at the last moment, the fence higher than it had seemed from the far end of the pasture. Magda pulled her knees as high as she could, gripping tightly with her legs. She girded herself; without stirrups to stand from, the horse's leap over the fence would slam her into the hard ridge of his withers.

She loosened the reins to give the horse as much of his head as he'd need to clear the fence. Tangling her fingers high and tight into his mane, Magda shrieked, "Heeya!" and with one last crush of her knees into his sides, they flew over the fence, and galloped away.

❧

"Nay, nay, I'd ken the Marquis of Montrose anywhere," the man said. He walked next to James, his wife bobbing her head at his side.

"I'm not the marquis," James said evenly.

James, Rollo, and Sibbald had been on the road for ten days, and the going had gotten increasingly dangerous. Crossing the southern border into Scotland brought them onto roads littered with broken men and Covenanter patrols. James refused to trade his horse for an animal more suited to his disguise, and they'd been getting more skeptical looks the farther north they rode. So much so that James was considering traveling by night instead, at least until they reached the safer Highland territory.

"But whyever are you dressed so, m'lord?" The villager looked back and forth between the well-dressed men and James, clothed as a groom in threadbare trews and bonnet, riding ten paces behind Rollo and Sibbald.

"I'm not the marquis, good man." His voice was steady and slow. "Although, I am certain the marquis would be touched by your loyalty." James nodded sagely to the villager, allowing himself a small smile at the man's joy at this last bit of information.

Giving a wink to the man's wife, James kicked his horse into a trot to catch up to his companions. His smile broadened to hear the woman's gasp behind him, scandalized by the familiar gesture.

"We approach Dumfries," Sibbald said. "A cup of ale and a proper bed at the Globe Inn has much to recommend it."

"And sleep the night in a Covenanting burgh?" Rollo asked.

"Aye," James jested, "you could buy your bed with that king's commission sewn into your saddle, and awaken to the sight of some of those red-coated Parliament soldiers."

"We press on then," Sibbald grumbled. "And easy it will be for you, lad. You've a younger arse than I."

"Don't fear, old man, if your arse can hold you just an hour or so longer, I know of a hunter's bothy on Maxwell land. I can't promise ale, but we'll spend the night dry at least."

A small farmhouse appeared to their left, the shutters slamming closed at their passing. James and Rollo exchanged a silent look.

"I'd push as far as we can every day now," James added. "It grieves me to see our country torn so."

"Is Clan Maxwell Royalist or Covenanter?" Rollo asked.

"Let's hope we'll not have the opportunity to ask, aye?" James replied, and spurred his horse into an easy canter.

Chapter 20

She'd stopped just once. Sweat had slicked her horse the color of burnt sienna, foamy ropes of saliva hung from the corners of his mouth, and Magda worried she would lame the animal. But she hadn't rested fifteen minutes before she heard the distant rumble of hooves, and she hopped back on, ignoring the agony between her legs and the streak of blood on the saddle blanket.

Still triumphing after landing the initial jump out of the paddock, she hadn't been completely prepared for the low stone wall surrounding Campbell lands. Castle Gloom sat higher than she'd realized, the ground sloping sharply down outside the castle perimeter. Her horse had landed the jump over the outer wall solidly, but Magda had slammed down hard onto his back with the unexpected shock of a missed step. She'd felt the dampness a moment later, though she'd guessed instantly that her pubic bone had sliced through her skin with the impact.

"Shit!" she hissed, spotting the water as she emerged from the trees, and she slammed sloppy kicks into the animal's sides. She heard shouts now, distant but closing in.

Panic squeezed Magda's chest. Her body trembled violently, as all rational thought was subsumed by primitive terror.

A large lake blocked her way. The choppy surface was a tempest of deep blues and blacks under the sunless sky. She tugged her reins, regretful of the pain she knew she was inflicting, but she had to pull her horse's head away from the shore. She barraged her horse with kicks now, wringing every last bit of energy out of him, hoping to ride around the lake.

She was being hunted, tracked easily from Campbell lands. Magda realized she'd galloped off, unthinking, leaving deep tracks across soft glens and scraping hard lines down gravelly hills. The trail she'd left must have been nothing short of an engraved map to her current location.

Horror dawned on her that there was no way to outrun the men who hunted her. She was trapped. It was impossible to return the way she came—even now she imagined she heard the rustling of riders through trees—and yet the lake filled the horizon, no visible curve to indicate land on the other side, simply water as far as she could see.

Magda pulled her horse to a halt, her heart thundering in her chest. She instinctively patted the animal on the neck, an apology for brutalizing him, and for the bruising she'd given his mouth with all of her tugging.

She needed to gather her wits. She dared not think what would happen if she were captured. Campbell would not forgive a second escape attempt. Magda knew she couldn't outrun these men, but if she'd only get ahold of herself, she might be able to outthink them.

She remembered a foxhunt she'd gone on as a teenager. It had been her first and last, so horrified she'd been at the sight of the terrified animal tearing under bushes and through trees. She'd thought angrily, if the dumb creature would only go to ground, throw off the hounds somehow. When it was done, the master of the hunt had merrily smeared its blood across her cheeks as her father looked proudly on, and it had been all Magda could do to choke down the bile that had risen in her throat.

Magda studied the lake, and Peter's face came to her—freckles and orange hair and the lank body of one full grown yet not fully a man—and the memories ran her through with fresh anguish.

She was cornered, just like that fox had been, and she felt herself start to shut down, beginning to feel the quiet dread of acceptance.

And then, as if summoned by remembrance of her brother, she saw it. Magda slid from her horse and squinted into the distance. The day's flat light had played tricks with the dark water and the shadowy trees all around, and she hadn't spotted it before. An island in the middle of the lake. Far, but not too far for a good swimmer.

And even as she felt a flicker of hope, her heart sank. She hadn't swum since Peter's accident.

Images of James came in a rush. Him sitting so still on the riverbank beside her, listening with care to the story of her brother's death. The sun had picked shades of amber in his brown hair. His hand had almost just touched hers in the grass.

Was James already dead? The grim thought sputtered briefly, and Magda just as quickly stifled it. She knew in her heart that James was still out there. He had to be out there. The memory of him was too vivid. His firm nod of understanding, accepting without question the pain of her loss, and the absence of any blame. She saw him in her mind's eye, and he revived her.

Her brother had drowned to save a stranger. Magda knew Peter would have struggled until the end. And she knew too that, more than anything, James would want her to struggle now. Nobody had come to save her, but she would fight to save her own life.

Magda slapped her horse hard on the rump, and the beleaguered animal took off as far and fast from his abusive rider as he could. Scraping her heels against the muck of the shore, she hastily covered her tracks and sent up a silent prayer that the horse would make too big a trail for her pursuers to ignore.

Magda stepped up to the water's gently lapping edge, and it bit at her toes, numbing them instantly. Freezing damp crept along the soles of her slippers and the rawhide shriveled, tightening around her feet.

She had no choice now, she thought grimly. She'd chosen her path, and it was straight into the lake. And fast too, if she didn't want to die at the hands of the Campbells, or by languishing in the icy lake. She knew she'd be hampered by her clothing, yet disrobing now would render useless whatever false trail the horse had lain for her. Fear threatened in the back of her mind, and crushing it, Magda dove in and pounded out as strong a crawl stroke as she could.

Lake vegetation grew thick in the shallows and brushed against her, ghostly and delicate, and she forced thoughts of Peter from her mind. A thick strand tangled her foot, pulling her slipper from her like a creature grasping hungrily from the deep. Renewed panic skittered up her spine as she kicked and slapped frantically at the water.

Magda was aware of the shore behind her, and sensed that the men had yet to break through the trees, but she knew she didn't have much time.

The lake got deep quickly. The thick wool of her dress reluctantly absorbed water and it slowly grew heavier, until the fabric swirled between her legs, beckoning her under. Hysteria gripped her, hammering her pulse and robbing her breath, and Magda stopped to tread water, clawing the dress from her body as if it were some foreign entity attacking her, purposely pulling her down to drown.

She sensed the rustle of trees at the lakeshore and knew the men were dangerously close. Wadding her dress beneath her feet, Magda pressed it as deeply as she could beneath the surface. Pulling a calming gulp of air into her lungs, she slid under the water and exploded forward. Encumbered only by her thin muslin shift, she kicked and stroked, skimming easily just beneath the surface.

The rhythmic kicking and exhaling composed her, and Magda was able to swim underwater for long periods of time before coming up for air. The sounds from the shore had quickly dispersed. It seemed the men didn't think swimming across the lake a viable escape option.

Magda thought one last time of that glorious horse, and was grateful. She hoped the men never found him, imagined that maybe he'd live out his days beloved by some farmer's daughter. But she knew better than to dream of happy endings, she thought, as she kicked and pulled her way toward what she hoped was the island.

❁

She'd crawled to safe ground and hidden beneath a cluster of low brush at the island's shore. Despite the violent shivers that wracked her, Magda felt her consciousness slip away and a pleasant emptiness slide over her.

A hand, hot and dry against her pale, wrinkled skin, tugged at her, and Magda came awake to the feel of the ground sliding beneath her.

A man knelt in the twilight, holding her foot, and she was instantly on the defensive, kicking at him, yelping, and trying desperately to skitter back into the bushes. He seemed monstrous.

A fringe of wiry white hair sprang from around his otherwise bald head, making him look a madman. A thick, shining scar ran down the side of his face and perfectly bisected his left eye, which twitched sightlessly, its dull, milky whiteness appearing eerily luminous in the day's dying light.

Magda screamed.

"Hush, child," he said, and the gentle creak of his voice gave her pause. She studied him. The man wore a rough black cassock, faded with age and cinched off at his waist with a hank of rope. Magda looked again at his hair and realized it wasn't that he was balding. It was a tonsured monk who held her foot in his hand.

He smiled hesitantly, and the right side of his face creased into well-worn lines around his mouth and at the corners of his eyes. But on the other half of him, the waxy cord of his scar buckled his skin in two, cutting the expression from his face.

"Come, Magda."

"How do you know me?" she asked, the familiar trill of alarm heightening her senses.

"I am Brother Lonan," he said gently. "And I've been expecting you."

"Lonan?" Confusion and shock dulled her senses, and she let herself be pulled to standing. "Wait." She jerked away from him, her tone taking on a note of hysteria. "The Lonan who knows James Graham?"

"Indeed," he chuckled. "I am that very Lonan." He tucked her icy hand in the crook of his elbow. "And now it's to the Warming House with you, before I lose you to another faint."

"But how did I get here?" She did her best to walk, her chilled legs shuffling slowly. "Why did you bring me here?"

"First things first, child." Lonan patted her hand and guided her to a squat stone building. The small size, low ceiling, and enormous hearth declared its sole purpose to be heat. He steered her to a large leather chair by the fire. She sat, mesmerized by the flames, dancing tall and warming her to the bone.

"But how did you find me?" she asked, as he slathered a foul-smelling paste on her extremities. She shuddered to think what sort of rancid animal lard was currently warming her through. "I hid in the bushes."

"Yes," he said, and Magda had to avert her eyes from his grotesque smile. "You dragged yourself under cover, leaving a path in the sand like a turtle from the sea to lay her eggs."

He slowly wiped his hands on a rag tucked in the rope of his belt. Using a pair of crude tongs, Lonan began to pull strips of heated linen from a cast-iron pot and laid them out along a blanket by his side. "If this is how you hide, my child, I count you doubly blessed. It's a wonder you made it here at all."

"What about the painting?" Magda struggled to keep her emotions in check as all of her questions and fears and worries of the past weeks boiled to the surface.

Lonan looked up at her with a kindly smile. "What about the painting, child?"

"The painting. You know." She pulled her feet out from Lonan's hands. "You were the one who did that portrait of James. How did you do that? I don't understand why I'm here."

Lonan *tsked*. "You'll injure yourself further, child. Your feet are shredded and in need of warmth and cleansing."

He tenderly took her feet back in his hands and, cupping her heels in his palms, said, "All in good time, Magdalen. You will understand all in good time."

Maybe it was her exhaustion, but although she wanted to protest further, she found she trusted the old man. Magda let him finish in silence then, watching as he bound her feet with the soothing linen bandages, transfixed by his age-spotted hands and knobby fingers covered with patches of wiry white hair. Despite herself, her own mind gradually grew quiet.

"Ah," Lonan said, as he tied off the last of her wrappings. He'd been kneeling in front of Magda, and as he rose creakily to his feet, she prepared to catch him if he toppled.

He took a small handkerchief from his pocket. "Lest I forget." Unfolding it, he produced a small square the color of seafoam. "This is for the wound under your skirts."

Wary uncertainty flashed in her eyes.

"There's no shame about it." Lonan pressed it into her hand. "I smell the blood, child. This is a natural styptic. It will speed your healing."

She stroked it between her fingers, and it was cool and spongy, with a lush velvety texture only possible in nature. "What is it?"

"It's merely touchwood, dear."

She shook her head, confused.

"If I tell you it's a fungus that grows like a shelf from the sides of trees, will you still place it between your legs?"

"Certainly not." She stiffened her back, trying to muster the picture of robust health.

"Well," he said, amusement quirking his features, "then I suppose I mustn't tell you that."

Relief at her successful escape had loosened something in her belly, and she laughed.

Lonan joined her, and his scar once again deformed his features, one half of him joyful and the other misshapen into a grimacing mask.

Magda forced herself to hold his gaze, though she had to fight herself from flicking her eyes to the left side of his face.

"You're wondering what happened."

She raised her brows in mock innocence, and he met her charade with patience.

"To my face, child. I can see you're wondering what it is that befell me."

"Well, I . . ."

"Do not be ashamed. Wonderment is what drives men to more and greater things. *'It was through the feeling of wonder that men now and at first began to philosophize.'*"

Magda looked baffled.

"Aristotle's words, not mine. I am not nearly so circumspect."

Lonan eased himself into a chair by the hearth and began. "'Twas the Battle of Glenlivet, many, many years ago. I was just a lad yet. I'm a Gordon by birth, you see. Perhaps that is why, to this day, despite being a forgiving man of God, I have no affection for Clan Campbell. But that is a tale for another day," he added ominously.

"It was my first battle, and I bore a virgin sword, as it were. Yet, unlike the other lads, more fascinating to me than any war play was how faith was enough to gird two thousand men and lead them to triumph over an army ten-thousand strong.

"Though many men were heroes that day, to me the greatest champion was my uncle. I'm no crusader," he confessed in a lighthearted tone, "and the lion's heart of my youth has faded into something closer to the lamb's, but those questions of battle, why men fight and what gives them courage, those are questions of which I'll never tire.

"I was injured that day—gravely, as you can see—and though I know now it was the frenzy of battle that numbed me to my wounds, at the time I felt certain it was God's hand at work. That the cross hanging at my neck and the holy water dampening my shirt was the only armor I needed.

"You could say I found God at the edge of a sword."

Lonan lifted his hands to the fire, and Magda could see the pain in his joints writ on his face.

"I've since that day devoted myself to scholarly inquiry that I may better understand we human animals. I'm a bit of a mendicant, I confess, but other holy men are always happy to take me in, sharing books and food in God's name, in places just like this." His hand shook with age as he gestured to the room around them.

"So *where* is this?" she asked.

"Do you ask of this island, or of this time?"

Magda froze at his implication, and Brother Lonan continued without pause.

"First things first, the island. But"—he handed her a tin cup filled with golden liquid—"I insist you drink this, child. It will help."

Skeptical, she brought the cup to her nose and inhaled a smell like peat fire and the sea, biting through her senses. She took a tentative sip, and it was like liquid smoke slipping down her throat. It curled through her body and warmed her, uncoiling muscles in its wake.

"What is this?" She sipped again, deciding that the flavor was toasty, and faintly salty.

"I once made my tonics by mixing pink centaury with whisky but, in my age and wisdom, I have simplified it. Magdalen," he said, pouring a measure of liquid into his own cup, "you have before you a dram of whisky. And, may I say, it calms the nerves as efficiently as any herbal tincture.

"*Slàinte mhath*, child," he added, raising his cup to hers. "I bid you welcome to Inchmahome Priory."

He sipped for a time in silence, and Magda let herself enjoy the pleasant buzz that hummed through her. Leaning her head back, she unclenched her jaw and slowly allowed herself to consider the pain between her legs, the ache in her bottom, and the stiffness between her shoulders.

"That was the Loch of Menteith you just swam. Most simply choose to arrive by boat." An amused appreciation played on the right side of his face.

"Robert the Bruce himself favored Inchmahome. He came often." Lonan gestured to the walls around them. "It's in disrepair now, as you can see."

She glanced up at the ceiling arching low overhead. The claustrophobic feel was only intensified by the thousands of stones used for bricks, their thin, irregular rectangles pressing down from above, seeming ready to crumble at any moment.

"Once the province of Augustinian monks," Lonan spoke, pulling her attention back to him, "Inchmahome welcomes all scholars, including the occasional wayward Dominican," he said, gesturing to himself with a smile.

"Some say that a spit of land on Menteith's southern shore was built by fairy folk." He shrugged with a hint of condescension.

"I see," she said, the whisky giving ease to her voice. "You only believe in time travel. Nothing so preposterous as fairies for you."

Her attempt at humor was met with sternness.

"Time travel is a law of physics, not an abomination to Christianity," he said, alluding to the old Celtic beliefs. "The nature of time is as intertwined with the universe as the beat of the tides. It is in the service of God and His people that I apply my scholarship to it, as I would to any other course of study."

Lonan considered her as he would a child, and he softened. "But I demand too much of you. Come." He pulled himself to the edge of his chair and slowly stood. "I will show you your room. You and I have much time together yet."

And, with that ominous statement resonating in her, Lonan walked Magda to the small cell she would call her own.

❋

The men had long returned to Castle Gloom and their furious chief, short a wench and one stud horse.

The lace was the first to rise, tickling the surface of the lake with its tattered, stained fingers. Gradually the green plaid rose to meet it, the wool thick with water and moving sluggishly, like some angry spectral body exhumed from the deep. It bobbed there for a time, on the choppy waves, until it disappeared again, pulled slowly back to the bottom.

Chapter 21

After he'd been recognized outside Dumfries, James and his men had traveled by night, resting as best they could by day. They had purposefully steered clear of Edinburgh, not far from Falkirk to the east. It was near dawn when they approached what appeared to be a simple crofter's cottage near Falkirk Moor.

"How can you know they're friendly?" Rollo asked, reining in to study the cottage. Red light flickered intermittently through a crack under the door.

"I suppose there's naught I know for sure, is there?" James replied cavalierly, eliciting a scowl from Rollo.

James slid off his horse, and Sibbald, shrugging his shoulders, joined him. While James helped Rollo dismount, the colonel tied off their horses with a long lead. The animals immediately set to grazing.

"I do know," James said, "that there was a time this particular cottage was a Royalist outpost."

Rollo eased to the ground, where he began to pound life back into his legs. "Let's hope the Covenanters haven't beaten us here."

"I'll see who's keeping the fires burning," James said. Before his companions could stop him, he was knocking on the door as if for a pleasant afternoon visit, rather than the predawn refuge they sought in a war-torn country.

The door opened, and Rollo and Sibbald at once put their hands to the swords at their sides, wary and alert.

Though he was the same height as James, the man filling the doorway was much wider. Where James was lithe muscle, this man was pure, thick brawn. A small peat fire crackled in the hearth at his back, illuminating him from behind, casting his already dark features into frightening blackness.

"The Graham, is it?" he growled in a thick burr. "James Graham of Montrose?"

"Indeed," James replied in a friendly tone. Though his posture remained at ease, James's right hand was tensed, fingers curled toward the sword hilt at his side. "And whose acquaintance do I have the pleasure of making?"

The man let out a laugh sounding much like a roar, and grabbed James into a bear hug. The man pushed James away and, holding his shoulders, avidly studied his face as if James were his long-lost brother.

"I am Alasdair MacColla Ciotach MacDomhnaill." He clapped James hard on the shoulder. "Alasdair the son of Colla the left-handed, of the Clan MacDonald."

"I know my Gaelic, Alasdair MacColla," James replied, "but you still haven't told me who you are."

MacColla roared another laugh, "Aye, Charles warned you were a canny one."

Grinning broadly, he added, "I'm the man come to help hunt for Campbells."

MacColla gestured to the room behind him. "Come, come. We've much to discuss, and I'd do it proper, with a *skalk* and porridge."

"*Skalk*?" Rollo's voice came from the darkness.

"The man means to drink whisky for breakfast," Sibbald said. "I could use a morning dram myself," he added, striding to the door.

The men passed around the quaich, and by the time the shallow wooden bowl was empty, they were at ease.

"The Campbells took our land. They took my father prisoner. And, when I was forced to seek refuge with the Clan MacDonald in Ireland, they took my country from me." MacColla polished the empty quaich with a corner of his tartan, his bushy black eyebrows furrowed in thought. "And now 'tis time for me to take something from the Campbells."

He raised his head and looked levelly at James. "I've come to fight by your side, and I've sixteen hundred Irishmen who stand with me."

"Good Lord," Sibbald blurted.

Rollo leaned forward in his chair, intrigued. "And where are all these men?"

MacColla wove his thick fingers together and stretched his arms in front of him, joints popping. Leaning back, he placed his hands atop the crown of his head and said, "I've installed my men in Lochaber, where they're currently enjoying a spot of Cameron hospitality."

James barked a sudden laugh. "I'm certain the young Lochiel is well pleased by that turn of events."

"Och," MacColla dismissed him good-naturedly, "'tis good for the wee Cameron lad."

"Wee lad," James mused, looking at the enormous man sitting across from him. "I suppose." Satisfaction creased his eyes. "I am pleased to hear that Ewen sides with us."

Sibbald rose. "If you two are going to gossip like milkmaids, I'd settle the horses and be off to bed."

"Sit, old man." The humor was gone from MacColla's voice. "The beasts can bide a wee. I've news yet. Campbell's kept busy since Aberdeen."

Leaning forward, he locked eyes with James and said, "I've word that he took your woman."

"Impossible," James said. "Napier, my brother-in-law, took her back with him to Montrose."

"No, the lass was taken from under his nose. Campbell has her," MacColla said. "He was given a commission of fire and sword, and he rides south, killing every Royalist in his path. He burnt the House of Airlie to the ground, and last word is that he's returned to his own castle."

The amiable effects of the whisky bled from James's eyes and voice. He edged forward in his seat, his features chill and focused. "Campbell took her to Inveraray?" he asked sharply.

"No, his other castle, Gloom. The bastard uses the old name." MacColla shook his head in disgust. "He seeks to intimidate by any means. Despite the men at his back, the Campbell is a soft and weak lump of flesh, and it angers him.

"I am sorry, Graham," he added. "If she's lucky, your woman is already dead."

❂

They were to rest through the day, and travel by night. The sound of snoring filled the small room, but James lay sleepless, fingering the strip of blue cloth once torn from Magda's dress. They'd shared just two kisses, and yet the thought of her seared him.

"You think of the lass." Rollo spoke softly in the semidarkness. They'd pulled the shutters tight, but daylight snuck in through cracks, throwing haphazard blades of light around the room.

"No . . ." James hesitated, and could feel his friend's stern look on his shoulders. "Aye," he admitted, his voice tight with pain. "I think of the lass."

The vividness of his memories shocked him. The silk of her heavy hair tangled in his hands, the flush of her wide, just-kissed mouth. Visceral images and sensations that sheared through James with a wanting and regret he hadn't realized in himself.

"I was a fool," he said in a tight whisper. "She came like a gift from the Fates, and I foolishly entrusted her safety to another."

"Napier is not just any other person, James. You cannot blame yourself."

James's silent energy vibrated through the room, charging the air like lightning before a storm.

"She must be special indeed to have caught the eye of an inveterate bachelor like yourself," Rollo attempted lightheartedly.

"Extraordinary," James replied at once. After a pause, he repeated, "Magda is extraordinary."

"And what does your family think of her?"

"Och, my family gets along with most. You know my sister. Margaret was thrilled to have another woman's life with which to meddle."

"And is Magda much like your sister?"

James laughed, quick and low. "Not that you could say, no. Do you know, the lass plays golf?" James sat up eagerly, tucking the blue strip of cloth into his breast pocket. "Aye, she truly can play. She gave old Tom Sydserf a thorough trouncing." He chuckled quietly, a distant look in his eye. "And shooting from the rough? Magda . . . well, at first you'd think she was a starchy, queenly sort of lass. Very upright. But she got in it at Montrose.

You ken the gorse near the tenth hole? Well she got into trouble, and damned if the lass didn't hunker down, waggling her haunches like a wee rabbit, and she took her shot and that ball sprang out like a rousted bird."

James's smile went slack. Hands restless, he once again took the cloth from his pocket and rubbed it idly between his fingers.

"I see we've a problem then," Rollo said gravely.

"Aye," he replied, knowing well what his friend referred to. To search for Magda now would be to waylay their current plans. They had a king's commission, thousands of Irishmen, and the north full of Highlanders ready for battle. To chase after a woman who might already be dead was a potentially ruinous complication. And yet it was clear that James would choose no other path. "We've a problem indeed."

They sat silent in the room's gloomy half-light for some time, then a canny smile slowly spread across James's face. "Although . . ."

"Tell it, James. What do you have us in for now?"

"Spiriting Magda out from under Campbell's nose and the war we wage are not necessarily at cross-purposes. A mere minor detour on the way to Perth, aye? Not to mention a pleasant way to provoke the Campbell."

"MacColla will be pleased, at least," Rollo said. "We abscond with the lass, and Campbell has no choice but to follow us north."

"One could even say it's to our advantage."

Rollo paused for a moment, then asked somberly, "But what if she's dead, James?"

"She's not dead," he growled. "I feel . . . I feel I'd know it somehow. But if she is . . ." He inhaled sharply. "If he's harmed Magda in any way, I swear I'll take his life even if it means my own. Campbell's house will crumble around him."

❧

At first Magda was frustrated and angered by Lonan's unwillingness to discuss his painting, or anything having to do with her time travel. Her relentless questioning had only been met with amused silence, or the occasional "In time, child." So she finally decided to just give in to the experience, trusting that the laconic brother really would tell her "in time."

At first she'd found monastery life startlingly rigorous, but as the weeks passed, Magda grew to find great comfort in the daily routine. So much so, she wondered if that weren't part of some greater lesson Lonan was teaching her.

The cycle was the same every day: up at dawn for matins, close each day with vespers, with every hour in between rigidly accounted for. Brother Lonan had stressed to her the importance of numbers in the order of life, and the monks put a premium on such precision. *Prime* stood for the first hour and for those prayers said at 6 a.m. *Terce*, the third hour, meant psalms at nine. *Sext* was the sixth-hour contemplation at noon, and so on.

Magda tried to feel some greater *something* surrounded by all this worship, and though she didn't think she'd be signing up for the convent any time soon, she did find an inner calm that had eluded her since Peter's death. Admittedly, facing her fears in the lake had done much to open her to the experience, but somehow the simple rhythm of life at Inchmahome Priory had thrown her old world into greater relief.

She had chided herself that a couple of kisses from some handsome Scotsman, and she was ready to forsake the modern world and live in the past as if it were some sort of living history book. But now Magda saw some kernel of rightness in the desire to stay. She was grateful to Lonan that his reticence had forced her to put out of her mind life as she knew it, to face instead life as it came to her in the moment.

Her old world had been so caught up in trivia, things that, at the end of the day, held nothing for her soul. Her family's never-ending pursuit of status. The rush of life in Manhattan, where she was surrounded by millions of people, not one of whom she could call in a crisis. And even her job. She loved the art she worked with, and yet it hadn't been about the paintings in so long. If she truly looked inward, she had to admit that her work had come to serve other purposes: pursuing a raise, jockeying for invites to the right openings, or—and this shamed her—keeping a sharp eye for possible mistakes made by her peers to save as fodder for some later advantage.

She'd lost sense of herself when Peter died and realized now she hadn't known who *that* Magda was, the Magda who was an empty shell of herself, walking through her daily grind at work, returning to her tiny studio every night. The Magda who would clearly drop everything at a chance for life. Being pulled back in time had been her excuse—she'd told herself it had been beyond her control, that life was something that happened to her.

But now it was time for Magda to wrest back her lost control. She pushed up the long draping sleeve of her borrowed cassock, trying to knot it at her elbow for what felt like the hundredth time that morning, and stirred the great pot of boiled oats in earnest.

As it turned out, the room where Lonan had bound her feet on that first day was one of the few with heat. The kitchen, though, was another, and that had become her primary refuge, even though the only culinary skills required by the monastery involved stirring oats and cleaning fish. Striving for simplicity, the monks ate poached fish and those godforsaken oats at every meal, and she fantasized now about any number of exotic foods, thinking with a smile that, at this point, she'd even be game to try black pudding.

The monks all played a part, each as he was able. Scholars like Lonan spent their days at tasks like illuminating manuscripts or maintaining the library. Most other men managed the physical labor of the island, gardening, fishing, repairing. The list of things that needed doing was endless.

Many of the men had taken vows of silence, and Magda had become accustomed to their language of gestures that, in many ways, was much easier to understand than the thick brogue of the old Scots.

Magda had assumed that all monks were like Lonan, inspired to monastic life from some quiet conviction, or to pursue a life of contemplative study. But she'd been shocked to hear that some families donated a son in return for blessings. Though, seeing the carnage wrought by men like Campbell, she thought perhaps that wasn't such a bad fate.

Lonan stood in the doorway. Magda didn't know how long he'd been there, silently watching her. His appearances were rare so, tapping her wooden spoon at the side of the pot, Magda set aside her current task to visit with him.

"Our time grows short, child."

By now, she had a good enough sense of Lonan to know that such ominous pronouncements weren't to be taken lightly. In their weeks together, Lonan had not yet once discussed the nature of time, Magda's appearance, or, for that matter, the part Lonan played in it all, having painted the portrait that had been her portal into the past. She'd long stopped pressing him on it. Seeing the somberness on his face now, though, Magda thought perhaps the moment to ask him just one more time had arrived.

"I found your journals," she ventured.

"I know." A mischievous light wrinkled the corners of his eyes. "I left them for you, after all."

She gave him a quizzical look and was met only with placid silence, so she continued, "You wrote something like, *time abides*. What did you mean by that?"

"Time doesn't flow like a river, child. It simply is."

Magda raised her brows. Now that he was finally willing to talk, she wanted more than just this abstruse explanation and hoped she wasn't going to have to pry every sentence out of him.

He sighed. "Everything man needed to know was within his grasp thousands of years ago." Lonan pulled a three-legged stool from along the wall and eased himself onto it. "The nature of time, astronomy, mathematics, these are things that were mastered millennia ago. The Indus Valley civilization, the ancient Babylonians, Hittites, Mayans, Persians. Magda, you have studied these peoples, their symbology.

"Despite the rigid exterior you present to the world"—he smiled fondly—"you are raw to it. Art is the soul of the universe, and your study has opened you to its ebbs and flows. This is why I think the portrait pulled you through.

"No," he said firmly, in answer to her silent question, "I did not pick you, Magda. I merely etched symbols on a canvas, then painted the image of our James."

"Why him?"

"Aside from the fact that we share a common enemy?" he asked, a devilish light in his eyes. "A monk I might be, but I've not forgotten the battles of my youth. My uncle, though a man of God, was ever a man of his clan. And we Gordons harbor no love for the Campbells, this brute in particular."

"But why choose to paint James," she pressed, "and not the king, or some other clan chief?"

"I am surprised that you need ask that, child." Lonan tilted his head knowingly. "You of all people recognize the heroism and charisma that is the marquis. But I will spell it plain for you. Few truly great men have walked this earth. Sometimes the Fates need a nudge, to lend these men aid, to empower them."

"But for what?"

"For some later, greater purpose," he answered mysteriously. "You see, child, our James has this capacity for greatness, for great success. But there is also the possibility of great sacrifice. And it's upon this latter path James finds himself, marching inexorably toward tragedy. That is, until you crossed it. The moment you laid eyes on his portrait, history came to a crossroads and the universe near vibrated with it."

"But I lived hundreds of years after his death."

"I told you, child. Time is not some fugitive, racing in a straight line ever forward, discrete moments never to be experienced again. Think of time as a circle. It merely is, and you, Magda, you found yourself at the center point of that circle."

Lonan shook his head in awe. "Think, how many thousands of people viewed that portrait in the last how many hundreds of years? And yet it was you it called through. You must have touched the portrait, engaged the symbols in some way."

"But," Magda interrupted, "that doesn't explain how you know things are going to happen. You've alluded to things. Like, expecting me, or leaving the journals for me."

"Ah, yes," the brother's grin was uncharacteristically broad. He fumbled in the deep pocket of his cassock. "Wine of opium, child." Lonan pulled out a small brown bottle filled with dark liquid. "I discovered long ago a tincture of opium and sugar opens my senses to the universe. It was only when I began sketching and musing in my books that I discovered I had the power to . . . to see things."

"Isn't that . . ." Magda couldn't help but laugh at the absurdity. "Isn't that laudanum?"

"Aye," Lonan said sheepishly, his childhood brogue momentarily slipping though, "I suppose it is at that."

"Well, what am I supposed to do, then?" Magda worried the

overlong cuff of her threadbare sleeve between two fists. "Does this mean I'm supposed to stay? How on earth am I supposed to be able to help James?"

"That I cannot say, child." Lonan rose to leave. "I'm unable to see your fate here, only its necessity."

He paused at the door. "We brothers may choose the study of life over the living of it, but we are not without wisdom. Augustine of Hippo taught '*Victoria veritatis est caritas.*' 'Nothing conquers except truth and the victory of truth is love.'

"You love James Graham, do you not?" he asked tenderly.

"I—" Magda faltered, tears filling her eyes. "I suppose I do."

"Then you'll know what's best, child."

Lonan left Magda, the room silent but for the thick burbling of oats.

❊

Her bed had never felt so uncomfortable, and Magda spent hours tossing and turning. The monks retreated to their cells early each night, and though she usually passed the time reading by candlelight, tonight she'd found herself eyeing the same line over and over again. Rather than waste what was a luxurious allowance, she'd blown out her beeswax candle and attempted sleep.

Magda froze at the sound of shuffling just outside her door. She strained her ears in the dark, and her heart began to pound as a terrifying thought unfurled.

Campbell must have found her.

She inched back on the bed, the blanket pulled tight below her chin, as the door creaked open.

It was a man. He extended a candle into her cell. Though his face was cast in blackness, the wavering flame made his shadow flicker along the open door, exaggerating his height and the stolidness of his stance.

As Magda's eyes adjusted, she began to make out his shape.

The shadows coalesced in the dark.

Then she saw his tartan, and knew. This man was not a monk.

Chapter 22

"Is it you, hen?" His voice was a husky whisper in the dark.

"James?" Magda nearly shrieked his name. "Is that you? How did you find me?"

She sprang from the bed, knocking into him in the dark. "Are you alright?" Magda rubbed his arms and patted her hands to his chest to assure herself that he was truly there, whole and healthy before her.

"Hush," he said, laughing quietly as he quickly pulled her door to. "You'll waken the entire priory. 'Tis I indeed, and I'll have you to myself till dawn if you'd but keep your voice down."

She heard the rasp of wood on stone as he slid her chair in front of the door. "That will do," he mumbled. A thrill shivered up her back as she realized that he intended to lock them in.

He placed the candle on the room's only table and strode to her. "But what of you? The bastard didn't touch you, did he?" His voice was cold steel, but his touch on her was gentle, stroking her arms and face as if she were a fragile piece of glass.

She shook her head. "No," she whispered. "He didn't hurt me."

"Are you certain? Come, let me look at you, Magda." James angled them toward the candlelight, and she thought she'd never seen such a beautiful man.

The flickering glow warmed one side of his face, and she saw that James had changed since she'd last seen him. When she'd first met him, his face was smooth-shaven, all relaxed lines and fluid expressions. It had been impossible not to think him handsome in his fine waistcoats, his basket-hilted sword ever at his side.

But it was a harder man who stood before her now. He even

appeared rougher on the surface, his stubbled jaw and shadowed eyes speaking of weeks on the road. His clothes had changed too. He'd snuck to her room, his head and feet bare, and Magda let her eyes roam along the deep green and blue plaid of his tartan and the solid lines and slopes of his muscular calves.

She looked up to face him, and the want that smoldered in his black eyes sent tremors of anticipation and fear and excitement through her.

James wore a shirt of coarse linen, and though it was belted loosely at his waist, Magda could still discern the outline of his chest and arms in the darkness. Her gaze lingered on the flex of his lean muscles as he took her hand and pulled her close to him.

His skin was warm, and her pulse skittered at the feel of his strong, callused fingers enveloping hers.

James had unleashed something dark in himself. Magda sensed it now and felt an untapped well stir in answer, the sudden force of her desire, feral and raw, shocking her with its intensity.

The energy crackling between them became almost unbearable, and Magda heard herself speak. "You came back."

"It seems you've become a habit with me." His voice was low, and tight with desire.

James gently pulled her back to stand close to the bed. His touch grazed up her arms, and he slowly began to walk around Magda, trailing his fingers along her breastbone, across her shoulder, down her spine. "Safe," he murmured. "You're safe." Pausing at her back, he slowly lifted thick handfuls of her hair and traced light kisses up her neck and along the curve of her ear. Magda felt his tongue flick along her earlobe, and a steady pulse thrummed to life between her legs.

James continued his walk around her, poring over every inch of her, his touch light, as if awed by the sight of her.

"I was terrified I'd lost you," he whispered.

He stood once again in front of Magda and gently pushed her hair away from her neck and off of her face. James drew his fingers around the outline of her cheeks and, taking her chin, leaned in to brush a kiss against her mouth.

"Och, Magda, my love," he said with sudden tenderness. He raised her face to his. "How can you not know it? You're my compass. Leaving you was the greatest error of my life. I'll not make it again."

His eyes glittered in the dark, steely and sure. "And, on this, Magdalen, I am dangerously serious." He spoke her name like an oath, and the sound of it on his lips sent a shiver through her.

"Be with me." His strong fingers twined around hers, his hands warm and dry in the chill of the room, and she longed to feel those hands holding her, knowing her.

She nodded mutely, not trusting her voice to speak, and pulled her body taller, drawing close as if for a kiss.

"No, lass. Not just like this." He cupped her chin. "Truly be with me. When I thought harm had come to you . . ." James touched his forehead to hers. "It's not just my country I serve now." He pulled away sharply, intensity honing his voice. "Let me serve *you* now." He took her hands in his and pulled them to his chest. "When I thought you'd come to some harm, I was a man undone. Be with me. We will be handfast. Brother Lonan will bless our union, and when this madness ends—and I pray it will end soon—I shall take you to Montrose and marry you properly, making you my bride in front of all and sundry."

She looked at him, looked at this man who not too long ago had been a stranger, as foreign to her as the cruel and savage time he lived in. And Magda thought then that she'd never felt so treasured. So understood. So loved.

"Okay." Her voice cracked. Suddenly nervous, she fought the trembling of her hands in his.

He stared at her, eyes grave in the darkness. "Is that aye or nay, hen?" The moonlight caught the edge of his strong jaw, set in a determined line that made her body flush with nervous anticipation.

She matched the somberness of his gaze. Magda hesitated. She knew what this meant. What it would mean especially to James, the implications for his time. And she took those rational concerns and set them aside. The moment felt right. He felt right. And for once in her life, she would take a risk. She would take what she wanted and follow her heart. "It's aye."

His mouth plunged to hers then, taking her with a ferocious kiss. Magda gasped with need, fumbling her hands over him, desperate to know him, to feel every inch.

He pulled away, and his hands went to his belt. His eyes didn't waver from hers as he unbuckled, and leather and sporran clattered to the ground. With a swift flick of his wrist, a cloud of wool followed, cascading heavily to their feet.

Magda glanced down and her heart pounded to see his shirt straining tight as he grew hard before her.

He kissed her again before tugging the coarse linen over his head and then stood before her gloriously naked. She ran her palms over the iron ropes of muscle at his biceps and back, and felt his erection heavy against her belly. Magda raked her nails down his back as something deep and primal stirred to life. He moaned in response and clutched her close, then she felt cool air pebble her skin as he stripped her bedgown from her.

James grew still. Surfacing from a haze of blind lust, Magda opened her eyes to the sight of him poring over her. "You're so beautiful," he whispered, swooping her into his arms, wrapping her legs around his waist. She felt his erection insistent against her bottom and groaned.

"Handfasting"—he cleared his throat, gathering himself— "handfasting is a Lowland ceremony." He eased her down to sit at the edge of the bed then knelt on the floor in front of her. "Not a proper wedding, aye?" She felt suddenly shy, exposed, sitting naked before him. Eager to close the distance, to end his frank scrutiny, Magda extended her hands to him, but James gently put them aside.

"And though I may be versed in the world of the court, it's a Highland tattoo sounded by my heart. And Highlanders have a tradition . . ." he began, then stopped to trace his hands down the length of her legs.

She could hear his wanting of her in the tight rasp of his voice and, shyness forgotten, reached for him again. James smiled, not meeting her eyes, intent only on her body. He cleared his throat and began again, "'Tis called the *glanadh nan cas*. The washing of a bride's feet on the eve of her pledge." He wrapped his hand around her foot, pale against his ruddy skin in the moonlight. He stroked it and, with a quiet inhale, froze, feeling the thin web of scars from the injury Lonan had tended what felt like so long ago. James carefully kissed along the old wound, and then rested her foot atop his thigh, the muscles of his leg solid and reassuring under her.

"Generally it's one of the bride's maids who attends her." There was a small pan of water at her bedside. James took it, dipped his hands, and brought a small puddle of cool water to her other foot. His thumbs kneaded leisurely down its length, water beading slow tracks along her skin. He reached her heel then moved higher, the calluses of his palms coarse against the thin skin below her ankle, and Magda shivered, her body piqued from the many sensations.

"But as there were no maids at hand, I didn't expect you'd mind a break from tradition. Considering the circumstances, aye?" His eyes finally met hers, a slow smile spreading across his face, and Magda swayed with the force of it. Hunger and intent sharpened his gaze. She was desperate now to hold him, to be held by him.

A gasp parted her lips, and he fixed his attention on her mouth, the smile gone from his face. James slowly rose to her, his gaze devouring the length of her body. He ever so gradually closed the distance between them, as if their joining were a fixed thing, inevitable, like gravity pulling two bodies together as one.

He took her shoulders in his hands and laid her back. His eyes were hooded as he hovered over her, the set of his jaw and the coiled muscles of his shoulders speaking to some dark urge, primal and predatory. Magda thought he'd take her then, half on the bed, their feet still resting on the ground.

His hands went to her breasts and cupped them tentatively. With a growl in the back of his throat, he leaned in to flick his tongue over a nipple.

Her breath became shallow, and at the sound of her light sighs, James nibbled at her, then sucked Magda hard into his mouth, abrading her tender skin between lips and teeth. He moved his attention to her other breast, kneading it in his hand, then ducked in to taste her, rolling her nipple on his tongue.

Magda threaded her fingers through his soft brown hair, pulling him more tightly to her, whimpering with her growing need. "Oh, James," she gasped, and realized she'd chanted his name over and over.

"Please, James."

He rolled to the bed, sweeping her up on her knees to straddle him. Magda eased back along his body until she found him, and rubbed slick against his hardness.

James stared at her, his black eyes intense, sharp with the force of his hunger. He rubbed his thumbs along her thighs, and the gesture flashed back to the moment Magda first passed through the portrait, when she'd landed astride him just that way.

A devilish smile lit his eyes, and she was overcome by a powerful feeling of love, and rightness, and completion.

"Please, James," she whispered again.

"Aye." His voice was ragged as he clutched her hips in his hands. "You're mine. I'll make you mine." Never taking his eyes from hers, James gave her a slight lift. "For now." He drove hard into her. "For always."

Magda gasped with the shock of him, at the newness of him full and large inside her.

He wrapped his arms at her back and pulled her toward him, silencing her moans with his mouth. James thrust his tongue hungrily as he began to move inside her, slowly at first, his cock slicked with her want.

Magda came almost immediately, collapsing onto his chest and clamping her teeth down onto the hard flesh between his shoulder and neck.

James flipped Magda onto her back, one hand pinning both of hers over her head, while the other slowly teased her breast. "You're not finished yet, lass," he warned, his voice a sultry growl.

She wrapped her legs around his back in answer, writhing her hips to grind even closer. She rubbed against the base of him and already felt the gathering in her belly again, her muscles tightening like a cord strung tight through her center.

Magda tensed beneath him, digging her heels into his back. "Aye, that's it," he said, voice hoarse. James held himself deep in her, and Magda felt him pulse inside her as he held himself back. "Let go of yourself," he rasped. James nibbled along her ears and neck and shoulders, giving gentle thrusts as he breathed, "I'll make you mine again and again and again."

He intensified, driving into her harder, and faster, and Magda felt the world slip away, and the edges of her vision faded to black, blood pounding just beneath the surface of her skin. She arched into him with the force of her orgasm, and James crushed his mouth to hers, letting himself finally find release.

They lay there for some time, their breathing and heartbeats gradually slowing. Magda shivered as the sweat cooled quickly in the chill night air. James reached down and swept his tartan off the floor and flicked the heavy wool over them, pulling her more tightly to his side for warmth.

"I've decided to stay," she said, breaking the silence.

James leaned in to nuzzle at her neck. "You'd best stay, hen," he said as he gave a gentle, playful smack to her bottom.

Magda giggled and snuggled closer, nestling one leg between his as he lay on his back.

James beamed. "This is what I wanted, aye?" He traced the lines of her face in the dying candlelight. "An easy smile on your lovely face."

Automatically, she began to deny the compliment, and he placed his finger over her mouth. "Hush, hen. If I've a notion to call you the bonniest in all Scotland, then I shall." He studied her, his black eyes solemn in the darkness. "And you are, Magda. The bonniest I've seen. You came to me like a torch in the darkness, and I've not been the same man since."

Feeling the blush creep into her cheeks, she smiled and nipped his finger between her teeth.

"Ah, a wee fox, is it?" James pulled his finger from her mouth and traced her lower lip with his thumb. He leaned in to kiss her slowly.

"And this spill of satin, russet like leaves in autumn," he said, raking his fingers through her hair. "I should have paid heed. Not a hen, but a fox, I see." He grabbed her bottom and nipped at her neck, his husky laugh echoing low off the stone walls.

Magda giggled again, and sat up slightly to lean on her elbow, head in hand. Her face grew serious as she thought about what he'd said. A ready smile is the last phrase she'd have used to describe herself, and yet something had happened to her since meeting James.

Through the years, she'd adopted a reserved exterior, taking refuge in formalities and solitude. But James hadn't been fooled. He'd cajoled and teased with a nonchalant charm that masked his own true nature, thoughtful and noble, until he'd shattered her world. She was, she thought with a quiet smile, rendered quite literally naked, and was surprised by the comfort she'd discovered in her own skin. Magda felt loose and expansive, discovering that easy laugh he claimed to cherish.

Magda studied the man lying naked by her side, and the knowledge that he watched her do so sent a flash of heat licking up between her legs. She slowly pushed down the plaid he'd used to cover them and traced her fingers over James's stomach, the ridges of his belly like hard islands of muscle. She drew her fingers lower still, to the line of hair below his navel.

He shivered as she moved lower, feathering light touches up and down his thighs and all around, grazing everything but his growing hardness. Emboldened by a new spring of confidence, Magda was taking great pleasure in teasing him.

James reached up to take her mouth with his, but she pushed him back down instead, tormenting him as she rubbed closer and closer, until she took him into her hand. He gasped, and she answered with a devilish smile. His skin was like silk under her fingertips, and the mere feel of him, and of his body's aggressive response to her touch, lit in Magda an urgent need to feel James again in her, and over her.

"Take me in your mouth." Her voice was breathy, greedy.

Reaching up to kiss her, James heard his own voice groan in response. Never, he believed, had a woman so embraced a man as Magda did now. Never had a woman so inflamed him. He felt at once humbled by such a great gift, and nearly blinded by the lust that pounded through his veins.

James steadied his breathing. He'd need to control himself lest he finish before he even got started. The tartan slipped to the floor as he slowly turned Magda on the bed and held her beneath him.

James marveled at her long pale body under his, and at her broad mouth smudged dark from his kisses, and he was devastated by his want for her. For a moment, it was as if he'd forgotten what to do. James merely stared, overwhelmed by the beauty in his hands.

"Please."

James heard her plea in the dark, and he was nearly unmanned. He kissed her lightly on her neck and down her chest, lingering to taste each breast, small and round in his palms. Then he kissed down her stomach, smooth and warmed amber by the flickering candlelight.

James moved lower, raking his fingers lightly through the thatch of hair between her legs as he kissed down her thigh. Magda moaned, arching up to press against him. He kneaded her, felt her damp with desire in his palm. Magda whimpered her protest as James dragged his hand away and continued to trace tongue and lips down her leg. Reaching her foot, he began to kiss up along her other leg, moving more urgently now, hungrily working back up between her thighs.

With an eager moan in his throat, James took her in his mouth, and Magda cried out, her breath coming in quick, shallow gasps. She threaded her fingers in his hair and pulled him more tightly to her, and James felt ready to explode with want for this woman. She was so open beneath him. So miraculously perfect. Magda stiffened, held her breath for a moment, then bucked her hips up. She shouted his name, and James felt his body surge harder in response.

His lips parted, hungry to taste all of her, and James crawled up the bed, covering her body with his own. Kissing her deeply, James took her again.

Her body still pulsed from her climax, and he held motionless inside her until once again her hips began to rock, urging him on. He felt himself close to the breaking point, and eager to prolong it, James effortlessly scooped Magda off the bed.

"Oh!" Her face betrayed a glimpse of surprise, and then re-newed appetite, as James strode to sit in the chair at her door, not once pulling from her. Magda rocked into him as he stroked his hands up her back, sucking at her mouth and breasts, his words of love and lust murmured over the creak of the wooden chair.

He felt her body tense again and he pulled her mouth to his for a frantic kiss. He drove into her one last time and then they froze, suspended in time, as the world fell away around them.

Chapter 23

Dawn sidled through her cell's slit of a window, casting a slice of yellow light along James's naked shoulder. Magda dared not move, savoring the opportunity to stare unabashedly at him. She was struck by the difference in his features. Awake, the man was all bold charisma. It was how she pictured him in her mind's eye, and it was what she'd fallen in love with. But to watch him sleep, his face still and at peace, she saw how classically handsome he was. It was as if his broad personality overshadowed his fine features. She took in the sight of those thick brown lashes resting on his cheeks, his strong jaw, and the long, taut body forged by a lifetime of swordplay and horsemanship.

His eyes opened, and Magda gave a start.

"Hi," she whispered.

James held her with his gaze and, cupping her cheek in his hand, silently leaned in to kiss her deeply.

"What did I do to deserve that?" She tucked her blanket under her arm and nestled happily onto her side.

"What did you do?" Cocking his brow, he reached over and pulled her easily on top of him. "What did you not do?" His laugh rumbled low and sexy in the quiet of the room.

"I hope I didn't shock you," she said, suddenly unsure.

"Shock me?" James rolled her to his other side, and leaned his face close to hers. "Oh, Magda, my love." He kissed her gently on her brow. "The only shock has been discovering how deep is my love for you. It's as if I've discovered raging depths, having only known water's frozen surface."

Fighting not to smile, he added with mock gravity, "As for last night, I invite you henceforth to shock me at your leisure, hen."

Magda didn't appear completely certain, so James pressed on. "I suppose, in my"—he cleared his throat—"*understanding*, there are some women, aye, who are perhaps more likely to, say, lie politely until the man's deed is done."

A smile split Magda's face, a very unladylike snort escaping her. "Haven't I been polite?"

"Oh, aye, most accommodating." He traced his fingers down her arm, and Magda's skin pebbled at his touch. The playfulness in his eyes darkened. He took her hip in his hand and pulled her firmly to him, already hard and insistent between them. Her muscles, though sore, roused at once to life, and she felt fresh dampness between her legs, mingling with last night's musk.

"And I'd have you accommodate me once more before breakfast."

❁

She woke this time to the sight of James standing naked at the window. Magda stretched, staring at his muscular back and legs as he craned his neck to see out.

Hearing her movement, he turned and gave her a languorous appraisal, his gaze slowly raking over her body, eyes narrowing with admiration. "What say you, love? Seems a bonny day for a handfasting."

She gave him a tentative smile, inexplicably nervous in the light of day. "So . . . a handfasting. Is it like a marriage then?"

"Och, no." He was at the bedside in an instant, on his knees before her. "I vow I shall give you a proper wedding." James swept the hair from her face, tracing his finger around her cheekbones, her lips. "I shall drape you in gold and silk finery, feed you with my own hand the finest of foods. No"—he took her hand, twining his fingers carefully in hers—"this is but a handfasting. Some in Scotland see it as but a promise, a betrothal like, while others see it as a union true. But we"—he gave a squeeze and brought her hand to his chest—"we shall give it our own meaning. I shall pledge myself to you until such time as I can give you my heart in the grandest of ceremonies. Before all of Scotland, if I could."

Certain again, she gave him a wordless nod as she blinked the sudden sting from her eyes. He laughed then, a joyful sound, and she giggled, unable to stop from joining him. He stood, inhaled deeply, and announced, "I'm a man starved."

"Me too." Magda smiled unabashedly at him. "Do you think they still have breakfast?"

"Och," he strode back to the window, "by the sun in the sky, I'd say the brothers broke their fast hours ago."

As if on cue, chanting rose up through the window, a low, resonant hum rumbling through the priory grounds. "No, hen, by the sound of it"—he stood silent for a moment—"if we rush, we can make the noontime meal."

"How do you know so much about this place?" Magda rose to dress, tamping down the instinctive and momentary shame at standing naked before him. As if sensing her discomfort, he flashed her a warm smile and set to gathering his clothes from the floor. "And you haven't told me how you knew I'd be here," she added.

"When I heard you were captured, we went straight for Campbell lands. It wasn't long before we heard of your escape. To say you vexed the Campbell would be understating the matter, aye? He combed the lands around Castle Gloom for days." Magda watched in awe as James deftly wound the yards of tartan around his waist. "I heard tell they lost your trail somewhere around the loch. It was then I remembered this spit of land. I'd hoped . . ." He stopped short, wincing with the pain that flashed in his eyes. Still holding the loose end of his tartan in one hand, he stepped to Magda and tangled the other in her hair, pulling her close to steal a quick kiss. "I'm just thankful you found this place. That I found you."

He finished tucking the length of wool around his waist. "And a braw thing indeed it was, Magda. Campbell's men discounted outright that a woman could escape by water. But I knew at once. And I know too what that would have cost you."

He swept the last of his tartan up over his shoulder. "I couldn't wait. I had to come for you in the night. I had to see with my own eyes you'd made it safe. Though," he added with a laugh, "I dare say there's at least one in my party who's sore put that our plans to raze Castle Gloom were waylaid."

Magda joined him in the open doorway, silent for a moment. He smoothed the top of her borrowed cassock, tucking it more snugly under her belt. "And the next order of business will be to get you some proper clothing, my wee mendicant."

She placed her hands on his arms to bring his attention back to the matter in question. "But you didn't answer how you know so much about this place."

"As improbable as it may seem, my family owns these lands. Aye," he said to her incredulous look. "I speak truly."

Tucking her arm snugly in his, he led them back down the hallway. "I'll not know if yours is a path touched by providence or serendipity, hen, but I welcome the stroke of luck all the same."

They walked toward the distant sound of chanting, their footfalls echoing off the empty stone corridor. "My family has long owned this island, and I've a mutual agreement with the monks, allowing them to stay."

Reaching the door to the dining hall, James added in a rushed whisper, "The Augustinians ignore my choice of church, and I ignore their lack of funds."

They shuffled into the dining hall as unobtrusively as possible. It was a long, low building, chill and dim despite the noonday sun, filled with the sounds of many men's voices chanting as one, a great, deep droning that vibrated over the stones. A single table spanned the far end of the room, with four tables extending perpendicular from it. Magda had gathered that important people and guests sat at the high table, and that's where they headed now. Though the monks didn't look up from their prayers, Magda nonetheless felt her cheeks burn with embarrassment, the walk from door to table feeling an eternity.

The chanting silenced abruptly just as Magda's chair scraped back from the table, and she shut her eyes and held her breath for a moment, willing the excruciating self-consciousness to pass.

"Sit, child." She heard Lonan's kind whisper, and inhaling, Magda settled herself at the table. "You've arrived at least a century too late for the Inquisition. I vow no harm will come to you for being tardy to a meal."

The twinkle in Lonan's eyes and a quick under-the-table squeeze on the knee from James put Magda at her ease.

"You are to leave us, I sense. Both of you."

Magda looked to James and, holding his gaze, nodded. Despite the serious stillness of his features, James gave her a wink and Magda felt a flare of wanting him blast through her.

"I suppose my work is done," Lonan said.

Thinking his comment a tongue-in-cheek reference to getting her and James together, Magda's eyes shot to the old monk, but he merely sat there, slowly chewing, looking straight into the distance.

"And quite a lot of work you've done, aye?" James set to twirling his spoon in a bowl of gluey oats, the ghost of a smile wrinkling his eyes.

This time she knew she heard sarcasm and kicked James beneath the table. Though there was a low murmuring in the hall, most of the men were silent, and Magda was mortified that undue attention be brought to her.

"Look around you, lass." Lonan gestured to the monks sitting at the lower tables. "Many of these men are hermits, living in isolation, their prayer as their work. I, though, I have my scholarship, in service to God and to my country. I also have an obligation to tend to those injured in body and mind, to nurture the soul of the wayward traveler. And you, dear Magda, were nothing if not wayward. But now"—smiling, he looked to James, and Magda thought she would miss the old man, scar and all—"now you have found yourself in good hands."

Lonan turned his attention back to his food and casually added, "Though I would bless your union. I'd not have all these efforts end with your two souls living in sin."

Magda stuffed the spoon in her mouth to silence her surprised laugh. She'd known the old man would be capable of wit.

"Well, my good brother, that is a point which we'd like to discuss with you." James took and held her hand under the table.

"Yes," she added, looking at him for strength. "We . . . we'd like to be . . ."

"Handfast?" Lonan smiled. "I know, child. I've readied the chapel for you." Magda and James exchanged perplexed looks, but the brother merely looked innocent, chafing his hands over the coarse sleeves of his cassock. "And I dare say the chill there will be more easily borne on a full belly. We'll proceed the moment we finish our meal."

"So soon?" Magda asked. She wanted this handfasting, was

ready to pledge herself to James. Felt, in fact, that she already had. But there was a part of her that thought there might have been more ceremony around it. She knew it wasn't to be her real wedding, but still, she wanted at least to wear something other than modified monk's clothing. She didn't even have a proper mirror with which to prepare herself.

"Aye, this soon," Lonan replied. "For you'll be off to Perthshire, if I have the right of it."

"Is that where we're going?" Magda looked to James. With all that had happened in the past hours, she hadn't thought to actually ask him where they'd be off to next. She realized a part of her had hoped they'd return to his home in Montrose.

"Old man"—James shook his head—"some day you'll show me how you do that. Aye, hen. Perthshire it is."

"But . . ." She turned to Lonan. She was about to pledge herself to James, and yet was she ready to say good-bye to her time, forever? "What if I need to find my way back . . . back to my own home?"

"Then you have only to find me once more. Don't fear, child." He put down his spoon and reached to cup her cheek. "I'll not be far when you need me."

"But I never found out what I'm supposed to do." A hint of panic pitched her voice. How was she to know what to do to help James?

"Magda dear, all you need remember is this." Brother Lonan gently took her hand. His grip was cool and dry, but firm, with knuckles bulging knobby with age. "It is only in letting go of our fears that we come to know the heart's true path."

"Who said that?"

"Lonan Gordon." The monk smiled broadly. "For once those are *my* words, Magdalen. And you may quote them yourself."

❀

The wind howled outside, fingering its way into the chapel despite the modest stained glass rosettes serving as windowpanes. The day was overcast, but light shone in from the west, throwing muted golds and blues onto the wooden altar. Magda studied the patterns in the glass above and wondered at the effort and cost that would've been needed to bring such a measure of luxury to this remote a place.

James took her hand, and she turned to the man she was to bind herself to. He'd told her this was a sort of union, that they'd have a proper wedding when a more suitable time presented itself.

She glanced down. Lonan had strewn a handful of wildflowers, tiny blue buttons, to brighten the old timber planks of the aisle. Magda nudged them with her toe, battling a sudden wave of melancholy. She'd been so swept up in the passion of it all. Reuniting with James again, seeing him safe before her, had overwhelmed her. Her need to hold him had been the only real thing last night. Making sure he was real, and whole. The frantic need to kiss and touch in the dark.

But now, in the light of day, she thought about what she was doing. Did this mean she was forever forsaking her world for James? She thought of her parents. What would they think? How would they handle it? She'd simply disappeared. Would they think she'd been kidnapped? Were they out there somewhere gathering funds even now, waiting by the phone? Or would they think she'd just run away, that she'd met a man and eloped to some exotic and faraway place. She hoped so. The last was actually not too far from the truth.

Her parents' response to her disappearance was almost too painful to think about. They might not have been close, but the prospect of losing two children in one lifetime was too much to bear.

She turned her mind to Walter instead. What would he have made of all this? She glanced around, at the old crucifix over the altar, the hammered bronze chalice. She smiled a little. He'd be in heaven surrounded by so many artifacts. What had he thought when she didn't show up that Monday? Her smile faded. How long had he waited to call her parents? Or would he have called the police first? There'd been a day when people wouldn't have thought twice about calling her brother, but she'd had nobody that close to her since his death. She blinked back the haze of tears clouding her vision.

"Are you still certain of this?" She felt James's breath at her neck, his voice a low whisper in her ear. "Certain of me?"

She looked at him. Truly looked at this man who wanted her, only her, by his side. He stood tall beside her. The dust of travel still clung faintly to his blue and green tartan. Though clean, his shirt was worn, with faded stains at the cuffs. If she strained, she recognized her musk, faintly overlaying the scent of trees and sea that was so distinctly James. His hair had grown a little since she'd last seen him, the color of flax and earth resting along his broad shoulders.

"Yes." She cleared her throat and said more loudly, "I'm certain."

"A fine thing that." Lonan's voice echoed up the aisle. "And are we ready then?"

The brother stood before them and, as they nodded, he began to wind a red cord about their joined hands. "In this binding, I join you. Under the eyes of God, in the eyes of the Holy Kirk, and so too by the ancient Gaelic law of *lánamnas foxail*, do you pledge your troth to one another, and so bind yourselves as handfast spouses?"

"Aye." James held tight to Magda's hand.

"I . . . yes." In the rush, they hadn't discussed the wording, and she found herself stumbling over the unsaid phrase *I do.*

"And James, shall you keep and maintain her with meat and drink, and find and keep her in all necessary garments and ornaments?"

"I think I can accommodate that, aye." She heard his quiet chuckle at her side.

"And so, James Graham and Magdalen Deacon, do I declare you pledged to one another."

Magda heard the words and wondered if she was married. It had been so brief, so businesslike. She didn't quite feel married. She knew it was just a handfasting, but still, she'd expected more. Perhaps it was that her parents weren't there. She'd always thought her father would be there to give her away. And her mother. How crushed her mother would've been to know her only daughter had been married and she'd not had the opportunity to plan it. And what an event *that* would've been. Magda should've been amused, but she just felt a little sad.

"Magdalen?"

"Hm?" She looked at James. He tucked his thumb down to stroke the palm of her hand, his brows raised expectantly as he waited for her to answer.

She met his gaze, so steady and so focused on her. In it, she saw everything he promised, saw his heart opened to her, and she knew this was right. No matter the future, no matter the past, this felt right.

"'Tis time you kissed me now."

Magda found herself beaming back at him then. And she kissed him.

Chapter 24

It had been a leisurely ride north to Perthshire, and for the first time Magda truly began to absorb the land around her. It was more idyllic than any pastoral painting she could've imagined. Blair Atholl, the small parish they temporarily called their home, was all gently rolling glens and lush trees surrounded by the Grampian mountain range in the distance.

MacColla had rallied his troops from the west, and while James spent his days busy with them, Magda explored. Water flowed from higher ground to feed many of Perthshire's waterways, and she often discovered small burbling falls or gently rushing streams, hidden gems that never ceased to delight her. The River Garry wound through the heart of Blair Atholl, and a particular stroll with the river in sight had become her favorite.

Weather during the summer months was as unpredictable as ever, and Magda appreciated those mornings that dawned sunny and clear, where she could take the thick woolen arisaid from her shoulders to savor the feel of the sun's rays.

The days were much longer than when she'd first arrived. She rarely caught the sunrises, which came earlier than ever. The sunsets happened well past supper now, and she loved nothing more than watching the sun drop behind the mountains, warmed by the nostalgic feeling of childhood summers and evenings that went on forever.

Their party was hosted quite graciously by Clan Donnachaidh. Although Alexander Robertson, the chief of the clan, was too young to join James in his fight, the family showed them every hospitality. James had, without pause, introduced Magda as his wife, raising Will Rollo's brows, but making her heart thrill. As a result, they got to share a lovely room overlooking the gardens of Blair Castle, and though James was immersed in training the massive force MacColla had brought from Ireland, they had their nights together, and Magda savored every moment. Increasingly, she'd caught him staring at those mountains in the distance, his usually easy features furrowed in thought, and she knew that this serene interlude would soon come to a close.

Wanting to be unobtrusive, she'd stayed far from James and his field practices during her walks. But Magda found that her curiosity was getting the better of her, and one day found herself walking toward where she knew James spent his days.

She crested a rise and gasped at her first sight of the Irish encampment. MacColla's forces were night and day from the Highlanders. The Irish traveled with their women and children in tow and had taken over one of the glens, now a vast sprawl of humanity, with dirty faces and threadbare clothes and chaos all around.

"Quite a spectacle, aye?"

Magda jumped. Placing her hand on her pounding heart, she turned to see James standing just behind her. A light breeze swept along the hilltop, clinging James's tartan and sweat-dampened shirt to his body, and Magda's breath caught at the sight of him.

"Sorry, hen. I saw you walking the hill like some fey wraith and thought I'd catch you as you reached the peak." A mischievous light flashed in his eyes. "What say you?" James clapped his hand on her bottom and grabbed her to him. "Have you peaked yet?"

"Stop it!" Magda swatted at him playfully.

"Aye, we can't let the Irish see us indiscrete up here. Though, by the looks of all those striplings running about, they're well versed in the mechanics of indiscretion." He nodded down toward the glen below. "It seems each Irishman brings five sons, if he brings a one."

Shading his eyes, James looked up at the sky. He hadn't shaved that morning, and the sun glinted gold off the whiskers of his strong jaw.

"Midday is upon us." He opened his sporran and took out a cloth-wrapped mound. "Would you join me? Though I fear all I have is a cold oatcake and some dried meat." He gave a sheepish shrug to his shoulders.

"I'd love to," she said as they sat in the grass, "but I think I'll pass on your feast there."

The grass was cool and slightly damp beneath them, but the sun was warm on their shoulders, which touched gently as they leaned into each other. Their peaceable silence was interrupted only by Magda's stray giggles at the sight of James struggling to chew and swallow his lunch.

Bagpipes jarred to life, as they invariably did, cutting across the valley like a knife. Listening to the notes keening and tripping along, Magda couldn't tell if the tune was joyful or mournful, and she realized that was precisely the reason the pipes were so uniquely Scottish. In their music—as in their landscape and their lives—jubilation and desolation lived in tandem, Scotland's warp and woof.

She couldn't help the tears that stung her eyes, filled as she was with emotion, its roots as likely from joy as from sadness.

"The tune is called 'Flowers of the Forest.'" James wrapped his arm around her shoulders, clutching her tight to him. "Do you know the story, hen? Of the Battle of Flodden?"

She looked at him, her knit brows asking for his explanation.

"Well you'll know King Henry the Eighth of England, aye?"

"Of course."

"Well, the Battle of Flodden was a bloody battle. And mayhap one of the largest ever fought on our land. 'Twas between Henry the Eighth and Scotland's King James the Fourth, well over one hundred years past now."

Nestling his chin on her shoulder, his voice was wistful over the drone of the pipes. "The Scots army was hewn into a mountain of dead that day, with King James himself cut down."

He sang a line from the song, his voice low and cracked, "*Sighing and moaning, on every green loaning, the Flowers of the Forest are all withered away.*" James inhaled deeply, letting the title's meaning hang, punctuated by the shrill cry of the bagpipes. "They say up to ten thousand men died that day. Every hearth in all Scotland felt the devastation, both Highland and Low. King James had been a good man, aye? A noble man, fair and kind."

"That's not always enough." Fear made Magda's voice waver. It was impossible not to think of her own James, her own good man.

"Aye, but he was braw too," James said, mistaking her meaning. "He was struck by one arrow and five swords that day, and yet he stood to slay five with his pike. And when that was shattered in his hand, King James took up his sword and slew five more."

She suddenly felt *his* sword, its hilt cold and hard leaning into her hip, both a reminder of battles he'd fought and a portent of what might come.

"It will begin soon now," he said. James took her hand in his and traced the lines of her palm. "Once the fight begins, we'll be on the move. Magda"—he looked in her eyes—"I think it best you return to Montrose—"

"No." She pulled her hand away and sat up to face him. "I will not leave you. I can't leave you." They'd finally reunited, and the prospect of parting again terrified her. She feared for his safety, and for hers apart from him. But mostly she feared the hazy destiny that loomed possible on the horizon. The outcome so nonchalantly described to her, by Walter, at the Met, what felt like a lifetime ago.

"Och, hen, don't fret so." Stroking her hair from her eyes, he cupped her chin and kissed her cheeks.

"But you don't understand, James. Something bad happens. I *know* something is going to happen."

He stilled. "What do you know?"

"I'm not sure when it will happen, just that you get captured. I just don't know, James." Magda's voice grew louder, and she spoke with uncharacteristic intensity. "It could be today or it could be in twenty years, but Walter said you . . ." Her voice hitched. "You get captured and hanged."

He was quiet for a moment. "And so it may be." James gave her a quiet smile. "But you're here now, so I don't suppose you'll let that happen, worked into a lather as you are."

"Don't joke about it," she snapped.

"Nay, hen, I'll not joke." He took her hand back into his and sat in silence.

"You can't just leave me," she said abruptly. "What if I was sent back for a reason? Maybe even to save you?"

He studied her face, and she could tell by the light in his eyes that the prospect of Magda saving him both touched and amused him. But it didn't matter, she thought, so long as he didn't abandon her in the middle of seventeenth-century Scotland. To worry over his fate from afar, waiting powerless to hear the possibly dire outcome, wouldn't be much different than returning home and reading about him in the history books.

"Whatever morbid destiny history once augured was altered when you came to me. I feel it, aye?" He laced his fingers in hers and squeezed hard. "'Tis you, Magda. You've changed it all."

James thumbed tears from her face that she hadn't realized were there. "Come now, don't be so melancholy," he told her. "The first battle comes soon. I'll keep you close at Blair Castle, and bring you with me when we march on. I can't know my future, but somehow that is what feels right. Travel with my wife, just like our Irish friends, aye?"

"Yeah, about that wife thing."

"Och, I know it wasn't done proper. I'd have us joined before all and sundry, with you in a grand gown and the pipes crying our joy to the skies." Frustration knitted his brow as he looked into the distance. "I want a proper wedding for you, Magda."

He looked to her, and she thought she saw an unfamiliar flicker of vulnerability in his eyes.

"If you'll have me?"

She nodded silently, smiling through the tears that still dampened her face.

James kissed her gently. "It seems I've won myself a marquise after all. Magdalen Graham, Marquise of Montrose. And when these troubles are over, we'll have a true wedding, and it shall be the finest in all Scotland."

Sighing deeply, he folded his square of cloth and returned it to his sporran. "But first you'd best accustom yourself to those oatcakes, hen. My plan is to harry the Covenanters, up and down and through the Highlands. I'll not be contented until I see snow on those passes." He nodded to the Grampian range in the distance. "The Highlanders will welcome a march through the sleet. The Lowland gentry, though, in their heavy cloaks and cobbled shoes, will not."

He gave a resigned shrug. "So, my love, as for the dried oats, I fear you've not seen the last of them."

She gave him a brave smile, trying to force out all other thoughts. But Walter's words came to hum at the edges of her mind, faint, like the pipes' ghostly echo.

Captured. Imprisoned. Hanged.

❁

"But my men grow impatient. You forget, they fight for money, and each day that passes is more coin squandered." Leslie took a healthy swig of ale. "If they dispersed now, it would take me months to gather a like force."

Campbell sucked the venison from his teeth, and stared flatly at the general. "'Tis my coin, Leslie, and my decision."

"But we've word that the Royalists stir north of Perth. Graham even now trains an army of men."

"An army?" Campbell laughed. "He's a boatful of Irish refugees and some filthy Highlanders." Campbell dragged a thick slice of bread through the stew in his bowl. "No, Elcho is already poised, ready for what troubles those savages might bring."

"Elcho is a lordling with a mob of untested men."

"*Lord* Elcho has a Covenanter army of six thousand foot and seven hundred horse. I don't care how brilliant Graham is. If he's foolish enough to challenge those numbers, it will be a rout, regardless of Elcho's preparations."

Campbell belched and pushed away from the table. "No, as much as I'd like to exact retribution from Graham and his bitch myself, you and I stay here. Elcho will obliterate the northern Royalists.

"Mark my words, Leslie." Campbell pursed his thin lips into a thoughtful sneer. "The Lowlands will be the only place of any relevance in Scotland, and the Lowland people its only threat."

Chapter 25

"Ready!" James shouted, and hoped his orders would carry to the men on the far reaches of the line. To pit his twenty-four hundred men against a force near seven thousand strong, he'd drawn his troops into a long and shallow front. Only three men deep, it stretched far along the floor of Tippermuir valley—long enough, he prayed, to avoid being outflanked by the Lowland general.

Sibbald and Rollo manned the left and right flanks, and James and MacColla held the center. They had but three horsemen, a knot of axe-wielding Highlanders, many men bearing sword and targe, and some with no weapons at all. James had gleaned a few lucky score of muskets, and it was these that he would use in the first assault, shot from the center of the line.

He'd momentarily silenced the piper. The air was charged, amplified only by the rasping of breath and hissing of steel poised in scabbard.

"Gentlemen!" James shouted. "It is true you have few weapons while your enemy has many." He locked eyes with as many men as he could, and thought in that moment that his heart would break for love of them. They stood brave and eager for battle, seeing their lack of arms not as an obstacle, but a challenge.

"But many stones lie upon this moor, and I say: Take as stout a one as you can manage." The men began to buzz, and James raised his fist in the air. "Run to the first Covenanter you meet." They cheered him, and his voice grew louder. "And strike him, and take his sword." James yelled above the din. "And then, gentlemen, I believe you will be at no loss how to proceed!"

Whooping and battle cries thundered down the line. "Silence!" he yelled.

The enemy Covenanters had begun their advance, and the hollow echo of approaching soldiers pressed toward them like a wall of sound.

"Prime!" James ordered. The sound of clicking metal was shrill in his ears as hundreds of men pulled back on the cocks of their muskets and methodically primed their weapons. They pressed hammers forward, opened priming pans, tipped powder flasks, poured, returned hammers.

The acrid smell of gunpowder subsumed everything, drowning the stench of unwashed men.

"About!" James called, and was roused by the sight of so many men moving in unison. Swinging their muskets butt first to the ground, pouring a measure more of gunpowder into the barrels, plucking lead balls from between their teeth to drop onto the powder.

"Draw ramrods!" There was a great screeching as his men withdrew their rods from channels beneath musket barrels, and plunged them down to seat bullets firmly against powder.

"Aim!" The snap of metal reverberated down the line, one single, tremendous sound, as James's men pulled their muskets to full cock.

"Fire!" he shouted, and flinched at the deafening boom. Black and gray smoke filled the air, and James whooped at the unexpected rush of exhilaration and the sensation that he was raw and alive to everything around him.

Lord Elcho, the enemy general, had taken a standard approach to the battle and, hoping to draw James's men from their ranks, was sending a cavalry unit as his first advance.

But the band of Highlanders and Irishmen had cut their teeth far from those military colleges favored by rich, young lords. They didn't know that proper infantry like themselves were supposed to fear men on horseback.

Rather, James and his men merely fired their single round and then, with looks that ranged from unimpressed, to impatient, to disgusted, threw down their muskets and charged the horses head-on.

The valley was choked with smoke, and at first the Covenanters only heard James's men. Many hesitated at the blood-chilling chorus of shrieks and cheers and howls, as if they were to stand witness to some epic Gael force risen from the dead.

James roared his own battle cry and ran beside his men as they exploded through the dense cloud of gun smoke, leaping and whooping, mad with delight and fury, and hundreds of their enemy soldiers turned their horses and fled from the sight.

Unfettered by horse or musket, James felt the rage of battle course through him with a newfound intensity and clarity. He dashed and leapt, cutting a path along the uneven terrain, and as his feet pounded directly along the Scottish soil, more than ever before he felt as one with his country.

Just as his feet were linked to the beloved ground, so too did the sword in his hand seem to extend effortlessly from him as if a part of his own body. He and his sword arced and sang through the air, cutting down any foolish enough to stand in their way.

His enemies fled. Lord Elcho frantically tried to regroup, but the horsemen who'd fallen back collided with the Covenanter foot soldiers who'd remained on the field, and the results were catastrophic. With James and MacColla carving a path through the Covenanters from the middle, and Rollo and Sibbald holding their flanks, they routed the enemy.

James found MacColla in the center of the valley, standing and laughing at the outrageous vision of Highlanders throwing stones at their retreating enemy.

"'Twas a braw day, Graham." MacColla clapped him hard on the shoulder.

"Indeed." James nodded, sharing his good humor. "Though I'd wager you could walk from here to the gates of Perth without touching your foot to the ground." Bodies of Covenanter soldiers littered the field. James scanned his troops and shook his head in disbelief. "What of our casualties?"

"I know of but one man lost," Rollo said, riding up from behind. "One man for one thousand Covenanters."

"Extraordinary," James murmured as he took in the devastation around him.

"I'll get you a full accounting by day's end."

"Aye, do that. And where has Sibbald got to?"

"He took himself one of those Covenanter ponies," MacColla

said. He looked around the field as if struck by possibility of pro-
curing his own spoils. "It looked to me like the old man rode
east."

"To Perth?" James pulled off his bonnet and shook the sweat
from his head.

MacColla merely shrugged.

"Rollo," James said, "we need to arrange a quick surrender with Perth. I'd not have it suffer the same plundering as
Aberdeen."

"I understand." If they were to avoid the plundering that could
happen after battle, they needed to broker the town's surrender as
soon as possible. Rollo turned his mount and was off at once, his
horse picking a tentative path through the carnage.

❖

"Aye, and the Irish were shocked that our James is no blustering
bonnet-laird!" MacColla leaned over and clapped James hard on
the shoulder for what must have been the twentieth time that evening. The man was built like an ox, and James thought sure he'd
have a bruise by night's end.

Young Alexander Robertson and his family hosted a celebra-
tory dinner for them, seating James in an honored place at one
end of the table, with Magda and MacColla sitting to either side.
He was becoming quite fond of MacColla and his bluster, though
the man did have a startlingly vicious streak in battle that James
thought he'd best keep an eye on.

They dined in Blair Castle, and James found the Great Hall a
warm welcome indeed. The room was simple but gracious, with
high ceilings and a fire roaring in the hearth. Sconces and can-
delabra chased the gloom from the hall and filled it with a warm
golden light.

"Why, James can't be called a bonnet-laird what with all the
Graham landholdings." Alexander placed his cutlery down, contemplating the issue in earnest. Though already named chief of
his clan, he was a young fourteen and his title was more honorific
than realistic as yet.

"No, lad," Rollo said. "I think the MacColla's meaning has
more to do with James's battle courage and acumen." Rollo's usu-

ally hard-edged voice was kind, and belied the great pain he must have been enduring. James knew at what cost his friend sat a saddle for the day, and a number of times he'd caught Rollo pounding the feeling back into his rigid, bent legs.

"Aye, but I curse the Campbell." MacColla slammed his fist on the table. "The rogue was too much of a coward to face us himself."

"I've a feeling he'll not let this day stand." James poured himself another glass of Bordeaux. "Bide your time, friend. You'll get your chance at revenge against the Campbell."

The glee that had suffused James was subsiding, and he grew thoughtful. They'd only lost one man to the Covenanters' thousand. It was the first time he'd seen a Highland charge in action and he was awed. And sobered.

"Over a thousand dead," Alexander marveled, as if reading James's mind. "Never before have so many fled from so few."

"Wise words from a young mouth, lad." James raised his glass in a toast. "You'll make a fine chief."

❧

As the dinner guests began to disperse, James once again addressed his young host. "I've a gift for you, Alexander."

James walked to the corner of the hall and retrieved his musket from the shadows. "I owe you a great debt for the hospitality you've shown us. I find this is no longer of any use to me," he said, and holding the barrel pointed toward himself, James handed him the gun.

The boy merely looked at him, incredulous.

"Aye." James smiled. "My bullets are spent, lad. I've my broadsword, and that will more than suffice."

Alexander took the musket gingerly into his hands. The butt of the rifle was made of wood the color of cocoa that James had polished to a fine patina, and it was short compared to the barrel, which swept forward in a thin, elegant line. Other men in his acquaintance coveted firearms with elaborate carvings or even ivory inlay, but James prized simplicity in a weapon, and his plain iron matchlock was polished to a bright silver sheen.

"Use it well, lad." James smiled. Alexander beamed in reply, moved by the gift. "I'm taking our fight deeper into the Highlands," James said. "It's the weapon of a Highlander I'll use now."

❀

James leaned down and traced his fingers through the water. "Touch it," he told her.

"I'd rather not."

Magda had been out of her mind with fear during his battle, and she was left uncharacteristically prickly the next day. It had all been so loud—louder than she could've ever imagined—with those godforsaken bagpipes keening all the while, making her think she'd tear her hair out. Not knowing, amidst the distant shots and screams, if James lived or died. And the only thing she'd been able to see on the horizon was a thick cloud of gray smoke hanging like an evil portent over the battlefield.

She'd been unable to relax, or even speak, through dinner, alternating between utter euphoria over James's safe return and bitter resentment over her decision to commit herself to this life of dangerous uncertainty.

He had been eager to lie with her that night, but Magda couldn't shake clear the anxiety, confusion, and fear that fogged her. So, he had woken her early the following morning and, with a wicked glint in his eye, had spirited her away for a long ride in the countryside. When they'd reached their destination, the sight of Loch Tay glimmering before her hadn't done much to soothe her nerves, and she wondered what James had been thinking to bring her to a lake, of all things.

James put an arm around her shoulder and gently pulled her down to squat at the water's edge. "Touch it," he whispered.

"But . . ."

"Och, hen, for me, aye?"

She turned to him, this otherwise strong, handsome warrior, looking at her with the eager intensity of a child, kneeling beside her as if Magda were all that mattered in the world. Not battle, not politics, just her good opinion.

She reached down, and her breath hissed in with the shock of it. "It's warm!" Magda couldn't help but laugh, astonished.

"Aye." He smiled broadly in return, the sun picking out high-lights in his hair, soft and loose in the morning's gentle breeze. "The wind blows in from the south and traps the warm water at the top. And since this wee bay is shallow for a ways out"—he shielded his eyes with his hand and looked into the distance— "you've warm water for swimming in the summer months."

He stood and stripped. James had long traded his armor and trews for a tartan in muted green and blue. He wore a Highlander's bonnet now, in which he'd pinned a sprig of oats twined with the swatch of blue he'd torn from her skirt what felt like so long ago. Magda stared at the sight of him. Though she hadn't wasted time memorizing his naked body, they had always lain together in some sort of shelter, lit by nothing brighter than a candle or what ren-egade sunlight graced them. But now the afternoon sun mottled his body with light and shadow, etching sharp contours around the ridges of his muscles.

He strode to the water's edge and dove in. For a single heart-beat, Magda knew panic skittering up her spine. Then James sprang above the surface, swinging the curtain of wet hair from his eyes, joy writ clear on his face.

"Come in, hen."

"I . . ." She raked her fingers through her hair in distress. "You know I can't, James."

"But you can, Magda." He waded closer to shore. "I know what this means to you. But I know you've the strength to do it, and I think it important that you know it too."

He emerged from the water, and she was mesmerized by the drops of water on his skin, reflecting the sun like so many tiny crystals.

"So, my love," he said, undressing her gently but surely, "you can." He ushered her to the water's edge and, not dropping her gaze, made sure of her assent. "And you will."

Magda tentatively stepped in, trying to force all thoughts from her mind but for the sensation of the lake's surface bobbing along the length of her calves.

James swooped her into his arms, and she shrieked a startled laugh. "A bonny sight you are, wearing naught but the breeze." He walked in up to his thighs and jostled her and made to drop her, with Magda laughing and kicking, stretching to the water to try to splash him.

"You've no hope, lass. I've got you. I'm a kelpie, aye? Or have I not told you?"

"A what?"

"Oh, you've not heard the story of the kelpie?"

She shook her head, eyeing him suspiciously.

"Well, they say kelpies make their home at the bottom of lochs and rivers." He walked in deeper and Magda felt the water kiss her hips and ankles. "But they're canny creatures who can change shape at will. And a kelpie in want of a wife? Och, lass, beware. He'll go to ground, roaming the land in the shape of a magnificent horse, to capture himself . . ." James paused dramatically. "A comely lass like yourself perhaps?" Magda giggled as he dipped her backward to steal a kiss at her throat. "To bring as his bonny bride to the kelpie's watery home."

James looked around him as if on guard, and finished in a whisper, "And some say that's why the loch is so warm. Not from sun, nor from the shallows, but from the mason he'd brought home one day, captured to build a chimney for the kelpie's young wife who pined for her life on land, but was instead doomed to live forever, cold at the bottom of the loch."

Magda listened, relaxed, and before she knew it James had eased her in, the water lapping and clinging just above and between her breasts.

When she'd swum across Lake Menteith, Magda had been fleeing for her life. She'd known only the burning of her lungs as she fought to stay as long as possible underwater. Experienced only terror when she'd instinctively opened her eyes in the water to see blackness all around, imagining the lake a thing of evil capable of taking her as it had her brother. She'd pulled her arms and thrashed her legs, kicking and lurching beneath the surface, her efforts seemingly in vain in the lake's vast darkness.

When she'd fled Campbell that day, she hadn't felt the water cradle her softly as it did now. Much older memories came to her at once, like some primal knowing, as she embraced again the sensuous feeling of floating weightless, naked, every part of her caressed by the water.

James held her from behind. His arm snaked slowly around her chest to take her breast in his hand, to chafe her hard nipple between his knuckles. He kissed and bit slowly, his tongue warm on the chilled, exposed column of her neck, the damp of his mouth mingling with the beads of water that clung to her.

James pressed hard against her back, and then slipped between her legs, skin dragging on skin, until he slid into her, the sudden slickness pulling him deep.

The water swayed with them, following the slow rock of their bodies, and thick waves slapped gently against their shoulders.

Though the water was shallow, James was the only one who could touch the bottom, and Magda floated weightless, her toes ever so slightly brushing the velvety soft mud of the lake bottom. She wondered at discovering this joy, at how rich a gift to delight once again in water, and for a moment she felt the hot ache of unshed tears.

Magda experienced the familiar coiling in her belly, but it was somehow different this time. This time she found comfort as much as pleasure, and as she tensed and released, her body rippled around James just as the waves undulated and whorled outward across the water.

Chapter 26

The seasons didn't change with a bluster. Rather, winter crept over the Highlands, displacing autumn, slowly bleeding sun and color from the land around them.

James and his men had spent September intoxicated with their triumphs. They'd marched from the decisive battle at Tippermuir back to Aberdeen, securing another significant—not to mention emotionally charged—victory. They'd been joined by the Earl of Airlie's second son, Thomas, who'd wanted to avenge the burning of his family's home at the hands of the Campbell. Despite reinforcements, the Royalists remained a scant force: merely fifteen hundred men and fifty horses compared to Campbell's massive cavalry.

Numbers hadn't mattered to James, though, when a Covenanter soldier shot down a Royalist drummer boy before they'd even reached the field. Infuriated, he'd used the Covenanter overconfidence against them, splitting horse from infantry, to win the battle tidily.

But this time, James chose to make an example of Aberdeen at battle's end. Though he'd ordered no bloodshed, he allowed his soldiers to pillage the town, raiding cattle and stealing stores of corn and oats.

From there, MacColla, Rollo, and Sibbald had left to find new recruits while James restocked, melting candlesticks, thimbles, even metal bands from wine casks, in order to make as many bullets as possible. Bullets that he'd turned around and shot at Campbell's primary seat at Inveraray Castle, in a brief interlude on their way to Tor Castle.

By the time they reached Lochaber and Cameron country, the December air had the bite of winter and snow dusted the mountains on the horizon. Despite his threats of subsisting solely on dried oats, James had taken good care of Magda on the road, and they'd lived well off the land, supplementing their meager stores with fresh game and berries. He'd also introduced her to more exotic fare, like arctic bramble and sorrel that, though sour, tasted delicious mixed with what eggs they could occasionally scare up.

Sitting by the blazing hearth, Magda was nonetheless pleased to be back under a warm roof, thrilled to rest for a while at the Cameron's Tor Castle, and embracing oatmeal porridge with renewed zeal.

"I'll leave after Hogmanay," James said, and Magda at once pushed his words from her mind. Life on the road had been hard, and it finally became clear that they'd both be safest if she took shelter with the Camerons. But until the day came when they had to part, she was determined to enjoy the peaceful respite.

"That will give us time to regroup," James continued. "Gather what supplies we can carry. I need to scour the countryside for clothes enough to outfit my men for snow."

He and the young Cameron laird Ewen sat near her by the fire. They'd all but ignored Magda, engrossed as they were in talk of battle, and she had been more than content simply staring at the flames, savoring the feel of a chair, rather than a horse, beneath her.

They would have Christmas together, and New Year's. But Covenanter forces were gathering, and James predicted that soon both the weather and the battles would become dangerously bitter.

"Your woman is a welcome guest in my home."

"And I thank you for that, Lochiel," James told Ewen, using the laird's term of address. "I know not how long we'll be away. We'll be constantly on the move now."

"In return, my desire is to join you in your fight with the Campbell."

"I'd pinned my faith on your support," James replied. "But it's not just the Campbell I battle. I go to fight for Scotland." He leaned forward, intent. "For peace, and for the freedom of her oppressed and enthralled subjects."

"Aye," Ewen growled at James's ornate words. "But will there be a battle?"

"But of course, Cameron." James laughed, nodding at the young man's passion.

At the sound of the laird's intensity, Magda turned to look at him. Though she estimated Ewen was still in his late teens, he was large, with strong hands that she imagined he'd grow into nicely someday soon. He raked a hand through the black hair hanging loose to his shoulders, and Magda thought he'd likely develop into a very attractive man.

Searching for a resemblance, Magda looked over to Ewen's uncle, who sat by the light of the window playing chess with a blond, bookish young man whom they'd referred to as the laird's foster brother. Neither bore a likeness to Ewen.

She had, however, noted a similar swagger when comparing Ewen and his grandfather. It seemed the lairdship was in transition to the younger man, and she'd gathered that his grandfather, though a vigorous old man, had been feeling his years of late, and at the moment had retired for an afternoon rest.

"I've many men who'd go happily to the fight," Ewen said. "Some number of swords, and pikemen plenty."

"Campbell marches east, eager to take vengeance for the damage done to his holdings at Inveraray." A smile flickered across James's face, remembering, and then he was somber once again. "I have word that a massive Covenanter force has gathered at Inverness. We've chosen mobility over firepower, and that is what will enable us to intercept Campbell before he reaches the rest of his forces."

Magda shivered at his words. She had tried not to listen, but couldn't avoid it. She tried to deny it, to force the topic from her mind, but it was impossible to silence the fear, a constant drumbeat hammering in her core.

❁

Though Christmas in the Highlands was a much more somber occasion than what she was used to, Magda had been moved by the simplicity of the Cameron family's celebration and was feeling contemplative when they gathered round the hearth after supper.

She was feeling pleasantly muzzy and full from a large supper and many cups of wassail, a mulled ale drink that filled the great room with the sharp scent of apples and spices. She'd stuffed herself on mincemeat pies and oat bread, followed by a hearty slice from the black bun, a dessert rich with fruit, nuts, and a healthy dose of whisky. She'd been skeptical, wondering just what it was about holidays and fruitcakes, but the black bun was delicious, despite its ominously dark appearance.

As in many Highland homes that night, candles had been lit in every window to mark the way for travelers, and tall shadows danced along the rough-hewn stone of the castle walls.

"I imagine fine courtiers like yourself don't bother with such nonsense as the *Cailleach* log."

Magda scowled. It was that girl Mairi, trying once again to ingratiate herself to James. She was lovely and petite, with a curtain of dark hair hanging smooth down her back, and Magda thought she'd throttle her if she caught the girl flirting with James one more time. She'd been told Mairi was Ewen's intended, though she didn't see any signs to support that. The laird, though gracious to all, seemed to have a mind only for the upcoming battle.

"Quite the contrary," James said, his tone icily polite in a way that both surprised and reassured Magda. He was urbane and politic when he needed to be, and she imagined James would be as magnificent a sight working the court in Edinburgh as he was in the woods with broadsword and tartan.

"Graham family holdings may not be of the Highlands, but neither are they Lowland. Rather, they lie just between, a wedge that runs from the Montrose seaport, to Stirling, to the Ochill Hills. A courtier I may be, but I am a Scotsman through and through. Edinburgh may be Scotland's spine, but the Highlands are her soul, and it's those traditions I value above all."

Ewen gave a quick nod in assent, and turned to Magda. "Do you ken the *Cailleach* log, lass?" His deep voice was kind, and she thought how Mairi didn't seem to deserve him, no matter how gorgeous she was.

"I . . . no . . ." Magda hedged, and the studious-seeming teen she'd heard referred to as Robert chimed in.

"It's a Highland tradition, dating possibly from pagan times. A face is carved into the *Cailleach* and then burned." He used his finger to outline the crude features of an old woman etched in the wood. "It is the burning of the Spirit of Winter. As the *Cailleach* log burns to ash, so too does the bad luck and enmity of the past year."

Magda wondered at this strange boy. He seemed as different as night and day from the laird, and yet they couldn't have been separated by more than a few years.

James surreptitiously took her hand, lacing his fingers through hers, and his smile warmed her more than any hearth fire could.

"Aye," Ewen chimed in, "they claim she lives at the top of Ben Nevis itself. So old is the *Cailleach*, her plaid is faded to white. And at the start of each winter she scrubs this great plaid of hers, and so too is Scotland washed white for the season."

"You best not have burnt the log without me."

Everyone had been listening in rapt silence, and Magda gave a start at the sound of the old man's voice booming through the room.

Ewen's grandfather walked in, gait and grimace betraying the stiffness of his limbs. Ewen rose from his seat by the fire to offer it to his elder. "We'd not dare," he said, and took the log from Robert to place on the fire. While most watched the flames lick and snap at the dry wood, Magda caught a furtive look shared between Mairi and Ewen's grandfather that turned her stomach. Mairi's chin tucked low, her mouth a teasing pout and the devil in her eyes. The old man's tongue flicked out to wet the thin skin of his wrinkled lips. Surely, Magda thought, she didn't just see what she thought she saw.

James's whisper in her ear interrupted her thoughts. "The little chit thinks to butter her bread on both sides, I see."

Amused, Magda bit her cheek to school her face into an impassive mask, all the while thinking that if she could kiss James full on the mouth without causing a scandal she would.

❦

"But why aren't you . . . merrier?" Magda asked James as they lay in bed. He looked at her quizzically, so she elaborated. "Well, it's a happy holiday after all, right? I mean, in modern times, we say

'Merry Christmas' to celebrate, and we exchange presents."

"The good cheer begins come Hogmanay," James said. "The days before New Year's, aye?" he added, seeing her confusion. "You think you've a full belly now. You'll have black buns and sun cakes and mincemeats aplenty come New Year's. I imagine you'll see Ewen's clansmen become quite boisterous, the lot of them.

"And"—he grabbed Magda and pinned her beneath him—"as for presents, who's to say you don't have a gift, hen?"

"A . . . really?" Her expression quickly crumpled, and she said, "But I have nothing for you, James."

"Are you in my bed?"

Magda nodded.

"Have you a stitch of clothing on you?"

Smiling, she shook her head slowly.

"Then you have given me my gift. And, before you fash yourself"—James put his hand to her mouth to stop her interruption—"'tis nothing I bought, aye? I've not exactly had the opportunity to take in the shops of the Royal Mile, eh?"

"Not exactly, no."

"So then." He leaned over to scoop his sporran from off the floor at their bedside. He pulled out a small sheet of paper folded in a neat square.

"What's this?"

He raised his brows in answer, indicating that she should see for herself.

It was a poem, a handful of stanzas long, written in an elaborate, sloping script. It took her a moment to get the hang of the old-fashioned handwriting, but by the end, she was reading fluidly, gripping James's hand in hers.

"I'd leave you with a token." He gently guided her chin until his eyes met hers. "I need you to know, Magda. To know how I love you. But to know too how I'm driven to what I'm about to do."

"But . . ." Tears flowed hot down her cheeks as she remembered the words she'd heard what felt like a lifetime ago. *Captured and hanged.*

"Hush." He stroked her brow, thumbing the tears from her face. "You and my country may both be twined in my heart, but it's your love that girds me in my fight. And I *will* return to you."

Magda slept fitfully that night, knowing that she'd wake and be one day closer to their parting. His last stanza had run her through, filling her with love and fear in equal parts.

I'll make thee glorious by my pen
And famous by my sword:
I'll serve thee in such noble ways
Was never heard before;
I'll crown and deck thee all with bays,
And love thee evermore.

Chapter 27

The wooden bed frame scudded across the floor as Campbell heaved his body over the wench. She'd gasped at the weight of him—he was a stately man—but she'd deserved to feel his might, the little harlot.

Just as the Marquis of Montrose would feel his might. He'd had a run of luck with his mad band of Highlanders and Irishmen, but now five hundred Covenanters camped at Inverness, blocking the road north like a cork stopping a bottle. Graham's Royalists were last seen in Lochaber, and there they would die.

Campbell would march, trapping the Royalists between his two Covenanter forces. Graham would be hemmed in like an animal, with the mountains blocking him from behind, their snow-covered peaks robbing him of any hope of escape.

Craning his head to take a bite of the wench's neck, he plowed harder. He would crush Graham against his larger force as a ram battered a gate. Like that gate, Graham's Royalists would splinter into a thousand pieces.

The woman whimpered beneath him, and Campbell heaved up to glare at her. Her pitifully small breasts bobbed like peaches as he thrust into her. And she didn't even have the courage to meet his gaze. He had a lesson to teach, though. Since Graham and his men had dogged him like a plague of bloody midges, he'd had to reassert his authority at Inveraray. He'd caught this trollop with a smirk on her face, but his biting mouth had quickly wiped it away. One more go-round and she'd think twice before smirking at his back ever again. He doubted his body could peak again so soon, but strumpets like this one didn't know the difference.

He would show her, and he would show them all. This time he wouldn't send some trembling lordling into battle, nor would he send General Leslie. Campbell made it his particular purpose to crush those unwilling to bow to him. He'd start with this wench, but he'd end it with James Graham.

Chapter 28

She recognized it immediately. Magda's heart thudded in her chest as she wriggled her way behind an oversized armchair to get a closer look at the painting. It had been a part of Walter's anonymous bequeathal. They'd labeled it merely "Nature Painting," a minor, almost crude, work by an unknown artist. Though it hadn't been one of the works she'd restored, there was no way she could've missed it. It wasn't every day you came across a seventeenth-century painting, over five feet long, featuring three dogs attacking a bear.

She'd been trying to lay low in the Cameron household, taking breakfast in her room, retiring early at night, and had avoided the other women as best she could. Most of them spent their days in the great room, gossiping and doing needlework, and Magda was terrified they'd grill her at the first opportunity—about James, about where she came from, about what must've seemed like a strange accent and strange ways.

James had deflected such scrutiny as best he could, telling them a story about Magda's religious father, various missionary expeditions, and vague references to family in Ireland. She had to laugh at his ingenuity, spinning the name Deacon as he'd done. Even her father would've been genuinely amused at that one. Skip Deacon was philanthropic, yes. But religious? Not so much.

She felt a pang at the memory of her father. Her parents no longer existed. They were centuries away from being born. Yet somewhere out there she did have ancestors who were very much alive, growing their families, making their livings. It was an eerie thought. Perhaps they had in fact been religious people. She knew that many surnames originated in such a way, people like millers and masons taking the names of their jobs.

She dampened the memories of her parents and thought again of James. The one for whom she'd abandoned her blood family. The person she longed to see more than any other. The Camerons had been more than hospitable to her, but the polite pleasantries felt empty when the only thing on her mind was James's safety. The smiling nods and wishes good-day all seemed so inane when what echoed over and over in her head like a morbid mantra was Walter's *"Captured, imprisoned, and hanged in Edinburgh."*

Eager for something, anything, to occupy her mind, she'd decided to explore the castle. Her "Nature Painting" was hanging in the library, a room that was its own phenomenon. Dark-paneled wood, a fireplace large enough to stand in, and a number of books that would be impressive for a modern collector, to say nothing of an old Highland laird.

The thrill of recognition began to subside as she insisted to her herself that, though stumbling into this painting was mind-blowing and against all odds, it was nonetheless an acceptable circumstance. Just a piece of art, likely with no hocus-pocus or time-traveling portal. Still, she kept her hands fisted firmly at her side, not about to touch any more strange artworks.

Though the dark colors and masculine theme were well suited to hang in a library, the painting really was quite rudimentary. The bear's and dogs' lips peeled back to reveal perfect white fangs, and none of the animals seemed to bear weight. They simply floated on the canvas like two-dimensional cutouts.

"What a pleasant surprise, Lady Magdalen."

"Oh!" Magda jumped, slamming her hip into the side of the chair just behind her. "Ow!"

"Oh dear," Robert said. The boy looked genuinely stricken. He was one of the very few people she'd encountered in the castle who didn't bustle around like he owned the place. "My apologies."

"Please don't worry." She sidled out from behind the chair. "You startled me. And, please, just Magda is fine." "Lady Magdalen" made her feel like some sort of religious figure.

"Thank you then, *Magda*." He smiled, and she thought how . . . *pretty* . . . his features were. Lithe limbs, shining yellow blond curls, and impeccable grooming set him apart from the average seventeenth-century man in her acquaintance. Granted, many of those men had been soldiers on the move, so she had to allow them some leeway.

"Pray tell, what is your peculiar accent?" His head canted to the side, questioning, and Magda's stomach knotted.

"My . . . accent?" James hadn't explicitly forbidden Magda from disclosing her true origins, nor did she have any reason to doubt the Camerons, who'd seemed nothing but loyal and trustworthy where he was concerned. Although the story James had woven about her family seemed to explain away things like her accent and bearing, Magda still felt as if she stood out like some greatly displaced and alien creature. James was the only one she truly felt she could trust. She feared that the others—though they had seemed kind—might just put her to that burning stake James had so cavalierly mentioned when she'd first arrived.

"Aye, I can't place it."

Robert leaned in, and she instinctively stepped back, bumping once again into the chair. If she didn't know better, she'd think he was about to sniff her, like she was some hitherto undiscovered species of plant. His eyes swept over her and lingered overlong on her teeth. Pursing her lips shut, she ducked around him to the middle of the room, making as if to study the books.

The corners of his lips curving up slightly, Robert added, "I suppose it must be from all that travel."

"Yes," Magda said, cursing the blush she felt infuse her cheeks. "I suppose it must be."

He was quiet for a moment. "That is some painting, aye?" Having abandoned his original question, Robert walked over to rest his elbow on the chair. "Do you know much about art?"

"Yes. I mean, no." She struggled with her reply, thinking that a missionary's daughter probably wouldn't have much experience with art. "I mean, I just know what I like."

"And you like this one?"

She simply nodded, wary of where this was going.

"Did you know bears are actually related to the dog family? Family Ursidae."

"Um, no, actually, I didn't know that." They stood silently, studying it. "Really?" she asked suddenly, incredulous.

"Aye, really." Leaning in closer, he tilted his chin as if to look down along his nose, and Magda wondered if he was nearsighted.

"It's always struck me as a rather simple piece," he said. "Do you see that dog's tail? It's longer than the piteous bear's arm."

A clipped laugh escaped her. She nodded, warming to this peculiar young man and his awkward candor. "Or that thing." She pointed to a dark brown form snaking along the ground behind the bear. "Is that supposed to be a bear tail?"

"Or something else entirely?" he asked, awe in his voice.

Magda had to clap her hand over her mouth to silence a very unladylike bark of laughter.

"I imagine your father has done quite a lot of missionary work in the British colonies, in the Americas?"

Magda was thrown off by the abrupt, and dangerous, return to the original topic.

"Yes, some." Panic flushed her anew, and she wondered frantically at a possible escape strategy.

Just as she was about to stride purposefully over to pull a book from the shelves, he asked, "The southern colonies or northeastern?" Robert spoke slowly, as if her answer would hold great import.

She hesitated, then said, "Northeastern mostly."

"Aye." A strange smile bloomed on his face, and he appraised her with eyes that seemed to hold a secret. "I'd guessed the northeastern colonies."

Chapter 29

"They've got him," Donald said. The old man stood, hand on the hilt of his sword as if poised at that very moment for vengeance. Streaks of muddied ice soiled his trews, and a thick layer of frost weighed down his bonnet, making the wool hang heavily on his head. "They've got the Lochiel."

James had sent the Cameron laird and his uncle ahead to scout Campbell's exact position, while he'd continued to march his Royalists through the snow-choked Grampian range toward their point of attack. Last they'd heard, Campbell had been on the move, bringing additional forces from the west, thinking to trap James between Campbell's Covenanters and the five thousand more that awaited him in Inverness.

But Campbell hadn't wagered on Highland ferocity. Rather than be cowed by the icy conditions around them, James and his men had been invigorated. Jagged mountains stretched vast and desolate around them. White snow dusted the high passes and seemed to melt directly into the white clouds that dotted the clear blue sky overhead.

James led his men into the foothills, and it was as if they were a single magnificent, wild force sweeping up effortlessly to elude some cruder and more banal predator below. Then they climbed higher still, along the snowy passes, cutting and kicking steps into the mountain for their ascent.

"The Campbell has come to rest, and the bastard cools his heels close to Cameron lands. The Lochiel, och"—Donald pulled the bonnet from his head and scrubbed his face with his hand—"Campbell's reinforcements camp at Inverlochy, and I'd wager there are no less than three thousand of them."

Colonel Sibbald had approached and heard the last of Donald's report. "Close to Tor Castle?" he asked, rubbing his hip where he'd been wounded near two decades past. The lead shot was never removed, and James knew it troubled the old colonel when the weather was cold. The man seemed to be having a particularly tough time of it now, and James had smelled whisky on his breath more often than usual. He didn't want to say anything to him—Sibbald had been leading military campaigns when James was still in knee breeches—but his misgivings grew as battle neared, and he thought the man's life to be more valuable than his dignity.

"Aye," Donald replied, "they edge onto Clan Cameron's very lap, and it didn't please young Ewen overmuch."

"I imagine not," James said. He forced thoughts of Magda from his mind. She stayed at Tor with the Camerons, but he couldn't think of that now. Anxiety over her safety would do him no good. Retaining his focus would be the best and only way to protect her.

Shaking his head, Ewen's uncle slapped his bonnet against his thigh, releasing a small cascade of snow and ice. "The lad got it into his head to cut a few Campbell throats on our way out, and I think he got himself a few too." Pride flickered in Donald's eyes. "And then I spied it, a wee tussle ending with Lochiel pulled from one of the larger tents, the lad struggling like a roped bull, a pistol at his head and two Covenanter swine at his side." Donald smiled. "If I know my nephew, I'd say he went for the throat of the Campbell himself. Though that cur would've had guards posted."

James held Donald's gaze. "I'll not abandon Ewen." He looked away to the ragged peaks of frozen rock stretching far into the distance. "Inverlochy, eh?" And a shiver ran through him, followed quickly by a buzz of excitement, the lust for battle deep, and startling.

"We'll turn at once, of course. Double back on our position. Head over the Devil's Staircase, across the high passes to the north side of Ben Nevis, then we're on down to Inverlochy."

Donald barked a startled laugh, then stared in silence as he realized that James was serious. "But lad, we've just passed Glencoe. Inverlochy is ten leagues from here. It will take days for so many men to travel so far."

"So, we'll just have to make haste, aye?" James announced. He would hurtle his fifteen hundred men like an avalanche down the mountain to crush Campbell from the rear.

He quickly rallied the men as word carried down the line of their new destination. The Highlanders took the change of plans in stride. They merely regrouped and took a final meal before the last push, using the opportunity to share in the few brace of black grouse and snow hare that some MacDonald clansmen had hunted, as if they hadn't been truly hungry before the suggestion of it. They'd looked on in amazement, though, watching their marquis pounding dried oats into the snow to scoop them up on his *sgian dubh* for one last meal of frozen porridge.

❁

The Royalists jogged through the day and night. All rational thought had long been expunged from James's mind, leaving in its wake only the instinctive bobbing and leaping over the uneven terrain, and the rhythmic pumping of his legs, keeping time with the steady in and out of air in his lungs. Elusive wisps of white smoke danced in the bitter air, the breath of over a thousand men racing across the mountains.

A MacDonald clansmen guided them. When MacColla had first broached it with James, telling of an unlikely man who knew the lay of the mountains like no other, he had been surprised and amused. What better army than his own, after all, to be led to battle by a poet? Iain Lom MacDonald was a bard of the MacDonalds of Keppoch, and his artistic nature had apparently led him to many a day spent in those very mountains, contemplating the jagged sweep of the land and the vast bowl of the Highland sky.

James sensed a slight alteration to his internal rhythm, and his mind coming back to him, he realized that the men ahead paused slightly before canting to the right and resuming their pace.

As he approached he saw Iain lying in the snow, the man's face turned to the dawn sky as if to will the sun's wan light down to warm him.

"Iain, man." James dropped beside him, the trampled snow crunching beneath his knees. "Are you hurt?" He patted at the man's ankles and feet. "Cold then, is it?" James blew heat on his hands, then cracked away some of the ice that had frozen his thick beard. "Och, and to think they call you 'Bald Iain.' You with hair enough for a shearing."

Slowly the russet of his beard showed through, and James paused, renegade thoughts of Magda pushing to the front of his mind. Inexplicably, he thought of her dead brother, wondering if he'd had the same red hair as this man before him. And he wondered too if this stranger, who'd forfeited his life to rally under James, was someone's brother. Or husband.

"Leave me b-b-be," Iain whispered. He was already covered with a fine dusting of snow, and his lean body chattered, exaggerating the stutter he was known for. He gestured north before dropping his head back to the ground. "I c-can go no f-further. You've but to f-follow the northern slopes. The Camerons will see the way. Climb the peak at Meall-an-t'Suidhe. There y-you'll perch like a gold eagle high above Inverlochy to stalk your prey."

"You'll not get poetic with me, lad." James took the man's hands and chafed them between his. "Now up with you. Before the blood freezes in your veins."

"We've still s-some distance to go," Iain said. "Just let me be."

"I'll not." James opened his coat and pulled out a small leather flask that had been kept warm at his side beneath layers of clothing. "We need our bard among us. Who else to sing our praises after the battle, aye?"

Iain's eyes opened wide, his face frozen in shock. James looked at the container he held, its oblong shape much resembling a powder flask, and he laughed. "Don't worry lad, I'm not going to shoot you. 'Tis whisky I administer, not gunpowder."

He unscrewed the brass stopper and tipped it to Iain's mouth. "Though distillers are known to mix their whisky with gunpowder and set it alight. If the potion explodes they know they've made their drink too strong."

Iain turned his head to the side, sputtering a cough.

"Aye, that's the way," James said. "*Uisge*, the water of life, to warm a man through." He took a sip and shut his eyes to savor it. "Amber liquid, like a drink from the rising sun." He tucked the flask back under his vests, quickly rebuttoning his overcoat. "And you'd thought yourself the only poet among us." He pulled Iain up to sitting.

"You'll need something to absorb the drink, or it'll go straight to your blood." James rifled through his sporran and retrieved a small square containing the last of his dried oats. "I want to warm you, not get you in your cups."

"B-but what of you?"

"I've had my fill. Take it," he said, wrapping Iain's hand around the cloth packet. "I've choked down my last drammock for a time. Any more oats and I'll grow a tail like a horse."

Iain hesitated, but James insisted. "No, we'll sup well tomorrow. The Camerons will feed us all"—James laughed—"whether the Lochiel likes it or no."

"But I heard the Cameron laird was captured."

"A momentary obstacle." He grabbed Iain's free hand and hauled him to his feet. "Now off with us, lad. You're the one who'll guide us to our triumph."

Iain seem as buoyed by the newfound hope as by the shared sustenance. James broke into a slow jog, looking behind him to make sure the bard kept up. "Make haste, lad. With the MacColla cutting our trail, I fear we'll all end up in Ireland."

❋

They finally arrived after dark on the night of February first. His men were mostly quiet now, ordered to rest a few hours until their dawn attack.

James had made his decision. He would go ahead of the others. To strike Campbell's camp before rescuing Ewen would be signing the young laird's death warrant. James himself would go alone, before dawn, and retrieve the Cameron.

He kicked at the ice, studying the dead stumps rotted beneath. It appeared that a small stand of pines had once braved the high altitude, their gnarled roots still clinging tenaciously to the hostile mountainside. James looked around, studying his position. Although the Highlanders claimed to enjoy using the snow as a pillow, James didn't look askance at warming himself by a small fire. Despite the freezing weather, the run had soaked his shirt through with sweat, and he felt the chill creeping into his muscles. They were high enough above Inverlochy that the smoke wouldn't betray their location, and he'd do himself the small service of at least melting the ice that had hardened the wool of his trews into a frozen crust.

Will Rollo hadn't been physically able to march into the mountains, and James was in mind of him now. His friend's severity always had the ironic effect of putting James into good spirits. But Rollo had been a mix of sadness, regret, envy, and anger at not going into battle with men who'd become like his brothers. Rollo had felt the loss of that fellowship keenly, and he had James's sympathy because of it.

MacColla, with his boisterous brand of courage and hearty goodwill, had been great solace to him, though. After weeks on the road, MacColla's black beard had grown full, and with his height and broad shoulders, he seemed like some great, burly bear marching through the snow. It was MacColla who'd lead the charge that day, Irishmen, Camerons, MacDonalds, Stewarts, MacLeans, and more at his back. James hoped to join them all, Ewen Cameron at his side, by the time the battle was under way.

James kicked at the ice again and saw the fuel he needed. He had fashioned a hearth easily enough by loosely arranging stones atop the snow, and collected dead branches enough for kindling. Giving the fire its heart, however, was a problem. Pulling his *sgian dubh* from the cuff of his boot, James scraped into the hardened stump and the smell of pine sap filled his senses; the frozen gold shone dully in the moonlight, thick enough to keep a small fire burning through the night.

He mourned the loss of Magda's wee red fire starter she called a lighter. It had simply died one day, and she'd insisted there was to be no reviving it.

Hands chapped and frozen, he set to work lighting the fire. He'd had to be creative with tinder, but some woolen lint from the waistband of his trews worked nicely. Pulling a small snuffbox from his sporran, he retrieved a piece of char cloth, one of many squares of scorched black silk that had proven miraculously flammable.

He withdrew his flint from his sporran. The stone glimmered blue black as if it were a piece of the night sky made whole, and James took care not to cut his numbed fingers on its sharp edges. A few strikes of his blade and sparks showered onto the char cloth, which set to glowing and lit the tinder at once. Blowing steady encouragement on the tiny flame, James quickly added small scraps of kindling, and then stacked a careful pyramid of wood on top. He dropped in the slivers of pine sap and a burst of black smoke spewed out. James squatted, warming his hands over a fire set to last for hours.

"That's a bonny wee blaze you have there."

James nodded a greeting and shuffled over, making room for MacColla by the fire.

"You're off for the Cameron then."

"Aye, I'd not leave such a good man to the dogs."

"If he's still alive."

"Aye, if he's still alive." James nodded grimly. "Ewen is a canny one though, and strong. I'm wagering he lives still. The Campbell would think to use him to some end." They sat in silence, letting that last thought hang.

"I'd have you lead the men."

"And who else?" MacColla's white smile glowed eerily, his dark features otherwise imperceptible in the night. "'Tis a chancy thing you do, James. Not many would stroll into the Campbell's lair to retrieve a stripling laird."

"Which is why I'll let none see me," James replied, his cavalier tone belying the danger of his task.

"And, James?"

"Aye?"

"I'd thank you." Before he could interrupt, MacColla continued, "Never before have I seen so many men banded together. Different men. Men of differing religions. Men of warring clans. We all fight for different things. You fight for the king. My fight is against the Campbell. Others fight for the Highlands. But it's only you, James, a man not born to the Highlands, who has been able to unite all Highlanders."

"Not *all* the Highlanders." James's protest was lighthearted.

"Och, the ones that matter, aye?" Laughing, MacColla slapped him hard on the back, and James looked on his friend with affection.

He was humbled by the sincerity of MacColla's words. And by the responsibility. "I thank you."

"Godspeed, Graham." MacColla nodded thoughtfully, knowing

the danger they both faced. The Royalists were hungry, exhausted, cold, and outnumbered more than two to one.

"Aye, good man." James clasped MacColla's shoulder and gave a curt bob of his head. "Godspeed."

❁

Making a stealthy approach when traveling alone wasn't a challenge. He'd had to half run, half slide down the scree of the lower foothills, but the thin blanket of snow actually muted James's descent. He sent silent good wishes up the mountain to MacColla. Campbell's encampment was vast, its thousands of men well fed and well rested. The Royalists, however, enjoyed but a few hours' rest after their thirty-six-hour trek across the mountains, fueled by melted snow and what small provisions they carried on their persons.

He spotted what was clearly the Campbell's tent, and knew at once what had drawn Ewen to such an audacious attack. It was larger than the others, and it lay in the midst of the encampment, like a queen bee in her hive. It was Campbell's own cowardice, James thought, to safeguard himself so.

Dark shadows flickered along its walls, which glowed amber from the oil lamps burning within. James easily made his way among the sea of tents, taking cover in a swath of black shadow outside Campbell's shelter. Somebody was speaking, and he leaned in closer to make sense of the words.

"I know Graham is not a ghost who simply disappeared into the mist. You will tell me where he and his Royalist pigs have spirited off to."

James heard a sharp crack, followed by the scuffling of feet. There was a grunt—he thought it might be the Campbell—then a series of dull, wet-sounding smacks.

"You'll not test me, Cameron." Campbell sounded winded. "I'll beat you like the hound you claim to be." Another crack. "Now you'll tell me where they make their attack."

There was a shuffling, then the sound of heavy breathing. "I'll wipe that smile from your face," Campbell snarled, and James heard the sound of steel on stone.

"I like my blade sharp, the better to cut your—"

It was all James needed to hear. He regretted the absence of a plan, but thought the Cameron could use his assistance just then.

His sword was in his hand. A lifetime of practice lightened the steel, making it an extension of his arm. His grasp was firm and the leather grip familiar in his palm as his fingers nestled in the soft, quilted maroon cloth that lined the basket. Basket hilts bearing elaborate filigree work were becoming the fashion, but James had chosen simplicity instead, a thick steel lattice sturdy enough to protect his hand from his opponent's blade.

The deadly sharp metal cut easily through the tent with a mere sigh of fabric to betray it. James leapt in, simply appearing at Campbell's side. The man had a small dagger to Ewen's ear, and blood bloomed like a rose tucked there, with a thick rope of crimson already oozing down his neck. His black hair was slicked with sweat. The young laird beamed at James, the wide smile unsettling on his bloodied and bruised face.

Campbell swung around at once, striking broadly at James, blade swishing close to his torso.

"I think not, Campbell." James bounded backward. "Though that's some bonny footwork. Impressive for a man of your . . . *stature.*"

James circled his enemy. "I will just . . . relieve you of this," he finished quickly, swatting the knife from Campbell's hand with his broadsword.

"Funny," James said as he kicked the blade across the ground. "I'd have taken you for more of a garrote man." He moved quickly to Ewen's side. "Something more subtle than cutlery. Now I shall just avail myself of my friend here—"

Despite his heft, the Campbell managed to dart to the edge of the tent, pulling a pistol from atop his cot. Tearing open a paper cartridge of powder with his teeth, he began to load his gun.

As Ewen struggled to free his hands from their ties behind his back, James was there in an instant, severing his bonds with a single flick of his blade, as though the laird had been bound by mere ribbon.

A loud click reverberated through the tent. Campbell had cocked his pistol. James sprung across the room, landing the point of his sword on the quivering flesh of Campbell's neck, just as he'd taken aim at James's chest. The moment hung in time as they stood, poised to kill, caught in a stalemate.

The Cameron was a blur of red and green plaid, slamming into Campbell from the side. The men hit the ground hard, Campbell emitting a clipped grunt, his pistol discharging with a deafening bang.

Campbell's guard pushed his way into the tent. "What—?"

"Come, Lochiel." James pulled Ewen to standing. "We've no time now."

Before the guard could act, the two men disappeared through the hole James had made in the tent.

Dawn was beginning to lighten the sky to a slate gray, and the morning air was crisp, with the clean smell of snow to it. The sounds of Campbell's men rousing from sleep followed them as James and Ewen snaked their way around tents, racing from the Covenanter encampment.

There were shouts at their backs now. Spying a large rise, James dashed around the base to the left and then shot uphill. The trail was littered with large rocks, and while Ewen plowed a straight line, muscular legs pumping up and over rocks, James raced ahead, vaulting an uneven path up, springing from rock to rock as he crested the rise. He fell to kneel behind a gray and white mottled boulder. Straining, he could hear his Royalist troops on their descent from a brae not two hundred yards away.

Ewen appeared, collapsing beside him, and both men laughed quietly.

"We wait but a moment," James said, "then will join MacColla as the river meets the sea."

"Aye, a wave to crash over Campbell's wee picnic."

"You're bleeding, lad." James turned Ewen's head hard to the side to study his wound.

"Och, just a scratch." Ewen flinched back. "Though I thank you for arriving when you did."

"The pleasure's mine, Cameron. You owe me an ear."

James cocked his head to listen to the approaching fighters. "The sea is upon us." Their eyes met in broad smiles. "And now we shall exact our revenge."

"Aye, Graham. We shall indeed."

Chapter 30

She felt trapped, anxious to get out of there. The Cameron library, though amazing, only went so far to break up the monotony of Magda's daily life at the castle. The first weeks had been a wondrous peek back in time. Robert had been a mixture of politely unobtrusive and oddly amusing as he'd shared history and lore about Scotland and the various clans. But she couldn't monopolize him all day, and Magda found she wasn't really expected to do anything other than appear for meals. Since she was interested in neither gossip nor needlework, she thought she'd go crazy from boredom.

Magda traced her fingers along stacks of yellowed manuscripts and the leather spines of books, looking in vain for something that would be a quick, fun read. Somehow *Caesar's Commentaries* and Sir Walter Raleigh's *History of the World* didn't do it for her, despite the fact that James had told her they were among his favorites. She picked up Quintus Curtius's *History of Alexander the Great*, but wasn't very optimistic.

"Pardon?" a voice said at her back.

She startled, and turned to see the maid Kat standing there. She couldn't have been much older than Magda, yet hard work was already ravaging her, clear to see in her red, cracked hands and the number of wiry white strands that already marbled her tightly wound bun.

"My apologies, mum." Looking suddenly stricken, Kat bobbed a quick curtsy, and the cups on her tray clinked precariously.

"Oh, not at all." Magda rushed to push aside books, clearing a space for the tea. "This looks lovely."

And it did. The tray held a number of delicate pieces of china and silver. Cups and saucers, a small pitcher of milk, miniature spoons. Magda had her eye on a plate of shortbread sprinkled with thick granules of sugar, a sight which more than made up for the beige skin she spied floating atop the milk. The picture was completed by the yellow crocheted cozy that topped the teapot.

"Will that be all?" Clutching a handful of her dirt-colored linen skirt in one hand, Kat began to edge out the door.

"Yes." Magda pulled off the tea cozy, then paused and ventured, "I mean, no." Folding and smoothing it slowly onto the tray, she asked, "Are there any other rooms, do you think, that I might be interested in seeing?"

Kat looked at her doubtfully, and Magda rushed, "I mean, I saw that there was another wing to the house, but that seemed a little scary. Well, what I mean is, is there maybe a den or someplace else you know about?"

"Oh, aye." Kat nodded, finally understanding. "I don't know of dens, but the women all gather in the common room for needlework." She added brightly, "Would you like me to bring your tea there?"

"Oh, no," Magda said, deflated. "Never mind then."

"Ah." A slow smile brightened the woman's plump face. "I think I ken your mind, lass. And no, there's not much else than these rooms you've seen. But have you walked the lands around Tor?"

The idea was a revelation to Magda. It wasn't like she'd been a prisoner at the castle, yet somehow it hadn't occurred to her to go outside for a walk. A simple walk.

The look of wonder that crossed her face encouraged Kat to continue. "Aye, Lochaber can be quite bonny this time of the season. With snow on the mountains, there's a wee bite in the air, but naught too much for a brisk walk to take care of."

After borrowing thick, woolen stockings and an additional shawl, Magda was on her way. She'd walked for some time, crossing a glen hard with frost, then on to the low hills, picking her way along the red and yellowish green tangles of coarse grasses. At first the bitter air was a shock to her lungs and the cold stung her cheeks red, but once Magda started moving, the feel of her muscles working and her blood pumping invigorated her.

A wall of trees spiked along the horizon, and as she drew gradually closer she could hear a river rushing in the distance. Wary of getting lost, Magda had merely skirted the edge of the forest, until she spied an old drover's track. The path was thin, but etched deep through the trees, attesting to many years and hundreds of hooves being led from home to pasture and back again.

Hesitantly, she stepped onto the path, venturing in a few yards, and it took her breath away. To see the woods from a distance was one thing, but to be immersed in its hush was quite another. Scots pines were all around, and though their evergreen needles were similar to those of their American counterparts, they seemed somehow more ancient, with huge swells of roots that wrapped down and around each other to clutch at the ground like great claws, and gnarled trunks silver with frost and lichen. Birch trees studded the forest at random. Leafless in winter, they rose like skeletons from the loamy ground, bony limbs scratching among the pines like primeval ghosts of the forest.

Magda walked on, captivated, careful to stick to the trail. The rush of the river was louder now, and taking her eyes from the path, she looked around to see if she could pinpoint its origin. Her foot was stopped short and the air suddenly rushed around her as she fell to the ground, tripped by a root meandering across the path like a great snake. She felt the pain sear up her arm like fire crackling along a fuse, and with it came the immediate bone-deep knowledge that she'd done something very wrong to her right wrist.

Arm clenched at her side, Magda shifted to sit against one of the trees along the trail. She breathed slowly, and when the pain subsided into a dull throb, she opened her eyes again and studied her already swollen wrist. She'd instinctively broken her fall with her hand, which she clenched and unclenched now, as acute pain was gradually replaced by panic over whether or not it was broken and how, exactly, she would deal with that.

Gingerly, she touched the bones along her wrist and forearm and was relieved to find everything seemingly intact. The pain, though, was an angry pulse in her arm and hand, and she thought if a sprain was this painful, she couldn't imagine how excruciating a broken bone would be. Magda leaned back and, willing the throbbing to subside a little, simply focused on the feel of cold air on her face and the dappled sunlight as it shifted through the leaves overhead, brightening to orange then dark again on her closed eyes.

"Losh, but didn't I think a wolf got you, lass."

Magda's eyes shot open. Before her stood an old woman, grinning through the smoke of a pipe which she clenched between her teeth. Her wiry body seemed to stand straight and strong, despite the roughly carved walking stick that she gripped in her bony hand.

"Well, what's the keening about, then?" She hobbled closer, and Magda saw for the first time that the woman's eyes were a disconcerting shade of white blue. "I was sitting for my tea when I heard you howl like some injured beast." She tapped and nudged her stick against the thick root bisecting the path. "I'd half a mind thinking mayhap I'd find my dinner here, slain and waiting for me." She cackled, stabbing her cane into the ground for emphasis, pipe bobbing up and down in her mouth.

"Well, get up with you. The cold will seep into your bones and dull you to no good, and then a wolf *will* come for you. Come on," she said impatiently, whacking the stick against the tree above Magda's head. "Up now. No lass ever died from a staved wrist, aye?"

The old woman clearly expected Magda to follow her. Though relying heavily on her stick, she was already trekking off the trail and through the trees. Magda felt only a moment's worry before curiosity won out, and quickly caught up and stayed close behind the woman, eyeing the frizzy white braid hanging long at her back as they picked their way through the woods.

Her cottage was tucked in a small clearing surrounded by trees on all sides. Shadows fell long in the woods, and the house was cut neatly in two by sunlight and shade, one half luminous whitewash, the other a dingy gray. A chimney rose along the side, the old, roughly mortared stones charred deep black from soot at the top. A tendril of smoke spoke to a warming fire within.

Magda followed her into the shadowy interior, as much for the promise of that fire now as to satisfy her curiosity. There was only the single rectangular room, and the slimness of the lone wooden cot sidled in the corner attested to but one occupant. The clumps of dried herbs and flowers hanging along the far wall were as close as the cottage got to decoration. A tea service in a rosebud china pattern was jarringly out of place sitting atop a thick butcher-block table in the center of the room. Otherwise, the woman lived simply, with a few cast-iron pots hanging from hooks, a crude wooden trunk, and a rocker by the hearth.

She pulled a stool from under the table and sat, a little sigh of ecstasy escaping her. Her hands trembled as she wrapped them around the teapot to test its warmth. The old woman shot Magda a gratified smile and, pouring the tea, shooed her over to sit by the fire.

"Rest your legs awhile. You've given your body a good scare. Milk, lass?"

Magda shook her head. "Good!" the woman hooted. "I've none." Chuckling to herself, she brought Magda's tea and pulled the stool by the fire. "Och," she said, easing down, "I've had neither goat nor cow for years now."

"Please," Magda said, gesturing to the rocker, "you sit here."

"No, lass, no," she said dismissively. "My old rump knows this stool like I kent the cup of my husband's hand." She cackled again, fishing in her deep skirt pockets for her pipe.

"You'd be the one staying with the Camerons then. Magda. Have I the right of it?"

"I . . . yes." She smiled. Between the tea and the warm peat fire at her shoulder, Magda was warmed through, feeling oddly comfortable and affable with the strange woman. "How did you know?"

"I'm Gormshuil, lass." She held her gaze for a moment. "Aye, I suppose you'd not ken me. The years pass, and bones and names fade to dust." Leaning over, Gormshuil pulled a thin stick from beside the hearthstone, lit it, then held the wavering flame to her pipe. She gave a few encouraging puffs and added, "The laird asked about you. Rather, the laird's grandda did ask. The generations do pass, aye?" she muttered, sucking at her pipe.

"He asked if it were right to keep you under his roof. 'And why not?' I said. Och, the old man sometimes calls on me just to hear himself talk." She looked in the bowl of her pipe, then tapped the side hard. "But in return for my ears and words, the Camerons supply what I find wanting, which is not much these days." She pulled the pipe from her mouth and sipped her tea. "Not much at all." She gestured to the items in her hands and gave Magda a near toothless smile.

"But you, lass." Gormshuil rose from her stool and studied the clumps of herbs hanging along the far wall. "I ken what you're wanting. I can see the pain on your face. Writ clear around your mouth, aye? Sometimes muscle can scream louder than bone. I've something for it."

She took a dried plant from its hook. "This will help if the ache from your wrist robs your sleep. Crush the leaves in hot water, but not too much, mind. Or you'll sleep like the dead. Wouldn't want the Camerons to think I've killed you, aye?" She laughed and gestured for Magda to take the plant.

It was an angry, foreign-looking thing. The thick stem and spiked leaves gave it the appearance of a great weed, its once-vibrant green leaves and yellow flowers faded to ghosts of their former color.

"Eh," Gormshuil spat, "don't fret, lass. 'Tis just the henbane. It won't kill you. Stronger than wine, aye, but still weaker than the poppy. Take it, take it."

Magda took it into her hands. From the look of it, she'd expected something light as air, and was surprised at its heft. Unlike dried flowers that seemed fragile as parchment in hand, this dried herb felt solid, its leaves prickling the sensitive skin of her palms.

"It grows in the muck off Tor Castle. A wonder, aye? And it smells like the dung it grows in."

Before she could dodge her, Gormshuil grabbed her hands roughly and shoved the plant under Magda's nose. A stink like rotten eggs filled her sinuses, and nausea rolled through her.

The old woman merely hooted. "Well, girl, I see you're no healer. Here." She stole the plant from Magda's hand and returned it to its hook. Muttering, she knelt to rifle through her trunk, and Magda wished she were brave enough to look over the woman's shoulder to see just what was crinkling and clanking around in the old chest.

"Ah!" Gormshuil held up a small bottle, and the firelight illuminated a small measure of greenish liquid. Removing its stopper, she held it up to her nose then barked a laugh. "You shan't smell this one unless you really want to sick up, lass. 'Tis the same henbane, but this one's mixed with whisky, and the easier to swallow for it."

She offered it to Magda. "Hold your nose and just one drink, mind. Dare take more than a sip and you'll have the look of the dead to you. Who knows, aye? You may find some other need of it than just the pain in your wrist."

Magda somehow doubted that and, afraid to do otherwise, took the bottle from Gormshuil's hand.

Chapter 31

His men were all screaming now, howls and screeches like berserkers of old. James and Ewen sprang from behind the boulder and ran to join them, a wall of Royalists cascading down upon the Covenanter camp. James roared to his men to attack, while Ewen shouted over and over the Cameron war cry, *"Chlanna nan con thigibh a so's gheibh sibh feoil."* A call to his men to come and get flesh. And all the Royalists responded with renewed fury, barreling down on their enemy from above.

Many of Campbell's men had a startled, wild-eyed look to them as they struggled in vain to load muskets with cold and sleepy fingers. The whoosh and slash of Royalist blades came too quickly, and the first wave cut through a swath of Covenanters before they could finish loading their weapons.

The sun rose bright that day, and light cut over the edge of the mountains to cast long shadows below. Chaos ruled as the mobs of men drove into each other. The sounds of men fighting for their lives and the noise of swords finding shield and flesh thundered through the valley.

James quickly lost sight of Ewen, his attention focused only on whatever man was unlucky enough to stand in his path. He didn't carry a shield like many of the others, relying instead on his agility as its own weapon, and he carved his way forward, ducking and diving away from any sword that sought him.

A surge of screams and guttural cries sounded from the side, and James looked quickly to see his pikemen hacking brutally into the Covenanters' left flank. MacColla led the charge. Standing head and shoulders above many of the others, he worked his sword furiously, his thick, black brows furrowed in rage.

They were decimating Campbell's troops from the front and side now, and what was once a solid block of men shattered like glass into a thousand skittering pieces.

James's eye flicked to a familiar bit of plaid. He saw Sibbald from behind, the colonel's wiry frame and balding head of gray brown hair easily recognizable. The man stumbled, and James rushed forward to catch him at his side. He had a lethal gash across his chest and another low on his belly. Pulling him away from the worst of the melee, James tore off his coat and quickly retrieved the flask from his vest. The colonel nodded eagerly and eased to the ground.

James hoped it hadn't been the drink that had blunted Sibbald's wits and opened him to injury. But it's drink he would have, James thought, as the man breathed his last.

"Graham!"

He heard his name as he knelt to tip the flask to Sibbald's lips, and looked up to see the bard Iain gesturing wildly. Then James heard the hum of steel. He thrust the colonel to the ground, and was rolling even before he saw the blade coming at him. He leapt to his feet, sword in hand, and found himself face-to-face with a young Campbell clansman. Junior even to Ewen, the boy appeared no older than thirteen.

"Och, lad," James growled. "You've years yet." He inclined his head to the hills. "Go, and none will be the wiser."

Confusion and fear warred on the boy's face. The smears of mud on his cheeks and tangled mop of light blond hair made him seem even younger than his years.

"Come now, lad. Off with you." James gestured with his sword away from the battle. "You're young yet. You've years of lassies and adventure ahead of you. There will be time enough for fighting."

The boy bared his teeth into a scowl and rushed at James, his broadsword flailing wildly.

"Och, you lads." James grimaced, dodging the boy's thrusts, holding his own sword still in his hand. "It's not cowardice. Go now, boy, into the hills, and none will know."

The sword teetered heavily in the boy's grip, and he waved and twirled it, terror making him blind.

The youngster managed to nick him, and James looked down to

see his calf bleeding. His face darkened. "I beg you, lad." James feinted, and then slapped the flat of his blade onto the boy's thigh. "I'll not fight you."

The boy redoubled his efforts, swinging with abandon.

James hopped forward as if to thrust. "I'm sure you've a mother who'd rather see some bonny new grandbabes borne home than your lifeless body." He hopped forward again, edging the young Campbell backward toward the mountains. "So off with you now." He swooped his blade overhead to slap at the boy's shoulder. "The hills beckon. Truly. I don't find the killing of lads to be an honorable pursuit."

The boy pressed again and managed to get close, striking awkwardly at James's belly. He wrenched his sword down just in time to stop the boy's blade. The clash of metal reverberated up his arm as the young Campbell's sword grazed along his, stopping short with a clang at the steel basket of James's sword.

"I beg you, lad. We can pass the day right here, but I'll not fight you in earnest."

The boy swung his arm down at an angle, and James brought his blade up hard to block the blow. But the boy had feinted. His sword doubled back to strike at James from the other side, and the only thing left to stop James's blade was the boy's torso. James tried to pull back at the last moment, but it was too late to stop his momentum. The boy let out a wordless gasp.

"No!" James cried.

The young Campbell's sword clattered to the ground, and he looked at his waist, momentarily confused.

"Oh no, lad." James quickly resheathed his sword and caught the adolescent as he fell. "Oh, lad, I begged you."

James knew at once the wound was fatal, and painful as well.

"You're a braw fighter." James held him tightly, as if he could staunch the wound with his grip alone. "A braw fighter. You've brought great honor to—"

A long, wheezy exhale deflated the boy's body. "Forgive me." Tears spilled down James's cheeks. "Oh lad, forgive me."

By the time he returned to Sibbald, the old colonel also lay dead, spilt flask clenched in his hand, the snow around it stained deep amber.

He dropped to sit, looking around at the echoes of a battle run its course. They'd had a commanding victory. Royalists filled the Covenanter camp now, turning bodies, gathering stray weapons, or just standing dazedly, waiting for their minds to make sense of things and assure their pounding hearts that the threat was well and truly over.

James merely put his head in his hand and allowed himself to weep.

❈

Campbell glowered from the deck of his galley, standing despite the agony in his injured shoulder. The vessel was a stout seagoing *birlinn*, twelve-oars strong with a single sail. He rode at the bow and absentmindedly stroked the honey-colored wood. He'd always treasured the boat, such an obvious emblem of his wealth, but he'd thought he'd be using it to parade his triumph along the Highland waterway, not be subjected to this despicable flight.

The boat bobbed unevenly, and agony shot up his arm. Campbell fisted his hands, digging nails into his palms to take his mind off the pain. The Cameron had come at him like a bull, and he'd heard the bone snap like a dried branch. One look at the mayhem outside his tent and Campbell had backtracked to his craft, docked just where Loch Eil fed into Loch Linnhe. Then, when he'd caught sight of the Royalists cavorting along the hillside and rummaging through his tents, he'd taken to the water.

If the Cameron had been a bull, then the Marquis of Montrose had been a lion, clawing and gutting Clan Campbell of its men, killing sons enough to have repercussions for generations to come. Campbell's power was decimated, whole families wiped out, not to mention almost half his forces killed.

He looked to his oarsmen, rowing two men short. Those who remained pulled frantically, powered by their fear, as the triumphant whoops and cries of Royalist soldiers echoed along Loch Linnhe to sound the Covenanters' escape.

Lips twitching, he studied the Campbell crest and motto stitched onto his sail. A boar's head, and the words *Ne Obliviscaris.* Do Not Forget.

Chapter 32

Magda dashed to the room she shared with James. She'd just received word of his return, and news that he'd sustained some sort of injury. The healer passed her on his way out, and his grave nod sent a shiver up her spine.

She'd been sleeping so long apart from him, lying awake through long, cold nights, and wishing so hard for his return, yet she hadn't imagined it would happen in this way.

Once she'd even tried Gormshuil's henbane, in search of anything that would grant her rest and a blank mind. But though it seemed to lessen the ache in her wrist, the green concoction only gave her a fitful sleep, sweaty and filled with strange nightmares.

Fear blanched her skin a bloodless white against the dark blue and black plaid of the arisaid that seemed unable to warm her. All she knew was that even the most minor wounds could fester, threatening limb or life.

He sat on the bed, propped up against a half-dozen pillows that appeared ready to slide under his slumped weight. Foul herbal smells assaulted her, infusing the sharp stink of alcohol that hung in the room.

"James?" she said, voice quivering.

"Aye?" His eyelids fluttered open. His cheeks were flushed and eyes bright, and Magda wondered if he wasn't already fighting a fever. "My Magda," he said with a wan smile, his voice weak. "You'd rouse any man to life."

She raced to his bedside, but stood uncertainly, afraid to stir him.

"Come," he whispered hoarsely. "Give me your ear, hen." He coughed weakly. "I'd tell you one last thing."

She leaned toward him on the bed. All her buried anxieties spewed forth to light as she wondered, Was this it? Did her arrival spare James from one fate only to serve him another equally dire? Her heart an ache in her throat, Magda gently touched his cheek with her fingertips.

"Closer," he rasped.

She leaned closer still, fear for him making her tremble.

James grabbed her suddenly, pulling Magda roughly on top of him, and kissed her hard.

She kissed him back eagerly, inhaling his breath deeply into her own lungs, savoring again the smell of his skin, relief unspooling her muscles in one great shudder. Abruptly, she pulled away and began smoothing her hands over his chest and arms.

"But you're injured?"

Silent, he studied his calf beneath the blanket, then said, "Och, they're naught but scratches." He gestured to his upper arm. "I'd not even realized this one was there 'til the battle was well over."

"And you let me think . . . James Graham!" She smacked him on the chest. "How dare you? I thought you were dying."

"Only with love for you, hen." He grabbed at her again, trying to pull her back to him.

"Dammit, James," she said, fighting not to laugh. "Don't do that again. You'll hurt yourself worse than you already are."

"Och, they're nothing. Truly." He pulled his shirt off to show her a thin bandage wound around his biceps. "I was on my horse racing back to you before I realized the sting of it." Magda admired the slide of fabric on his skin, and the sight again of his naked body. He was leaner, yet the weeks of marching through the mountains had hammered his muscles into even more prominence.

She made to get off the bed. "Magda." His voice was suddenly earnest. "I need you here with me." He took her hand to stroke it lightly in his and stared at her in silence for a moment. "I need to see your bonny face instead of these dreadful images filling my mind of late."

"I'm here—" she began, when he grabbed her hip and put an arm underneath her legs. "Aye," he growled, "I need you, Magda." Her arisaid fell from her shoulders, and he bent down to nip at her breast underneath the wool of her dress. "And you'll not move from this place." James nibbled and kissed his way up her chest to nuzzle at her neck. "Until I say so."

Desire thickened his voice, and Magda felt the hot rush of her body's response. All the fear and anxiety and loneliness of the last weeks were submerged by her desire for this man.

Hungry for him, she grabbed and pulled his face to hers. He moaned in response, a primal sound deep in his throat that reverberated through her. She couldn't get close enough to him, felt suffocated by her thick layers of clothing. James ran his hand down her throat and the creamy expanse of her breastbone. Her skin pebbled and her nipples tightened in response to the feel of his hands, warm and rough on the cool smoothness of her skin.

She wore a simple tartan dress, with a tight bodice and low, square neck. He dipped his fingers down inside her gown to graze her nipple, and she gasped with the pleasure of it. The urgency to have him subsumed Magda, and she quickly rose to her knees and swung a leg over to straddle him.

Magda felt the hard ridge of him and ground her body into his. Kissing her deeply, he rubbed his hands up her back and eased his fingers into the ropes of hair gathered at the nape of her neck, loosening and freeing it. Magda shuddered as she felt the thick weight of it fall onto her back, and bit at his mouth with the joy of it.

James slipped his hand down into her dress again and, cupping her breast, released it from the tight bodice. The cool air on her skin was quickly replaced by his mouth, hot and sucking on her. Magda was lost for a moment, then heard the crisp tear of fabric and the popping of buttons as she realized she'd been bared from the waist up.

James hiked the skirts of her dress up and tore the blankets from between them, his movements heated, almost violent, in their intensity.

He slowed and, inhaling deeply, pulled back to hold Magda's gaze with his own. "I love you more than life," he said, and tenderly inched himself into her. The simple feel of him, filling her, made her eyes tear. She had to look away then, dropping her head back and closing her eyes, nearly unable to endure such pleasure.

James thrust deeply to the last inch and Magda felt heat tear through her. Breath came in gasps as her body remembered to pull air into its lungs. Her head buzzed as, someplace distant, she felt James pumping fast into her for his own release.

Not more than a quarter hour passed, yet Magda felt like she'd slept for hours, dozing, spent, leaning against his body, her forehead damp against his neck.

"Are you with me, hen?" he whispered.

"Oh yes." An unintended giggle bubbled up as the relief and realization that James was returned safe finally became real to her.

"Truly, you'd make a man forget his own name." He kissed her over and over, quick pecks along her face and neck, and Magda giggled in earnest. Her whole body was sensitive, her blood still thrumming just below the surface of her skin.

"But I think we'd best make haste for dinner." He tucked her hair behind her ears. "I have visions of the Cameron bursting in here to see what's detained us."

She rose reluctantly, and a rush of air replaced James's body, cold on her moist skin.

He flicked back the blanket to reveal bare legs and the wide strip of cloth wrapped around his right calf. James swung his legs over the side of the bed, and a fresh spot of blood appeared, fanning out bright and angry against the white of his bandage.

Magda gasped. "You need to stay in bed."

"Only with you atop me."

"Seriously, James." She studied her torn dress, and not sure what else to do, wadded it into a ball to deal with later. She opened a trunk at the foot of the bed and retrieved the only other dress in her possession. She'd been able to successfully avoid dresses in the more extravagant fabrics, and despite the judgmental once-overs of women like Mairi, the warm tartan wool was quickly becoming her favorite.

She clutched the dress to her breast, somehow more capable of argument when she wasn't completely naked. "You really shouldn't be up and around on that leg."

"Och," he muttered. He stood and shifted his weight from foot to foot, testing his wound. "Not when I hear Tom Sydserf's come to call."

Magda gaped at him, aghast at the nonchalance with which he treated his injury.

James looked at her and smiled. "Don't fash yourself on my account, hen." He hobbled to Magda. "I've had enough potions and salves to last me a lifetime of battles. You're the only medicine I need."

"Alright." She swatted him with her dress, trying to appear impatient. "Enough sweet talk."

Magda began to dress, watching from the corner of her eye as he flicked out the length of his plaid and slowly wound it round himself.

"Our Tom, reemerged at long last." James limped to a basin by the bedside and scrubbed water on his face. "Have you seen him then?"

At her nod, he continued, "It remains to be seen under what capacity my friend has decided to present himself. Hogmanay has passed, or I'd have wagered he'd some sort of holiday *dramatique* planned for us."

"No." Magda smiled, amused by the notion of portly Tom in any sort of theatrical endeavor. She brushed out the length of her hair. There was no way she could ever recreate the elaborate style perpetrated upon her by one of the Cameron maids, so down it would have to be. "He claims to have some news, though he wouldn't tell any of us till you returned."

"News, eh?" James made his way to the door. "Well, we'd best go down for dinner where we can hear it, aye?" His gaze roved down her body. "I find I'm suddenly quite famished."

He winked, and she was surprised to find that he was still able to make her cheeks flush red.

❁

"Aye, good man," Tom bellowed, already well into his third glass of brandy. "March south, I tell you. You'll receive a hero's greeting."

Will Rollo was with them, expansive at the thought of traveling once more. "I've heard murmurs that Charles has regained control over Parliament."

"Och"—Ewen glowered—"whose murmurs?"

Ignoring the young laird, Tom continued, "I'm told the Lowlands want to rally for you, James. You see"—he leaned in conspiratorially—"after chasing you to Oxford and back, I traveled for a fortnight in the border towns."

"Forsaking your dramatic career for one as a spy, is it?" James laughed.

"And why not?" Tom beamed proudly. "I had the honor of supping at Traquair House, in Peebles, where I met a number of prominent noblemen." His cheeks flushed crimson with his excitement. "The south is near filled with recruits anxious to take the bit and join you."

"Aye, James," MacColla chimed in, emphasizing his point by waving the dinner knife in his hand. "I expect your men have the right of it. Place your humility elsewhere." He took a bite of roast venison and spoke as he chewed. "We've trounced the Covenanters up and down these Highlands. No false modesty about it."

Magda looked down to saw at the hunk of meat on her own plate, biting her lip not to smile. MacColla's broad personality and manners ranged from startling to amusing. He caught her eye and, gesturing again with his knife, gave her an exaggerated wink.

"'Tis not false modesty, my friend." James pushed his plate away. "'Tis merely good sense. I question all intelligence." He picked up his drink. The leaded glass was thick with a slight taper to it, and it felt good and solid in his hand. Swirling his brandy, he eyed the thin ropes of tawny liquid left in its wake. "Most particularly those reports with such grand estimations of yours truly."

"And will *you* ride south with us?" Ewen asked of Tom, still wary of his enthusiasm. "I didn't see *your* face when we slept with the snow for a pillow, or ate rabbit tasting of winter's freeze."

Tom flushed to be called out so, and sat tall in his seat, inadvertently creating a gap between his breeches and the vest that strained over his belly.

"Easy, Cameron." MacColla laughed.

"Have another, lad," James said, reaching over to refill Ewen's glass. "It will serve you well."

"I ken you're like his family," Ewen told Tom. Then the young laird turned to James and added, "But how can you be certain you'll be greeted a hero with the word of just one—"

"Och, enough." James slammed his hand on the table. "I'll not scour the country in search of accolades. But I do see the wisdom of a southern campaign. And I will continue to rely on Tom for his assistance." James looked to his friend. "If you're willing, aye? I know you're no soldier, but I am in want of a trustworthy spy."

"It's high time for another adventure." Tom raised his glass to James. "I'd not miss the fetes in your honor, my dear Marquis."

"I remain ever at your side as well," Rollo said gravely.

"And what of you, MacColla?" Ewen asked. His brandy still sat untouched before him. "Do you still march with us?"

"No," MacColla replied nonchalantly, picking at the meat in his teeth. "I head west, not south."

Startled, James put his glass down hard. "This is unexpected, Alasdair."

"Oho! My Christian name." MacColla laughed. "I must be in your poor graces." He pushed back his chair, the wood screeching loud against the stone-flagged floor. "Aye, James, 'tis true." He kicked his crossed ankles onto the table with a small nod to Magda as if to beg pardon.

"'Twas a fight against the Campbell that I reckoned on, not a fight for the king, and that is the fight I shall continue to wage. I'll leave you some number of MacDonald swords, but I take the rest of my men west. To head south with you would be to put Clan Campbell at my back, and I'll not be sated until the Highland sod is manured with the blood of all Campbells."

James was silent for a moment, holding MacColla's gaze. "So, my friend," he finally said, "farewell it shall be." James raised his glass, and with a wistful smile added, "But first we drink together, to the destruction of an old enemy."

"Aye." A huge smile split MacColla's face, and he downed his brandy in one gulp.

"And let's not forget James," Tom said. "To James, whose military prowess and superlative leadership dogged the Covenanters hither and yon throughout bonny Scotland."

"Are you quite done, man?" Ewen glowered, holding his brandy impatiently.

"And may he finally reap the fruits of his battle cunning," Rollo chimed in, over James's amused protests.

"And journey safely south," Tom added, "to hear the first of accolades that will be sung of him for generations to come."

Even Ewen laughed then, the men suddenly giddy with drink and triumph.

Then James looked to Magda. She'd been sitting silently, turning the glass around and around on the table in front of her. She returned his gaze, anxiety chilling her green eyes, and the smile bled from his face.

Chapter 33

"If your troops cannot win this war—"

"'Tis your leadership we enjoyed at Inverlochy," Alexander Leslie snapped, straining for indifference in his voice. "*Our* troops would have fared much better had you not stubbornly rushed them through the snow in cloaks and cavalry boots."

Perspiration beaded above Campbell's lip, which trembled in anger. He'd summoned the general to Campbell's primary seat at Inveraray Castle and was anxious to get the man from his sight as quickly as possible. Leslie had been much aggrieved that so many of his soldiers had been killed, and had since tried Campbell to no end.

"Silence," Campbell hissed. "Or your treasonous words will cause that overproud head of yours to be severed from its body."

Steeling himself, he retrieved a handkerchief from his sleeve and dabbed at his brow. "If the troops you trained are unable to best the Marquis of Montrose, then I'll simply put a price on his head. Surely those"—distaste puckered Campbell's features—"Highlanders are as capable of treachery as they are of savagery."

Forcing the general to wait in attentive silence, Campbell meticulously folded the square of cloth and tucked it away. "Every man can be bought, Leslie. Find one who will deliver me James Graham."

Chapter 34

"As I recall," James said with a tease in his voice, "you claimed you dreamt of going on holiday to a warm isle and no horse riding." He kicked his mount into a trot. Loch Eil was already at their backs and it wasn't a long ride now to Loch Ailort, where they'd hire a boat, and propelled by the spring tides, head into the Sound of Arisaig to their destination.

"Yeah," Magda said, quickly catching up. "But this pony counts as a horse, James. You know what I meant."

"Oh, aye." He leaned far over the saddle and gave a squeeze to her thigh. "But some riding is necessary, aye? I'll not have you walking."

"But on a pony?"

"I'd not entrust my horse to some ferryman," James laughed. "'Tis but a short ride. And I *am* producing your requested isle."

"Yeah, but I had something more like Hawaii in mind."

"Ha—where?" James stood in his stirrups, eyeing the horizon. The spectacular edge of Scotland was visible in the distance, a glare of white on water with crags beyond, as Loch Ailort snaked its way out to the open sea. "As for the warmth," he added, "well, we've waited till spring and cannot wait any longer. The men are fully rested and we must be on our way. I'd not try Cameron hospitality any longer."

Magda was greatly relieved to feel the sand at her feet when they finally landed on the Isle of Eigg. James and the captain had gotten out, dragging the boat some ways through the shallows to shore. It hadn't been much more than a dinghy, and the trip would've been an anxious affair even if she hadn't had the nagging fear of water to contend with. James had made the mistake of telling her whales could often be seen this time of year, and Magda spent much of their crossing envisioning scenarios whereby they were flipped into the sea by a gargantuan, breeching marine mammal.

Once her heart returned to its normal rate, though, Magda looked around and was delighted. It was as if a comb had been dragged through a painter's palette, swirling together but not quite mixing basic shades of blue and beige and brown and red and green, the colors of ocean giving way to sand, beach grasses to mud, then onto the turf that stretched into an impossible shade of emerald in the distance.

"Charming, eh?" James came up from behind to wrap his arms tightly around her. The sound of gentle waves slapping at the retreating boat already faded in the distance. "Less than one hundred souls live here. We can go about unhampered."

His breath tickled her ear. "So shall we?" He nuzzled past her wind-tangled hair to kiss at her neck. "Go be . . ." He bit lightly at her shoulder. "Unhampered?"

"That sounds perfect," she purred. "No gunfire?"

"Nary a sword in sight, hen."

James knew of an abandoned farmhouse and gave her the option of a roof overhead, but Magda actually wanted to sleep outdoors. All of the camping they'd done, and she hadn't yet truly felt the joy of what it was to lie next to him, naked under a bowl of stars, without the fear of soldiers coming for them in the night.

They headed for the highest point on the island, setting up camp on a carpet of lush grass on the lee side of what James told her was the Sgurr pitchstone, an enormous black rock formation that jutted violently from the isle's soft green flesh like a broken bone.

Winter was well past, and the sun was setting much later now. By the time James settled them with a tent and small fire, it was late afternoon. A shelf of clouds hung low in the sky, breaking clear just along the horizon so that a thin band of white glowed luminous, gilding the sea in the distance.

"This would be a wonderful place for a house." She sighed contentedly.

"No, hen, this would be a miserable place for a house." The cool of the evening approached fast now, and he snuggled closer to Magda to share his heat.

She shot him an indignant look, and with a devilish smile in his eyes, he stole a kiss at her cheek.

"But why?" she asked. Magda sat forward, studying the lay of the land in earnest. "That huge rock blocks the wind. And there were those pretty yellow daisies all around. They're a little overgrown, but you could probably cut them back and transplant them to a little garden. It would be pretty."

"'Tis ragwort, and very poisonous indeed." Chuckling, he shook her shoulder gently, teasing. "I'm told you once tried to poison a platoon of soldiers with spindle berries too."

"Well, I didn't plan on eating the flowers, James," she grumbled. His bark of laughter in response made Magda smile despite herself.

"Come, hen." Sliding his hand to her neck, he gently smoothed errant hairs from inside her collar and then rubbed his hand down her back. "Time to rest."

"It's not even night yet," she protested. "And I'm hungry."

"Aye," he said, as he wound his arm tight around her waist. James kissed his way along her shoulder. "I'm hungry too." Nibbling at her ear, he whispered, "There will be time to fill our bellies later."

She gently tugged his arm from her waist and, lacing her fingers in his, clasped his hand and tucked it between them.

"I . . . do you mind if we just sit for now?" She searched his face. "I know it's supposed to be our special getaway and everything."

"Of course, lass." He tenderly cupped her cheek. "Is there something troubling you?"

"No, I . . . I just want to lie with you tonight."

He stroked his fingers lightly along her skin, silently considering her face. "As you wish, my love." He kissed each cheek, and then touched his forehead to hers. "Now, shall I muster some food on this homestead of yours?"

"Yes, please," she said with a light heart.

Their bodies tangled close that night, stretched on the soft ground with his tartan to warm them, his hand smoothing through her hair until their breathing slowed to a deep, dreamless sleep.

❀

They walked along the beach the next morning, and Magda giggled like a child, running and stomping and dragging her feet to
hear the sand hum at her touch.

"I've heard of singing sand," she said, "but I had no idea." She
plopped down. The sand was dry, yet still firm with the memory
of the sea. Magda rubbed her fingers through the soft, beige powder, eliciting eerie tonal sounds like whale song.

"This is beautiful," she beamed. "Thank you for taking me
here."

"Och, hen, you're the one who's beautiful." He kissed the top
of her head, then dropped to sit beside her.

"See there"—he pointed to an island rising black from the water, its evenly undulating hills suggesting the humpback of some
great sea creature floating along the horizon—"that's the Isle of
Rum."

"Ooh, that sounds like a fun one."

"Indeed." He smiled and raised a brow. "And just there, you
can see Skye." He gestured to a faraway island, a ghostly gray in
the far distance.

They sat in amicable silence for some time. Seabirds cawed
and swooped overhead, making quick dips, then bombing into
the water for food. A thin halo of foam hissed and sighed lightly
against the small black rocks and smooth sand of the shore.

"I think it's time, hen," he told her in a grave voice.

Fear at once prickled up Magda's back. These sorts of pronouncements from James were usually followed by random and
dangerous military missions. "For . . . ?"

"For putting a bairn in your belly. I ken you've been counting
the days," he continued. "That's what last night was about, if I've
the right of it?"

She nodded. Magda had been counting the days, doing what
she could to avoid a pregnancy. "But how did you know?"

"Och, I'm with you every night lass. I can count too."

"A bairn," she said. The word was foreign on her tongue.

Magda went quiet. That they would begin having babies as
soon as possible would be the obvious assumption, and yet it was

something she hadn't fully considered. She felt uncertain. Magda realized she had an idea of herself that she'd grown up with, a particular understanding of who she was that was etched at her core. She'd defined herself by her childhood, her home, and even her parents. To consider motherhood somehow set all of those elements into strong relief.

"I . . . I just need to think. But I do love you, James."

"And I you, lass." He laid her back gently, taking her hands in his, holding them in the cool sand over her head. "And I you."

They passed the rest of the morning with slow, hushed kisses to the sound of the surf.

Chapter 35

"They'll greet me as a hero, hen."

"Don't *hen* me," Magda snapped. The day had come for James and his men to leave the Camerons and head south, to a fate Magda refused to contemplate. He said he wanted to have a child, and she'd let herself see that as a sign they could finally settle down. Make a life together. She'd thought it meant an end to his campaigning—a sign that he'd escaped an unthinkable end on the gallows.

He gave an easy laugh and cupped her chin for a kiss.

She pulled her head back to look at him, her eyes sharp on his. "Really, James." *Is this it, finally?* The moment he'll need her help, and she'll be too far away? *Just like Peter.* "Don't go. Please. Or, if you go, take me with you. But you can't just leave me here."

"I shall return to you, scores of Lowlanders at my back, to quell this turmoil once and for all." He took her face in both hands and refused to let her go. "Truly, Magda," he said in a whisper, "it's but a momentary parting. I know you think there's some gruesome fate I'm to meet, but I tell you that is not the case."

"You can't know that."

"I have it on good word that all is lost for the Campbell and his Covenanters. All are ready to rise and march for me."

"But you can't just leave me." Her helplessness was turning to anger. Would their lives together always be this? Always goodbye? Would he still be rushing off to danger when they had children together? Rushing off to save the world? *Just like Peter.*

"Oho, pretty lass," he said playfully. "But I can." Her glare in response tempered the humor in his tone.

"Truly, Magda," he added seriously. "Regardless of my destiny, it is far safer for you in my family's care. You simply cannot march about the country with me and scores of fighting men."

"What if you get killed? No, really," she added bluntly, seeing the cavalier flash in his eyes. "What if this *is* the time? And you die? And I . . . what? I languish the rest of my days with a bunch of strangers, hundreds of years before my birth?"

Fear had been a constant drone, vibrating through Magda's every cell since she'd arrived. She was utterly exhausted from it, and she finally felt herself snap.

"I tell you, hen, I will not—"

"Or . . . okay . . . say you don't die this time." She pulled away from him and stepped back. "Is *this* what I have to look forward to? To you gallivanting off at every opportunity, leaving me to sit around and . . . what? Sit with the other women all day while I worry I'll never see you again? Should I be like . . ." She pitched her voice to a low hiss. "Should I be like Margaret? Napier is with you more often that he's with her. Is that what you'd have for me?"

"I'd not—" he tried to interrupt.

"I can't have your baby, James." Her voice was flat. Her feelings had ravaged through her, laying waste, leaving Magda feeling utterly empty. James might be her world, but without him this place never would be, and somehow it'd been the question of getting pregnant that had shed a harsh light on it all. Magda couldn't be abandoned there, couldn't envision bringing a child into a place so alien. Not if she might have to do it alone.

"I can't have your baby in some filthy bed with some leech-using doctor, and then sit around for the rest of my life having more babies and watching them play while I spend my days hoping and praying that you return home alive. I can't bear anymore loss, James."

"That will not be your life," he said evenly. His voice was steely, his body rigid. "You have my word. But for now, Magda, I must go. Just this once more. The wheels turn, plans are set in motion, and I cannot simply run from it all." He stepped toward her, and she flinched back to avoid his touch. Hurt flickered across his features, but he pressed on. "No man can know his own fate. But even if he could, my country's destiny is larger than my own. That is what I

need to attend, at this moment, above all else. But you have my
promise, I shall do all in my power to return to you. And I will be
a good husband, here, with you. And I will put that bairn in your
belly," he said, and Magda finally let him take her in his arms.

She didn't doubt any of that. Nor did she doubt that he'd get
himself killed with these crusades of his. Just like her brother had.
She couldn't endure that sort of pain again.

She wouldn't endure it.

❁

Summer was almost past, and MacColla had kept his word, leaving James a few hundred men of Clan MacDonald to stand at his
back. Rollo and Ewen rode with him, but he'd sent Magda with
Tom back to Montrose.

It had been hard parting as they did. There had been something
in her look that he'd not seen before. Defiance flashed in her eyes
on the day they left, replacing her usual desire to satisfy, appease,
accommodate. He found he loved her all the more for it. He would
prove to her that he wasn't just any man. Magda deserved an extraordinary life, and that was what he would give her. But turmoil
and uncertainty reigned in his country, and his first priority was
to ease Scotland into peace.

They marched south, not for battle, but merely to supplement
their forces. He would return safe, and spend the rest of his life
proving his love to her. He'd not let an army of nannies raise his
children as he'd been raised. He'd be by his wife's side, reminding
her every day, for the rest of his days, that she was his.

"What was that about?" Rollo trotted his horse up to James's
side. He'd started to wave at a woman peeking from a cottage
window, but when their eyes met, the woman simply began calling
frantically to her children to herd them inside.

Though they'd run into many friendly faces on the road, an
equal number got skittish at the sight of them, as if the mounted
throng were the angel of death itself, sweeping over the country,
looking for a place to land. James had been chilled to see that the
majority of those he'd seen had been women and children, compared to so few men.

But despite the occasionally wary greeting, most of the Royalists traveled merrily along, buoyed by pleasant weather and their leisurely pace. The terrain became easier as they approached the Scottish borders, and the hard Highland crags smoothed into the gentle rolls of the Lowlands.

"Aye," James replied, "the country's on edge, and why not? Nobody knows who marches for whom, or where the wind will blow tomorrow." He pitched his voice louder to be heard over the men as they broke into a rousing pub song, and Rollo spared a smile for him.

There had been much singing as they went, with the men crooning out ballads and battle chants, or the piper playing in time to the gait of the horses. James and Rollo laughed now, upon hearing the latest tune.

> He left his lady with gentlemen,
> And he kissed the lass in the stable.
> Are you wi' bairn, my chicken?
> Are you wi' bairn, my chicken?
> If I am not, I hope to be,
> E'er the green leaves be shaken.

"What say you, Rollo?" James grinned. "When songs of battle turn to songs of bairns, I think it time to rest for the night."

James read the relief clear on his friend's face. Rollo's great upper-body strength and custom saddle did much to mitigate the pain of such long marches, but at the end of a day's ride, James could always spot the agony writ in the furrow at Rollo's brow and in the lines that bracketed his mouth.

"Men!" he called. "Draw rein! We camp here."

"You'll camp here at Philiphaugh," James told him. He looked around at the smooth stretch of moor. The River Ettrick glared white in the late-afternoon sun, drawing a ragged line that rent the lush swath of green in two. "There's room enough for the cavalry and the Irish as well."

"What of you?" Rollo asked.

"I'll quarter at Selkirk, just across the river. 'Tis but a wee burgh but should be large enough to find most officers a roof for their heads."

Tents appeared, studding the moor like spring shoots, and the black smoke and charred smell of cook fires soon choked the air. His men seemed relaxed, unhurriedly setting up camp, squatting to chat, sharing pulls from flasks. James and the other officers gradually left Philiphaugh, crossing the river to find beds in Selkirk.

❁

Padraic O'Shaughnessy lay down for the night. He and his Irish brothers had mocked the Scottish tartan, but withstanding such extensive marching and camping, he finally understood why the Scots had such a peculiar attachment to their plaids. His saddle blanket was but a trifle when compared to the yards of wool the Highlanders rolled into every night.

He'd quartered his battle-scarred pony at Philiphaugh like the rest of the cavalry, but joined a dozen of his countrymen to camp the night in a copse away from the river. Imagining the air to rise cooler by the water, he welcomed the shelter the woods provided.

There was a small snap, and his head shot up. Heart pounding, his eyes searched blindly in the darkness until, eventually, the silence convinced him that what he'd heard was just a breeze in the trees. Or one from his group had been settling for the night. Or that perhaps he'd even imagined such a sound.

Padraic pulled the gray wool up over his shoulders, exposing a stretch of muddy boot cradled in the leaves. Tucking his arm under his head, he shut his eyes to rest.

❁

"We've found them, General."

"Nicely done, lad." Alexander Leslie smiled, revealing a row of small, square teeth. "Where?"

"At Philiphaugh, and the woods surrounding."

"So close?" Leslie smoothed a drop of whisky from his moustache and stoppered his flask. "The Fates smile upon us."

"Aye, and our spy at Selkirk claims Royalist officers are scattered through the burgh like bits of chaff on the wind."

"Ah." Leslie stroked his beard into a point. "An unexpected boon. Officers and their men separated by a river?" He barked a sharp laugh. "A foolish thing indeed to separate the beast from its head."

Leslie stood and stretched, turning each foot in small circles. He needed his wits sharp. The hour was late, but if they were to keep the element of surprise, they'd need to strike early. There would be little rest that night, but the gold he'd get in trade for Montrose's head would buy drink that would put to shame the horse piss he was currently forced to swill.

"Have all six cavalry regiments at the ready." Leslie's eyes narrowed, and his hatred and longing for retribution seeped into his features, transforming him from a merely small and crooked man into a devil.

"Rally the men," he said. "We blaze like the sun's fire at the dawn."

Chapter 36

"I'd not expected to see you so early." Rollo pulled up short at the sight of James. His silhouette was black and featureless as it emerged from the fog, a startling presence among the still-slumbering camp. Cold had stolen in during the night, and air bearing the chill threat of autumn collided with ground still warm from the summer sun, enshrouding Philiphaugh with mist.

"I'd hoped to see the men readied for another day of travel," James said, "but we'll not cover any ground this morning until the fog clears." He reined in close to Rollo's side, and each man could finally discern the features of the other.

"You'd be in a rush to get back to that woman of yours, I suppose." An uncharacteristically open smile warmed Rollo's face.

"Indeed, my friend"—James chuckled—"though I'll admit—"

There was a sharp popping, discordant in the still of the morning. In that instant between perceiving and knowing, James wondered if he hadn't heard a thunderclap. Time slowed as he turned to Rollo, the specter of a smile still clinging to James's face. His friend slowly crumpled and slid, as if deflating. The sight of scarlet seeping through the blue of Rollo's coat roused James to himself, a jolt of fury and energy suffusing him like lighting to the thunder that had just sounded.

Rollo hit the ground, and his horse, spooked, reared then bolted through the mist to disappear.

It was in that instant the chaos began.

Gunfire erupted, red flares flashing in the mist that was quickly blackening from the smoke of musket fire. James was blind to his enemy, but the noise pressed on him as if it rode on the fog, and he knew that they surrounded him. Startled screams tore through the camp, followed by wordless exhales and the dull sounds of bullets finding flesh, layering notes of terror to the gunfire's booming orchestra.

Tents popped and burst like living things as Campbell's Covenanter muskets found soldiers who would never wake from that night's sleep. Some of James's men managed to spring from other tents, racing to find family members they'd left encamped on the outskirts of Philiphaugh, which now raged with gunfire, flames, and shrieks.

"You!" James called to an older cavalryman whose sure hands were buckling his sword at his side. "Sort this man to rights," he said, gesturing to the still Rollo. Blood pooled black in the grass around him, and James couldn't bear to know at that moment whether his friend lived or died.

The old soldier knelt at Rollo's side, and James's eyes went to the camp, his gaze sweeping over the bedlam. Men raced like ants all over, their senior officers nowhere in sight. "Form a line!" James shouted.

The grim thought struck him that most of the officers had bedded at Selkirk and weren't there to give orders.

"Men!" he cried again. "Form your line!"

Many finally came to themselves and rallied. "To me!" James called. Retreating slightly, he raced them in the direction of Selkirk, entrenching behind a low knoll that rose like a knobby spine close to the bank of the river.

And then, as if they'd stumbled into the eye of the storm, the sounds of battle faded away and an eerie stillness fell around them. Some of his soldiers made as if to stand but froze at a look and a gesture from James. Stillness in battle could mean but few things.

There was a single shot from faraway, and James shut his eyes. Then another shot. And another. A chill crept along his skin. They heard another lone shot, as Campbell's men killed their prisoners one by one.

"It's done for, Graham. They've four thousand horses if they've a one." The voice behind him was ragged. James turned to see a MacDonald clansman squatting grimly behind him. The lad was still a teen yet, with a single smear of crimson marring his features where he'd used a bloody hand to wipe the sweat from his brow.

Dread spiked through James's belly as he thought of the hundreds of clansmen MacColla had put in his charge. He couldn't bear to tally the number of MacDonald men he'd lost that morning.

"Only those who ran fast enough could avoid capture," the young scout said. "We need to go from here, and now."

"No," James said. But then he looked down the line of men, a couple hundred at most, many unarmed and still half naked from their sleep. Irish and Highlanders most of them, and they dug through the dirt now, gathering stones and ready to fight.

"Aye," he muttered then, and eased his forehead into his hand. So many men lost, and all because he'd been blinded by such a string of victories. He thought of Rollo and wondered whether his friend lived or died.

Inhaling sharply, he whipped his head up to look at the MacDonald. "Selkirk! How stands Selkirk?"

"I've come from there. Covenanters are rousing every innkeeper and publican in the town, searching for Royalist officers."

"How do you fare in the woods, lad?"

"I cut my teeth sneaking through trees to escape blackguards like these Covenanters," the boy said, puffing his chest.

"I'm away to Selkirk." James jumped up and leaned one foot along the side of the low ridge. "Can you lead these men to safety?"

"Me?" Doubt muddled the boy's features. "Aye." He hesitated. "I can lead them. But"—he eyed James impatiently palming the hilt of his sword—"you cannot go, sir. Covenanter soldiers even now wend through the town looking for you."

James ignored the comment. "Don't fear, lad. You're fleet, a mere couple hundred men." He flashed the young man a smile. "You can fly from here."

He stared dumbly at James.

"You can lead these men through to safety." He nodded firmly, clapping the MacDonald on his shoulder. "You'll do it, lad. And now."

James vaulted over the rise and ran into the mist.

❁

He'd found a horse and raced it to Selkirk, abandoning the animal just outside the town's limits. Shouts and gunfire came only intermittently now, and James dreaded what carnage he'd find in the streets. No battle was lost that still raged, but silence portended only one thing.

He heard men approaching and ducked into the shadows between two buildings. James clung close to the wall, and the gray stone cooled his sweat-soaked shirt, gradually steadying his heart, which still pounded from his flight out of Philiphaugh. The sounds of the men's conversation amplified as they grew near, and then gradually faded away.

James spent a moment trying to orient himself, pinpointing in his mind where he stood in relation to the room he'd let the previous night. Gunfire cracked close, followed by more distant reports. Seconds passed, and shots erupted once more, and again they'd come from two different origins. It would be a volley, James thought, between two groups of men, and a volley meant some of his officers were still alive.

Looking right and left, he eased from his hiding spot and jogged toward the sound of musket fire. He slipped his hand into his sword's basket and wrapped his fingers around the grip. He may not have a musket to hand, he thought, but his sword would be all he needed.

He had to double back twice among the winding alleys of Selkirk, but he found them in short order. And he'd been correct in his assumption. A firefight raged between two knots of men, with a cluster of three of his Royalists holding their own against a like number of Covenanter soldiers.

James thought he'd need the element of surprise, some agility, and a tremendous amount of luck if he were to best three armed men. Their muskets would be impotent at close range, and it was how he would make his initial charge that James wondered at now. If he could get at the enemy between shots, he might have a chance. But with Parliament's sympathies and funds flowing to the Covenanter cause, the enemy's red-coated soldiers used paper cartridges instead of powder horns, enabling them to get off three, perhaps four shots in a minute. James estimated that would give him no more than fifteen seconds to strike.

The gunshots from his Royalists seemed to thin, and James thought he needed to act now before they ran out of ammunition.

"Blast it all," James muttered. When he saw the building, he knew what he had to do.

The wooden structure sat just to the side of the Covenanter soldiers. With its two stories and gabled roof, it was unremarkable but for one element: A single-story entryway protruded from its façade like a low-slung building in miniature, complete with its own peaked roof.

He scowled, preparing his body for a drop from such a height. "Blast it to hell," he repeated in a resigned whisper as he snuck around to the back.

Giving silent thanks that he'd taken to wearing his tartan to battle, he began to scale the rear of the building, his powerful legs free to stretch and reach with ease. A brick chimney flanked by two small windows on each floor made finding handholds simple, and James was soon pulling himself onto the roof.

He inched along on his belly, both to elude notice and to avoid slipping from its sharply angled slope. James edged as close as he dared, and peeked down to the top of the small entry hall below. It would be a single-story drop to its roof. Then, if he managed not to slide from its sharp peak, it would be another single-story leap to the ground. Where he'd take on three armed soldiers with naught but his blade at his side.

He cursed once more under his breath.

The Covenanters shot and reloaded and shot again, and began to work their way slowly forward as their relentless attack was answered less frequently by the Royalists. James could see his men in the distance, and their frantic gestures made plain their alarming lack of ammunition.

The Royalists spotted him then, and their eyes all went to James's rooftop. But the Covenanters had closed in enough to notice their enemies' focus shifting upward.

"Dammit, lads," James swore.

A Covenant soldier in a red coat turned to track the direction of their gazes and, spotting James, swung his musket to put him in his sights.

"Blast it," James cried as he leapt. He twisted to the side at the last moment to avoid getting rammed between his legs, but the rooftop below clipped him sharp on the hip instead. He immediately began to slide to the ground, clawing at a thin, spindled pinnacle to slow his fall.

The musket blast was loud at close range, and a hole exploded behind him as a bullet bit into the top of the gable.

The lip of the roof scraped hard along his lower back, and he grabbed it, managing to right his legs under him for the rest of his drop.

His feet hit the ground, the collision spearing pain up his calves, and James immediately bent to a crouch to absorb the rest of the impact. He rolled to the dirt at the sound of a cocking musket, and two more shots split the air almost immediately. James sprang to his feet and rushed the Covenanters, counting silently in his head the time it would take them to reload.

His sword was unsheathed and found flesh the moment he reached them, leaving two men remaining. One of his enemies had jogged out of view, and James could hear the tear and scrape as he reloaded his gun. The other stood not five feet from him, his loaded musket pointing at James's chest. The Covenanter's hand trembled as he swept it along the top of his weapon, pulling it to full cock.

The three Royalists James had come to save ran up from behind. The Covenanter turned his head in surprise, inadvertently tilting his musket up a fraction, giving James enough of a window to close the distance with a leap and cleave his broadsword high into the man's torso.

"Thank you, gentlemen," James said, a little out of breath. "That was a bit tight, aye?"

A crash sounded in the alley as the remaining Covenanter ducked behind a cart for cover. One of the Royalists flashed James a crooked smile and, pointing from himself to the cart, indicated that he would create a diversion. The man was tall and blond, and looked as if he was enjoying himself in his exaggeratedly loud approach to the hidden Covenanter.

James slunk around from behind just as he heard the scrape of a gun's hammer. The Covenanter rose, taking aim at the man in front of him. James swung his blade, a single, forceful strike, and his enemy fell, never knowing what hit him.

"And I thank you . . . James Graham, if I'm not mistaken." The blond man gave James another lopsided smile, a single dimple creasing his tanned face.

"Aye, you've the right of it," James replied. "And you gentlemen would be . . . ?"

"Jamie Ogilvy, second earl of the House of Airlie," the blond said, "and a pleasure it is to meet one who's felled so many Campbells."

"Ah," James replied. "The earl is your father?"

"Aye, I'm his eldest."

"Then you've my sympathies, good man," James said somberly. Magda had told him of the atrocities she'd witnessed when Campbell razed the Ogilvy estate, burning the House of Airlie to the ground.

"The kindness is appreciated, Graham, but what I'd most like is vengeance."

"Aye, we're not done yet." James looked around uneasily. "Though we should flee from this place if we're to live to fight again."

He turned to the other men, and they introduced themselves in quick succession: One was a Scotsman with the name Crawford, and the other was the Marquis of Douglas, the only southern noble to join them on the field. They'd been scouring Selkirk for survivors when they were taken by surprise by the handful of Covenanters.

The four men ran in silence from the town, hugging close to buildings to take cover whenever they heard voices. They spoke little as they moved swiftly out into the countryside, sparing their breath for the hard travel.

They'd gone for hours on foot, tracing a path along the banks of the Tweed, when Ogilvy stopped suddenly, his voice breaking the silence. "My luck's not left me yet." He cracked another of his cockeyed grins that made it look as if his mouth were too lazy to curve up on both of its sides.

"Oh, you're lucky, is it?" James looked with amusement at his companion.

"See for yourself." He nodded toward two saddled ponies grazing well north of Philiphaugh.

"So I see." James laughed. "Though I'll wager *your* luck was another's misfortune," he added, referring to the owners who'd presumably been killed in the battle.

The four men soon found themselves on a hilltop overlooking Peebles. It was a small burgh, whose buildings sprang up from the midst of a lush meadow as if cupped in a great, green palm.

"And this Neil MacLeod is a friend of yours?" James asked the southern nobleman as they studied the distant estate.

"Of true friends, I have few," Douglas said as he eyed Traquair House. It was a large manse on the outskirts of town, nestled in an idyllic spot among trees and the gentle curve of the River Tweed. "The MacLeod is an acquaintance, and a Highlander at that. I've no cause to doubt his allegiance."

"A Lowlander with Highland acquaintances, I imagine you don't count many among your allies." Ogilvy edged closer to the rise, as if the extra inches could help him discern friend from foe. His hair had come loose, and he held the dirty blond mass of it back from his forehead with a blood-crusted hand. "The Laird of Assynt is housed in Peebles?" He rolled on his side to face the other men. "What's a MacLeod laird doing in a border town?"

"A skeptic, eh?" Crawford had been eager to find safe harbor, and spoke in favor of approaching Traquair House.

"Aye," Ogilvy said incredulously, "as would you be if you'd had your home burned to the ground by just such a man keeping strange friends in stranger places."

"What takes him so far south?" James asked, ever on guard.

"When last we met, he claimed to be rallying men for you, James," Douglas replied.

"But why at Traquair House? The Earl of Traquair is a Stewart, and I've yet to glean his true allegiance." He looked up from the valley to the Lowland nobleman. The resounding defeat at Philiphaugh had the smell of a trap, and it had nagged at James since.

He would trust nobody until he could make sense of what treachery might be at work. "Are you certain of his hospitality?"

"Aye," Douglas replied, "he encouraged me and mine to partake of Traquair hospitality anytime."

"Truly, James." Crawford stood and adjusted his breeches and jacket. "The sun sets quickly now and I'd rather not spend one more night under the stars. I'm not so romantic a soul as you."

It became clear just how vast the mansion was when seen from up close. Its whitewashed stone was an imposing sight, glowing ghostly in the twilight. The façade was riddled with small square windows that emphasized the house's stout profile.

The MacLeod was a dour man of middle age, and though clearly he'd once been muscular, the skin had already begun to hang slack on his cheeks.

"My friend the Marquis of Douglas assures me we've your hospitality," James said. "I'm afraid we need to avail ourselves of it, despite the late hour."

"Och, what do you take me for?" MacLeod snarled, but it was unclear whether it was truly gruff good humor or something else that tempered his voice.

"You," he said to James, through lips that peeled into a smile that didn't quite meet his eyes. "No day passes that I'm not subjected to some tale of your victories. I'd hear tell from your own mouth, Graham. I'd also hear news of Philiphaugh. It seems you were routed without the MacColla to stand with you."

"Routed we were," James ventured in an even voice, "but not for want of MacColla, extraordinary soldier though he may be. Leslie discovered our position." The good humor that usually animated his face hardened, and James's black eyes flashed a warning. "Almost as though he'd expected us."

MacLeod laughed then, a spiritless utterance that chilled him. "Come, Graham, we've made a poor start of it. Food and whisky will set us to rights. But you men," he said to James's companions, "you must be weary from your travels. A maid will settle you in rooms for the night."

"Where, pray tell, is our host?" Ogilvy asked, not budging.

"Aye," James added, "I've long wanted to meet the Earl of Traquair. I've a question to put to him."

"He's gone away," MacLeod said simply. Two maids appeared to hustle the others to their rooms for the night. Ogilvy seemed hesitant to leave, but James dismissed his men with a shrug.

"That's unfortunate," James said. "You see, Cromwell and his Parliament and Campbell and his Covenanters all wish to overthrow the king."

He followed the MacLeod, who strode without pause toward the mansion's great room. "And yet," James continued, "Parliament accuses our host of being for the king, while the Royalists believe he's an enemy."

James stopped just inside the doorway. Though his tone was cavalier, his words were dangerous. "I'd hear it from the man's own mouth where his allegiance lies. And that of his friends," he added, his eyes glittering.

"I'd not question a man's loyalties when he's not here to speak for his own self," MacLeod said flatly. He turned and glared at James. "But you're here, are you not?" Another humorless smile split his face. "You're brought under this roof, so mayhap there's your answer, aye?"

They entered the room, cavernous and empty but for a long table and chairs. Night had fallen, and shadows clung to the fabric-draped walls, untouched by the candlelight that studded the table. Curtains in an indiscernible dark color bracketed a panel of windows whose dull, glassy eyes stared blindly into the blackness outside.

A fire burned low in the hearth, fronted by an enormous mastiff, his languorous pose belying the thick knots of muscle poised under fur and ready to pounce.

"Please," MacLeod said, pulling a chair from the table for his guest.

James sat warily, not taking his eye from the laird whose inscrutable ways had him at his guard. Two glasses waited for them on the table, thick leaded goblets each bearing a dram of whisky.

"To the king." MacLeod raised his in a toast.

"Aye," James said, "to Charles."

The wrong smell of it in his sinuses registered too late. No sooner had James placed his glass back on the table than he felt the effects. Buzzing came loud in his ears, and seeing MacLeod's expectant gaze, he knew.

"What treachery is this?" Clinging to the arms of his chair, James forced himself to stay upright. "Bastard, you've poisoned me."

"Not poison, no," MacLeod said.

"We don't want you dead, Graham." The voice came from the shadows. James heard the clicking heels approach at his back, though his body was unable to turn and see. "I'd not rob my fine countrymen from such a sight as your death. The execution of James Graham, Marquis of Montrose, would-be champion to his king and country? No, that shall be performed for a crowd of thousands. I'd not covet it for myself alone."

"Campbell," James bit out the name with disgust. "I'd know your snake's hiss anywhere. So you"—he managed to cant his head and catch the eye of the MacLeod—"you've played me false, is it? Is that how the wind blows here in the Lowlands?"

Campbell chuckled, the candlelight glistening on the damp of his thin lips. Elaborately settling and tucking his brocaded waistcoat, he sat by James's side.

James began to tremble violently, and the effort to remain seated took all his will. Numbness crept up his legs and deadened his hands, which were still clinging to the arms of his chair like lifeless claws.

"But"—James shuddered a deep inhale—"you're a Highlander. Why sully yourself with this . . . pig?"

"Oh, he has twenty-five thousand reasons to do so," Campbell answered for the laird.

"Aye," MacLeod added, "the bounty on your head is too great to ignore. For twenty-five thousand pounds you'd sell your own sister, I wager."

"Then . . ." James struggled, "you . . . wager wrongly."

"Och," MacLeod spat, "'twasn't just the reward. You've associated with too many Catholics for my tastes."

"I fight . . . with papist and Protestant alike." Head quivering, James's words were loosely formed now, spoken through lips nearly frozen with paralysis. "B-bigger than religion. For king. F-for country."

"King," Campbell said with a wave of his hand. "Your King Charles has fled. Parliament now wants his head for treason, so he's disappeared, some say to the Isle of Man."

Campbell took a small snuffbox from his pocket. It was crafted from horn, and the candlelight warmed the golden brown colors of its lid.

"It seems they've grown tired of him. Perhaps it's that he was born in Scotland." Campbell took a pinch of the powder and sniffed. "But Charles seems to have forgotten he's been sitting on an *English* throne these past years."

"No court . . ." James began. "None can try a king."

"Really?" Campbell absentmindedly picked the dark residue from under his thumbnail. "You must inform Parliament of that en route to Mercat Cross for your hanging."

James only gaped now, his body rigid but for the faint in and out of his breath.

"Oh yes," Campbell smiled. "Parliament has taken over, under the hand of Cromwell."

James sat like a statue beside him. Campbell caught his eyes and held them. "So you see, Graham, there is no one to protect you now."

Chapter 37

Magda tore frantically through the trunk, and was dismayed to see that it was filled with yet another pile of old clothes. Mildew and dust hung in the room, tightening her lungs. She dropped back to sit, wiping the damp from her brow.

She'd ridden back to Montrose in silence. James's uncertain destiny made her sick with fear. He seemed so intent on saving the world, just as her brother had. And Magda was terrified that, as it had for Peter, the day would come when James, with some gesture both foolish and grand, would get himself killed. She would lose him like she'd lost Peter. She'd barely survived her brother's death. Magda couldn't bear to go through such darkness and despair again.

She needed to protect herself from it. Needed to find her way back home.

She'd thought of his portrait as they traveled, and how it might once again be a portal for her, returning her back to her own time. It had disappeared from his room, but certainly it would still be somewhere in his possession, and she looked for it now.

She loved James—knew with regret and certainty that he was likely the only man she would ever love. She felt the sadness of leaving him already, profound and creeping steadily through her, deadening her to all other emotion.

The shadows grew darker, and she looked to the candle on the floor beside her. It was sputtering now, and she estimated she had but thirty minutes more until she lost the light. She had just one trunk left to go.

Magda knew as the lid opened effortlessly that this would be the one. Reluctance and eagerness both coursed through her. She leaned the lid against the wall and there it was, sitting atop a pile of someone's long-forgotten dresses. A portrait lying amongst the threadbare velvet and lace. His portrait. And once again it buzzed with the eerie energy she'd felt when it had sent her back in time. It was suffused with life, an almost sentient presence that spoke to Magda. Beckoned her.

Tentatively, she reached down and took the painting in her hands. The black background was even more ominous in the candlelight. It was cold under her touch, yet hummed with its own strange vitality.

She placed the painting on the floor to lean against the trunk. She stared at it, knowing with certainty that it was a door back to her time. Where would it land her? Would she be back in that same workroom, as if nothing had ever happened?

Was this it? Was this all there was to her time with James?

Nausea rolled through her at the thought. She realized a part of her had hoped to find the painting lifeless, had imagined that the decision would be made for her. But just as she'd wanted, the life Magda would lead was hers to choose. She could go forward in time, back to her workroom and her tools, back to her apartment, with hot showers and all the comforts she could imagine. So why was she claimed by doubt that left her feeling so empty and alone?

"Magda!"

She shrieked at the sound of Tom's voice.

He stood in the open doorway and scanned the room, trying to make sense of the scene. "What are you about, lass?"

Cold dread prickled through her chest at the vision of Tom. Distress furrowed his features, exaggerated in the spectral light of the single candle he held.

"They have him, lass. They have James. He had a price on his head. Some petty laird has betrayed him for gold."

"I . . ." Bile rose in her throat. "I . . ." Magda looked from Tom to the portrait at her side. Terror and love swelled in her in equal parts. *James.*

It was happening. What she'd feared most was coming to pass. James had been captured. The man she loved was going to be hanged.

And she was sitting here, rifling through trunks, thinking of abandoning him. Thinking about her old world, things like showers and work. How could she have forgotten how empty that life had felt after Peter's death? How life without love was a hollow procession of lonely days and unending, sleepless nights?

Magda dropped her hands from the painting as if stung. James would never abandon her. She wouldn't abandon him now.

She looked at the painting, edging away from it. She loved James, more than anything. To flee now would be an act of cowardice. She would no longer live her life in fear of loss.

She had to try to save him. If she succeeded, she would live with him and love him every day for the rest of her days. The time would come when she'd lose him, or James her, but Magda wouldn't let the fear of that day dictate her life.

"I can't leave him."

"We must run," Tom said.

She rose steadily to her feet. "We have to find him."

"There's naught we can do, Magda." Tom went to her and grabbed her shoulders, pleading. "We'll be lucky to escape with our own heads. Listen to me. We leave now, take shelter with the Camerons."

"You listen to *me*." Magda pulled from his grip. "They'll be expecting us to run," she said. "Campbell will be looking for us on every road out of here."

"The more reason to make haste, woman."

She heard herself say the words before she'd even thought about them. "James said you were once an actor."

"Aye," Tom replied, bewildered. "On the finest stages in all Edinburgh."

"Well then." Magda looked at the trunks all around her. "We need to find some disguises, because I need to help James."

❧

She hitched the creel higher on her back, and willed her muscles to cooperate. They'd traveled on horseback for as long as they dared, then as Magda and Tom had approached Selkirk, they'd had to adopt their disguises in full. Encountering a peddler family on the road, they had traded Tom's pistol and the last of his coin for a cart filled with pots and the basket she wore at her back, heavy with salt.

The town buzzed with excitement. Word had spread quickly about James's capture, and everyone had gathered to see the great hero, bound and helpless.

"I don't get it," Magda hissed. "What's the matter with these people?" Her arisaid began to slide off and she tugged it back over the crown of her head, her frustration with the scratchy, over-large garb only adding to her outrage. "They're Scottish too, right? James fought for *them*."

"Aye, Magda," Tom whispered, "Scotland is not so simple as that. You've Highlands and Low, and a mix of different religious beliefs, with clan grudges to leaven the dish." He was sweating profusely, the tan of his cloak already soaked to a dark brown at his back. "Not so simple at all."

James came into view, and Magda clapped a hand over her mouth to stifle her gasp. He'd regained control of his body, but remained immobile, hands trussed behind his back, tied to the seat of a cart. Despite his condition, he sat tall, sunlight picking gold highlights in his brown hair. Magda's throat closed as she forced her tears not to fall.

It was suddenly clear to her that worries over battles and babies could come later. She couldn't think of the future, or what it meant to be in the past. Magda only had the now, and what she knew in that very moment was that James was hers. She needed him by her side, and if that meant living in seventeenth-century Scotland, then so be it.

There was a challenge in his eyes as he discreetly scanned the crowd. They swept over Magda and Tom, and just when she thought James had missed them, she caught the hidden smile twitching his lips. That he'd seen her, that he knew she was there with him, gave Magda courage.

"Let's go," she said. "I think the show's starting."

Tom pushed the cart, and at once a wheel caught in the dirt-packed road. "I traded my pistol for this?" he grumbled, struggling to lever it up and over the rut. "Did you see the butt of it? Heart-shaped," he said wistfully, "like the rump of a French courtesan. And engraved too. It was a fine piece. Fine."

She silenced Tom with a glare, then looked around quickly to ensure nobody had heard. Though Campbell was nowhere to be seen, Magda was certain he was out there somewhere, lurking, and she made certain to keep her borrowed plaid draped over her head and pulled low over her brow.

They walked for some time, having no choice but to follow the growing mob, all angling for a glimpse of the Royalist hero before he was hanged. A handful of Campbell's men drove James's cart, pulled by a two-horse team. It was slow going, forced as they were to haul their load over drover's tracks whenever the dirt road faded into grass, but Magda made sure she and Tom kept the ragged jolting and dipping of James's cart constantly in sight.

"Had I known the intention was to march James all the way to Edinburgh, I would have posed as, say, a solicitor." Tom struggled with the wheels of his wagon. "Then I'd have had no need for this godforsaken thing."

Magda greeted Tom's nervous chattering with empty, unfocused stares. She'd made her decision to stay, and every bit of her was concentrated on James, as if he were some celestial body whose gravity drew her to him at all costs. In her mind, this was the moment. This was the single test, her chance to save James and live out her days by his side. Or she could lose everything. Magda somehow knew that, despite Lonan's assurances, in turning her back on the portrait, she'd lost her chance to return to her world. And now she could lose James forever too.

Campbell's men stopped frequently along the road and at every village and hamlet between Peebles and Edinburgh, and a distance of less than thirty miles stretched into a week of degradation for James. But despite the many humiliations suffered upon him, his posture never wavered. He always sought her in the crowd, managing to steal glimpses of her through the day.

Their peddlers' disguise was easy to maintain, and whenever Campbell's men stopped, Magda and Tom would set up keep not far from him. She was startled the first time someone approached her to buy salt, but was happy to lighten her load in trade for some bread and hard cheese.

On the morning they approached Edinburgh, rain fell far in the distance, looking like a gray veil billowing along the horizon. The weather followed close at their backs, and when they finally entered the capital, a gunmetal sky pressed in on the mass of granite buildings, robbing the city of color and shadow. Despite the gloom, Edinburgh throbbed with life, and Magda was overwhelmed by the bustle of what seemed like a remarkably modern city. The roads were narrow and buildings closed in on either side, many reaching higher than she'd have expected.

When Campbell's men turned the cart onto the smoothly cobbled stretch of Edinburgh's Royal Mile, a buzz swept through the crowd. The mob was expectant, and the sense of imminent change crackled in the air.

"I warned him of this," Tom muttered. "There was a time I warned him he'd end his days swinging from three fathom of rope, a day's diversion for the merchants of Mercat Cross."

"Where are they taking him?" Magda tucked her head toward Tom in an effort to make herself invisible. The crowd was growing now, a sickening crush of people smelling of sweat, smoke, and sewage.

"He'll be imprisoned at the Tolbooth, of course."

"So they're not going to hang him immediately?" she asked with relief. "There's still time to help him escape then."

"No, lass." Tom stopped abruptly, looking at her with pity in his eyes. "There's no saving him now. James is lost to us. None escape from the Tolbooth."

But Magda walked on, Tom's words merely a drone in her ears. She was certain now of what she had to do.

"This is Canongate," Tom whispered, catching up to her. "We're close now."

They creaked along for a time, struggling not to let the tide of people drive them too far from James. "Sweet Alba," Tom suddenly swore. Pulling his bonnet low, he pressed tight to Magda's side. "Look, quickly, to Moray House." He pointed to a building, two stories high. With its sharply pitched roof it was almost quaint. The elegant stonework around its windows was the only thing to announce it as a place of import.

Then a movement caught her eye, and Magda spotted him. Campbell, receding from a second floor window, disappearing from view as the curtain fell back into place. Even as adrenalin spiked her heart, relief that he hadn't spotted them flooded Magda. Just to make sure, she canted her body away from Campbell's building, only to accidentally knock into the person in front of her.

Magda felt the shadow pass overhead like a great cloud, and a dead chill crept over her. The crowd had stopped, and she looked up to see what she knew instantly could only be the Tolbooth. It was a solid, grim thing, constructed of gray stone, and looming high above the street. A boxy, two-story antechamber clung to the side of the building, topped by a balustrade gruesomely decorated with rotting skulls. One drew Magda's eye, and its wispy gray hair floating in the breeze seemed to ridicule her innocence. The skull angled toward the empty iron spike at its side, corroded black and waiting to be adorned.

The hum of the crowd intensified into loud and distinct calls, and people jostled roughly, trying for a final a glimpse of James.

It happened quickly then. He was whisked from the cart, flanked by burly Campbell men on either side. Planting his feet down hard, he struggled to hold them outside the doorway, frantically scanning the mob for sight of her, but it was in vain. James vanished into the blackness of the Tolbooth, and this time Magda was unable to stop the cry that tore from her throat.

Chapter 38

The wet reek of sewage assaulted James the moment he entered the Tolbooth. The wailing of men's voices echoed inside like the cries of feral animals. It took a moment for his eyes to adjust to the sudden dark pressing in on him. Raw stone gradually came into clarity, as did the handful of doors studding a hallway that disappeared from shadow into blackness.

A turnkey appeared, his hair pulled raggedly into a limp ponytail hanging down his back. He emanated the sour stench of sweat and vomit, as if he were the foulness of the place made manifest.

"The devil take you." One of the Campbell men thrust James toward the prison guard. "You'll soon rot with the MacDonalds."

James quickly righted himself. "And I'll see that the devil holds your place," he replied coolly. Straightening his shoulders, James mustered what dignity he could with his hands bound behind him. The turnkey grasped for his arm, and he flinched away. "I've no fight with you," James told him, and allowed the man to lead him to his cell.

Little light permeated the bowels of the prison. Torches sputtered along the walls, casting the two men in intermittent halos as they made their way, wending along corridors that seemed to branch ever outward like a labyrinth. The mad howling of men reverberated more loudly the deeper they went, and James wondered that perhaps he *was* off to see the devil, and that hell lay within the very walls around him.

The guard heaved open a door and they walked in among the prisoners. The acrid tang of urine was sharp in the dead air, making James's eyes momentarily tear. Cells crafted of brick and mortar lined the heavy stone walls like a honeycomb. Four iron doors loomed at the end of the passageway, each bearing a black slit proclaiming its occupant imprisoned in total darkness. Men, and what seemed the ghosts of men, were all around him. Some stared wild-eyed, ranting and grabbing for them through the bars of their cages, while others lay still, with their backs to the world as if willing death to claim them.

"Aye, here." The turnkey's voice was a startling rasp at his side. They'd reached an empty cell, and James was grateful to see he had bars instead of a door to hold him. Something skittered from out of the cell and the guard kicked suddenly and violently, just missing a large rat that raced into the shadows.

"You're to catch those," a voice scolded from behind. James turned to the prisoner inhabiting the cell across from his own. The man bowed his head. "The rats. You must catch them," he repeated. James noted the tight swell at the belly of the man's waistcoat.

Clicking a large square padlock into place, the guard locked him in. Though he'd girded himself, James couldn't help but feel his stomach turn at the sound.

Tamping down a spike of disbelief, James studied the small cubicle that was his cell. He inhaled deeply in an attempt to gather himself, realizing that his last days might very well be spent with nothing but his wits and a single bucket to rely on.

"The name is Ainslie," he heard behind him.

"I am James Graham," he said, meeting the other prisoner's eyes. "Marquis of—"

"We've no need for surnames here," Ainslie interrupted. "A title will earn you naught but death."

"Indeed?" James assessed the man. His bulging eyes and yellowed skin belied the gentlemanly clothing that now hung loose on his sinewy body. "Well, I am still pleased to make your acquaintance." He imagined Ainslie was once a young man of promise, and wondered what he could have done to suffer such a hideous fate.

"May I ask . . ."

"You may," Ainslie said at once. "Taxes."

"Pardon me?" James thought for a moment that the man had misunderstood his question.

"What did I do to find myself in the Tolbooth?" Ainslie brushed at a spot on his sleeve as if picking off a bit of dust in the midst of a drawing room conversation, rather than the filth of prison. "That was your question, yes? Well, sir, my crime is that I found myself unable to pay my taxes. An ill-conceived trust, one perjurious solicitor, and two purloined accounts, and here I stand before you, moldering like last week's bread."

"But what of escape?" James leaned against the bars of his cell. "Have you a mind for it? You seem at worst a wronged man, not a criminal."

"Escape?" Ainslie laughed. "Where to? Out the door, and I'd be mobbed and ransomed the moment my lungs met fresh air. Venture down and I'd be manna for rats."

"Down?" James asked in earnest, gripping the iron bars.

"They say another city lies tunneled beneath us." Ainslie spoke slowly, clearly savoring the sudden attention. "But I have my doubts as to whether a man could find his way out from there, and a death in the vaults beneath the Tolbooth is a death all the same, is it not?" He combed his fingers through the mass of his long beard, clearly hoping to appear civilized at all costs. "No, my poor, dear man. None has ever escaped the tyranny of the Tolbooth." Ainslie considered for a moment, then added as an afterthought, "Though there is half-hangit Maggie."

"Who?" James asked, startled by this absurdity.

"You've not heard of Maggie Dickson?" Ainslie smiled. "Aye, she too found herself imprisoned in Edinburgh's Tolbooth. The lass had been with child, and as the bairn's father was not her husband, she'd hid the truth. But truth, like a bad tooth, must come out, and come out it did. She was hanged for her offense. But"—he adopted a dramatic tone, and James wondered if Ainslie wasn't the perjurious solicitor he'd spoken of—"as her family was bringing her to be buried, they heard a banging on the coffin. They opened it, of course, and there lay Maggie. Angry and sore, aye, but alive, and live she did for another forty years."

James raised his brows in question, and Ainslie elaborated, "Her sentence was hanging, and hang her they did. You can be hanged but once for a single misdeed."

"Perhaps we'll be so lucky, aye?"

"As Maggie?" Ainslie asked. "No, friend, luck like that is a rare stroke indeed."

❀

"Do you need to practice it one more time?"

"No, I certainly do not," Tom told Magda, no longer hiding his impatience. He examined himself once more in the looking glass, ensuring that he truly looked the part he played. It had been easy to find himself a priest's cassock. A few coins slipped to a St. Giles washerwoman and he was as good as ordained. Suitable clothing for Magda, however, had been harder to come by. In the end, they'd settled for the simplest possible disguise. She'd pose as his impoverished attendant, requiring only that she skulk silently at Tom's side.

James had been in the Tolbooth two days now. Tom assured her that James's enemies would crave a very public hanging, and though Magda knew that bought them time, she couldn't help but dread that she might be on the verge of witnessing history as it had really happened.

Magda was amazed at how easily they could enter the Tolbooth with a few coins to grease the way. They'd sacrificed the last of their coin to the turnkey, insisting they give a condemned man his last rites.

"We've come to administer the viaticum, sir," Tom informed him in his most austere voice. "The last Holy Communion," he added when faced with the guard's dumb stare, "for a man on the brink of his death."

"Ach," the turnkey spat, "he was too long with the papists. And good riddance, says I."

"You too shall be forgiven," Tom intoned ominously as he glided into the cell, and James was forced to turn his back to hide the look on his face.

"*Nomini spiritus sanctu . . .*" Tom knelt at the door to the cell and began to pray in a loud, atonal voice, and the turnkey quickly cleared from the cellblock as if exposed to a contagion. Magda had a strong suspicion that Tom wasn't getting the words right, but she had to assume that the only people nearby who'd recognize the Latin mass would likely be behind bars.

"James," she gasped his name, instantly at his side.

"You're a sight, hen." A smile warmed his face, but she noticed the lines etched at the corners of his eyes and the tightness around his mouth, visible even through the week-long growth of his beard, many shades darker than the light brown of his hair.

"We don't have much time," she whispered, frantic. She dug clumsily in the pouch tied at her waist and pulled out a small stoppered vial. "Take this." She shoved it into his hand. "A witch, Gormshuil, gave it to me. It's henbane. It'll act like a poison. She said three sips will make a person appear dead. Sort of like *Romeo and Juliet*, right?"

"I think not, love." James gingerly placed the bottle back in her hands. "You forget, poison is what got me here, and I fear one poisoning is enough in this lifetime."

"Dammit, James," she hissed. "*This* lifetime is about to come to an end. Now take it," she commanded, slapping the vial back into his hand. "I don't know what you'll do when you wake up, or where you'll wake up, but . . . I can't think of anything else to do."

"I see it's unwise to cross you," he said, smiling at her verve. "*Hen*bane, aye?" He rolled the vial in his palm. "I knew I'd gotten to the heart of it with my name for you."

The scrape of wood on stone rumbled down the passageway as a guard opened the door to their wing.

James leaned down to take her mouth with his, and she clawed at the front of his coat, pulling him wildly to her. She poured her whole self, her whole focus into the knowing of him. The stubble of his beard, just long enough to be soft on her face. His lips dry on her mouth. The long press of his body, solid against her. Tears rolled down her cheeks, and she thought that, if he couldn't escape, this would be their last kiss, the one most seared into her, the one she'd be left with to kiss over and over again in her memory.

The dull clack of boot heels sounded on stone, and James pulled away. "You've not seen the last of me," he whispered, and he dashed the tears from her cheeks.

After the guard escorted Tom and Magda away, Ainslie's voice came from across the darkened corridor. "If ever I find my way free of this place, it seems I must convert."

James's response was uncharacteristically grave. "Faith is a powerful thing," he said, feeling the cool of the glass vial in his palm.

❀

"Guard!" Other prisoners joined Ainslie's chant. Many men in the Tolbooth may have longed for their own deaths, but it didn't mean they felt comfortable living among it. Having a dead body in the cellblock aroused feelings ranging from mild superstition to all-out hysteria.

"Bloody hell," the guard muttered, realizing his poor luck at being the one to discover a body. Clapping a hand over his mouth and nose, he kicked at James, who lay cold and motionless on the slab floor of his cell. The henbane brought with it a terrible stench, a foulness easily mistaken for the stink of death.

"How is he?" Ainslie asked. He'd grown increasingly agitated since James's collapse. They'd been chatting amiably when his speech began to slur heavily, and James lost consciousness soon thereafter.

"*How is he?*" the guard mimicked. "He's dead as a rail." Cursing, he laid James out flat, arms at his sides. "And that Campbell will be angrier than a wet cat too. Dead as a rail," he muttered, quickly rifling through James's pockets.

"What will you do with him then?" Ainslie spoke rapidly, his voice holding a note of alarm. He rubbed the near-empty vial where it hid in his coat pocket. James had tossed it to him, with a warning not to drink it. Ainslie fretted, not knowing if it was a soporific, or worse, he had in his possession.

"What we do with all you corpses. Aye," he said with a wink, "that's what you are to me. A corpse, or about to be one. Some get sold to the barber surgeons at Dickson's Close, for cutting." The guard grinned at this last bit, seeing Ainslie's obvious chagrin. "But first," he said with one last kick to James's side, "it's down to the vaults."

Chapter 39

James opened his eyes to utter blackness, and for a horrified moment thought he'd been buried alive. Shifting, he felt the crunch and slip of dry bones underneath him and, bolting up, slammed his head on the low ceiling. His stomach came to life roiling, and a wave of nausea stole his breath. Spinning onto his hands and knees, he vomited into the darkness. Mysterious hard edges cut into his hands, and knobs of bone dug into his shins and the tops of his feet, now stripped bare of his boots. Wiping the corner of his tartan along his mouth, James sent up a silent apology to the restless souls whose remains he'd just defiled.

The full memory of what he'd done came to him. Realizing he had no other choice, he'd choked down Magda's potion. It had been foul and sickly sweet, and he was now finding it to be all the more odious on the way back up. He spat into the blackness. His gut was completely empty, but he still couldn't eradicate the lingering taste of henbane from his mouth and nose.

They would have put him in the vaults underneath the Tolbooth. James knew it to be a nest of coffin-sized crypts, except this mausoleum housed no refined sarcophagi. It was merely a repository for corpses to rot into bone and dust. Looking from side to side, he opened his eyes wide. In the back of his mind, he'd hoped they would adjust, but not a shred of light made it to the cellars below the Tolbooth.

The sound of a small creature scurrying reverberated through the vault, sending bones to topple and settle loudly behind him. James instinctively patted his hand to his side for his small blade before he remembered he had no weapon, and, he thought, the guards would have stripped his pockets clean as well.

He sensed other creatures, almost definitely rats, making their approach. The smell of his own vomit came to him, and his stomach gave a belated lurch as he realized rodents would soon bear down on him, come to feed.

Hoping the vault wasn't any longer than a coffin, he edged back slowly until his feet hit open air. James eased backward, and when the lip of the cell was at his waist, his feet finally touched ground.

The scream of rusted metal rang through the chamber as someone opened a little-used door in the distance. His deprived senses quickly became aware of voices and the hint of a torch approaching. His surroundings emerged limned in faint gray light, gradually growing clearer as the torch drew closer.

He darted his eyes around him, taking in the small room and the crypts stacked in rows all around, three-high to the ceiling. The only exit from the chamber was the tunnel. A yellow glow flickered along its low walls, bobbing and swaying in time with the torchbearer's gait.

Even closer now, the voices assaulted him, and he realized how much the henbane had left his senses scraped raw. James shook his head and rubbed his hands roughly along his scalp to clear his mind. He focused on the sounds until he distinguished two distinct speakers. One would be a guard, he thought, at the sound of the thick accent. Rambling nonstop, cajoling a silent companion. The other man spoke infrequently, begrudgingly, in tones announcing him of an upper class. So the guard was selling him something. James's corpse, most like. He knew that many a guard turned a tidy profit selling bodies to teaching hospitals, or worse.

James opened his eyes wide, urging them to adjust to the approaching light. It would do him no good to be blinded by the torchlight. He stood on the hard-packed floor and swept his eyes over the wall of crypts. Desiccated remains emerged from the black shadows. Ashen silhouettes resolved into grimacing faces and empty sockets staring at him, crying a silent warning. He stifled a shudder, grateful that the vault he'd been placed in housed only bones. Reaching in, he took the largest one he could find.

Though its long, smooth heft was reassuring in his hand, he knew it wouldn't be enough. James scanned the room, spotting a small chamber along the top edge. Just inside the entry, it was one of the first the men would walk past as they entered from the tunnel. James grasped the crumbling brick lip of the crypt, and planting his foot along the centermost vault, he hoisted himself into the pile of bones easily five feet off the ground.

"What was—" the more effete of the two men stammered.

"*Ist!*" the guard ordered, and their strained silence choked the still air. A sudden clatter of bones was met with a gasp, followed by the sound of tiny feet scuttling along the far wall.

"Just the rats, aye?" The guard spoke again. "Come now, in here."

The men drew closer, and James found their voices an almost unbearably loud booming in the confined space. He turned his focus inward, forcing his overwhelmed and still sickened body to reconcile with its surroundings. A musty smell like damp wool made his sinuses twinge, but otherwise the chamber was surprisingly void of scent. His breath gradually steadied, sweeping extraneous thoughts from his mind. James eased his knuckles, loosening his fingers around the bone so his grip was firm, but not choking.

"And you claim he's deceased no more than twenty hours past?"

The one buying the body spoke, and James found the sound was no longer a shrill assault.

"Oh, aye," the guard assured him, "he's fresh yet, and not even stiffened. Just through—"

James leapt just as the men entered the chamber, landing on the taller of the two. The smoothed hair and fine feel to his clothing announced him as the client. James barely hit him, his weapon striking the flesh of the man's shoulder with a dull crack. The bone in his hand was old and brittle, and James felt it splinter wide up the middle as he struck. The man collapsed, but if it was from James's blow or merely due to a dead faint, he couldn't tell.

The guard threw down his torch and was on him at once. James knew instantly that the man would pose a much greater challenge than his companion had. He was shorter than James, but scrappy and tenacious, and managed to land a flurry of punches to his abdomen and side before James got his bearings.

He thought he'd heard a clatter when the other man fell, and hoped he'd carried a gentleman's sword at his side. Such a blade was intended less for fighting than for show, but anything would be a step up from a dead man's thighbone. James grabbed the guard around the shoulders and, pinning him in a boxer's hold, began landing heavy blows on his side, all the while creeping sideways toward the unconscious nobleman.

The guard, though, clearly relied on a fair amount of street-fighting experience. He tore away from James's grasp and swooped back in to butt him hard on the head.

James grunted as a flare of white light momentarily filled his line of sight. He'd heard his nose crunch, and the iron tang of blood filled his mouth and impaired his breathing. He stumbled backward, tripping over the other man who was still out cold on the floor. James purposely tumbled then, immediately pawing at the nobleman's side until he felt the ornamental scabbard at the man's waist.

The smallsword was a pleasant little weapon, shorter than a rapier, and James couldn't help the smile that spread over his face at the feel of its featherlight weight in his hand. A new fashion from France, such swords were more like jewelry than weaponry for a man, with their slender blades and decorative pommels and crossguards.

Bounding to his feet, he gave it an experimental whip through the air, and laughed then at the joy of wielding a blade that could dip and alight like a bird in flight.

The guard dove toward him, and James ducked back easily. He'd seen the hesitation flicker across the man's features at the sound of his laugh. "You could run, aye?" James told him, taking advantage of the man's uncertainty.

Unlike his broadsword, this weapon lacked a cutting edge, its needle-thin outline made for thrusting alone. And, as the man shook his head, thrust James did, hopping forward and forward again to plunge the sword easily into the man's torso. Gasping a curse, the guard lurched backward and clutched at his wound. He pulled his hands away and stared with disbelief at the blood covering them.

James dragged a sleeve across his face to wipe his own blood from beneath his injured nose. He counted himself lucky that his opponent was a simple turnkey and not a part of the city guard. Though this man clearly wasn't armed as a soldier would be, he did carry a dagger, which appeared now in his bloodied hand.

The guard rushed at him and then stopped short, seeing James's poised sword stance and the calm that smoothed his face. Sneering, the man bobbed his hand a few times then tossed up his knife, grabbing the flat of the blade in his palm. Planting a short step forward, he threw.

A clipped grunt escaped James as the dagger stabbed the dense muscle of his thigh. He was calm as he removed the blade and slung it back in a single swift motion.

Squinting, James picked up the torch and limped down the tunnel. The sound of the guard hitting the floor echoed along the stone passageway, his own dagger plunged in his throat.

The ground was cold on his bare feet, which slapped quietly as James jogged through the passage beneath the Tolbooth. Dozens of chambers and tight tunnels spurred from his path, but spying the footprints shuffled into the top layer of loose, dry dirt, he stuck to the original passageway and eventually spotted a narrow staircase cut into the stone.

James scaled it quickly, thinking he could always double back if need be. He came to a landing and braced the flat of his hand on the door there. The cold, corroded iron muted all sound, and James thought he was as likely to find a safe haven as a crowded guardroom on the other side. He startled when the door began to budge, and dove quickly back down the stairs. He flung the torch down the tunnel. It clattered and rolled to a stop, and James hoped it landed far enough away to conceal its light.

He plugged his fingers in his ears at the shriek of rust dragging along stone. A sliver of light cut down the stairs as the door opened. Motes of dust, dirt, and the powder of ancient metal whirled in angry currents, disturbed by the sudden movement. James tucked himself close along the stone wall and waited, tracing his palm expectantly along the thin bracket of steel that comprised his sword's elegant hand guard. A draft of fresh air carried muted voices down to him, and James mused he'd never thought Edinburgh had ever smelled so sweet.

The door screeched again, not as loudly this time, and James sensed it closing, shutting him off once again from the world. He knew he had but a moment to act. Bounding back up the stairs, James fled into the late-afternoon light, a grin on his face at the terrified shouts of laborers who'd thought a wraith had just escaped the tombs to cross their path. A ghost indeed, he thought, and ran to the one place nobody would find him.

But James didn't see the man rise from the steps of the neighboring Bellhouse to follow, intent drawing the stranger's face into tight lines and hastening his stride.

The Scottish could be a suspicious lot, and James knew that, come night, the only folk to be found in the graveyard off Greyfriars Kirk would be grave robbers. The Royal College of Surgeons was expanding, and with the increased demand for bodies, resurrection was a fast-growing trade.

It was late afternoon, and the sun struck Greyfriars Kirkyard at a sharp angle. White light illuminated tombs and trees from the side, making them appear more vivid, somehow beyond real. Long black shadows tapered from the bases of elaborate tombstones like specters emerging for the night.

Tall, tightly packed walls of tombstones closed in on either side of him, gray, elaborately carved monuments covered with macabre images of ill-shaped skulls and ominous epitaphs extolling the lives of brave husbands and loving wives. Oversized family vaults studded the graveyard, looming like small haunted dwellings frozen in time, the years moldering and blackening their names and their detail.

The elegant steeple of St. Giles Cathedral hovered in the distance, putting him in mind of Brother Lonan. He thought of Rollo too, wondering if he lived or died. That Rollo might be out there somewhere at that very moment, in the borderlands not too far away, struck him. But whether he suffered, thrived, or had already breathed his last, James had no way to know.

He let his mind turn to Magda then. Clever, beautiful, surprising Magda. Since they'd met, she'd flourished, like an elegant heron, once stiff and straight, who'd spread her wings to reveal the startlingly spectacular plumage beneath. It had taken a special kind of courage to snub her nose at danger, sneaking into the Tolbooth to administer him poison, of all things.

And it had taken love too. For surely that is the only thing that could fuel such recklessness. Just as he loved her. His chest swelled with it. It expanded him, ennobled him, somehow made him more than just a man.

"Graham." The voice behind him was furtive hush.

The smallsword was in his hand before he'd finished turning about. The blade may have been intended for decoration, but it made a pretty hum as it cut through the crisp autumn air. The terror on the man's face stopped James's hand short, and he halted the sword to touch a light kiss on the stranger's right ear.

"State your business, man." Pent-up energy hummed along James's veins, his body still coiled from his ordeal of the past days. "How is it you know my name?"

"I-I . . ." he stammered. James eased away his blade, realizing the man in front of him was a half-wit. A quick scan and blackened nails, filthy bare feet, and the dirty knees of his trousers hanging loose betrayed his status as a simple workman.

"Easy, lad." James resheathed his sword. His relaxed posture was intended to put the stranger at ease, but James scanned the graveyard all the while, looking for signs of movement or telltale shadows peeking from behind the towering tombstones.

"Mag-da—" the man began, his tongue thick in his mouth.

"What of Magda?" Panic shot through James, and he fought to keep a calm stance. "You've time. Say it, man. Who has brought you here?"

The man clapped a hand to his pocket, and James pulled his own hand back to rest once again on his sword hilt.

"M-Magda says Graham comes with me." He pulled something out of his pocket and thrust it toward James.

The button James had given her so long ago once again rested cool in his palm. Sunlight shimmered along the delicate gold filigree and made the blue enamel glow luminous.

"She says give Graham the button and Graham comes with me."

"So I shall," James told him, shaking his head at his wife's keen mind. Long stripped of his sporran, he tucked the button in his shirtsleeve. He gave the man a reassuring clap on the shoulder. "Graham comes with you, lad."

The man led him down the path at an aggravatingly slow pace. Irregularly paved stones wended through grass that was an eerily vivid green against the colorless kirkyard. They reached an alley, and James spotted the coach waiting at its end, just at the intersection of Grassmarket.

The carriage was backlit by the sun, lower now in the sky. Flares of white sunlight streaked across the black painted exterior, casting sinister shadows of carriage and horse along the alleyway. He saw her then, stepping out. She was lit brilliantly from behind, setting off warm, bright streaks in her hair. A breeze swept down the passageway, sweeping the long russet locks up to dance like flames on the wind.

As he approached, her features emerged from shadow. The slight curl to her lips belied the intensity in her eyes. She looked happy to see him, but relieved too, and not yet certain they were out of danger.

James leaned in to kiss her, and she gave the slightest shake to her head. Turning, Magda climbed back in the carriage. Blood pounding in his chest, he watched her. Took in the curve of her hip and the slight shift of muscle as she alighted.

James was quick behind her, pressing his body along hers, urging her in, and kissing the words from her mouth as the coach door slammed shut.

Chapter 40

Magda shut her eyes and inhaled, soothed by the distant ebb and flow of the waves. James had insisted they open the balcony door while they took their tea, despite the shocked protestations of his sister. The third-floor sitting room was small, but with charming furniture and a door that opened to a view of the sea, it was one of Magda's favorite places. Though the journey back to Montrose had been harrowing, and nice as it was to be safe for the moment with a roof over their heads, they'd gotten accustomed to feeling the air fresh on their faces.

Tom had arranged the carriage out of Edinburgh, but they could only afford to let it for the day. It had been enough, though, to hide James as he quickly changed his clothes, and they'd gotten outside the walls of Edinburgh disguised as a wealthy family. From there, they convinced a Queensferry fisherman to take them out from the Firth of Forth to sail directly into Montrose harbor. Magda had breathed a sigh of relief when they finally arrived at his home late the following night.

"Where is that woman?" Margaret exclaimed. "I called for her a quarter hour past." Chafing her arms, James's sister glared once again at the open balcony door. "Well," she announced, "you two may insist on taking a chill, but the premature cooling of this fine tea would vex a lesser woman."

Margaret had been bustling about since their return to Montrose, and Magda had been more than happy to let herself get swept along by all the commotion. They would stay but one more night before they had to leave, gathering the supplies necessary to be in disguise and on the run once again. In search of additional blankets, Margaret had led her to the same dusty storage room whose trunks Magda had so thoroughly rifled through. In a moment of whimsy, she dashed off a little something to store with James's portrait. Careful not to touch it, she laid a slip of paper atop the painting with the note: "*Property of the Metropolitan Museum of Art.*"

"We know well it is the rare concern that makes you peevish, Margaret." A mannered smile spread across James's face, which Margaret only greeted with a sisterly glare.

Though returned home, James still wore only a tartan and shirt. He'd simply smiled when Margaret gently hinted that he should dress like her husband, Napier, and don proper trews. And, looking at him now over the lip of her teacup, Magda grinned and thought she never would've guessed that a man could look so sexy walking around in what basically amounted to a skirt.

But James was nothing if not sexy. His skin glowed from so much time outdoors, setting off the smoldering cocoa color of his eyes. His nose was recovering from the break. It had been on the large side to begin with, and the injury left a small bump on the length of it, an appealing imperfection on his otherwise gorgeous face.

"Dear sister," he added, "don't you know, the sea air is good for the soul."

"I can see it through the window." She stood from her seat. "I don't know where that woman has got to. It seems I'll have to find my own shawl," Margaret muttered as she bustled from the room.

In deciding to stay, Magda had freed herself to experience fully how much James meant to her. Although his handsomeness did indeed make her knees buckle, she thought she'd burst from the love she felt for him. She'd contemplated his portrait and the exit it offered, and had come close to leaving him forever. But the instant she heard of his capture, she realized that she couldn't turn her back on him; if there were something she could do to save him, then that could be her only choice. And then Magda had seen him, and though he'd been bound and subjected to such humiliations, he was ever gallant and noble to the last, and she knew at once that she'd made the right decision.

James shot her a look at his sister's exit, and Magda gave him a quiet smile. She set her tea down and, knitting her brows, stared out toward the sea.

"Still not convinced, are you, hen?" Parliament's red-coated soldiers would be on the lookout for them now, and they needed to find a safe haven in which to disappear. Though Magda battled her own panic, James had been calmly reassuring her over and over again that they'd be safe once ensconced in a cottage on one of the Western Isles. "You know I will keep you safe."

"It's not me so much that I worry about," she said. Her eyes ran over the length of him. James could don the crudest of disguises, yet there would be no way to hide his audacity, his nobility, his courage. It shone in his eyes, and was clear in the way he spoke and the manner in which he carried himself. "You're pretty recognizable."

Though, she thought, one good thing about the seventeenth century was that no phones or cameras meant a person really could simply disappear into thin air.

"Aye, and that is why we leave tomorrow," he agreed. "Charles courts the Scottish from his hideaway on the Isle of Man, and I too shall have to be satisfied pursuing my political intrigues from afar."

"Don't joke," Magda said. "You told me they want to execute the king for treason. If Campbell can find him, he can find you too."

"No, hen," James said quietly. "It's not the Campbell who harries me now. He's fled back to his castle at Inveraray, a ruined man. He thought his wealth would buy him victory. He mortgaged his future to buy support, and now creditors bang at his door and his own son threatens patricide."

James got up to sit close to her on the rose-colored settee. "It's Cromwell I fear now. He wants to unseat the king and have Parliament alone rule us all." James gazed out the window into the far distance, his face dark. "I have a bad feeling about one who would claim the head of his own monarch. Accession to the throne is something divinely determined. It doesn't seem possible for a king to be guilty of treason. Treason against himself, is it?" James asked figuratively, shaking his head in disgust.

"Either way," he added, "the time for me to pursue overt action is over. I shall continue to agitate for the king, but sadly, it will have to be from a distance. For the moment, at least."

Magda glared at that last statement, but James was saved by a knock at the door. He studied her face as if he could convince her with his eyes alone. "Come," he called out, without looking from Magda.

One of the home's many maids opened the door. "A gentleman has come to call, sir." She bobbed a curtsy. "He didn't give his name," she added quickly, seeing the intensity on James's face. "He claims you fought together at Philiphaugh."

"How did he find you?" Magda asked of the mysterious visitor. But the look that swept James's features broke her heart. He would be desperate to speak with a former comrade. She knew he'd been haunted by regret and anguish from the battle at the border. He wouldn't have recovered from the deaths of so many good men. Would never recover.

"Aye," he said quickly, obviously eager to speak with one of the few survivors. "Send him up straightaway."

He looked back to Magda, a resigned smile curving his mouth, and put her hand to his lips. He was facing her when they heard the sickeningly familiar sound. His hand gripped hers tightly, and the peace that lit his eyes froze as all expression bled from his face.

"I'd have killed you months ago if it weren't for Campbell's incompetence."

James turned just as Alexander Leslie pulled his pistol to full cock with another loud click. He stared at Leslie until realization loosened his brow. "You'd be the Covenanter general."

"Very good, Graham." Leslie took a step forward, his arms extended straight in front of him, aiming for James's chest. "I *was* the Covenanter general, until Campbell, that stubborn and raging prig, misused my men. He thought his wealth—"

Magda shifted her weight, and Leslie's gun barrel was pointed at her head in an instant. "Still yourself. Don't think I'd not shoot a lass."

"Who knew"—James rose slowly, drawing Leslie's attention away from Magda—"that you'd have such principles?" He instinctively brought his hand to his side, empty where his broadsword usually hung. He'd not yet replaced it, and imagined it had fetched a tidy sum for some lucky guard along the way.

"Is that what you call it then?" Leslie's eyes roved the well-appointed room around him. "I say you're just like the Campbell. I say men like you use money, not *principles*, to achieve your victories." The Covenanter general was impassioned, and didn't hear the door ease open behind him.

"You can think what you like." James spoke through gritted teeth. "You're the one who fights for coin. Not I. My Highlanders and I were rewarded with dried oats for our bellies and cold-packed snow to rest our heads. And you come here to challenge *me*?"

Leslie didn't hear Margaret at his back. She'd glided in the room, snatching up the silver pot from the tea service as she entered. Magda tried to catch her eye to send a silent message, but James's sister saw nothing but the back of Leslie's head. Margaret cut across the sitting room like a great, silent blue-silken barge, outrage pursing her mouth tight.

"I tire . . ." Margaret said as she swung, "of your"—Leslie turned in what seemed like slow motion just as the teapot connected with his temple—"adventures, James.

"And *you*," she pointed at Magda with an accusing finger. "You mustn't overtax yourself."

James was across the room in an instant, standing over Leslie's limp body splayed on the Oriental carpet. Shaking his head in disbelief, he said sotto voce, "My sister takes every advantage of the trappings of her wealth."

Magda's laugh sounded relieved, but her eyes didn't leave Margaret, who studied her with disarming intensity.

"Fetch Napier," James called to a maid who'd rushed in upon hearing the commotion. She stood staring mutely at Leslie. "Fetch my brother-in-law. Make haste, now. Before he wakes." James nodded to the floor, which spurred the woman to action.

"Aye," James's sister said. The two women still stared at each other from across the room. "I've seen your belly." Margaret calmly gathered the teapot from the floor and placed it back on the tray. "You'll not hide it from me."

She walked briskly to Magda's side and put a proprietary hand on her abdomen. "And did you not know it?" Margaret asked. "Look at those cheeks. And I know your bosom wasn't nearly so large when first we met. Oh aye," she said responding to Magda's blush. "I can always spot a woman with child."

Tears pricked the corners of Magda's eyes as she gazed up at James, now standing above her.

"Is it true, hen?" Tenderly, he reached down and cupped her chin. "Could it be true?"

"I . . . I don't know," she stammered, even as she realized that she did know. Had known somewhere deep down that she carried James's child. A vision flashed to her, of a life with James on some small, windswept island, a plaid shawl pulled tight around her for warmth, children racing at her feet, their cheeks flushed with their simple life of green moors, sunshine, and the sea. All of her reservations about life in the seventeenth century dissolved and she thought only of James's smile, and felt the rightness of it all. "Yes, I think . . . I think I am."

"Really?" The question exploded from his mouth with a laugh. Sitting, he grabbed Magda and pulled her onto his lap. "So," he said, quoting the old marching song in an exaggerated Scots brogue, "are you with bairn, my chicken?" He kissed her full on the mouth, for all to see.

"So I've been downgraded from a hen, is it?" Then Magda laughed too, her immediate fears for their safety, for the moment, melted away. "I do love you, James."

"And I you." He took her face in his hands and gave her a brief, rough kiss. "Oh, aye, I do love you so."

Margaret turned away quickly and bustled back to the tea tray. "I know that . . . that *man*, Lonan was it?" Hesitating, she retrieved her half-filled cup. "That he handfasted the two of you. But I plan to throw you a proper wedding." She took a dainty sip and scowled at the cold temperature. "The seamstress has your sizing now, and I'd commission her before you grow too large. But we must wait," Margaret added with great consternation, "until that hideous injury on my brother's face subsides." She put the cup back down with a sharp clink. "As if his nose wasn't already large enough," she added in a mumble.

Magda simply laughed. "It's good to be home."

Chapter 41

"Tell me again, my swan." Napier backed off the balcony into their bedroom, pulling his wife with him. "Tell me how you did it."

He leaned in to nibble at the thick flesh at Margaret's neck. Its softness never ceased to entice him, and the low-necked gowns she favored were a constant torment, showcasing her suppleness as they did. "Tell me how you saved the day."

"Oh, Archibald," Margaret gasped. "I . . . I was so afraid."

"My sweet and delicate swan, you must have been terrified." He twined his long, thin fingers through her hair, releasing it from its tight bun. "What would I have done had you not found such courage?"

"I had no choice. Oh!" she cried, as Napier spun her around to bend her over the edge of the bed. His lean body folded over hers, an almost perfect match in height, if not in weight.

"Oh, Archie, I was so afraid. But it was the only thing I could do to save us."

"You brave, brave lassie." He deftly undid the row of buttons running down the spine of her dress. "My sweet bonny lassie." Napier loosened the bodice and slipped his fingers in and around the front, taking one of her large breasts full into his hand.

"Oh, Archie!"

They both stood, but Margaret's elbows and head rested on the bed now, as if that and the force of Napier's will were the only things holding her upright. He swept her hair up and over into loose tendrils on the mattress above her head. Napier could tell by the rapid rise and fall of her chest that she was breathless now. He could feel Margaret's eagerness for him, sensed her deep longing cut with the slightest bit of trepidation.

Margaret may have been a force to be reckoned with outside the bedroom, but inside she was as demure as a virgin, always startled and exhilarated by his overtures. Napier tenderly turned her face sideways, tracing his finger along her lips, inserting it into her mouth, and watched with a hooded and hungry smile as her eyes closed with pleasure and the flush spread from her breasts up to her cheeks.

"Do you want me, wife?"

"Oh . . . oh, aye," she said. And that too made Napier smile. She was so conscious of appearances, of place and class. Napier was always incredibly gratified to watch that propriety slip away whenever they lay together. To watch her blush, to hear her accent grow coarse, and see her face go wild with her passion made him want her beyond reason.

He took Margaret fast then, hiking up her skirt and hitching down his pants, unable to wait. Napier would take her slowly and properly later, but now he needed to be inside his wife. He pulled her close and thrust into her, ignited by Margaret's pleasured moans and the feel of his flesh against hers. She tossed her head back, and Napier saw the hot flush of her cheeks and watched as Margaret's lips parted to release a sound, sharp and feral, as her body tensed then loosened in his arms. He fell into her then, losing himself to her, and they collapsed together, sated, onto the bed.

"Oh, you are my Archibald," she purred when they'd finished. Napier gently pulled her all the way up onto their bed, cradling her body into his.

"And you," he said in reply, his love for her ragged in his voice. "You are my most adored, my brave and bonny Margaret."

Chapter 42

They entered their home with their arms wrapped about each other. It was a humble place, but made beautiful by the multitude of wildflowers they'd picked, blooms tenacious enough to brave the late autumn wind that whipped against the crags of the shoreline. Lavender, pink, and white blossoms twined along the rafters, and their sweet, fresh scents mingled with the rich sea air that permeated their life on the island.

Though James and Magda had been joined long ago in a handfasting blessed by Brother Lonan, the wedding ceremony they'd just held was a formal acknowledgment of their union. A few friends and family had come to give witness, and they crowded now into the cottage's main living area.

Of those who couldn't attend, they'd gotten news. MacColla still fought in the western Highlands, eager to avenge his father, seemingly unable to rest until he witnessed the total destruction of the Campbell clan. Ewen Cameron had relayed his family's regrets, but had sent with Napier a gift from his library, a bound copy of the poems of Lucan, whom he knew to be one of James's favorite authors. And James had been heartbroken to hear that the fine young Jamie Ogilvy had been captured after their escape from Selkirk, and was still imprisoned in the Tolbooth.

James thought too of all those who'd fallen, and drank a toast to Colonel Sibbald, noting that, though the old man would've appreciated the gesture, he'd likely have preferred whisky to the wine in James's hand.

Everyone had news, and some even had gossip about James himself to share. Speculation over his fate raged through Scotland. Apparently there were some who believed he'd been hanged in secret for Cromwell's personal entertainment, while others had him off gallivanting across France. It all amused him, so long as it kept their eyes away from his and Magda's hideaway.

All were dressed for the day in their finest. Napier wore a quilted waistcoat in olive green that set off the canary yellow of Margaret's dress. His eyes kept straying to the line of satin bows that ran from between her breasts down the front of the gown's tight stomacher, and the two of them seemed to think that their stolen touches went unseen.

Tom Sydserf was a grand figure in a doublet of navy velvet. He also wore buff-colored britches, tucked into fashionable wide-cuffed boots new enough to creak with each step.

James was overjoyed to see Will Rollo again, having only recently learned of his fate. He'd come the day before, still recovering, but alive and strong. Napier had received word that Rollo would attend the ceremony, but he'd kept his impending arrival secret, and the shock and elation of it had overwhelmed James. Though the bandage across Rollo's chest meant he could only wear his coat slung about his shoulders, his stoic face cut as handsome a profile as ever.

"I'd like to raise my glass." Tom's voice boomed over the chatter, and the room fell silent.

"Aye, a toast," Napier agreed. For the first time that evening, he stepped from his wife's side. "To the health and honor of the happy couple. If years ago you'd told us this day would come, we'd have doubted you."

"Aye," Margaret interrupted. "I never thought to meet a woman so capable of captivating my brother."

"Though I dare say he chose one from much farther afield than France," Tom mused into his wine glass. Magda watched Margaret overhear his comment, and saw the renewed speculation that sparked in her eyes. She gave her sister-in-law an enigmatic wink, then had to laugh at herself acting so like her husband. Soon she'd tell Margaret of her true origins, and she greatly looked forward to shocking her with the news.

They toasted for some time, but when the talk turned ribald, James pulled his wife out onto a modest flagstone terrace along the side of their cottage. The sun had long set and the moon outshone the stars that night, casting bright, silvery light in a shimmering line that connected Magda and James to the land at their feet and the waves beyond.

"I look at you and cannot believe my fortune." James stepped back and held her hands in his, admiring Magda in her dress. It was a gown of ivory satin with a straight bodice, simple but elegant. James had instructed his sister to spare no expense, and gold thread was embroidered at the neckline and along armbands above the elbow. Magda wore an arisaid over top, in matching ivory wool and lined with silk, tied at her waist by a thin leather cord with coral beading at the tips.

The ceremony had been smaller than he would've wished—James would have pledged his vows to her in front of all the world if he could have—but he took her at her word that the intimate celebration was all she ever could have wanted.

"Are you certain a life sequestered with me is what you desire?" Fear for their safety had led them to one of the more secluded Hebridean isles. He longed to have his library, to hear musical performances, and to drink fine wines, but the simplicity they enjoyed seemed to thrill Magda. Seeing her run barefoot along the beach, her hair flowing loose and her laugh rising in the air, had made this self-enforced exile worthwhile.

"You deserve a life rich with the sights and sounds of the world." Concern etched his brow. "And yet I find that my days of travel, roaming from royal courts to tangled wilderness, seem to have come to a close."

"James." Magda beamed, shaking her head in disbelief. "This is exactly what I want. Your roaming was just about the death of me. I love our new life, and I want to stay just here. I want to raise our children just here."

He placed his hand on her swollen belly. "How is it the Fates smile upon me so? You, hen, make me the happiest man alive. And I've a gift for you. Aye," he said, seeing the protest begin to furrow her face. "I'll not be refused. A husband has the right to give a gift to his bonny bride."

"But I didn't get you anything."

"Oh, but you already have." He took out a small rectangular parcel. It was wrapped in a bit of flannel, and had just fit in his sporran. James placed it in her palm and, holding his hand atop hers, said, "You've chosen to stay here with me. I can think of no greater gift than your very self. But this"—James looked down at their hands clasped around his gift to her—"this is my way of saying that I do not take lightly what you offer. I know all that you've sacrificed. You lost your brother long before we met, and in choosing to stay by me, you've now lost your future as well. A chaotic world it seems to me," James said with a small laugh, "but nonetheless magnificent for all its wonders."

"I don't miss it, James. That world—"

"You may not miss it now, but the day might come when you do. I just want you to understand that I appreciate all that you've sacrificed. I will spend my days trying to be a man equal to it."

He squeezed her hand and let it go, and the bit of flannel parted to reveal the gift beneath. It was a miniature portrait, done in oil on a small, square panel of wood. A young man bearing Magda's wide forehead, her aristocratic nose, and her full mouth. But it was his bright red hair that made him the image of Peter. The brother she'd lost.

Her tears came in a rush. The image was tiny, but somehow it was precisely those hair-thin brushstrokes, and the way they picked out the fine details yet omitted the broad ones, that made the portrait such an uncanny representation of her brother.

It was a shock to see his face again, but it filled her. James clearly understood her feelings for her brother and the profundity of her loss. Holding this tiny image that James had commissioned to honor Peter's memory gave her a feeling of completion. She mourned her brother, and it was James's recognition of the depth of those feelings that let her feel she could finally move on.

"Is it a good likeness?" he asked tenderly.

"Yes . . . I can't believe it. How did you . . . ?"

"Our fine Brother Lonan. I told him what you've said about Peter."

Magda smiled to hear her brother's name on her husband's lips.

"That you were a pair, but he with his bright ginger hair."

"You remembered."

"Of course I did, hen. You have me bewitched. I hang on your every word." His tone was more serious than playful. "Or do you not know it yet?"

"Thank you, James." She held the portrait to her breast. "I'll treasure this."

"As I'll treasure you, Magda." He cupped her cheek in his hand. "And, if you ever tire of me, well, you can see this wee painting as acknowledgment of your freedom. I know it's different for lasses where you came from, and I will try to make you my equal in every way, but you will always have this portrait, and the promise of the power Lonan assures me it wields."

"But I could never leave you." She leaned into James, savoring the reassuring solidity of him. Magda had come to know the hard feel of his body and his smell of musk and spices that she knew like her own self. "I know that now."

"And I will spend my every day trying to make myself worthy of that pledge, hen." He kissed her brow, then skimmed his lips gently down to take her mouth in a slow kiss. "Now, wife, shall we? Our party awaits."

Magda just smiled as James brushed the last of her tears from her cheeks. Everyone turned to them as they entered, and the open joy on their faces told her she was home.

Author's Note

I saw a portrait of the handsome James Graham, Marquis of Montrose, and knew I had to learn more about him. When I read C. V. Wedgwood's definitive biography, I was so swept up in his story, how this dashing nobleman, learned poet, and gifted swordsman transformed himself into one of the greatest military leaders in Scottish history, I literally wept to read of his death on the gallows on May 21, 1650. I knew then that I needed to rewrite his fate and send a woman back in time to save him.

Although this book was inspired by real events in James's life during the time of the Wars of the Three Kingdoms, Magda would say what I've done here is more impressionistic than realistic. My heroine is not the only woman to have done a bit of time traveling: In order to avoid slowing the plot, I have omitted a number of events and battles, greatly compressing the period between 1638 and 1650. I left out a brief period of imprisonment and a three-year exile, and perhaps most notably, I conflated the battle of Philiphaugh and James's last campaign at Carbisdale for my own final conflict.

Many of my characters are based on real people. Tom, Rollo, Napier, Margaret, MacColla, Sibbald, Leslie, Campbell, the Ogilvys, and King Charles each played a role in James's life. I've also included countless details based in fact: Van Dyck and the role of art and music in Charles's court; James, Sibbald, and Rollo's travels in disguise through Scotland; the burning of the House of Airlie; and the bard

Iain Lom and his part in the battle at Inverlochy are a few examples.

In order to avoid having a cast of hundreds, though, at times I incorrectly attributed words or feats. For example, although the Camerons played a great part in James's victories, it was Iain Lom, not Donald Cameron, who reportedly scouted the Campbells' position at Inverlochy. The capture and rescue of Ewen is also completely fabricated, and a case of this author merely wanting to spend a bit more time with the young laird.

Some of my quotes, however, actually paraphrase real historical accounts: A friend's nervous words at the Mercat Cross, parts of James's rousing battle speech, and of course his poetry are all things I cannot claim as my own.

And it's perhaps the things that really happened that are the hardest to believe. James truly did command such stunning victories, truly did lead his men on a thirty-six-hour jog through snowy Highland passes, and sadly, he truly was betrayed, captured, paraded through Scotland, and hanged.

To discover the many other elements rooted in fact, and to see paintings of the real people who inspired my characters, please visit my website at www.VeronicaWolff.com.

Turn the page for a preview of the next
historical romance by Veronica Wolff

Warrior of the Highlands

Coming soon from Berkley Sensation!

Haley rubbed her finger over the blade. Metal was a curious material. It assumed the body's heat and yet would never be mistaken for a living thing. She turned it in her hand. It was the oddest weapon she'd ever laid eyes on.

Who was the man who'd held this weapon? she wondered, projecting her mind to another time. Circa 1675, the catalog read. *Whose blood had it drawn?*

The filigree patterns at its base remained vivid, but the knife's edge was nearly serrated from corrosion. Though she knew it still had a bite, Haley couldn't resist tentatively scraping the pad of her thumb along the tip, and she gasped when it nicked her. She raised the cut to her mouth and breathed in the sour tang of steel that clung to her damp palm.

Another blade, sharper and colder, invaded her thoughts. It was years ago now but in a single heartbeat, Haley was back—reliving the moment that had changed her forever.

She fingered her scar, grazing lightly along it, as if it were some ghastly length of twine with the give of flesh beneath her fingers. The tissue had no feeling, and she could almost imagine it wasn't a part of her body. Yet she could never forget it. Would never forget that other blade, once pressed hard to her throat.

Her breath hissed sharply from between her teeth. Deep inhale, sharp exhale. *The breath sweeps the mind clear*, she could hear her father say. He'd been so helpful after the attack, using his experience and sheer will to pull his daughter back from the darkness that had enveloped her. Just thinking of her dad brought a smile to her face. The love of her family had brought her back, but it had been her father's police academy training—leavened with some good old South Boston street fighting—that had helped Haley control the feeling of vulnerability that had paralyzed her.

She put the strange dagger back on the table and took a rubber band from around her wrist to pull her hair back tight. Haley cursed herself. She really needed to figure out her dissertation, not get sidetracked by some weapon. She'd come to the museum that day for inspiration, and Sarah had let her into the second-floor storage area to peruse what few artifacts they had that might be germane to Haley's thesis on seventeenth-century Britain.

Her advisor had threatened that Haley was in danger of losing her teaching stipend. She'd been in the graduate program for three years now, and though she'd managed to eke out a chapter here and there, she needed to establish her argument and finish the thing.

A thick hank of black hair slipped free, and Haley roughly tugged the elastic out and pulled the coarse mass back into place. She tapped her finger between her teeth. She needed a breakthrough to catch her advisor's attention. Something fresh. Something she could even milk into a journal article or two and get the heat off of her for a little while.

Dr. Clark had just about lost his patience. Haley's interest in early modern weaponry didn't help matters, skewing, as they did, so dangerously close to what he considered military theory. And with a fellowship co-funded by the History Department and the Department of Celtic Languages, Haley had no choice but to position herself as a pure Reformation-era Scottish historian. Period.

As much as she'd prefer studying old broadswords.

Muttering a very American expletive, Haley snatched the weapon back off the table anyway. She leaned back and, slouching low in the chair, stretched her legs out in front of her. It was gorgeous. And inexplicably buried deep in the museum's archives with so many other gems in the Harvard collection.

On the surface, it looked like a simple dagger. An elegant, though stout, dagger. But Haley had known instantly what she was looking at. It was what was known as a "combination weapon." Wary of gunpowder's unreliability, early modern arms makers created guns capable of multiple jobs. A spear that shot bullets. A hunting trousse with a small pistol flush against its machetelike blade. She'd once even seen an elaborate museum piece that was a sword, cane, hammer, and musket rest all in one.

Many of the combination weapons were clunky—they would have been ostentatious displays of wealth, not something one would've relied upon for day-to-day hunting or fighting. But this one was stunning, extraordinary. It was only when she held it in her hand that she could sense the hollowness of the blade that would've served as the barrel of the pistol. And if the owner weren't inclined to bullets, the tip of the knife could separate and shoot from the base like a lethal steel arrowhead. The flintlock mechanism that acted as cock and hammer was almost completely camouflaged by the elaborate etching on the blade, and by the fine hounds' heads crafted at the T-shaped crossguard above the hilt.

Haley smoothed her palm along the flat of the blade, marveling at the intricate pattern. She shivered.

The air-conditioning must've clicked on. She set the dagger down, pulled her cardigan over her jersey dress, and was distractedly buttoning the sweater to the top when she noticed it. Picking the weapon back up, Haley squinted closely at the hilt. She held it up to the light. Something was etched at the base, and it was unlike the filigree work on the blade.

She darted her eyes around the storage area. Seeing she was alone, Haley licked her thumb and smudged it along the bottom of the handle. Something was engraved there, but it was obscured by black tarnish. She huffed her breath on the metal and used the hem of her dress to polish it. The letter *J* appeared. And then *L. V. E.*

It was an inscription. *For J.*

W something something.

Could it be "with love"? Who on earth would give their lover a dagger?

Haley roughly buffed the cap of the hilt to a dull sheen, pausing only with the ache in her arm. *For JG, with love from Ma.*

"Ho-ly crow!" she exclaimed as her phone vibrated to life, buzzing along the top of the table like an angry insect.

Putting her hand to her pounding heart, she glanced at the text message.

You're late. Get your butt over here.

Rolling her eyes, she muttered, "What, is the beer getting warm?" She stuffed her phone in her bag, gathered her notes, and, with one last look at the dagger on the table, made her way out.

"Dr. Brawn," Haley said, leaning her elbows on the front desk and smiling broadly at one of the Fogg Museum's conservators.

"Dr. Fitzpatrick." Sarah Brawn smiled right back. They both knew they were still years from the coveted PhDs, but they'd met in a first-year graduate seminar and, sharing a love of pizza and peculiar artifacts, had been friends ever since.

"I think I've got it. An idea for my dissertation," Haley clarified, seeing her friend's confusion. "Thanks again, by the way, for pulling that dagger for me. It helped get the juices flowing. Those combo weapons blow me away."

"Ooh, sock it to me. I assume you've got the title?" They enjoyed whiling away the hours contemplating grand titles for their yet to be complete dissertations, that being so much more fun than the actual writing.

She nodded enthusiastically. "Might to Power: British Firearms and the Forging of an Empire." Haley's tone was appropriately grand. "You know, how it was only with the rise of gunpowder that they were able to build an empire? That way I've got my focus on the seventeenth century, but I can also study all those cool old flintlock weapons."

"Hasn't that gunpowder idea already been done to death?"

"Hey," she said, feigning chagrin. "I'm still working on it."

"I mean . . . *nice*!" Sarah was thoughtful for a moment. "But forging really sounds more like a sword thing—"

Haley put up her hand to change the subject. "Meet up with us later?"

"Clan gathering?"

She nodded, pulling a long and well-worn scarf from her bag to wind around her neck.

"So that means it must be Sunday."

"Pigskin and pints at Paddy's," Haley smiled. "The countdown to the afternoon game's begun."

"You Fitzpatricks, you're like clockwork."

"Where football and my brothers are concerned? Yes." She scowled at the door as someone let themselves out and a blast of autumn air in.

"Don't you mean football, your brothers, and sports bars?"

"Yeah, yeah, and you're so above it all, right?" Haley readjusted her heavy canvas messenger bag, slinging it over her head and across her shoulder. "Come on, come out with me. I'll buy you a slice." She elongated the word *slice* into as enticing a one as possible.

"Some other time, yes. Tonight? No. We've been over this. I am not interested in getting set up with one of the Fitzpatrick boys."

"Hey, we're good people!" Haley said, laughing. "And the Pats are playing."

Grinning, her friend merely waved her fingers in good-bye, her nose already tucked back in her book.

❈

"Doc!" a chorus of voices shouted as Haley entered. Though far from being a fully realized professor, Haley's family had taken to calling her Doc the moment she began grad school. She looked around at all the welcoming faces, letting her eyes adjust. The place smelled of beer and fried things, and it brought a smile to her face. She may be in the ivory tower now, but she was South Boston through and through.

Three tall Fitzpatrick men were at her side in an instant, and two more waved at her from the table, beckoning with frosty plastic pitchers sloshing with whatever the beer of choice was that day. Sam Adams, if she knew her brothers.

The Fitzpatrick bunch took over Paddy's every week for the Sunday games, and were a fixture many other nights besides. Though the clan had grown to include some friends, a few cousins, one wife, two girlfriends, and the invariable men they tried to set their only—and baby—sister up with, the family resemblance among the siblings was unmistakable. The dark, wiry "black Irish" hair and pale skin with a perpetually rosy flush to the cheeks.

Daniel Jr., aka Danny Boy, clamped Haley into a hug, and the smell of fish filled her senses. She looked up and smiled into the eyes of her oldest brother. His hair was pulled back in a short ponytail for his gig as a short-order cook in a seafood joint. Tall and with his cleft chin, Haley couldn't understand how the most charming of them could be so completely single.

Colin and Conor, the twins, vied for a spot by their sister. They'd been the biggest troublemakers of all the six kids—holy terrors, her mother used to sigh—and now they were the most stable of the lot. One was married, the other might as well be, and they'd left their dates seated to come and scruff Haley's hair and take her bag and unwind the scarf from her neck.

"C'mon, beautiful." Danny pushed his way back between their brothers to undo the top of the sweater still buttoned tight around her neck. "Loosen up a bit."

"A beer will help!" Gerry shouted from the table, raising his glass in a toast and flashing a wide, gap-toothed grin. His free hand fumbled with the crumpled pack of cigarettes he wasn't allowed to smoke inside.

"Yeah, Doc!" Jimmy shouted. He beamed at her from his seat, his arm wrapped tight around his girlfriend, Maggie. Haley had to laugh at the sight of him, the tips of his ears already red with drink. They protruded almost comically from his head, accentuated by his buzz-cut hair, which was regulation cop, just like Dad's. "Get in out of the cold."

"Yeah, it's colder than a nun's t—"

"Gerald Patrick!" Her father's voice boomed from the other end of the bar. "Jesus, Mary, and Joseph, boy. You kiss your mother with that mouth?" He approached Haley, a pint in one hand, a basket of curly fries in the other, and leaned down and bussed her on the cheek. "My day has greatly improved with the vision of you, darlin' girl. I'm glad to see your work could spare you of an evening." More than forty years had passed since her dad had stepped off the boat from his native Donegal, but he'd never lost the warm Irish burr in his voice.

"And I take it Mom's at bridge night?" Even though they'd all stayed local, Haley's mother had been unhappy to see the last of her kids leave the nest and had taken up all manner of hobbies since. And their mother had been the only one surprised by how much fun she was having now.

"And where else?" Danny ushered Haley to a seat.

"Time to focus, people." Gerry poured himself another.

"Gerry has twenty bucks on the over," Danny said.

"I say he's crazy." Conor looked at his sister intently. "What do you say? You've always been good at picking the line. Will the game go over fifty-four points?"

Haley took a deep pull of her beer while she considered. "Dallas hasn't gotten their running game going yet," she said with the same gravity she approached her scholarship. "I think it's going to be a shoot-out, so yeah, I'd side with Gerry on this one." She raised her pint to the brother in question.

"Listen up!" Jimmy reached over the table and stole Gerry's lighter from his hand. "Hey, attention, people." He clinked the old metal Zippo on the side of his glass. "I said shut up, you dips." Jimmy swatted the nearest brother on the head.

"What the—" Danny recoiled and smoothed his hair back down into his ponytail.

"Apologies, ladies." Jimmy ignored Danny and nodded at the women. "But we have an announcement. Maggie, love?"

His girlfriend shyly pulled her hand from beneath the table. Directing her words to Haley, she said, "We were waiting for you to get here. I wanted you to be the first—the first to hear."

"You'll have a new sister!" Jimmy shouted, and was at once drowned out in cheers and a few female shrieks.

"Really?" Haley leaned in to her, genuinely pleased. "I've got to see the ring."

Colin spoke above the din. "And when are *you* going to make an honest woman of *yourself*, Doc?"

Haley didn't deign to give him a look, and merely kicked her brother beneath the table. She held Maggie's hand, shifting it under the light, setting the small diamond to twinkling. "Oh, guys, it's beautiful."

Maggie's sweet face bloomed into a smile. Between the strawberry blond curls that framed Maggie's delicate, heart-shaped face and the six-two length of Haley's swarthy brother, she couldn't wait to see what their kids would look like.

"And look." She wriggled her ring off and angled it up to the dim bar light. "Jimmy knew my size, and even inscribed it for me."

Haley took it from her, focusing on the tiny script. *James loves Maggie.*

"The lout couldn't think of anything more creative," Gerry said.

"Shut up." Jimmy threw his brother's lighter back at him. "Her fingers are small."

"No." Haley frowned at them. "It's simple and perfect. It says it all." She turned to Jimmy. "It's lovely. Just perfect."

"Blessings, kids." Her father raised his glass in a toast. "May the road rise up to meet you."

"Get comfortable." Gerry leaned low over the table and winked at Haley.

"May the wind be always at your back."

"And here we go," Danny muttered.

"May the sun shine warm—"

A roar erupted in the bar, and all eyes went to the TV screen. The Patriots had scored a touchdown, and soon everyone's attention was back on the game.

James loves Maggie, Haley thought, warm inside at the thought of it. Jimmy was a good guy; he deserved every happiness. Her eyes were on the screen, but her mind began to drift.

Another, much older, inscription popped into her head. Just who would dedicate a dagger to their sweetheart? *For JG, with love from Ma—*

J. Not a lot of J names in Scotland. Haley wracked her brain. She decided it was safe to assume the recipient had been a man, making him in all likelihood another James, or Jamie.

But *Ma* would be harder to pin down. You'd have Mairi, Malveen, Margaret, Marsali.

James loves Maggie.

"Hey Mag!" she heard Gerry tease. "Give your new brother some sugar."

Mag.

With love from—

"Magda?" Haley exclaimed. The bar had fallen momentarily silent and everyone turned to her, but for Gerry, who was scanning the bar for whomever this new girl might be that his sister was greeting.

"Sorry. Just thinking." Haley hid her face in her glass as she took a big sip.

"You need to focus," Colin scolded her.

"You need to *will* them to win, Haley." Conor nodded somberly in agreement.

JG, she thought. *James Graham's wife was named Magdalen. But the dagger was dated 1675. Graham was hanged in 1650.*

JG could be any one of thousands of men.

But how many of those would have the resources to buy such an extravagant weapon?

"Hey, Doc." Gerry snapped his fingers in front of her. "Earth to Haley."

"I tell you, she needs to focus." Colin gravely shook his head.

"Huh?" Haley looked at them blankly. "Oh, yeah, yeah." Shifting, she stared blindly at the flat screen hanging in the corner.

Maybe the piece was misdated.

But it was a flintlock pistol. Anything prior to 1650 would probably have used a matchlock mechanism.

"I have to go." Haley stood suddenly, screeching her chair along the sticky barroom floor. She was going to drive herself crazy. There was no way on earth that dagger had belonged to the famous war hero, hanged in Edinburgh in 1650. She needed to buff the rest of the thing off; then she'd see it was Margaret or Marjory or Martha who'd given the strange gift, and then Haley could stop spinning out. She swore to herself she'd once and for all focus on her dissertation. Just as soon as she figured out this one little mystery.

Her pronouncement was immediately met with grumbling and dire predictions.

Danny stared at her in disbelief. "It's bad mojo to leave before halftime."

"You have only yourself to blame if they lose," Colin said.

"Aren't you going to celebrate with us?" Jimmy attempted, in the most masterful tack of all.

"No, really, guys, I need to chase something down."

"We'll only release you if you're referring to a male student in that school of yours." Gerry stretched his leg along the side of the table as if to halt her escape.

"Stop fooling around," Conor said, "and sit your butt down, Doc."

"Really. Sorry, everyone." Haley reached over to give Maggie a big hug. "Welcome to the family."

"She's really leaving?" Conor asked his father in disbelief.

"God help her!" Danny shouted.

"Leave the girl be." Her dad nodded sagely. "She's got more important affairs to tend than a mere football game."

Haley scampered back out into the cold, winding her scarf about her neck as she went, the sound of hooting, cheering, and teasing about "affairs" at her back.

Enter the rich world of
historical romance
with Berkley Books.

Lynn Kurland

Patricia Potter

Betina Krahn

Jodi Thomas

Anne Gracie

Love is timeless.
penguin.com

M9G0907